Home and Away

Other Books by Rochelle Alers

ALONG THE SHORE

BREAKFAST IN BED

HAPPILY EVER AFTER

HEAVEN SENT

HIDDEN AGENDA

HIDEAWAY

HOME SWEET HOME

THE INHERITANCE

ROOM SERVICE

THE BEACH HOUSE

THE SEASIDE CAFÉ

VOWS

TAKE THE LONG WAY HOME

ROCHELLE ALERS

Home and Away

KENSINGTON PUBLISHING CORP.
kensingtonbooks.com

Content Warnings: miscarriage, racial slurs, hate speech

DAFINA BOOKS are published by

Kensington Publishing Corp.
900 Third Avenue
New York, NY 10022

All Kensington titles, imprints, and distributed lines are available at special quantity discounts for bulk purchases for sales promotion, premiums, fund-raising, and educational or institutional use.

Special book excerpts or customized printings can also be created to fit specific needs. For details, write or phone the office of the Kensington Sales Manager: Kensington Publishing Corp., 900 Third Avenue, New York, NY 10022. Attn. Sales Department. Phone: 1-800-221-2647.

ISBN: 978-1-4967-4274-2
First Trade Paperback Printing: January 2025

ISBN: 978-1-4967-4275-9 (e-book)

10 9 8 7 6 5 4 3 2 1

Printed in the United States of America

My son, do not forget my teaching, but keep my commands in your heart.

—Proverbs 3:1

Dear Reader,

I can't remember at what age I became acquainted with the game of baseball, but as a Black girl growing up on New York City's Upper West Side a half block away from Central Park, my tender ears were bombarded with the incessant talk about the Brooklyn Dodgers. It hadn't mattered that New York City had three baseballs teams: Yankees, Giants, and Dodgers, but it was the latter who had become the darlings of the residents along my block. Yes, in those days we were defined by blocks rather than neighborhoods—and mine was more racially diverse than the two bordering ours. I suppose that made the Dodgers favorites because they had the most diversity when it came to Black and Latino players.

During the summer months radios were blasting the games through open windows, and I would sit on the stoop of my building along with my friends and listen to the play-by-play, cheering when there was a home run and grumbling when the game ended in a loss. There were a lot of losses in those days, despite the incredible talent of the team that had come to be known as the Brooklyn Bums. "Dem Bums are bums," had become the catchphrase for sportswriters, but that all changed when the Brooklyn Dodgers won their first World Series in 1955. It was like Mardi Gras, fireworks on the Fourth of July, and the ball coming down in Times Square to celebrate the New Year—all in one. I can recall a woman hanging out of her window screaming excitedly at the top of her lungs, and if there hadn't been railings outside her window, she surely would have fallen four flights to the sidewalk.

However, I do remember my aunt who would come up from Florida every summer to spoil her nieces and nephews.

One summer she took me with her to Ebbets Field to see the Dodgers play, and the only thing I can recall about that outing was the long subway ride from Manhattan to Brooklyn that seemingly took forever—the only longer ride was to Coney Island—then taking a trolley ride to the ballpark. I was too young and exhausted to take note of the game.

It wasn't until I was old enough to read about Jackie Robinson and his impact on the teams that had been exclusive to White baseball players, that I was able to understand why he had become a hero for Black people. After Jackie, there was Roy Campenella, Don Newcombe, Jim "Junior" Gilliam, and Sandy Amorós. It wasn't only these players I remember to this day but also Carl Erskine, Sandy Koufax, Pee Wee Reese, Johnny Podres, Gil Hodges, Carl Furillo, and of course Duke Snider. I don't know why, but their names are imprinted in my memory like a permanent tattoo. They had become my boys of summer whenever I sat on the stoop listening to the games whenever me and my friends weren't hanging out in Central Park.

It was the boys on the block who played stickball. They couldn't wait for their mothers to toss out an old broom that had lost its usefulness, to remove the remaining straw and use the handle as their bat. Pensie Pinkies or Spaldings were used as balls because of their high bounce, and manhole covers doubled as bases. Play was only halted when a car came down the block—albeit very slowly because kids were always playing in the streets.

For me those were the good old days when a city kid did not have to leave his or her block to enjoy their summer vacation. But then there were drawbacks because the mothers who did not work doubled as sentries and were snitches, telling other parents what they had seen and overheard about their children. The worst punishment, other than a spanking, was having to stay in the house for an extended period. I didn't deliberately misbehave, but I was okay with staying in because it gave me time to complete my summer reading. My local public library allowed me to take out twelve books at the same time, and it had become a challenge to read all of them before the beginning of the next school year. It was during one of those summers that I read about Jackie Robinson and the other men who had played in the Negro Leagues. When I'd mentioned this to another aunt, who was a schoolteacher and my piano teacher, she showed me photographs that she'd taken of Jackie Robinson when he still played for the Dodgers; she had invited him to meet her first-grade class at the Bank Street School for Children. The expressions on the children's faces were ones of pure joy.

Many years later I was able to see Jackie Robinson in person when he visited an office building where I worked for a literary magazine, and my heart did a flip-flop when I couldn't stop staring at this tall, incredibly handsome, graying Black man who stopped everyone in their tracks once they recognized who he was. By this time, I'd transferred my allegiance to the New York Mets, because as a fan of the former Brooklyn Dodgers I knew I could never root for the New York Yankees, our crosstown rivals.

I've become a Mets fan for life, regardless of their winning or losing seasons, because they remind me of my beloved Brooklyn Dodgers. I watch every game and I'm always gifted tickets for Mother's Day and my birthday to attend at-home games, while proudly wearing my orange and blue paraphernalia.

And it is through my love of the game that I knew I had to write about the Negro Leagues and the players who played the game as well as or better than their White counterparts, and the women who loved and supported them. *Home and Away* is a work of fiction, but for me it is real—as real as the men who loved baseball and were content to form their own leagues for their race and for their people. It was also real for Black players who were faced with extreme racism during a time in our country's history when they were called derogatory names like *nigger, boy, and coon*, and the only thing they wanted was equal treatment as a man. Although some of the words in this novel are offensive, they were necessary to make the events even more real.

Happy Reading,
Rochelle

Chapter 1

Leaning back in her chair, Harper Fleming closed her eyes as she attempted not to lose her temper. Her first impulse after meeting with the paper's editor in chief was to tell him that he was a sanctimonious sonofabitch, and she hated his shit-eating grin as he tried to downplay the reason she'd been passed over as the sports reporter, for the second time in six years. She knew it had to be because she was a woman. In his narrow-minded opinion, she was perfect for covering local politics and social events for the biweekly. He didn't have to say outright that female reporters were better suited to cover events in a ballroom rather than a men's locker room, but nonetheless she got his message loud and clear.

Harper had lost track of the number of times she had chided herself for allowing herself to be lured away from a position with another newspaper to work for the biweekly because she'd felt obligated to support the Black-owned periodical. She had given the newspaper everything she had as a journalist, and for the editor it was never enough. Even when she had assisted the investigative reporter in uncovering the identity of the murderer of a social justice advocate, she received a measly pat on the head, as if she'd been an obedient puppy, while the editor continued to extol the brilliance of the other reporter at many of the staff meetings. Harper wouldn't have felt so disappointed if her colleague had given her some credit, because the murderer wouldn't have been apprehended without her assistance, but what followed was crickets from the egotistical coworker.

This is not to say she begrudged her colleagues whenever they broke a story, but Harper was tired of attending political meetings and covering the fundraisers for candidates vying for power in a city where politics have always been muddled.

"I know you're disappointed, Harper, but—"

"I'm not disappointed," she countered, cutting him off. "Right now, I couldn't be more pleased with myself because I'm quitting. I've already been approved for vacation, so that means you have my two weeks' notice. And to quote Edward R. Murrow's sign-off, 'Goodnight and good luck.' "

Pushing to her feet, Harper walked out of the office. The sound of heavy breathing from the paper's editor followed her. Harper knew she had shocked him with her resignation, but she was beyond caring or worrying if he could get anyone to replace her. That was no longer her problem.

Enough was enough until it had become too much for her. What she didn't want was to come into work angry and add to the ongoing hostile workplace environment. She was aware that many on staff were disgruntled about long-awaited raises, but for Harper it was a long-promised promotion. She'd begun cleaning out her desk several weeks ago. Somehow, she knew intuitively that she wasn't going to be promoted, and the time had come for her to leave. Not only was her career on pause, but also her love life.

She'd been seeing the same man off and on for a year. The relationship was going nowhere because he claimed he didn't believe in commitment. At first, this didn't bother Harper, but now, at thirty-three, she had come to the realization that she'd given up a year of her life making herself available for him whenever he called. Earlier that morning she had deleted and blocked his number from her cell phone. Now that she was leaving the newspaper, he wouldn't be able to contact her there.

Harper gathered her tote bag and walked out of the office for the last time, brimming with confidence. She took the elevator to the street, walking a block to her car in a nearby parking lot. Before starting up her car, she sent a text message to her father telling him she had quit her job and she'd talk to him later. Instead of driving to her apartment, she headed in the direction of her parents' house in a Chicago suburb. She knew her father wouldn't be home because, as a television baseball broadcaster for the Chicago White Sox, he followed the team for home and away games.

In the past she had spoken with Daniel Fleming at length about her frustration working at a dead-end job. He reminded her that she had options, but only if she decided to exercise them.

You're so right, Dad, she thought, before starting up the SUV.

Tapping the screen on the dashboard, she activated the Bluetooth feature and her parents' number. It rang twice before she heard her mother's voice.

"Hi, Mom. Is it all right if I come over?"

"Of course. Is something wrong?"

Harper knew it was impossible to fool her mother. School clinical psychologist Martell Fleming claimed she knew more about her children than they did about themselves, so it was a waste of time to try and conceal things from her.

"Not tonight, Mom. In fact, everything is wonderful."

"You quit your job."

"How did you know?"

"Harper, honey, that's all you've been talking about every time we get together. That one day you're going to get up enough nerve to say *I'm out*."

"I put in for a vacation, so that's going to serve as my two-week notice."

"Do you plan to look for a position with another newspaper?"

"Not right away. I need to get away and clear my head, so I'm going to call Grandpa Flem and ask if I can spend time with him this summer."

"You know he's going to love that."

Harper smiled. "And I'm going to love seeing him again." She had reconnected with her grandfather last Christmas when she, her parents, and her brothers and their families went to Tennessee to celebrate the holiday with Bernard Fleming. Two years ago, after burying his wife, he'd sold his house and moved to Nashville.

"Every time I call and ask how he is, Bernard tells me he's doing well," Martell said, "but I keep telling your father that at seventy-nine and soon to be eighty, the man shouldn't be living alone."

"He's not as isolated as he was in Memphis," Harper said in defense of her elderly grandfather. He had moved to a community where he quickly made friends with several neighbors.

Bernard and his wife, Nadine, a retired corrections officer and schoolteacher respectively, had taken over the small family farm that had belonged to his parents. It was where Harper and her brothers spent their summers gathering eggs from the chickens, feeding the hogs, and weeding fruit and vegetable gardens. She couldn't wait for the end of the school year when she was able to leave Chicago for Memphis to run barefoot, pick berries, and help her grandmother prepare meals. Those days were branded in her memory like a permanent tattoo, a constant reminder that her childhood was as close to perfect as it could get.

It wasn't that she hadn't grown up privileged, because her father was a professional baseball player who'd signed a multimillion-dollar contract, which had afforded his family the luxury of living in an affluent Chicago suburb. She and her siblings had attended private schools, and subsequently enrolled in prestigious private colleges. Her mother worked as a clinical psychologist for a public school district and was also a partner in a private practice with a social worker whose clients were substance abusers.

Harper would have been willing to trade all the luxuries at home to live on what had been her great-grandparents' farm in rural Tennessee near Memphis. She'd looked forward to waking up at dawn to the crowing of the rooster and walking barefoot in the wet grass before the sun rose high enough to dispel the dew. She also loved accompanying her grandmother to the garden to pick the fruits or vegetables for what she planned to cook for the day. Harper didn't know why, but everything she ate seemed more delicious because it was home grown.

Now she planned to return to Tennessee, but not to the family farm near Memphis. Instead, she was going to visit a small community of retirees to spend time with Bernard Fleming, and hopefully relive her childhood. She loved listening to him reminisce about his father, who had played in the Negro Leagues. Kelton Fleming was good enough to play for Major League Baseball once Jackie Robinson broke the color barrier, but a series of incidents had derailed his career, which resulted in him walking away from the game he had loved more than anyone or anything in his life.

"How long do you plan to stay in Nashville?" Martell asked Harper as they sat in the alcove of a spacious ultramodern kitchen.

She peered over the rim of the crystal water goblet, meeting her mother's large, dark brown eyes. Martell, who had recently celebrated her fifty-eighth birthday, could easily pass for a woman at least ten years younger. She'd cut her hair shorter, worked out several days a week, and had modified her diet to include more lean meat, fruits, and vegetables.

Harper's father would repeat ad nauseam that it had only taken a single glance at his teammate's cousin to know he wanted to marry her. After a whirlwind courtship lasting less than three months, Daniel Fletcher married Martell a week before the beginning of spring training.

Harper set the glass on a coaster. "I'm not sure. When I talk to Grandpa, occasionally he will mention something about his father playing in the Negro Leagues, and I can't stop thinking about writing a book based on Kelton Fleming's life as a Black baseball player before Jackie Robinson broke baseball's color barrier."

"Would it be biographical?"

"I don't know. I'd have to wait and see what he's willing to tell me. There are times when I bring up the subject of his father playing baseball and he'll just smile and nod. That's when I suspect there are family secrets he would prefer remain hidden."

Martell's eyebrows lifted slightly. "I can't imagine what would be so horrific about his father that he wouldn't want to talk about it."

Harper smiled. "We'll just have to wait and see. If it's that horrific, then it can't be biographical. I don't want to disclose something about Dad's family that could taint his career as a sports commentator." Her father, who had spent his entire baseball career playing for the Chicago White Sox, had become an analyst and then a commentator for the team following his retirement.

"Maybe you should let your father see what you've written, to get his approval."

Harper shook her head. "That's something I won't do. If I'm going to write a book, then whatever is written will be between me, a book publisher, and editor."

"What if it's scandalous?"

"How scandalous, Mom?"

Martell lowered her eyes. "Adulterous affairs, secret babies, illegal abortions, and murder."

Throwing back her head, Harper laughed with wild abandon. "You have to stop watching those true crime shows, Mom." She sobered up when her mother glared at her. "I don't know how much Grandpa knows about his mother and father, but if it's anything salacious then I won't include it. Better yet, I will write a fictional account and change names and places to conceal their identity."

"That sounds better," Martell agreed.

"It sounds better, because it won't be about your family," she said to Martell.

"We are not talking about my family, Harper. I know who my folks are and what they have done. This isn't about me."

Harper knew her mother was concerned that her social standing would take a hit if Harper were to uncover something about her husband's family. Martell Fleming would never admit it, but she was a successful social climber and well-respected wife of a professional ballplayer who gave her a lifestyle she never could have imagined while growing up in a blue-collar factory town in Ohio known for having a double-digit unemployment rate after several factories closed or relocated following prolonged union strikes. She also wondered if Martell knew something about her husband's family she did not want made public.

However, when it came to family secrets, Martell Fleming had enough to fill a dumpster. She claimed relatives with criminal records spanning decades, if not generations, and who had spent more time in prison in their lifetimes than on the outside. However, Martell had hit the proverbial jackpot when a distant cousin who played for the White Sox invited her to attend a game being played against the former Cleveland Indians, now known as the Guardians, and ended up catching the attention of third baseman Daniel Fleming.

"I'm going to call Grandpa when I get home to ask if I can come and stay with him for the summer."

Martell smiled, the expression relaxing the lines of tension around her mouth. "You know he's going to say yes."

That was what Harper hoped for. It was early May and spending the rest of the summer months and, if necessary, beyond that in Nashville would come as a welcome change from being in Chicago, jobless and with no boyfriend.

Martell paused. "I know I'll probably not see much of you this summer, so why don't we go out to dinner at Lawry's before you leave."

Harper knew her mother didn't like eating alone when her husband was out of town, and Martell had selected one of her favorite steakhouse restaurants. "We can do that tomorrow. I need to call Grandpa and let him know I'm coming down, then clean out my fridge, and forward my mail before I leave." Pushing back her chair, she circled the table and kissed Martell's cheek. "I'll see you tomorrow."

She waited until she was in her apartment to call her grandfather. The phone rang three times before she heard, "Talk to me."

Harper smiled when hearing his familiar greeting. "Hello, Grandpa. I'm calling to ask if I can come down and hang out with you for a while?"

"How long is a while, grandbaby girl?"

Harper felt tears prick the back of her eyelids whenever he called her that. "What about for the summer?"

A beat passed before Bernard said, "Aren't you working?"

"Not anymore, Grandpa. I quit my job today."

There came another pause. "What are you going to do?"

"Right now, nothing. I'm going to take the summer off and plan the next phase of my career. You know I've been talking about writing a book about your father when he played in the Negro Baseball Leagues. You said your father used to talk to you all the time about his life when he was a ballplayer."

"Not only did my father talk incessantly about his days as a baseball player, he also wrote everything down. It's taken me a while to unpack everything I had shipped from the farm.

There was an old trunk filled with his notebooks and lots of my mother's faded photos and handbills from the 1930s and '40s."

Harper felt a shiver of excitement sweep over her with this disclosure. Now she did not have to rely on her grandfather's oral history, but written documentation. "How many, Grandpa?"

"A lot, Harper."

"Have you read any of them?"

"Not really. What I did do was put them in chronological order."

"Why didn't you read them, Grandpa?"

"I didn't want to relive the experience of my father going on and on about his ballplaying days. Those were the times when I'd just tune him out. It was as if he'd become so obsessed with the game that I suspected at one time it had taken over his whole life. Even my mother would whisper to me that she thought he was losing his mind whenever he picked up a bat and would begin swinging at an imaginary ball."

Her grandfather did not want to revisit his father's life on the page, but it was different for Harper. She'd read books and watched documentaries about the Negro Leagues and the stories of African American baseball, but to read an eyewitness account of the game was akin to having a genie grant her fervent wish.

"What condition are they in?" she asked.

"Surprisingly, they are in good condition. Some pages in the older ones have begun to turn yellow though. What saved them was that he wrapped them in oilcloth, and then in burlap before packing them away in the trunk."

"Thank you, Grandpa, for not throwing them away."

"Not to worry, grandbaby girl. I never would've thrown them away without telling you or Daniel. I also found your grandmom's cast-iron frying pans. I know you were asking about them after she passed away."

Harper had believed her grandmother's fried chicken, pork

chops, and cornbread were the best she'd ever eaten because of the cast-iron frying pans. When she and her family had gone to Nashville for Christmas it was only three months after Bernard had moved from Memphis, and several rooms were still filled with boxes he claimed he was going to take his time unpacking.

"Have you finished unboxing everything?"

A deep chuckle came through the earpiece. "Not yet. I still have a few more."

"Leave them, Grandpa. We can open them together and then figure out what you want to keep or donate to charity."

"That sounds good to me. When are you coming down?"

Harper thought about what she had to do to close her apartment for the next five months. "Wednesday."

"Wednesday it is. It's going to be like old times when you used to spend the summers at the farm, only this time there won't be any animals."

She noticed he'd mentioned animals and not his wife. Harper knew Bernard Fleming did not like talking about his late wife, because then he would lapse into a funk for days. He and Nadine had been married for more than fifty years and he'd claimed she was the love of his life.

"See you soon, Grandpa."

"Okay."

"Love you."

"Love you more," Bernard said.

Harper ended the call as she stared out her bedroom window. Her grandfather finding his father's notebooks was like winning the Powerball. Whenever she opened someone's journal or diary she'd become a voyeur, reading the innermost thoughts and desires of the writer.

She never knew her great-grandfather, but after reading the journals, there was no doubt she would discover who Kelton Fleming was.

Chapter 2

Harper left Chicago at five o'clock in the morning, knowing it would take her more than seven hours to drive to Nashville, Tennessee. She planned to stop midway between the two cities in Columbus, Indiana, to eat, refuel, and stretch her legs. She'd called her grandfather the day before to tell him to expect her the following afternoon.

After stopping in Columbus, Indiana, for about forty minutes, she was back on the road, singing along to the tunes on her phone's playlist. Harper smiled when she saw the highway sign indicating the number of miles to Nashville. Not only was she looking forward to reuniting with her grandfather, but also the city's delicious Southern cuisine, featuring authentic soul food and barbecue.

Her phone rang and her father's name appeared on the navigation screen. Tapping a button on the steering wheel, she activated the Bluetooth feature. "Hi, Dad."

"Hi, yourself. I just got in from LA and I want to talk to you about you quitting your job."

"Well, I finally did it."

There came a pause before Daniel Fleming said, "Good for

you. Now, if you want me to put in a word for you at some of the networks I—"

"No, Dad," Harper said, interrupting him.

"I don't want you to think of it as nepotism, Harper, because you have the—"

"Don't say it, Dad," she said, cutting him off again. She knew her father was going to say she had the chops to make it as a television sports analyst. All she had to do was apply to several sports networks. The instant she'd announce herself as the daughter of Hall of Famer third baseman Daniel Fleming, she would be viewed differently from other candidates vying for the same position. And if hired, she did not want to set herself up for resentment from those who believed if she wasn't Daniel's daughter, she wouldn't have got the job.

"Okay, sweets, I won't say it. Your mother said you're going to take the summer off and stay with Dad."

"I'm on my way to Nashville right now."

"Do you need money to tide you over until you find another job?"

Harper blew out her breath, shaking her head. "No, Dad. I don't need money." She didn't know why Daniel Fleming believed he had to be financially responsible for her. She'd graduated from college without having to apply for student loans, and she'd lived at home until getting a job and saving enough money to rent a studio apartment. She'd driven her mother's older-model cars for years until she purchased the SUV to celebrate her thirtieth birthday three years ago.

Fiercely independent, Harper had learned to budget her earnings, saving ten percent of her take-home pay each month. As the beneficiary of her grandmother's insurance policy she'd become even more financially secure.

"I was just asking."

She smiled. "And I thank you for asking, but I'm good."

"I'm going to ring off now because I'm beginning to feel the effects of jetlag."

"Get some sleep, Dad. I'll talk to you in a couple of days to let you know how Grandpa is doing."

"I'm glad you're going to stay with him. I stopped in to see him when I was in St. Louis a couple of weeks ago. Although he appeared thinner, he seemed to be feeling well."

"Don't worry about your father, Dad. I'll take loving care of him."

"Thanks, sweetie. Talk to you soon."

Later, Dad."

Harper tapped the button, ending the connection. Although she appreciated her father offering to give her money, she did not want to depend on her parents financially, which wouldn't allow her to feel like an adult. As the youngest of three, and the only girl, she had to challenge her parents for independence; they raised her differently from their sons, who were permitted more freedom when it came to selecting out-of-state colleges, while her choices were limited to the state of Illinois. It hadn't mattered how much she pleaded and begged, they wouldn't give in, and that was when she vowed it would be the last time she'd permit her parents or anyone else to control her life.

She bypassed downtown Nashville and drove in the direction of a community populated mostly by retirees. Nine hours after leaving Chicago, Harper maneuvered into the driveway of a modest one-story ranch house and came to a stop behind her grandfather's Ford Taurus. The front door opened before she could get out of her vehicle. Harper smiled when he came over to greet her. Bernard Fleming was the quintessential Southern gentleman, who believed it was incumbent upon men to take care of women. Harper wanted to tell him he was a dinosaur, because some of the men she dealt with were looking for a woman to take care of them.

Daniel Fleming was right about his father losing weight. It hadn't been six months since Harper last saw her grandfather face-to-face, and he now appeared frail. Bernard, standing at an even six feet, had always been slender, but unlike most people who put on weight as they aged, it was the reverse for him, despite always having a hearty appetite.

I hope he isn't sick. Harper shook her head as if to dispel the thought as she hugged her grandfather. "It's so good seeing you again."

Bernard Fleming smiled down at his granddaughter. He didn't believe he would ever get over the shock that Harper looked so much like Nadine. In fact, she could've been his late wife's clone. Harper was several inches taller than her petite paternal grandmother, but that was the only difference. She had inherited Nadine's slender figure, round face, and flawless brown complexion with orange undertones that reminded him of autumn leaves. Her wide-set dark brown eyes were laughing even when she wasn't.

He kissed her cheek. "That goes double for me. I know you must be tired from all that driving, so come into the house and rest yourself."

Harper eased out of his embrace. "I just need to get my bags."

Bernard nodded. "I'll help you with that," he said when Harper pressed a button on her car's fob to open the hatch. Walking to the rear of the SUV, he removed the wheeled Pullman and waited for Harper to take out another smaller wheeled monogrammed leather case he knew contained her laptop. He smiled. It was the last gift Nadine had given her granddaughter before her passing.

"Even though the calendar says it's still spring, it definitely feels like summer down here," Harper remarked as she closed the hatch.

Bernard nodded again. "Even though folks keep talking about global warming, there are those who claim they're just talking out the side of their necks. It was the same back in the day when Noah warned folks to stop sinning because a flood was coming."

"For most folks seeing is believing, Grandpa."

"Sure, you right," he said under his breath.

Harper laughed. "It's funny that I don't remember some of the colloquialisms germane to the South until I stay here a while."

"Like y'all for you all?"

"Not so much y'all because I tend to say it, too."

"That's because your daddy was raised down here and I always say you can take the boy out of the country, but you can't take the country out of the boy."

"That's what makes him so popular to millions of baseball fans because he intersperses Southern colloquialisms into the game commentary."

"Your father grew up listening to Yankee games play-by-play with Mel Allen's catchphrases. He used to say that if he couldn't play baseball, then he wanted to become a commentator."

"He was lucky because he realized both of his dreams."

"That he did," Bernard said, smiling. His son had become a professional baseball player and was inducted into the Baseball Hall of Fame, something that wasn't possible for Kelton Fleming because of his race and the times. Daniel was a baseball phenom, and his agent had negotiated his last ten-year contract with deferred payments spread over twenty-five years.

Things were different for Bernard's son when compared to his father. There were times when Bernard had tended to tune Kelton out whenever he reminisced about his time playing in the Negro Leagues. Now that Harper wanted to write about those glory days when Black men played the game, often better than their White counterparts, Bernard knew even though his father was no longer alive, his story would be told accurately by his great-granddaughter.

It wasn't until after Kelton's passing that Bernard found a letter addressed to him about his notebooks. Kelton had indicated he wanted his son to read them because there were things he wanted him to know about his time when he played the game, but Bernard did not want to relive the stories he'd heard over and over again. He'd almost forgotten about them until he sold the farm and moved everything to Nashville. When he opened the trunk, it was as if it was a portal to the past—a past Harper would bring into the future.

He held open the screen door for Harper. "Are you hungry?"

She smiled at him over her shoulder. "No. I stopped to eat something. I'd like to wait a few hours before I take you out to dinner."

Bernard set the Pullman next to the table in the entryway. "I have to watch what I eat, because the last time I had a checkup my blood pressure was a little high."

"How high is high, Grandpa?"

"I forget the numbers, but I knew something was wrong when I'd get lightheaded and had to sit or fall down."

Harper met her grandfather's eyes, wondering if there was something else going on with him other than hypertension. "Are you taking medication?"

Bernard ran a hand over his cropped white hair. "Yes. And I'm also on a strict diet because my cholesterol is also little high."

She wanted to ask him how his health had deteriorated so quickly when six months ago he'd announced that he passed his medical checkup with flying colors. "You're going to have to let me know what you can or cannot eat."

Bernard's snow-white bushy eyebrows lifted. "You're going to cook for me?"

Harper gave him an incredulous stare. "Of course. Did you expect me to order takeout?"

A sheepish expression flitted over Bernard's features. "I only asked because there is someone who cooks for me."

"Who, Grandpa?"

"A lady friend."

"You have a lady friend?"

"Yes. She's a widow who lives across the street."

Harper paused as she carefully thought about what she wanted to say. She didn't want to interfere in her grandfather's personal life. She didn't want him to resent her, but she felt it incumbent to assume some responsibility for his well-being. "You can tell your lady friend that your granddaughter will prepare your meals while she's here."

A beat passed before Bernard said, "Okay. I'll tell her."

"Good. Now I'm going to take my things to my bedroom and then shower. Once I'm finished you can show me your father's notebooks."

Picking up the Pullman and the case with her computer, Harper walked into a bedroom with a double and two twin beds. During Christmas she had shared the room with her sister-in-law and niece. It was a time when the three-bedroom house was filled with Flemings spanning four generations. There was constant activity with young children challenging one another for the television remote, and the kitchen was crowded with Harper, her mother, and sisters-in-law preparing enough food to feed a small army, while Bernard, his son, and grandsons were content to sit on the back porch discussing sports and politics. It was only one of a few times that the entire Fleming clan was able to get together because her brothers were both active-duty military career officers and they never knew when they would be reassigned to a different base.

Harper opened the Pullman to take out a change of clothes and a quilted bag with her beauty products. She'd noticed a layer of dust on flat surfaces in the bedroom and planned to set aside a day when she would have to give the house an overall dusting and vacuuming. She knew if her grandmother were still alive the house would've been spotless.

A lukewarm shower revived her. Wearing a tank top, shorts, and flip-flops, Harper made her way to the all-season sunroom at the rear of the house. Bernard sat on a rocker watching a television resting on its own stand.

She folded her body down to a cushioned chair next to him. "When did you get this one?" she asked, pointing at the television.

Bernard gave her a sidelong glance. "I bought it after Christmas, once I realized having one TV in the house wasn't going to work with kids fighting over which shows to watch."

Stretching out her legs, Harper crossed her feet at the ankles and noticed the red polish on one of her big toes was chipped. Like Martell, she had a standing appointment at her favorite salon for her hair, manicure, and pedicure. While her mother had her hair cut, Harper had decided to let hers grow shoulder length because it was easier to style into a ponytail when she was pressed for time, rather than having to use a curling iron before leaving the house.

"It did get a little crazy with them arguing and constantly changing the channel," Bernard elaborated. "I did feel sorry for them when Craig told them to tone it down or they would be on lockdown for the rest of the week."

Harper laughed softly. "That's because Craig is a badass marine."

Craig, three years her senior, had joined the Marine Corps after graduating from college and was recently promoted to captain, while thirty-eight-year-old Daniel Jr., a West Point graduate, had achieved the rank of lieutenant colonel. Both had survived several deployments and were now permanently Stateside.

Bernard pointed to a plastic bin in a corner of the sunroom. "Dad's notebooks are in there if you want to start going over them."

Harper found it hard to draw a normal breath as she pushed off the chair. The anticipation of reading what Kelton had written nearly overwhelmed her as she walked on shaky legs to the container filled with notebooks chronicling the life of her great-grandfather as a Negro baseball player.

Sinking down to the carpeted floor, she removed the lid and stared at stacks of composition notebooks. She read the inscription on the top one: *Property of Kelton S. Fleming—1936*. Bernard said he had put them in chronological order, and she assumed 1936 would be the first one. She opened the tattered cover and saw the corners of the pages had yellowed, and some were frayed, and realized it was necessary for her to wear cotton gloves to keep the oil from her fingers from causing further damage to the brittle pages.

Harper knew her grandmother owned several pairs of white gloves for whenever she attended church services, and hoped that she'd be able to find some among the clothes Bernard had packed away.

She returned the notebook to the bin, replaced the cover, and then walked back to sit next to Bernard. "I'm going to need gloves whenever I read them."

"I remember packing away some with your grandmother's clothes. I know women don't wear gloves anymore, but my Nadine would never go to church without her hat and gloves even when they were no longer fashionable."

Harper nodded, smiling. There were outdated styles and customs Nadine held on to like a rabid junkyard dog. She only went out to eat at a restaurant for what she thought was a special occasion, like birthdays or anniversaries, preferring to cook at home. She attended church services every Sunday, rain or shine, and afterward there was always a home-cooked dinner. Her house was spotless, and she hated it when someone dropped by unannounced. If she hadn't invited you into her home, that meant she would not open the door for you.

"I'll look for her gloves later. Meanwhile, I'm going to check in your fridge to see what I can fix for tonight."

"I have some chicken and frozen fish filets."

"What about vegetables?" she asked.

"I'm not certain what's in the vegetable bin, because I haven't gone shopping in more than a week."

Harper wanted to tell Bernard that was because he was relying on his lady friend to cook for him. She wasn't certain what the woman was feeding him, but now that she was here, she would monitor her grandfather's diet. "After I take an inventory of your pantry I'll go shopping tomorrow. And I want you to tell me what you like or don't like."

Bernard smiled and a network of tiny lines fanned out around his large dark eyes. "I like everything, but it depends on how it's prepared. No more fried chicken, fish, or pork chops. And what I really miss is ham hocks in my greens."

"Don't worry, Grandpa. I can use smoked meat that is high in lean protein and low in fats and carbs but will give the greens the same taste."

"Nadine always said you would become a wonderful cook."

"That's because I learned from the best."

While Martell's cooking skills were adequate, they could not compare to Nadine Fleming's, which on occasion had prompted Martell to allow Harper to take over cooking whenever she'd volunteered to make dinner.

Bernard closed his eyes as he pressed his head against the rocker's cushioned backrest. "I really miss her, Harper. I thought it would get easier, but it hasn't. I thought selling the house and farm in Memphis and moving here would stop me from thinking about her so much because everything there reminded me of her, but I was wrong. There are times when I still feel her presence—especially at night when I'm in bed. We may have had our difficulties over the years, but there was never a time when we would go to bed angry. I would kiss her goodnight and tell her that I loved her, and she would say she loved me, too."

Harper bit her lip when she heard the passion and depth of emotion in his voice. "Grandma told me over and over that she was the luckiest woman in the world because you had chosen her to be your wife."

Smiling, Bernard opened his eyes. "That's something I hope for you, Harper. That you meet the man who will make you happy that you are his wife."

Harper wanted to tell him he was more hopeful than she was, because falling in love and marrying did not top her wish list. She wanted to feel secure in her career before embarking on marriage and eventually motherhood.

The doorbell chimed throughout the house, and Harper stood up. "Are you expecting anyone?"

Bernard also came to his feet. "It's probably my friend asking me what I want her to fix for me."

"It's all right, Grandpa. It's time I let her know that she doesn't have to cook for you."

"That's okay, grandbaby girl," Bernard said. "You wait here, and I'll tell her."

Harper curbed the urge to disobey her grandfather to see the woman who had assumed the responsibility for feeding Bernard. Had she done it because she was being altruistic, or did she have an ulterior motive? Bernard Fleming didn't have to rely on a fixed income to make ends meet. After serving in Vietnam, he returned home and became a corrections officer at a state prison. After retiring with a modest pension, he took over his parents' farm and eventually sold it at a profit, which afforded him the opportunity to purchase the house in Nashville without securing a mortgage. He didn't believe in buying anything on credit and even paid cash for all his automobiles.

She didn't have to wait long for Bernard to come back. "She wasn't too happy, but says she understands."

"Do you pay her to cook for you?"

He shook his head. "I offered, but she refused to take my money." He squinted at her. "What are you thinking about, Harper?

"What makes you think I'm thinking about anything?"

"You have the same look on your face that Nadine would have when she was contemplating whether she should say something or not."

"You've got me there, Grandpa. Your lady friend wants to become the next Mrs. Bernard Fleming."

Harper didn't need to tell her grandfather that he was still an incredibly attractive man, and women, regardless of their age, always gave him a second look whenever he walked into a room. There were times when he was mistaken for someone from Southeast Asia with his near-straight hair, dark brown complexion, aquiline nose, and full mouth.

"That's never going to happen. Fleming men marry for life. It was the same with my parents and it continued with your father. When I asked Nadine to marry me, I knew she was the woman I wanted to spend the rest of my life with. To be honest I'm too old to even think about trying to figure out another woman."

"Now you sound like your son, Grandpa."

"That's because he's a Fleming man," Bernard said, grinning.

Harper nodded. "Why don't you finish watching television while I see if I can find something to make for dinner."

"Okay." Bernard paused. "I'm glad you're here."

"Me too."

CHAPTER 3

It took Harper nearly two weeks to read what had taken Kelton Fleming eleven years to document: when he'd left home for the first time in 1936, to the day when Jackie Robinson took the field on April 15, 1947, and broke Major League Baseball's "color line." To say he was a prolific writer was putting it mildly. He had meticulously documented every place he'd visited and included detailed facts about those he'd met and interacted with during his ballplaying days.

She had established the habit of rising early to shower and dress for the day. Then she'd prepare breakfast for Bernard after he returned from what he called his early morning workout, which consisted of driving to the local high school and walking laps around the track before the beginning of classes. She assumed the responsibilities of cooking, doing laundry, and cleaning the house, which had freed Bernard up to watch his favorite movies and sporting events. However, she was annoyed when her grandfather entered the shed behind the house to take out a gas-powered lawnmower and other garden equipment to mow the front and back lawns. He also pruned several trees, and when she asked him about doing yardwork, he claimed he only did it twice a month. According to him, working outdoors kept him from thinking about his late wife.

Harper hadn't come to Nashville to upset her grandfather's daily routine, but to bond with him as she'd done more than twenty summers ago. The year she celebrated her sixth birthday, her parents had dropped their children off in Memphis to spend the summer on the farm. The ritual continued until Harper turned fifteen, when she went to a sleepaway camp that was more of a finishing school for young women looking to marry well. She had learned to set a table for casual and formal dining, and to design menus for afternoon teas, luncheons, buffets, and sit-down dinners.

She had come to resent Martell, who insisted she return to the camp every year until she graduated from high school. Even though she wasn't able to attend an out-of-state college, Harper felt as if she'd been given a reprieve because she was able to live on campus. It had given her a foretaste of independence for the first time.

Harper also noticed that Bernard's face wasn't as gaunt as it had been two weeks ago. She hoped that he was beginning to regain some of the weight he'd lost. He enjoyed the varied egg white omelets, fresh fruit cups, and baked muffins she prepared for breakfast. She had also purchased an air fryer and she was able to make fried chicken without the added oil, and the lean cuts of meat that Bernard claimed he missed eating. Whenever she made pork chops in the air fryer, she removed most of the fat before serving them to her grandfather. He had also given her a list of what he wanted her to prepare, and she attached it to the refrigerator. It had begun with sweet potatoes, cornbread, green beans with white potatoes, collard greens, cucumber salad, lima beans, and oxtail stew, before he added what Harper thought of as questionable: red beans and sausage. Although beans were a reliable source of protein, she had reservations about the sodium content in the smoked ham and andouille sausage. Not wanting to squelch his enthusiasm for what he liked to eat, Harper said she would agree to prepare one cheat meal per week. What she didn't tell her grandfather was that she had to find the appropriate substitutes for the ham and sausage.

She had set up her laptop on a table in the corner of the expansive sunroom that now doubled as her temporary home office. After reading each notebook, she typed up notes and set up a storyboard for the novel. Kelton Fleming's writing had permitted her a glimpse into the past, beginning when he left home at eighteen to become a baseball player. What she hadn't been prepared for was reading about what he encountered as a Black man traveling throughout the South in the 1930s and 1940s, and the reaction to Negroes playing baseball in Mexico, the Caribbean, and South America. Kelton, who had been an avid reader, recorded the exploits of players whose names would become synonymous with the history of the Negro Baseball Leagues.

Kelton also wrote about intimate details of his own life, including encounters with different women he had slept with before marrying. Harper found herself reading one incident over and over because she couldn't believe what he'd written and decided to exclude it. When her mother had mentioned adulterous affairs, secret babies, and illegal abortions, Martell did not know how right she'd been, because the pages of several notebooks had described the events in vivid detail.

Even before beginning to plot the novel, Harper had decided to not only change names, but also dates and cities to protect her family's reputation. She closed her eyes and massaged her forehead as she thought about how she wanted to tell her great-grandfather's story without compromising his reputation.

"Are you okay?"

Harper glanced over her shoulder to find Bernard standing several feet away. She'd been so focused on the stack of notebooks resting on a chair that she hadn't heard his approach. "I'm good, Grandpa." She told him only a half-truth. Reading about his father's adulterous affairs and his mother forgiving her husband repeatedly troubled Harper. She wondered why her great-grandmother had been willing to turn a blind eye to her husband's philandering. Was it because she truly loved him, or was she more in love with the idea of being married to Kelton Fleming, superstar of the Negro Baseball Leagues?

Bernard walked over and sat on a stool next to the table. "I just came to tell you that I got a call from one of my army friends. Some of us who belong to Tennessee Vietnam Veterans of America are planning to get together for a Memorial Day reunion in Chattanooga. This year we decided it's going to be a dudes-only trip, so we can be ourselves."

Harper wondered if they had excluded women so they could relive past exploits with other women. She met his eyes. "Do you plan to drive?" Harper knew it would take two hours to drive between the two cities.

"No. We're hiring a driver who's going to pick up a couple of guys in Memphis, me here in Nashville, and one more in Murfreesboro."

Harper smiled. "How long do you plan to stay?"

"A week. We're going to check into a hotel and figure out what we want to do each day."

She hoped spending a week with his old military friends would give Bernard the opportunity to not dwell on losing Nadine. Harper did not want to minimize the effect of his loss, because going to bed and waking up beside the same person for more than fifty years was a monumental feat, when some couples weren't able to stay together for five years.

"Good for you, Grandpa. Do you need help packing?"

Bernard grunted under his breath. "No. I may be old, but I'm not helpless."

Harper grimaced. "I'm not implying you are, but I just want to make certain you pack enough to last you a week."

He rested a hand on her shoulder. "I know you're worried

about me, and I appreciate that. But now that you're here, I'm feeling better than I have in months."

"That's good to know." She wanted to remind her grandfather that hypertension and elevated cholesterol levels were life-threatening health issues, and even more so for a man his age.

Bernard dropped his hand. "I'm going to let you get back to work, while I go and pack."

Harper nodded. She had typed a draft of several chapters and felt ready to begin writing. Kelton Fleming was now Moses Gilliam, who had lived with his family in the fictional town of Nichols, Tennessee. She'd chosen to give him the name as a nod to Moses Fleetwood Walker. The professional baseball catcher was historically credited with being the first Black man to play in Major League Baseball. He, although mixed-race, was open about his Black heritage, unlike William Edward White, who had passed himself off as a White man. The name Gilliam was homage to James William "Junior" Gilliam, who'd been a second and third baseman and coach in the Negro Leagues and had spent his entire major league baseball career with the Brooklyn Dodgers—and then the Los Angeles Dodgers when the team moved to California. The notebooks were filled with the mention of different women, and Harper decided to also change their names and portray them as supporting fictional characters in Moses's life.

Leaning back in her chair, she stared through the mesh on the screen and gathered her thoughts. It had taken her days to produce a title for the novel, beginning with a listing of more than half a dozen potential titles before narrowing it down to two. She'd discovered Kelton to be optimistic, believing good things came to those who wait. While he'd experienced setbacks, he had been able to overcome them with positivity and perseverance.

The seconds ticked before she selected the final title: *Home and Away.*

Nichols, Tennessee
May 30, 1936

Moses Gilliam refused to show fear or back down as he stood in front of his father, staring at the bulging vein in the older man's forehead and the spittle forming at the corners of his gaping mouth. In the past he had feared arousing Solomon Gilliam's quick and unbridled temper, but not today. He was prepared to walk out of the house where he'd been born and raised. If pushed to his breaking point, he'd leave and never look back.

He didn't know if Solomon would attempt to beat him, as he'd done in the past until Moses had decided enough was enough and put a stop to it. The year he turned sixteen, not only was he taller than his father, but he'd also put on muscle from working after school as a part-time helper for the man who owned the local general store. He swept and mopped floors, delivered groceries, lifted fifty-pound sacks of flour, grits, and rice, and everything else the store owner wanted him to do. Moses resented the man calling him *boy* and ordering him to use the outhouse rather than the bathroom at the back of the store whenever he needed to relieve himself, but that hadn't mattered because the money he earned and saved was what he needed to begin his new life away from Nichols, Tennessee.

Moses didn't want to end up like his grandfather or father, who had left the house before sunrise, returning at dusk after working long hours in a coal mine. He'd watched his grandfather die a slow, agonizing death coughing up blood and coal dust, and it had become the same with Solomon, whose chest rattled whenever he took a deep breath.

No, he thought. That wasn't the life for him, because unlike his father and grandfather, Moses had choices. Not only could he read and write well, but he also had twelve years of schooling thanks to the encouragement of his mother. If Daisy Gilliam hadn't stood up to her dictatorial husband and insisted their only son finish high school, Moses knew he would've gotten up every morning and accompanied his father and the work crews to the mines.

Solomon's hands balled into fists. "You're not leaving my house until I say you can."

Moses shook his head. "The days when you can tell me what to do and not do are over, Pop. I'm my own man now, and I'm going to do what's best for me. Working in a coal mine is not what I want for my future."

"Hitting a ball is?"

"Yes, Pop. They tell me I'm good enough to play in the Negro Baseball Leagues, so I'm leaving for Memphis to join one of the teams there."

"You'll never make it, and before you know it, you'll find your dumb ass right back here working in the mines."

"I don't care what you say because I'm leaving."

Solomon took a step, bringing him less than a foot from his son. "Over my dead body you will."

"And it will be your dead body if you don't get out of the way and let my son walk out of here."

Moses heard the distinctive racking of a shotgun at the same time as Solomon. They both turned to see Daisy pointing the deadly weapon in their direction. He couldn't believe his soft-spoken mother had threatened Solomon. There weren't too many times when she did not defer to her husband, allowing him to make all the decisions in their nineteen-year marriage. The exception was insisting her son get a decent education because she hadn't wanted him to succumb to the debilitating disease that had taken the life of her father, who died much too young, and had now afflicted her husband, despite his denials that it wasn't an occupational illness.

Solomon's mouth was smiling, while his eyes, an odd shade of green, gold, and gray resembling a cat's-eye marble, were cold as chipped glass. "You wouldn't shoot your husband."

Daisy's impassive expression did not change. "Yes, I would. I will blow your behind to hell, and then tell the sheriff that I had to defend myself because you were beating me. Everyone knows that you're as mean as a rabid dog when you drink, and you hit your kids. That's why our girls left home at fifteen and sixteen to become wives and mothers rather than teachers or nurses. But that's not going to happen with my son, Solomon."

"You forget, Daisy, that he's also my son."

She slowly shook her head. "No, Solomon. Moses has always been my son, and you knew that when you married me. You were aware that I was carrying another man's child, but you promised to raise it as your own, not because you wanted the baby in my belly. It was always about me. You just couldn't stand that I preferred your best friend over you. Meanwhile, I've stood by and allowed you to beat our children into submission, but it stops today as sure as my name is Daisy Loretta Gilliam. Now, step aside and let Moses walk out of here to live his life by his own rules, or so help me they will carry you out with your body filled with buckshot."

Moses recognized something in his mother's eyes that hadn't been there before: determination. She had promised him that she would support his dream to become a baseball player, and she now willingly challenged her husband even if she had to threaten his life to make that a reality for him.

His mother had known he was a good athlete even before the scouts came around asking about him. Word had gotten out about his incredible ability to hit home runs. It hadn't mattered whether the pitcher threw a slow curve or a fastball, but whenever Moses's bat contacted the ball, it sailed over the heads of the outfielders and out of the ballpark. He knew it wasn't just luck, but the ability to visually track the ball in the fraction of a second from when it was released from the pitcher's hand to when it would reach home plate. Some people were gifted with total recall, or the ability to mimic sounds, but for Moses it was hand-eye coordination.

He studied religiously in school, worked hard at his part-time job, but he practiced even harder to learn how to hit. Moses knew he wanted to become a baseball player the first time his grandfather had taken him to a ballgame the year he celebrated his eighth birthday.

He glanced over his shoulder and met his mother's eyes. "It's okay, Mama. Pop knows I'm going and there's nothing he can do about it." Moses shifted his attention to his father once again. "I'm leaving, but if I hear that you laid a hand on my mother, then I'm coming back to beat the shit out of you. I've stood by and watched you beat my sisters, but that's not going to happen with your wife."

Moses's heart was beating so fast that he suddenly felt lightheaded. It was the first time he'd challenged his dictatorial father and hopefully the last. He was leaving for Memphis to start a new life and he prayed that he wasn't leaving his mother with a man who had not only physically beaten his son but also his daughters. If Solomon had hit his wife, it was never in front of their children, and he hadn't left visible bruises.

Daisy lowered the shotgun. "You better head out or you are going to miss your bus."

Moses nodded as he hoisted the duffel over his shoulder, filled with a half dozen changes of clothes, a Bible, books, and the notebooks his mother had given him to write down his experiences as a baseball player. He had saved every penny he earned, and with the few dollars his mother had secretly given him whenever her husband gave her money to cover household expenses, he now had a total sum of almost two hundred dollars. And for Moses it was a small fortune.

He walked out of the house and into the bright spring sunlight, coming to a complete stop when he saw the White man leaning against the side of a shiny black car. It was the scout who had come to see him play and subsequently given him the opportunity to try out with a local team, where he hit a home run each time he came up to bat.

The man straightened, flashing a smile with a mouth filled with large white teeth. "You didn't think I was going to let my best prospect sit in the back of the bus all the way to Memphis."

Moses's impassive expression did not change, because he knew Edgar Donnelly viewed him as a meal ticket, a talented Black ballplayer he could exploit to a make as much money as he could. "I don't know what to think, Mr. Donnelly, because I'm not a mind reader." The scout opened the sedan's rear door, and Moses ducked his head to get in, but stopped when he felt the man's hand on his arm.

"Put your things in the back and get up front next to me. We don't want folks to think I was the chauffeur for a nigger."

Moses went completely still. "You call me that again and you'll find yourself driving to Memphis without me. I'm not a nigger, boy, or whatever name you tend to call Black men." He knew challenging the man like he did could cost him a chance to play baseball. Moses realized that if he had uttered those words in the company of other White men, he could have been beaten or even lynched for not knowing know his "place."

Donnelly's face turned beet red with the reprimand. "Sorry. It won't happen again."

Even though the man had apologized, Moses knew it would be short-lived. He was a Black person, but what he hated most was being called a nigger. Nodding, he left his duffel on the floor behind the passenger seat, and then got into the automobile that still had a new car smell. It was obvious the scout was paid well for signing players to various Negro Leagues teams to own such a fine car.

"When am I going to see my contract?" Moses asked as Donnelly started up the Duesenberg SJ.

"There's no need for you to see the contract. As your agent I will go over everything to make certain you will get what's coming to you."

Moses turned to stare at the profile of the man with features that appeared much too small for his fleshy face. "When did you become my agent?"

"When the owner of the Eagles wanted to sign you."

"And you did this without talking to me first? I thought I was going to Memphis on a trial basis."

"It's too late for that. Some of the owner's people came to see you play, and reported back that you should join the team."

Moses struggled not to lose his temper. It was obvious Donnelly thought that he would be all too happy to sign away everything because he valued playing baseball above everything else in his life. However, the man was so focused on making money that he had not taken the time to know who he was dealing with.

"I will not put my signature on anything until I can read it."

Donnelly shifted into a higher gear, increasing his speed when he reached a paved road. "Do you think I would cheat you?"

Moses stared out the windshield. "I told you before

that I'm not a mind reader. It's not enough that we can't play in the Major Leagues because of our race, but we're still being short-changed when White men who own Black teams continue to take advantage of us because we're all too happy to show everyone we are as talented—and some even more talented—than Babe Ruth, Ty Cobb, or Lou Gehrig."

"You seem like a very intelligent young man," Donnelly said after a strained silence. "Would you have become a coal miner like your father if you decided not to play baseball?"

He wanted to tell the supercilious man that he *was* intelligent. Probably a lot more intelligent than he could have imagined as a young Black man growing up in Tennessee's coal country. "No. I would go to college to become a doctor or lawyer."

Donnelly gave him a quick glance before returning his attention to the road. "Really?"

Moses wanted to laugh in the man's face. Was the idea of a Black man going to college so unbelievable to him when there were hundreds of adults graduating from Black colleges and universities every year?

"Yes. Really. I graduated at the top of my class in high school, and I was offered partial scholarships to attend Fisk and Howard Universities."

"So, you're really smart."

Moses smiled for the first time since getting into the luxury automobile. "Smart enough to know if I'm being cheated."

Donnelly sat up straighter. "I'll go over the contract carefully before you see it, and if there is anything you don't agree to, then we can discuss it before you agree to sign it."

"Are you open to negotiating something I'd like to see included in the contract?" Moses knew he was treading on thin ice because as a Black man in the segregated

South he had little or no influence when it came to demanding what he wanted from a White person. However, what he did know was his worth. He was worth a lot to the Memphis Eagles; at high school he'd been touted as the Black Babe Ruth.

"I'm open if it will benefit both of us. Remember, when you make more, I make more as your agent."

"At least we can agree on that," Moses said under his breath. He knew he had disappointed his mother when he'd chosen baseball over college. However, she was willing to support him because she knew playing ball was something he'd wanted to do all his life.

"Why don't you relax?" Donnelly said. "It's going to be a while before we get to Memphis. We'll have to stay overnight midway, and I'll drop you off in the Colored section of town where you can get a room, because we won't be able to stay in the same place. I'll pick you up at ten and that should give you enough time to have breakfast before we get back on the road."

The arrangements suited Moses; he'd wanted to tell the man he preferred being around his own people because then he could be himself. He was more comfortable being with Black folks and also felt safe around them. Having his own room meant he could begin writing in his notebook—stories he would pass along to a generation of the future Gilliams.

Moses got out of the car when Donnelly stopped in a little dusty town that barely made the map. He retrieved his duffel and walked up the rickety steps to a two-story rooming house that was sorely in need of a coat of white paint. A sign out front advertised clean rooms with meals included in the daily rate.

Moses didn't know how much he would be paid once he signed the contract, but until that time came, he knew he had to be careful when it came to spending his meager savings. He couldn't afford to squander his money by checking into a place with more comfortable amenities. He opened the front door and walked into what passed for a reception area. A hanging ceiling fixture and several table lamps provided enough illumination for Moses to notice faded wallpaper and mismatched tables and chairs. A middle-aged Black woman wearing wire-rimmed glasses smiled at him. Her two front teeth were ringed in gold.

"Evening. I'm Bettina Jackson, the owner of this fine establishment. And what can I do for you?"

Moses returned her smile with a friendly one of his own. "It's nice meeting you, Miss Bettina. I'd like a room with a bathroom."

"Having your own bathroom is going to cost extra."

"How much extra?" he questioned.

The woman pushed her hands into the pockets of her bibbed apron. "A dollar extra."

"How much is the room?" Moses asked.

"Two dollars."

Moses nodded. Giving the woman three dollars wasn't too much for him not to share a communal bathroom with strangers. "What time is breakfast?"

"We begin serving breakfast at eight in the dining room. The cook makes grits, eggs, ham, bacon, fried fish, and biscuits."

He wanted to tell the woman that she was singing his song. There was nothing he loved better than eating fried fish and grits for breakfast. "I'll have the fish, grits, eggs, and biscuits."

"Whiting or catfish?"

Moses couldn't believe that he had been given a choice. "Catfish."

Bettina smiled again. "I'll let him know to take some out of the icehouse." She held out her hand. "You need to pay in advance, because in the past some of the roomers would run out without paying."

Reaching into the front pocket of his khakis, Moses took out several folded one-dollar bills, counting out three and handing them to Bettina, while repocketing the rest. He couldn't understand why Black folks would cheat one another when it was something they never would attempt to do when dealing with Whites.

Bettina slipped the money into the pocket of her dress under the apron. Picking up a bell off a table, she shook it vigorously. "I'll have someone show you to your room."

Seconds later, a beautiful young woman appeared, and Moses stared at her as if she were an apparition. Her straightened hair was parted in the middle and pinned in a bun on the nape of her long, slender neck. He was mesmerized by her delicate features, her complexion the color of a shiny copper penny. She smiled at the same time she demurely lowered her eyes.

"Karleen, please show Mr. . . ."

"Gilliam," Moses said, unable to stop staring at Karleen.

"Please show Mr. Gilliam to the room with the private bathroom."

"Yes, Mama."

Moses followed Karleen to a staircase leading to the second floor, his gaze fixed on her rounded bottom in a pair of blue jeans that were too small for her voluptuous hips. She'd tied the hem of a sleeveless white blouse at the waist, leaving an expanse of visible skin at the small of her back. He wasn't a virgin—an older woman he'd encountered the year he'd turned sixteen had seen to that—yet Moses was very discriminating when it came to having sex with a woman. He'd never attempted to seduce any of the girls at school, because he knew most of them were saving themselves for marriage.

Daisy had lectured him about getting a girl pregnant because it would be certain to derail all his plans to play baseball and, like the other men in his family, he would be forced to go to work in the mines. Along with his notebooks, his mother had also packed several condoms. She'd warned him if he didn't use them, he could have to face the responsibilities of becoming a father before he was ready. She had been forthcoming when she told him she had given another man her virginity to spite Solomon, and how when she'd told the man she was pregnant, he'd left town the following day. Although Solomon had married her knowing she was carrying another man's child, he'd never let her forget that he had saved her reputation.

There were times when Moses was as randy as a goat but opted to use another method to assuage his buildup of sexual tension. He'd begun masturbating.

"How long are you staying, Mr. Gilliam?" Karleen asked, as she peered at Moses over her shoulder.

"Just the night, ma'am."

She giggled. "There's no need to call me ma'am. I'm not that old. I'm willing to bet that I'm just a few years older than you."

Moses knew she was flirting with him, but he had no intention of reciprocating. He was on his way to Memphis to become a ballplayer and he couldn't afford to lose focus by getting involved with a woman. Even one who was as attractive as Karleen.

She opened the door to a room at the end of the long hallway. "I changed the bed, and there are clean towels and facecloths in the bathroom. If there is anything you need just let me know. My room is at the top of the stairs on the right. Just knock on the door and I'll get you whatever you need."

He walked into the room, finding it more than adequate with a full-size bed, a chest of drawers, an armchair with a footstool, and a small lamp on a bedside table. "Thank you. I don't think I'm going to need anything."

Moses waited until Karleen turned and reversed her steps, then closed and locked the door. After a restful night's sleep followed by a substantial breakfast, he would be more than ready to meet Donnelly and the owner of the team looking to sign him to a contract to play for the Memphis Eagles.

CHAPTER 4

Moses was more than ready to meet the owner of the Memphis Eagles when he walked outside the rooming house to find Edgar Donnelly sitting in his car waiting for him. He'd slept well, and after shaving, showering, and dressing in a pair of dark slacks, white shirt, and a lightweight tan jacket, he went downstairs to the dining room and ordered his breakfast of fish, grits, eggs, and buttery biscuits. After storing his duffel on the rear seat, he settled himself on the passenger side beside the scout-turned-agent.

Donnelly gave him a sidelong glance before he started up the car. "How were the accommodations?"

Moses smiled. "Wonderful." He had no intention of engaging in small talk with the man because he didn't want to develop a personal relationship with someone who was responsible for him earning a living. He'd heard the expression over and over that he shouldn't shit where he ate, and that meant he had to keep a distinct separation between the two.

"Are you excited about meeting the owner?"

Moses stared straight ahead. "No."

"Why not?" Donnelly asked.

"Because he's probably another big-city hustler looking to take advantage of men who want to become baseball players more than anything else in their lives and because of that they are willing to accept whatever is doled out to them for the privilege to play in the Negro Leagues."

"Not all owners are hustlers, Moses."

"You think not, Mr. Donnelly?"

"Not the owner of the Eagles. The team's owner has earned a reputation of being one of the most honest and generous ones in the leagues. Most of the players stay with the team after their initial contracts expire because not only are they paid well, but they are also treated well."

Moses wanted to tell his agent that seeing was believing. There were things he wanted in his contract that would benefit not only his rookie status but also when he'd become a regular team player.

Donnelly had hinted that the more money he earned, the more he would receive in commission, but Moses had read in Black newspapers that some players left the game because they were unaware of the language in their contracts that indicated they could be fired for vague infractions based on the owner's interpretation. Gambling and game-fixing topped the list because of the fixing of the 1919 World Series between the Chicago White Sox and the Cincinnati Reds in exchange for money from a gambling syndicate led by Arnold Rothstein. The incident, known as the Black Sox Scandal, ended with eight men being banned from playing professional baseball for the rest of their lives. Inasmuch as Moses wanted a career as a ballplayer, he knew he'd never accept money to throw a game, no matter how much he was offered.

Moses had found himself enthralled with stories about gangsters, mobsters, and outlaws. He had scoured magazines and newspapers for articles about Al Capone, John Dillinger, and Bonnie and Clyde, which disturbed his mother because she believed he was focusing on becoming a criminal. However, Moses knew at an early age that Capone, Dillinger, Baby Face Nelson, and Ma Barker's criminal careers were spawned by Prohibition and the continuing Depression. He didn't know why he had an intense interest in criminal activities, but he was fascinated by the men who'd been employed by the Bureau of Investigation, which recently had been renamed the Federal Bureau of Investigation, to end the careers of gangsters and mobsters topping their Most Wanted list.

The Great Depression affected everyone, including the coal industry where production fell from a high of 608 million tons in 1929 to a low of only 359 million in 1932. The Depression worsened the already bleak economic situations of Negroes because they were the first to be laid off from their jobs and suffered an unemployment rate two to three times higher than Whites.

The Gilliams were more fortunate than other Black families because Solomon hadn't been laid off. Moses's mother grew her own vegetables and raised a flock of laying hens in the small plot of land behind their house, so there was always enough food on the table. Daisy, a dressmaker, had also taken in laundry for the wife of the owner of the mine, which had cemented her husband's opportunity for continued employment. She claimed she wasn't above becoming domestic help for someone if it meant keeping a roof over her children's heads. She wanted her children to finish high school because that had been denied to her when she'd had to drop out in the tenth grade once she discovered she was pregnant. Moses was able to achieve what she hadn't accomplished, but her daughters weren't so lucky: They left school to marry and escape their father's unbridled temper and whippings.

There were times when Moses attempted to stop his father from hitting his sisters, but Daisy told him not to interfere because she didn't want him to incur Solomon's wrath. She knew he hated the boy he begrudgingly claimed as his own.

Moses and his sisters had left Nichols, and if word got back to him that Solomon was abusing his wife, Moses would send for her once he began earning money from playing ball. He promised to write to her as soon as he was settled, and she also promised to write back. Solomon was illiterate, so Moses knew his father wouldn't read her mail. Solomon could recognize two- and three-letter words, had learned to sign his name, but he'd found extreme difficulty in learning to read. Frustrated, he'd dropped out in the sixth grade and went to work in the mines with his father.

"Are you ready to meet the team's owner?" Edgar Donnelly said, interrupting Moses's thoughts.

"I am," Moses answered truthfully.

He did not want to admit it was something he'd wanted and prayed for as long as he could remember. The first time he found an old baseball and then fashioned a bat from a discarded broomstick and hit the ball into the air for what seemed to him like miles, he knew he wanted to become a ballplayer. Then, when his grandfather took him to a game to see men who played the game and looked like him, Moses knew he had found his calling. Up until that time, he'd heard names like Babe Ruth, Rogers Hornsby, and Lou Gehrig. But after attending that game and many others to follow, Moses wanted to know more about the Black men who were not accepted into the major and minor baseball leagues because of racism, which had established a color line. The result had forced them to form their own teams. His interest in gangsters, mobsters, and outlaws shifted to Black baseball, and he read everything he could find written about them, which hadn't been much, especially since he didn't have much access to Black newspapers.

However, he did become obsessed when researching Moses Fleetwood Walker, and his brother Weldy Wilberforce Walker, who were the first two Black players in the Major Leagues. They had played for the Toledo Blue Stockings in the American Association in 1884, which at that time was considered a Major League. There were other Black American players who joined the International League, but 1888 was the last season Blacks were permitted in any minor leagues.

Moses wasn't certain whether he'd been named for the baseball player or for the Hebrew prophet who had brought the Israelites out of bondage in Egypt to lead them to the Promised Land, yet he had come to revere his name.

"Well, you won't have to wait much longer, because we'll be in Memphis in a couple of hours, and after meeting with the owner, there's no doubt life as you know it will change completely."

Moses stared out the side window. "I just want to be paid what I'm worth." He didn't want to be like some players who continued to stay with a team despite knowing they were being cheated by unscrupulous owners who claimed because profits were down, they were forced to cut the salaries of their players. He hadn't wanted to forgo the opportunity to attend college to become a doctor or lawyer, only to become an athlete with a tenuous future where he could be cut, fired, or even injured before turning twenty-five. Rather, he left Nichols to make his mother proud.

He was born the year World War I ended. Now there were rumors of more turmoil in Europe with the meteoric rise of the Nazi Party and Adolf Hitler as party chancellor because of the weakness of democracy in Germany and the ongoing conditions of the Great Depression.

Moses was only eighteen, and he did not want to concern himself with national politics or world affairs. He'd come to accept the so-called separate but equal laws of Jim Crow throughout the South. He lived in a segregated town, attended segregated schools with all-Black teachers, and adhered to the WHITES ONLY and COLORED ONLY signs. And because of Tennessee's Jim Crow laws that enacted school segregation, supported segregated railroads, public accommodations, street transportation, and outlawed interracial marriage, Moses had made certain to limit his interaction with Whites.

That was, until he'd been approached by Edgar Donnelly after the man had attended a baseball game where Moses's school was competing with another school for the state's Negro baseball championship. Moses was surprised when his coach asked him to stay after the game because someone was interested in him. Coming face-to-face with Edgar Donnelly shocked him when the man introduced himself and extended his hand to Moses. It wasn't until later that he discovered Donnelly wasn't a Southerner but someone who'd been born and raised in New York City and was hired as a scout for the Memphis Eagles's new owner. The team's former owner had committed suicide after he'd discovered his wife had run off with his brother.

Moses had taken the proffered hand with the knowledge it was the first time he'd shaken hands with a White man. Despite the friendly gesture, it hadn't precluded Donnelly's calling him a nigger. He didn't know if the epithet was one he used frequently, but it was one word Moses refused to acknowledge for himself.

"As I said before, the more you make, the more I make."

"How much of a percentage do you intend to charge me?" Moses asked.

"I was thinking of fifteen percent."

Moses shook his head. "That's too much."

Donnelly gave him a quick glance. "How much do you think I should charge you?"

A beat passed, then Moses said, "I was thinking more like eight. That's almost half of what you planned to take."

There came another moment of silence before Donnelly said, "What if we compromise and agree on ten? For one hundred dollars you make I'll get ten, leaving you with ninety."

Moses pondered his explanation. He wasn't certain how much the owner was willing to pay him for an initial one-year contract, but even if he earned a monthly salary between one and four hundred dollars it would be comparable to working as a coal miner, and with less health risks. However, life in the Negro Leagues was hard; some players might play in as many as three games a day and only earn four or five hundred a month, while White players in the Major Leagues, even if they were playing doubleheaders, were earning thousands. The highest salary in the 1930s was $80,000 for Babe Ruth, who played for the New York Yankees, while most other White players could expect to earn between five and six thousand a year. If he were to earn five thousand dollars a year and didn't squander his money, he could become financially secure for years to come.

"I'll think on it," Moses countered. He didn't want to tip his hand about how much commission the agent would make until he discussed the terms of his contract with the team's owner. He wasn't a slave or a commodity to be bought or sold, but someone with the physical and mental ability to satisfy human wants and needs, now that baseball had come to be known as America's "national pastime."

Moses had witnessed his mother's struggle to provide for her family when she got up early to work in the little patch of earth that passed for the family's garden, before seeing her children off to school. Then she would go and pick up laundry and spend hours scrubbing on the washboard and hanging wet laundry out to dry before ironing and folding it to be returned to the woman who believed she was above doing her own laundry.

There was never a time when her hands were still. Even when she sat down at the end of the day to listen to the radio, she would knit socks, gloves, hats, and scarves for her husband and children to ward off the cold during the winter months, or she'd busy herself hemming, sewing zippers on the garments she made on the sewing machine with a foot pedal. The first thing Moses wanted to purchase for his mother was a newer model machine to replace the treadle, because several years ago many of the miners' homes had been updated with electricity and indoor plumbing to appease the workers who were threatening to strike for higher wages and better living conditions.

Coal companies did not want a repeat of what had occurred during West Virginia's coal wars, which had sparked a series of violent outbreaks throughout the state, beginning in 1920. Violent conflicts between coal miners and owners erupted throughout coal mining regions in the country and resulted in casualties, predominantly for workers. If they weren't killed in riots, then it was cave-ins, or black lung.

Daisy Gilliam had sacrificed a lot to put up with her

abusive husband, and Moses wanted to pay her back for what she had surrendered to make Moses into the man he had become and to help him realize his dream of becoming a baseball player. And if it was about making money, it wasn't only about himself, but her. He didn't know whether she would ever leave her husband—that choice would have to be hers alone. Yet Moses knew he had to be ready to accept her whenever she decided she'd had enough and made the decision to divorce her husband. She was in her mid-thirties and still young enough to start her life over. She always talked about going back to school to earn her high school diploma and even go to college to become a schoolteacher. But that would only become a possibility if she were single again.

Solomon had argued that he didn't need book learning because he earned enough to take care of his family and viewed education as a waste of time and money. Whenever he talked like that, Moses wondered what it was that Daisy saw in the man to make her accept him. It could've been because other girls were chasing him; he was one of the more attractive boys in their town and was a sharp dresser. Daisy had been keeping company with another boy when Solomon decided he wanted to take her out. After a while they were going steady, but something occurred between them that forced Daisy to break up with Solomon and she went back to her old boyfriend. She knew it would cause tension between the two men because they'd grown up as friends. Daisy had slept with her old boyfriend to spite Solomon because she had promised to remain a virgin until married, but it was too late when she discovered she was carrying a baby that wasn't Solomon Gilliam's.

Moses had promised himself that he didn't want a repeat of his parents' lives, so he focused on what he needed to do to secure his own future. He knew men who were already married with families by eighteen. Moses wanted to wait before becoming a husband and father. There was no way he would be able to take care of a family if he wasn't able to take care of himself.

The remainder of the drive was silent, and for that Moses was grateful. He wasn't comfortable talking to Donnelly; he didn't want the man to know what he was thinking. Folks called it "picking one's brain." The less he said, the less Donnelly would know about him.

Moses became alert when Donnelly maneuvered into an alley behind a row of shotgun houses in a Colored section of Memphis. He believed they would conduct business in an office building or even a house that wasn't covered with a rusted tin roof, and at that moment, he felt as if he'd been duped by unscrupulous businesspeople looking to take advantage of his age and naïveté. Had they lured him away from home because, like the pied piper, they believed he would follow them anywhere? However, he did see a pickup truck parked in the alley and several workers dressed in coveralls sitting on the ground talking and eating. It was obvious they were taking a break.

Donnelly cut off the Duesenberg's engine. "Well, we're here."

Moses gave him a direct stare. "You're going to leave your car here?" The shiny luxury automobile appeared incompatible with its impoverished surroundings.

"Sure. No one's going to bother with it. These folks know who I am."

Moses wondered how many times the scout had driven prospective players to this section of town where even respectable Black folks wouldn't be caught after dark. There were men—old and young—sitting on wooden crates on lopsided porches, watching all the comings and goings.

He got out, retrieved his duffel, and followed his agent up the back stairs to the clapboard house built on stilts. Donnelly knocked on the door a couple of times, followed by three more taps before it opened and an incredibly beautiful Black woman dressed in the height of fashion stood in the doorway. The woman was wearing a light blue linen suit that was the perfect contrast with her velvety mahogany complexion. Smiling, her lush mouth outlined in vermilion lipstick, her straight teeth appeared even whiter against the brilliant red lip color.

"Come in, Edgar," she said, leaning to press her cheek against his.

Moses was stunned as Edgar Donnelly hugged the woman longer than he deemed necessary. He stared as if in a trance, not realizing he'd been holding his breath until he felt tightness in his chest that reminded him to exhale. There was something so familiar in the body language of the two and he suspected they were more connected to each other than just by business.

Donnelly removed his straw hat and ran a hand over thick wavy black hair. "Winnie, I'd like you to meet our latest prospect, Moses Gilliam. Moses, this is the owner of the Memphis Eagles, Miss Winnie Chess."

Moses's impassive expression concealed his shock as he dipped his head, then met the large, light brown eyes of the woman who, if he signed the contract, would become his boss. "It's a pleasure to meet you, ma'am."

"No, Moses, it's my pleasure to finally meet you. Edgar has been talking about you for months, and I'm so glad he was able to convince you to come to Memphis so we could talk about your future with the Eagles."

I like her. There wasn't anything Moses didn't like about the woman who smelled as good as she looked. He assumed she was older than his mother, but probably not by much. But then, makeup was able to conceal imperfections. She was tall for a woman, only three or four inches shorter than his own six-foot height, and very slender. Her hair was styled in finger waves that framed her oval face perfectly.

Suddenly Moses felt awkward as he glanced around the room furnished with a coal stove, bed, wardrobe, and a round table with four chairs. He noted a trio of kerosene lamps on the floor several feet from the stove. There was no doubt Donnelly and Winnie were city sophisticates, while he was a country boy from a coal mining region who had never traveled more than ten miles from Nichols.

He didn't know whether to continue to stand or sit, but Donnelly solved his dilemma when he pulled out a chair for Winnie and seated her before taking one next to her. "Sit down, Moses. We need to discuss business because I'd like to be on the road back north before sundown."

Moses wanted to ask Donnelly where he expected *him* to be at sundown, but he decided to hold his tongue. He knew he had a lot to learn that could only be accomplished with patience and observation.

Setting his duffel on the floor, he pulled out a chair and sat opposite the couple who were exchanging furtive glances with each other. Winnie, lacing her fingers together, smiled at Moses. "I assume you're surprised that I'm the owner of the Memphis Eagles."

Moses nodded. "Yes, ma'am." Not only was he shocked that she was the owner, but he wondered if there was something physical between her and Edgar Donnelly, although neither wore rings. Judging from Winnie's speech pattern it was obvious that she hadn't been raised in the South.

Winnie leaned forward; her long spiky lashes coated

with black mascara fluttered as she met Moses's eyes. "I need you to tell me why you believe you can become a baseball player."

Moses was slightly taken aback when he replayed her words in his head. "It's not so much what I believe, but what I know," he countered confidently. "Mr. Donnelly would not have asked me to come here to meet you if he didn't believe I could make the team."

Winnie sat back and gave him a long, penetrating stare. "You're right about that." She paused for a full minute. "Now, it's time I tell you what I want and expect from you."

CHAPTER 5

Winnie couldn't believe her good luck when her business partner had sung the praises of a young man he'd seen play baseball at an all-Colored school in rural Tennessee. It was the first time Edgar had appeared so excited about a potential prospect for the team they owned and managed together.

She hadn't seen Moses play, but if his batting skills were comparable to his appearance, then no doubt they had stumbled upon a sure winner. With his smooth, dark brown complexion, large expressive brown eyes, and evenly balanced masculine features, it was obvious he'd have girls and women giving him a second glance. At thirty-seven, Winnie was nearly twenty years his senior, old enough to be his mother. It didn't matter how much she found herself attracted to him, nothing would become of it. He had two strikes against him: age, and—once he signed the contract—he'd be her employee. She had made it a practice never to become involved with any of the players on the Memphis Eagles. She also did not mix business with pleasure when it came to Edgar Donnelly. He was her business partner and she made certain never to cross the line where it would become more than that.

"I'd like to sign you to a six-month rather than a yearlong contract," she announced outright.

Moses blinked slowly. "I thought it would be a one-year contact."

Winnie smiled. "It will be six months, with an extension for another six with an increase in salary depending on your performance." She paused. "I will pay you two hundred dollars a month for the first six, and if your batting average increases exponentially where the team wins more games than they lose, then I will double your salary to four hundred. That's equitable to what many veteran players are making in the Negro Leagues."

Moses stared at Donnelly. "How much are you charging for commission?"

Winnie exchanged a glance with her partner. "What have you agreed to?"

"Ten," he said, meeting Moses's eyes.

"That's a little high, Edgar," Winnie said, smiling. "We can't take all his money because I'm certain he needs to send money back home to take care of his family. Do you have a wife, children, or girlfriend?"

Moses shook his head.

"That leaves you to do whatever you want with your money. What if we start out with five percent, then once we negotiate your extended six-month contract it can increase to, say, six or even seven?"

She was aware that Edgar always started high, and it was up to her to counter his percentage with a lower one to make herself appear more favorable to the players. It was a game they'd played seamlessly since purchasing the failing team. So far, it had worked because they had gained the support of many of the players to work even harder to win games.

Moses blinked again, and the gesture was reminiscent of an owl perched on a tree in the backyard of the house she had inherited in Harlem, New York. She had complained to Edgar that owls represented sinister and ill omens in paintings she'd seen in art books, and then there was the superstition that the hooting of an owl foretold someone's death. She was able to relax and forget about the owl once Edgar reassured her that the bird of prey was responsible for ridding the property of rats without them having to put out poison to kill the rodents. However, it still bothered her to watch Moses stare at her and then slowly close his eyes to blink.

"If we agree, then I will have a contract typed up later today and we can go over it together before we sign it—after you've gone through batting practice. Meanwhile, you can stay here tonight. Someone will come back tomorrow to drive you over to a baseball field where you will take batting practice."

"What about a uniform?"

Winnie rested a hand over her smooth throat. "You'll be supplied with one. I'm not certain what the policy is with other teams, but we take good care of our players. However, let me remind you that there will be a great deal of travel. There are times when you may play two or three games a day. You're a Southern boy, so I don't have to tell you to stay away from White women, and most of all do not fuck one, because we won't be responsible if you're caught and lynched. You will also have the option of traveling once the summer season is over to play winter ball out of the country." Winnie noticed Moses's expression did not change when she'd said *fuck* rather than *sleep with*, and in that instant, she realized he was more mature than several of the older players she'd met with since purchasing the team. She knew a few were resentful they had to rely on a woman for their paycheck, but in the end, if she hadn't bought the team then their days of playing baseball were over if they weren't picked up by other teams.

"Which countries?" Moses questioned.

"Mexico, Cuba, Puerto Rico, the Dominican Republic, and Venezuela. If you're interested and willing to travel abroad, then you'll need a passport." Moses nodded again. "I'll get the application for you to fill out, but that's something we'll do once you officially join the team. I don't know how much you know about barnstorming, but you'll be on the road a lot of the time in various cities, playing against a local opponent, or even another barnstorming team."

"I read that Babe Ruth also did some barnstorming with Bob Meusel after losing the 1922 World Series," Moses said.

Winnie's penciled eyebrows lifted slightly. "It appears as if you're quite familiar with the history of baseball."

A hint of a smile played at the corners of Moses's mouth. "That's because I read a lot."

"He graduated at the top of his high school class," Donnelly stated.

"So, you must be very smart," Winnie crooned.

"I am smart," Moses said confidently. "If I didn't want to play ball, then I would have gone to college to study medicine or law."

Winnie sat up straighter. "You prefer playing ball than becoming a Black doctor or lawyer? Why?"

"Because I know I'm good at baseball. I don't know what kind of doctor or lawyer I'd be. There's going to come a day when Black men will be allowed to play alongside White players, and hopefully I will live long enough to see them compete with Josh Gibson, Cool Papa Bell, and Buck Leonard."

"I hate to burst your bubble, son, but that's not going to happen for a long time," Donnelly interjected.

Moses frowned. "You can't say that unless you have a

crystal ball where you can predict the future. And please don't call me *son*, because you look nothing like my father."

Winnie felt the rising tension between the two men, which was palpable. What she didn't want to do was take sides because it would end badly. She needed Edgar to front for her in the South, while she also needed a new home-run hitter to offset the team's losses. The Eagles had good pitching and adequate fielding, but scoring runs had become a problem. Even when there were no outs and the bases were loaded, strikeouts were preventing runners from scoring. Even additional batting practice hadn't helped, and right now Moses Gilliam had become her last hope.

"Edgar, please. That's not necessary," she said in a hushed tone. There were times when he'd unintentionally say things that were derogatory to her people. While she'd tried to school him on how to interact with Black folks, he would occasionally slip up and say something insulting or belittling.

He dropped his head. "Sorry about that," he said, apologizing.

Winnie did not have to tell him to apologize because he knew she was the one who had afforded him a level of affluence he never would've had if he hadn't met her. She'd taught him how to dress, what to say when interacting with prospective players, and which fork to use when sitting down to eat. He was the great-grandson of immigrants who came to America to escape Ireland's potato famine and found positions as housekeepers, and factory and dockworkers, while she was the descendant of free people of color who had escaped slavery through the Underground Railroad to settle in New York.

Winnie had become one of a few women to own a baseball team; her hero was Effa Manley, who managed and co-owned the Newark Eagles. Although Manley wasn't Black, she had been born into an interracial family. While her mother's Black husband wasn't her biological father, Manley continued living as a Black woman, which had raised her status in Winnie's eyes.

As a nurse, Winnie no longer worked shifts in a hospital, yet she'd continued to use her skills when becoming the live-in private duty nurse for an elderly, widowed, bed-ridden judge who had been the direct descendent of a wealthy Dutch family who had settled in New York's Hudson Valley. Aside from the monies she derived from her divorce settlement, she had been the beneficiary of her patient's Harlem brownstone after he passed away. His children and grandchildren hadn't contested the will because they'd inherited the bulk of his estate.

Edgar had become an equal partner once he contributed enough capital for them to purchase the Memphis Eagles. One of his uncles, who'd belonged to a New York City Irish mob, had been arrested for bootlegging, prostitution, and bookmaking. He had given his favorite nephew money to hold on to for him before being arrested and subsequently sentenced to a ten-year stint in Sing Sing Prison in upstate New York. His uncle died two months after being incarcerated. Edgar, who'd admitted having a crush on Winnie when they attended the same Brooklyn junior and senior high schools, asked her to go to a New York Yankees baseball game with him after running into her at Macy's several years later after graduating when they both were Easter shopping. She'd agreed once he told her his wife didn't like baseball, and it was the beginning of many more games they attended together at either Yankee Stadium in the Bronx or Ebbets Field in Brooklyn. She couldn't believe she'd found a friend who was as fanatical about baseball as she was.

Edgar had used a portion of his uncle's illegal

earnings to purchase a dress factory in the Bronx. When she'd approached him about investing in a Negro baseball team, he jumped at the opportunity to own a team—even if it was in the Negro Leagues.

She knew he wanted more than friendship, but Winnie wasn't willing to cross that line because in addition to Edgar being White, he was married with children. She had married briefly after graduating from nursing school, but it didn't last more than two years. The even-tempered lawyer she'd married had been living a double life. Unbeknownst to her, he had hidden his homosexuality until one day she came home before her shift had ended to find him in bed with another man.

She packed her clothes, walked out of the apartment, and told him she was filing for divorce. However, she did save his reputation by not disclosing his proclivity for sleeping with men. The settlement she received was enough for her to save for the proverbial rainy day. However, luck was with her when several years later she inherited property from her deceased patient in a residential neighborhood that had been owned by well-to-do White families before the turn of the twentieth century. There were several apartments in the brownstone she'd rented out to Black young professionals, and the income was more than enough to offset taxes and maintenance expenses. She'd subsequently taken out a mortgage on the brownstone and that, with the money from her divorce settlement, was enough for her to go into business with Edgar as co-owners of a Black baseball team.

If she had reinvented herself as a businessperson, so had Edgar, as the owner of a factory. He married a schoolteacher, purchased a house in Brooklyn Heights overlooking the East River with views of downtown Manhattan, and when at home he drove his children around in the Duesenberg. As co-owners of the

Memphis Eagles, Winnie and Edgar were financially stable, but she believed they could do and live even better if they were able to sign a player whom they would be able to tout as the "Black Babe Ruth." While Edgar believed the color line for baseball would never be broken, Winnie thought differently. Things always changed. Nothing ever remained the same.

Donnelly pushed back his chair and stood up. "I'm going to head out now, because I want to be home in time for my wife's birthday." He rested a hand on Winnie's shoulder. "I'll see you later on in the month."

Winnie patted the hand on her shoulder and smiled up at Donnelly. "I'll call you once I get back to New York."

She waited for Edgar to leave to give Moses her undivided attention. "What's bothering you, Moses?"

He blinked again. "What makes you think something is bothering me?"

"It's the way you've been staring at me."

Moses wanted to lie and say he was curious about her, but he decided to be truthful. "Why did you decide to buy a baseball team?"

Winnie angled her head. "Would you have asked me that if I were a man?"

He averted his gaze, knowing she had read his mind. In his limited experience, women were not in business. Some found employment as teachers, clerks, or nurses, while the few he'd encountered worked in restaurants, beauty shops, and factories.

"No, ma'am, I wouldn't. I'm simply curious why you would want to own a baseball team."

"To make money. Isn't that the reason anyone goes into business? And as Black folks, we will never be able to compete with other groups until we are able to achieve ownership of something that will allow us to become financially independent. There are people who've come to this country with not much more than the clothes on their backs, and it didn't take them a generation to achieve what we haven't been able to in more than three hundred years."

"That's because we can't change the color of our skin," Moses said, meeting her eyes. "If that were possible, then we would have the same opportunities as other immigrants who come to this country for a better way of life."

Winnie's smile did not meet her light brown eyes as they bore into his. "Now that you realize that, what are you going to do about it?"

A slight frown creased Moses's forehead. "I don't understand."

"What you must understand, Moses, is that if you're not able to come in through the front door because of the color of your skin, then you must develop a strategy to get in another way. Edgar and I are kindred spirits because not only are we former classmates and friends, but we both love baseball. Edgar is my representative here in the South and I don't interfere or second-guess him when he decides what's best for the team."

"But you did when he mentioned his commission."

"That's because regardless of our business relationship I will not permit him to take advantage of my people."

"He must do very well with his commissions to drive a Deusenberg."

Winnie lowered her eyes as she shook her head. "Being part-owner of the Memphis Eagles isn't his only business. Owning a baseball team is like a hobby for him."

Now Moses was confused, but then he didn't want to overstep and ask Winnie anything that was too personal. "Other than playing baseball, what do you suggest I do to achieve financial stability?"

"Don't spend your money gambling or on loose women. Try and put away a little each month, and before you know it, you'll have enough to buy property."

He slowly blinked. "Are you saying I shouldn't invest it?"

"If you want a repeat of the Crash of '29, then go ahead and do it, but I suggest you buy land. The more the better, because land doesn't depreciate like other goods."

Moses was more confused than before. "You're telling me to buy land, but you bought a baseball team."

Winnie glared at him. "The team isn't the only thing I own, Moses. I recently negotiated to purchase the row houses on this street, with the intention of renovating them to allow these folks to live in decent housing. The workers will replace the roofs, install indoor plumbing, replace floors, and put up walls for a modicum of privacy. Of course, I will have to raise rents, but it won't be so much that they won't be able to pay it. I've already hired a manager who will make unannounced inspections to make certain renters are maintaining the property, and if not then they will be evicted."

"You're a landlord." His question was a statement.

"No, Moses. I'm a property owner, and I don't intend to waste my money on folks who don't mind living in squalor. They will have to stop using the backyards to dispose of their garbage, and if their children break something then they will be responsible for it to be repaired."

Moses digested what he'd just heard and decided he was open to buying land, but at no time did he want the responsibility of becoming a landlord. He would become a farmer and grow his own crops, like his mother.

"It's a lot to think about," he said.

Winnie pushed back the cuff on her suit jacket to glance at her watch. "It's not as much as you think. I must leave so I can get your contract typed up. As I said before, you can stay here for the night. If you're hungry, there's a little place about ten minutes down the road that serves decent food. One of the coaches will pick you up around eight, so try and be ready when he comes. He's all bark and no bite, so just do what he says, and you'll get along well."

"Will I have to stay here after tonight?"

"That all depends on how well you do with batting practice. If you pass, then you'll stay in a house with other players who don't live in Memphis. If you don't make it, then I'll arrange for someone to pay for a bus ticket back to Nichols." Winnie stood, Moses rising with her. "There's a key on a shelf in the wardrobe. You'll need it when you go out and come back. The doors lock automatically behind you, so you'll have to use the key to get back in. Before you leave tomorrow, just put the key back on the shelf in the wardrobe."

Winnie Chess didn't know that Moses had no intention of spending more than one night in the row house because he hadn't left Nichols for Memphis just to turn around and live under his father's roof again, especially since he'd turned down offers to attend Fisk and Howard Universities. There was no way he was going to work in a coal mine; he'd vowed that generational cycle would end with him. It wasn't as if he didn't have options: He could join the Great Migration of Negroes to cities in the North to work in an automobile factory. He'd heard that Henry Ford paid his workers five dollars a day for a forty-hour workweek for both Black and White workers. He'd also thought about going West. There had been another migration when dust storms devastated the Plains states and thousands left the region and headed for California. Moses was anxious to visit a state with sun, mountains, sand, and surf.

He waited for Winnie to leave, the door locking

behind her. He didn't know what to make of her; he'd never met someone who knew exactly who they were and what they wanted from life. He found her beautiful, but she also possessed an overabundance of confidence. He wondered if she'd lectured all the players on the Memphis Eagles about the evils of gambling and loose women.

The more he thought about it, the more the idea of becoming a farmer appealed to him. He would plant his own crops, raise hogs, chickens, and milk cows, and what he didn't use he'd sell. Farming was backbreaking work, but if he were to save enough money to buy a tractor, then he would be able to work the land himself.

Removing his shoes, he lay on the bed and stared up at the ceiling covered with tarpaper. Winnie was right about the structures being hovels, because although the house in which he'd been raised belonged to the mining company, it was habitable. Resting his head on folded arms, Moses closed his eyes and felt the tension he hadn't known was there, slipping away until he was relaxed enough to fall asleep.

Moses slept through the sounds of hammering and sawing. When he woke up the room was shrouded in afternoon shadows. He opened a door at the back of the house and discovered a toilet in a small shed that also had a makeshift shower. After relieving himself, Moses changed into a pair of denim coveralls and scuffed work boots. With enough money to cover his meal, he slid the duffel under the bed and left the house.

Twenty minutes after walking along a dusty unpaved road, he saw the restaurant Winnie had mentioned. He was hot and thirsty. Moses thought of the ramshackle structure as an oasis in the desert. When he opened the door, he was greeted with the sound of blues coming from a jukebox and the distinctive aroma of fried chicken. Waiting until his vision adjusted to the dim interior illuminated by low-watt lightbulbs, he noticed two men sitting at a bar and a trio of others at a table in the corner.

A heavyset woman, hoisting a tray on her shoulder from which wafted mouthwatering aromas, smiled at him. "Whatcha want, sugah?"

He said the first thing that came to his head. "Dinner."

"Well, you came to the right place. Rest yourself and someone will be right with you to take your order."

Moses found an empty table and stared at the initials carved into the wooden surface. Some were outlined with hearts, and he wondered if the couples were still together. A younger woman, who was the spitting image of the one serving the men at the other table, approached him. "What you want?"

He took a cursory glance at her sullen expression. "I'll have fried chicken, collard greens, sweet potatoes, and cornbread."

"What about dessert?"

"What do you have?"

The woman rolled her eyes at the same time she exhaled an audible breath. "We got pie, cobbler, and cake."

Moses wanted to tell her that if he owned the restaurant she never would've been hired because of her bad attitude. "Cake."

"What you want to drink?"

"Pop. Coca Cola," he added when she glared at him.

Turning on her heels, she walked away, dragging her feet as if they were too heavy for her. Moses was more than willing to put up with her attitude because he needed to eat.

"Did she take your order, sugah?"

His head popped up and he smiled. "Yes, ma'am."

She winked at him. "Don't worry, sugah, I'm gonna

take good care of you, because I know that trifling-ass gal ain't good for nothing but to roll her eyes and suck her teeth."

Moses nodded. He didn't want to comment or get into what he knew was a family squabble. He'd left Nichols where the family dynamics were always tense, and now that he was on his own, he felt as if he'd been freed from the shackles of domestic turmoil.

He didn't have to wait long for his dinner, and after picking up a knife and fork he cut into the crispy breast of the chicken and took a bite. It was perfect. He took his time eating, enjoying every mouthful. He was halfway through the meal when he ordered another piece of chicken and cornbread to take with him. The to-go order would become breakfast, because if the coach was scheduled to pick him up at eight, then he didn't want to begin batting practice on an empty stomach.

Moses was glad he hadn't worn a belt because he would've had to loosen it several notches. He was full—in fact, satisfied—when he retraced his steps and returned to the row house. Young children had replaced the men sitting on porches, and he avoided their gazes.

He returned to the house and unlocked the door. Walking in, he found a box of matches, lit several lanterns, and set one on the table. After retrieving his duffel from under the bed, Moses took out a pocket watch, notebook, and unzipped a case filled with pencils. His hand was poised on the cover as he wrote his name and the year.

Once he began writing he couldn't stop. The words poured out on the pages like sand in an hourglass. He lost track of time. When he closed the notebook, he felt tightness across his shoulders from sitting in one position while hunched over the table. It was too early to go to bed, and if he'd had more illumination than the kerosene lanterns offered, Moses would've read one of the three books he'd brought with him. The buildup of the day's heat had not abated with the setting sun, and he was faced with the dilemma of remaining indoors or sitting out on the front porch. However, the former won out when he stripped off his clothes down to his underwear and lay on the bed to wait for sleep. He needed to be rested and alert when he stepped onto the field at batting practice.

CHAPTER 6

A shiver of excitement flowed through Harper as she reread what she had typed, hoping and believing she'd captured the essence of Moses Gilliam's personality. Although he'd been only eighteen, someone that age in the 1930s was quite different from today's youth. He'd had to grow up much faster.

What she did admire about Kelton was his resolute belief that he could become a baseball player. From what she'd read, he was able to live out his dream to play in the Negro Leagues. She stared at the faded photograph of her great-grandfather and smiled. To say he was handsome was an understatement. This is why she'd written that Winnie had found him extremely attractive.

Now that she'd completed introducing Moses, Harper decided to take a break for a few days and think about what she'd written. She found herself so immersed in the story that she realized she needed to take a step back or it would consume her to the point she wouldn't be able to eat or sleep. Although she saved what she'd written on the laptop and a thumb drive, Harper also wanted to print out the pages, and that meant purchasing a printer and reams of paper.

It was close to midnight when she turned off the lamp on the table and retreated to her bedroom. If Moses was stiff from sitting in one position for a long time, it had been the same with her. The tension in her neck and shoulders made moving her head difficult. What she needed was a full-body massage. If only she could find a spa offering those services, then taking a day off from writing would be worth the sacrifice.

She hadn't given herself a deadline for completing the novel; however, she wanted to have most of it finished before returning to Chicago by mid-October, because she'd prepaid her rent up until the end of that month. It was now late May and she had close to five months to write at her leisure.

Harper had structured her day to prepare breakfast for her grandfather, do laundry every three days, give the house a thorough cleaning, and shop for groceries once a week. She discovered prepping lunch and dinner meals in advance had saved her a lot of time when all she had to do was put them in the oven or microwave.

After taking a hot shower, she slathered a lightly scented cream on her body, slipped on a cotton nightgown, climbed into bed, and fell asleep within seconds of her head touching the pillow. However, dreams plagued her relentlessly with images of what Kelton had encountered during his years in the Negro Leagues. There were people, places, and things he'd dealt with that made Harper uneasy about putting them down on paper. But it was too late to retract what she planned to write because Moses Gilliam had become all too real for her to minimize what he'd experienced during his lifetime.

She also thought about how her father would react once he read what she had written about his grandfather. Would he approve of the fictional account of Kelton Fleming's life, or would it serve as a wedge between him and his journalist daughter? What Harper did not want to do was sugarcoat the incidents but phrase them in a way where Kelton's anonymity would be left intact. He was her great-grandfather, and she did not want to air her family's dirty linen even if it meant the novel would remain unpublished.

"You look tired," Bernard said, as he stared at her across the breakfast table.

Harper touched a napkin to the corners of her mouth. "That's because I didn't sleep well last night."

"What's bothering you, grandbaby girl?"

She laced her fingers together. "I couldn't stop dreaming about what your father wrote in his notebooks."

"Was it good or bad?"

"Both, Grandpa. I was hoping you had read his journals, because then you would be able to tell me what I should put in or leave out."

Bernard lowered his eyes. "That's not going to happen. My father's life was his, and if there were some things he didn't want to talk about, then that never bothered me. He was a good father and husband, and a positive role model for me when I decided to marry and have a family."

"Don't you think it's odd that your father had one child? In those days folks usually had big families."

"I don't know about my mother, but after Nadine became pregnant with Daniel, we decided to wait a few years before having another baby. Even though we tried over and over it never happened, so we counted ourselves lucky that we had a son to carry on the Fleming name."

Harper had asked her grandfather questions she'd known the answers to after reading the notebooks, because she wanted and needed to know how much Bernard knew about his father. It was apparent he didn't want to know about his father's relationships with different women, and she wasn't going to be the one to disclose it to him.

"How's the book going?" Bernard asked after a comfortable silence.

"It's going well. I'm able to use your father's entries as a blueprint for a fictional character I'm calling Moses Gilliam. I didn't use the names of people he met, or the places and dates where Kelton played. I even changed the locale of towns in foreign countries where he'd played winter ball."

"I don't know if I told you, but my father learned to speak Spanish and it served him well whenever he played in Latin American countries."

This was surprising to Harper because there hadn't been a mention of it in Kelton's entries. "Did you ever hear him speak the language?"

"Only once when we saw some Mexican migrant workers who were on their way to pick oranges in Florida and tried to order groceries from a store. Pop stepped in as translator and the store owner and workers both thanked him effusively. When I told him that I didn't know he spoke Spanish, he winked at me and said there were a lot of things I didn't know about him. Then he gave me a look and I knew the subject was closed, so I left it at that."

Harper decided to include in Moses's character the ability to speak Spanish, although her great-grandfather hadn't documented it in his notebooks. What he'd written proved to be enough fodder for Harper to develop fictional characters for her novel.

If she second-guessed herself about giving up her position at the biweekly, it was short-lived. She didn't have to punch a clock, attend meetings, interview people whose egos surpassed their intelligence, or attempt to make sense of gibberish spewed out by politicians who'd had too much to drink at a fundraising event. Then there was the paper's editor, who'd ignored her request to cover sports. Harper knew at thirty-three she had taken a risk to quit her job at the newspaper when she didn't have another position waiting for her. If not now, then when? When she'd chosen to major in English as an undergraduate and journalism as a graduate student, she had been aware of the number of media available to her. She could write for a newspaper or magazine. However, it was television that proved more enticing because it meant heightened visibility.

She had been willing to start at the bottom and work her way up, while refusing to use her father's celebrity status to advance her career. She'd interned at a local newspaper, writing about local news before she left to get a position at the Black-owned biweekly. The editor knew she was Daniel Fleming's daughter and had promised her he would assign her to cover sports whenever the sports reporter went on vacation. She waited patiently but the opportunity never materialized; she suspected the editor was a misogynist who believed women had no place in the locker room. Well, that was no longer an issue because she didn't regret her decision to quit. Now she was able to write about a relative who lived his life as a baseball player in the Negro Leagues.

It wasn't the first time that she wondered, if Kelton Fleming had decided to forgo baseball to attend Fisk or Howard University, how different his life would've been. He wouldn't have traveled to Latin American countries where he'd learned to speak Spanish.

Pushing back his chair, Bernard stood up. "I'm going to help you clean up the kitchen before I leave."

Harper waved her hand. "Don't bother, Grandpa. I've got this. I'm not going to write today. I am going to take my time doing things around the house."

Bernard usually helped her clean up after breakfast because he knew she wanted to begin writing right after they finished eating. "Are you sure?"

She smiled. "Yes, I'm sure, Grandpa. Why don't you get your things, so your friends don't have to wait for you." Harper stood up and came around the table to hug Bernard. "I want you to enjoy yourself and not worry about me."

Dipping his head, Bernard pressed a kiss to her forehead.

"Thank you, grandbaby girl. It's been a blessing having you come and stay with me."

"That goes double for me." She patted his chest. "Love you."

Tiny lines fanned out around Bernard's eyes, when he smiled. Half-hooded eyes, like the ones she'd stared at in photographs of Kelton Fleming, stood out to her. It was the only feature, other than his height, that he had inherited from his father.

"Love you more."

Harper knew she'd always loved her grandmother, but now that Nadine was gone the affection she felt for her grandfather was more acute than she could remember. As a corrections officer working different shifts, Harper hadn't known when she would see him. It was different with Nadine, who as a schoolteacher always had the summers off. Bernard had been drafted and fought in the Vietnam War, but he rarely talked about what he'd experienced in the jungles of Southeast Asia. He returned home physically unscathed, yet Harper suspected he hadn't escaped psychological trauma because whenever someone mentioned his military service, he became mute. Meeting up with his former military friends was something he needed, to bond with men who'd shared similar experiences.

Harper's head was filled with thoughts of what she planned to write to continue Moses's story when she maneuvered into a parking lot behind a strip mall in the Nashville suburb. After cleaning up the kitchen and seeing Bernard off, she called several spas to see if she could secure an appointment for a massage. Luckily, one of them had a cancellation and the owner said she could fit her in with a massage therapist, but she had to be at the spa within the hour. She booked the session for the massage and a facial. Spending the morning at a spa was exactly what she needed to renew her feelings of well-being.

Before leaving the full-service spa, she made an appointment for the following week for her hair, manicure, and pedicure. Then she walked out knowing she had made the right decision to distance herself from Chicago. She'd fallen into a rut, with one day merging into the next, her going into the newspaper office for staff meetings, updates, and assignments. Aside from attending fundraisers and political rallies, sharing dinner with her mother, and maintaining a standing appointment at her favorite salon, nothing in her life had changed dramatically. She wasn't dating nor open to seeing anyone after her last relationship fizzled. It had taken strength she didn't know she possessed to keep from saying exactly what was on her mind during the paper's staff meetings.

One time she'd suggested the newspaper could save money by not renting office space and allowing the staff to work from home, with the savings used for staff raises. The editor had shut her down before she could finish. It hadn't mattered to him that advertising revenue had decreased and circulation was down; and even after the periodical had gone completely online, Harper knew it was just a matter of time before the biweekly would cease to exist.

In hindsight, she was glad she had gotten out now. She'd left on her own terms and not because she'd been forced out, carrying a banker box full of her possessions as she left the office for the last time.

Harper decided to eat out rather than go home. With her grandfather away for a week, she didn't have to prepare three meals a day and opted to take advantage of the time to explore some of Nashville's eating establishments. She drove past several restaurants and decided to stop at Martin's Bar-B-Que Joint. It had been a while since she'd eaten authentic barbecue.

The interior featured a rustic-industrial vibe offering authentic Southern cuisine with draft beer on tap, whiskey, and cocktails. Beyond the dining room, in the rear, was an enormous beer garden with lots of seating and a stage for live music. She hadn't taken more than a half dozen steps before coming face-to-face with someone from her childhood. Although it had been twenty years, Harper could never forget the first boy she had a crush on. However, Cheney Sanders was no longer the tall, lanky boy who wore glasses and would occasionally come to her grandparents' farm to play basketball with her brothers. Here he was in the flesh, as tall and handsome as she remembered.

Three years her senior, Cheney hadn't paid her much attention because to him she was Craig and Danny's little sister. He had viewed her as an annoyance, just like her brothers did on occasion, whenever she wanted to follow them around. Yet at twelve, she had imagined herself a princess who'd found her prince in Cheney and together they would live happily ever after.

Cheney Sanders went completely still, unable to believe the woman standing only feet away was someone he remembered from his childhood. There was no way he could forget Harper Fleming because she looked exactly like her grandmother. He had sat at Miss Nadine's table enough times to remember the woman who had treated him like one of her grandsons.

"Harper." He didn't realize he'd whispered her name.

She smiled and nodded. "Yes, Cheney, it's me."

"What are you doing here in Nashville?"

"It's the same thing I should be asking you," she countered, her smile still in place.

"Are you meeting someone for lunch?"

"No. Why?"

"Because I'm also eating alone. Do you mind sharing a table so we can catch up on old times?" he asked.

"Of course."

If Harper was curious why he was in Nashville, he wondered the same about her. His father and uncle had owned and operated a local home improvement company in Memphis and Cheney met the Flemings for the first time when he'd accompanied his father to their farm to replace the roof on the main house and build a new structure for Miss Nadine's chickens. Mr. Bernard had introduced him to his grandsons and granddaughter, who'd come from Chicago to spend the summer.

Cheney had bonded quickly with Craig and Danny. They would occasionally get together on weekends to shoot hoops or swim in the lake near the farm. Harper rarely joined them on their outings because she was kept busy helping Miss Nadine in the garden or kitchen. What he did recall about Harper was her crestfallen expression whenever her brothers told her she couldn't come with them. He suspected they wanted to talk about something they didn't want their sister to overhear.

It was the same for Cheney because his twin sisters were six years his senior and were inseparable. By the time he'd reached adolescence they had left home for college. Not only were Dionne and Dahlia identical twins who did everything together, they'd also fallen in love with and married brothers. He was now an uncle to two nephews and three nieces.

He seated Harper and rounded the table to sit opposite her, silently admiring her flawless bare face. She hadn't worn any makeup and her complexion glowed like polished golden-brown citrine. His interaction with Harper had been limited to sitting at the same table whenever the Flemings invited him to share dinner with them, while he'd been much too intent on eating Miss Nadine's food to give her much of a passing glance. That was then, and this was now, and Cheney found that he couldn't stop staring at her.

Harper met Cheney's large hazel eyes behind the lenses of a pair of round black wire-framed glasses. Even as a child she'd been transfixed by the color of his eyes that would appear even lighter when the summer sun darkened his tawny-brown complexion. He was only thirty-seven and graying prematurely. His cropped hair was liberally salt-and-pepper as was his trimmed mustache and goatee. To say he'd aged like fine wine was an understatement. She silently admired his tailored blue suit, starched white shirt, blue-and-white striped tie, and black slip-ons.

"What are you doing in Nashville?" she questioned, repeating what he'd asked her minutes before.

"I live here now."

"Where did you live before?"

"Falls Church, Virginia."

Her eyebrows lifted slightly. Harper knew that Falls Church was one of the more expensive cities to live in in the US. "How long did you live there?"

"Too long. I moved to Arlington after my divorce until I decided it was time to come home."

Harper had noticed he wasn't wearing a ring, but that didn't mean he was single. Either he'd remarried or had opted not to wear one. "Why didn't you move back to Memphis?" She'd asked him yet another question. And in that instant, she'd become a reporter interviewing a subject.

Cheney angled his head and stared at something over her shoulder. "Except for some distant cousins, most of my family left Memphis. My parents moved to a retirement community in Tucson to be closer to their grandchildren, while both my sisters are married and live with their families in Santa Fe and Albuquerque."

"Why New Mexico?"

"It's where my sisters attended college and met their husbands. Enough about me," he said, smiling. "What's been going on in your life?"

Harper wanted to ask Cheney where he wanted her to start and decided not to elaborate on her personal relationships. "Right now, I'm spending the summer with my grandfather, who moved here from Memphis after my grandmother passed away."

"I'm sorry, Harper. Your grandmother was an exceptional woman."

"I know," she said at the same time, forcing a smile. "I

miss her, but it's my grandfather who isn't taking the loss well."

"That's understandable, for a couple who spent so many years together."

She had to agree with Cheney. His parents were still married after more than forty years and it was the same with hers, who'd recently celebrated their fortieth wedding anniversary, while her brothers weren't shy about admitting to being in love with their wives.

Harper told him about majoring in English and journalism in college, and after a short stint teaching high school English, then working for two newspapers, she still hadn't fulfilled her dream of becoming a sports reporter and/or analyst. "I kept hoping my editor would assign me to cover some of Chicago's professional sporting events, but it was all in vain, so I decided to quit."

"Didn't he realize you're the daughter of a baseball Hall of Famer?"

"Of course he did, Cheney. I don't know why, but I think he's a misogynist who is of the belief that women don't belong in locker rooms."

"Can't your father put in a good word for you?"

Harper gave him an incredulous look. "That's what I don't want, Cheney. If I'm going to make it as a sports correspondent, then it's not going to be because I'm Daniel Fleming's daughter."

Tiny lines fanned out around Cheney's eyes when he smiled. "I was hoping you would say that."

"If that's the case, then why did you ask me that?"

"I asked because I wanted to know what you're made of."

"And that is?"

"A woman with a fighting spirit."

Harper wanted to tell him there was a lot of fight in her and as an emancipated, independent woman, only she would determine what she wanted for her future. It was as if she'd always had to fight for what she wanted but, in the end, she'd been the one who had to compromise. When she'd called her grandmother to complain that her parents wouldn't permit her to attend an out-of-state college, Nadine reminded her that they were still financially responsible for her but there would come a time when she'd be able to make her own decisions about her life and future. Nadine had ended the call saying she would help her any way she could. It wasn't until after her grandmother had passed away that Harper realized what the older woman meant when she'd named Harper as the sole beneficiary of Nadine Fleming's life insurance.

The death benefit had provided her with a measure of financial stability; she was able to walk away from one position before securing another, and she hadn't regretted it either. What she would've regretted was getting up every morning and going into an office she'd come to resent with a passion. Resentment, bitterness, and regret were things she strived to avoid at all costs.

A waiter approached their table and Harper quickly scanned the menu. There was so much she wanted to sample, and when Cheney suggested they share a Big Brother Sampler, she agreed. The spareribs, brisket, and sides of baked beans and hush puppies were more than enough for two people. Cheney ordered craft beer, while she decided on sweet tea.

CHAPTER 7

Harper could not remember when she'd last enjoyed a man's company as she listened intently while Cheney told her about going to Morehouse College as an undergraduate. After graduating, he'd enrolled at Georgetown Law School for his JD. He was hired by a prestigious DC law firm as a litigator, working an average of sixty hours a week, while earning more money than he had time to spend. He had married, but the union ended abruptly before they were scheduled to celebrate their fifth anniversary.

"Did you suspect your marriage was in trouble?" she asked Cheney.

Cheney shook his head as he met her eyes. "Not initially, but then Michelle admitted to me that she felt like a widow because she never got to see her husband. There were nights when I didn't get home until midnight whenever I was working on a big case. It was the same with weekends when I'd go into the office and spend hours there. I promised her that we would have a date night where we would go to our favorite restaurant and then check into a hotel to try and recapture some of the magic we'd experienced when we were engaged, but even that rarely materialized. Meanwhile, I was clueless because I thought she was happy working as a dental hygienist and occasionally inviting her coworkers over for a cookout or dinner party.

"Her telling me she'd gone to a lawyer to file for divorce was a wake-up call to the fact that my work, and not her, had become the priority in my life. The divorce was uncontested and when I offered to give her the house in addition to a generous settlement, she turned me down saying the only thing she wanted was for me to pay her legal fees." He held up his hand. "And before you ask—I had no idea that she'd been involved with another man, who was her boss and was able to give her what I didn't or wouldn't, and that was myself. It was as if she wanted to make a clean break."

"I'm so sorry your marriage didn't work out," Harper whispered.

Picking up his mug, Cheney took a long swallow. "It's okay, Harper. It's the past and I make it a practice to never look back."

Harper nodded when she really wanted to reach across the table and hold his hand, doubting that he'd want her pity. She hadn't had the best luck when it came to dating. However, she hadn't been aware that any of her former boyfriends had cheated on her. If they had, then they hid it well.

"I've laid bare my soul, now it's time for a little cross-examination," Cheney said, smiling.

"What if I decide to plead the Fifth," she countered.

"Pleading the Fifth means you have something to hide."

Slumping back in her chair, Harper gave him a long, penetrating stare. "There's nothing in my life I feel I need to hide." She didn't have anything to hide, yet after reading Kelton's journals there were incidents in his life she felt compelled not to disclose in print, because she wasn't certain if it would affect how Bernard would think of his father. "I'm single and right now I'm not involved with anyone. I live alone, I'm currently unemployed, but I'm also solvent."

"When was the last time you were in a relationship?" Cheney asked.

"It's been a while."

"In other words, you dated?"

Harper decided honesty was best if she and Cheney were to become friends. Despite her childhood crush on him, she now viewed him differently. Her heart hadn't beat a double-time rhythm when seeing him again. Neither did she find herself unable to speak when in his presence.

She nodded. "There were months when we didn't see each other and that's when I realized I'd made myself available whenever he called, and after a while, I decided to end it."

"Good for you. No one likes to be taken for granted."

Like your wife, Harper couldn't help but think. Cheney had put his career ahead of his wife and in the end, she had decided enough was enough and filed for divorce. It was the same with Harper with all the men she'd dated. When she thought about it, her last boyfriend wasn't the only one who had refused to be in a committed relationship. She had to accept some of the blame because she'd warned him once they started dating that she needed space, and she didn't want him to attempt to control her life.

However, Harper was never one to second-guess what she said or did, but owned it even if it didn't turn out to be what she wanted. She considered a mistake to be a learning experience, and hopefully she wouldn't repeat it.

"You asked why I'm in Nashville and it's because I'm spending the summer with my grandfather. Grandpa sold his farm after my grandmother passed away and he bought a house in a community with other retirees and semi-retirees."

"So, it's like old times when you used to spend the summers with your grandparents."

Nodding and smiling, Harper said, "Yes, it is. Right now, Grandpa is spending time with his Vietnam buddies, so I have all next week to myself."

"Who can forget it's Memorial Day weekend with all the

flags and bunting all over the city. Speaking of the military, did your brothers ever serve? Because I remember them talking about becoming lifers."

"Both are currently in for life. Craig is a captain in the Corps, and Daniel is an army lieutenant colonel. They were deployed for several missions, but thankfully they returned unscathed."

"I'm sorry I didn't stay in touch with them once I graduated from high school."

"I'll let my brothers know you asked about them whenever we email one another."

Cheney reached into the breast pocket of his jacket, took his cell phone out, and handed it to Harper. "Put your number in my Contacts and when I send you a text you can give me your brothers' email addresses."

Harper tapped in her number and gave Cheney back his phone. "How long are you going to be in Nashville?"

"I hope for a long time because it's my home. I bought a house six months ago after I was hired as a legal counsel for an organization advocating for abused women and their children."

"That's quite a change from litigating on behalf of corporations and defending the rich and powerful."

"You think it's a step down because I've chosen to represent victimized women and their children?"

"Oh no," she said quickly. "I think it's wonderful. So many women in those situations are too afraid to seek help because they fear not only for themselves but also their children if their abuser decides to retaliate."

"So, you approve?"

Harper lowered her eyes. "I don't think you need my approval, but if you're asking for it, then of course I approve. I'm blessed because I've never been in a situation where I've been physically, verbally, or emotionally abused by a man, but that doesn't stop me from advocating for women who want to stop the vicious cycle of domestic abuse."

Cheney ran a hand over his goatee. "And most times the abuse is cyclical, spanning generations, and that becomes the greatest obstacle facing the social workers and psychologists when counseling their clients. Some women are willing to remain in an abusive relationship because they've witnessed their mothers and even their grandmothers go through the same thing."

"When do you get involved?" Harper asked him.

"Usually when the abuser ignores the protection or restraining order. Most times I ask the judge to lock them up a minimum of thirty days and hopefully that will give us enough time to be able to relocate the woman and her children to a safe house."

"What if she doesn't want to go?"

"You're asking a question that I can't answer, because it's impossible to get inside the head of someone who has become almost immune to the abuse. I hadn't worked there a week when I saw a woman come in with bruises all over her body, and the fading ones looked like tattoos from a distance. That's when I called my sisters and asked if their husbands had ever put their hands on them. They denied it and thought I was crazy to ask, and then I told them if they ever did I was going to kill them."

"You didn't mean that, Cheney."

"I meant every word, Harper. Witnessing women and children who have become punching bags for men who feel the need to exert power over the vulnerable made me aware that I do have a dark side."

"Everyone has a dark side. It's just that we can't let it control us."

"That's what I've been working on. I don't want to unload on you, but seeing the underbelly of human depravity with the bruised and battered bodies of women and children has changed my view of my fellow man.

"Have you made plans to do anything this coming week

until your grandfather comes back?" he asked, deftly changing the topic of conversation.

Harper wanted to tell Cheney that, other than writing, she didn't have any plans. "Not really."

He winked at her. "Is that a yes or a no?"

"It's a no."

"I'd like pick you up on Sunday and take you to see my fixer-upper, then I can put something on the grill for us to eat before taking you back home."

"You bought a fixer-upper?"

Grinning and exhibiting straight white teeth, Cheney nodded. "Yup. When a realtor took me to look at houses, I couldn't tell one from the other because they appeared to be cookie-cutters with the same mirror images of open floor plan, kitchen, and bathroom. If I was going to spend six or even seven figures for a house, then I wanted it to look like a home and not one designed for a magazine layout. I did find one with six bedrooms and seven bathrooms that is a little more than forty-four hundred square feet. It's been vacant for years, and uninhabitable. The prior owners were asking a lot more than I was willing to pay, but then in the end we were able to negotiate a price to which we both agreed. It has more space than I'll ever need, but the upside is now I have enough room for when my parents, and my sisters' families come to visit. Then came the renovations. It took a contracting company more than three months to renovate the house to accommodate my lifestyle."

"I don't know why, but I figured you would've done most of the work yourself," Harper said. "I remember you used to help your father and uncle whenever they did renovations."

Harper was right about his father teaching him everything he needed to know about repairing or remodeling a house, from roofing to installing plumbing and electrical wiring to bring the house up to code. His lessons began the year he turned eight, when he spent summers and weekends in his father's workshop. As he grew older, he'd accompany him on construction projects.

"Dad used to talk to about me taking over the business once he retired, but that was just a pipe dream; he knew I always wanted to be a lawyer. My bachelor uncle didn't have any kids, so once Dad decided to retire, he and Uncle Jack sold the business. And I would have tackled the renovations if I didn't have anything else to do. Even though I don't go into the office every day, I'm always available for staff meetings, court appearances, and I'm also on-call in case of emergencies. The house needed a new roof, windows, plumbing, and electrical work. The wood floors were refinished, and there's a deck off the back where I spend most of my time whenever I'm home. It would've taken me five or maybe even six months to complete if I'd had to do it myself."

"Do you plan to have people over for the holiday?"

Cheney shook his head. "No. Why did you ask?"

"It's the Memorial Day weekend, the official start of the summer season, so I figured you would host a cookout."

"I've made it a practice not to invite folks to my home. Not because I don't want them to know where I live, but because of the clients we serve. A counselor might inadvertently tell a client where I live, and she in turn could disclose this to her abuser if under duress. And as they say, the shit would hit the fan."

"Are you afraid of threats?"

"No," he said truthfully. "It's just that I prefer to keep my professional life separate from my personal life." What he didn't want to disclose to Harper was that he had been threatened several times during court proceedings when he'd asked the judge to give the abuser jail time for repeatedly ignoring a restraining order. Since he didn't live in a gated community with onsite security, Cheney had decided it was best not to invite his coworkers to his home. The exception was the agency's director, who was not only his boss but also a former high school classmate.

Harper laughed. "Do you realize that you sound like my grandmother? She taught school for thirty years, but never did she allow any of her students or their families to come to her home."

"That's where you're wrong, because Miss Nadine was my third-grade teacher."

"You were the only one, because your father brought you with him when he came to make repairs, and because you had bonded with her grandsons, which made you the exception. She had a *don't drop by unannounced* policy. Even if you saw her looking at you through the window, she'd never open the door."

"Well, you are going to become my exception because I'm inviting you to my home."

Harper inclined her head as if he were royalty. "Thank you, Mr. Sanders."

"You're most welcome, Ms. Fleming."

In that instant, Cheney realized he liked Harper—really liked her because she was so easy to talk to and unpretentious. He marveled that he was able to open up to her about his failed marriage, and talking about it made him aware of his shortcomings as a husband. He thought buying a house in the country would make a girl who'd grown up in a row house in a blighted neighborhood in rural Kentucky happy. His mistake was not having taken the time to know that the woman he loved enough to make her a part of his life and future wasn't interested in material things. All she wanted and needed was to be loved.

Harper reached for her handbag and took out her wallet. "Even though I don't have a job, I know that you do, so I'm not going to take up anymore of your time."

"Don't do that, Harper."

She gave him a questioning look. "Do what?"

"Take out your wallet. Whenever you're with me I don't want you to pay for anything."

She froze. Nothing moved. Not even her eyes. "I'm not a pauper, Cheney."

"I didn't say you were. Please, Harper, don't embarrass me." He leaned over the table. "Put your wallet away," he whispered.

Cheney had lost track of the number of times he'd seen women pay the restaurant check when their dining partners either pretended interest in their cell phones or purposely left the table to use the restroom whenever the bill was set on the table. Then there were women who'd pass enough cash under the table to make it appear as if he were paying the tab.

His father and grandfather had lectured him relentlessly that if he couldn't afford to take a girl out on a date, then it was up to him to wait until he had enough money to pay for everything. Sharing lunch with Harper wasn't a date, even though it felt like one.

Cheney had dated women following his divorce, but never long enough to become a relationship, because neither were looking for a commitment. If he hadn't had time for his wife, then Cheney was aware that it would be the same with the women he dated. After selling the house and moving from Falls Church to a rental in Arlington, his life had become even more predictable. It was work, home, and work again. Cheney craved a different lifestyle, but he hadn't known how to make a change. It came when he returned to Memphis for the funeral of a former high school student. The most popular girl in their graduating class had been killed by her jealous boyfriend before he'd taken his own life. The following day Cheney was approached by a former classmate who was a social worker and asked if he would be willing to move back to Tennessee to provide legal counsel for a program dedicated to advocating for abused women. Cheney told her he'd think about it.

And he did think about it, for a long time. The year he celebrated his thirty-fifth birthday, Cheney likened himself to a hamster on a wheel going around and around aimlessly until he burned out completely. He finally called Sabrina Watkins, asking if she still wanted him to work for her agency, and when she said yes, life as he'd known it changed forever.

Cheney paid the check, then rounded the table to help Harper to stand. "I'll walk you to your car."

Harper noticed Cheney's closeness when he rested a hand at the small of her back as he led her out of the restaurant and into the brilliant afternoon sunlight. She told him where she'd parked and he dropped his hand and walked alongside her, making her blatantly aware of the differences in their height. She was five-five in ballet flats, and Cheney was at least several inches above six feet.

She stopped next to the blue metallic Nissan Rogue with charcoal-gray interior and smiled up at Cheney. "Thank you for lunch."

He stared at her under lowered lids. "And I thank you for your company." Dipping his head, Cheney kissed her cheek. "I'll be in touch."

Harper closed her eyes as the scent of Cheney's masculine cologne wafted to her nostrils. The fragrance was a blend of sandalwood, bergamot, and patchouli, of which the latter was her favorite. When she opened her eyes, she found Cheney staring at her as if she were a stranger. What she hadn't expected was for him to kiss her. Even if it had been a chaste one.

"What do you want me to bring?"

"Nothing, Harper."

She slowly shook her head. "I'm only one generation removed from the South, so I know when folks are invited to someone's house, they never show up empty-handed."

His taut expression softened. "You can bring dessert."

Harper was glad he mentioned dessert because she would go through the listing of her grandmother's recipes she'd stored on her laptop. One summer she'd helped Nadine collect recipes written on scraps of paper and write them on index cards and put them in alphabetical order in a metal box for safekeeping. It was after her grandmother had passed away that Harper took the box, retyped the recipes, and stored them on her computer's desktop and backed them up on a thumb drive.

She opened the door to her vehicle and slipped in behind the wheel. Cheney closed the door and stepped away as she started the engine and backed out of the lot. When she'd called a spa for an appointment, Harper could not have imagined running into someone she'd known as a child when she spent her summers at her grandfather's farm outside of Memphis. After returning to Chicago, she'd found herself counting down the days until she'd be able to go back.

Each summer had blended into the next one. Then her entire world changed when she was eleven going on twelve. Cheney Sanders came to the farm with his father and uncle. It had only taken a single glance at the tall, lanky teenage boy for Harper to believe he was a prince come to life with his tanned skin, shimmering eyes, and hair that the intense summer sun had turned a sandy brown. He'd barely glanced at her, but Harper didn't care, because she had committed his image to memory.

She saw him again the following two summers when he'd come to the farm to hang out with her brothers. He didn't come back the year she turned fourteen because he'd graduated from high school and left to attend college in Georgia. A lot had happened in the near twenty years since she last saw Cheney, and once again it was summer when they would reunite. She'd stay in Tennessee long enough to write and complete her novel before returning to Chicago to plan the next phase of her life.

Cheney had planned for her to come to his house on Sunday, and that meant she could devote all day Saturday to writing. She drove back to her grandfather's house and parked in the driveway. Bernard had put his car in the garage until his return, and she hoped he was enjoying his reunion with his army friends.

Kelton Fleming had fought in World War II, Bernard in Vietnam, and now Kelton's great-grandsons had made the military their careers. Kelton had written in vivid detail of what he'd experienced fighting in the South Pacific, his enlistment derailing his baseball career, but when he returned to the States at the end of the war, he was never the same man who'd put on a different uniform than the one he'd worn as a player in the Negro Leagues.

Harper unlocked the door to the house and kicked off her shoes, leaving them on a mat near the door. Walking on bare feet, she made her way to her bedroom and flopped down on the bed. She lay motionless as cool air flowing from an overhead vent feathered over her exposed skin. Bernard had grown up in Memphis, where window and portable fans were the only way of cooling the rooms at the farm during the intense and sometime relentless Southern summer heat. But the house in Nashville had been built with central air-conditioning divided in different zones.

Harper didn't want to admit it but she had eaten too much. Even though Cheney had eaten more than she had, spareribs, brisket, baked beans, and hush puppies were much more than she normally ate for a midday meal.

Whenever she consumed more than one meat in a single sitting, she always felt lethargic and knew her dinner would be a salad with lots of veggies. She retreated to the sunroom and then went online to order a printer, ink, and reams of paper to be delivered to the house. She'd become slightly paranoid that if her laptop were hacked, or crashed, that she wouldn't be able to retrieve what she'd written. The delivery was promised for the following day, and after rereading her notes she felt confident she'd able to pick up where she left off with Moses Gilliam.

As she waited for her computer to boot up, Harper found that she couldn't stop thinking about Cheney Sanders. She wondered if he was as shocked as she was, seeing him after so many years. She couldn't remember if they had exchanged more than a hundred words during summers in Memphis; and now it was as if they were friends catching up on what had been going on in their lives.

Although she still found herself attracted to him, Harper knew nothing would come of it. Her plan to spend time in Nashville had an expiration date, and once she completed the novel, she'd return to Chicago, where she would have to begin looking for another position as a journalist. All thoughts of Cheney vanished as she inserted the thumb drive into the port and began typing.

CHAPTER 8

Moses was up at dawn; he'd shaved, showered, dressed, and had eaten his leftover chicken and cornbread. He also returned the key to the shelf in the wardrobe and was standing on the porch when the baseball coach walked up.

"You Moses?"

"Yes, sir, Mister . . ." His words trailed off.

The man was medium height and solidly built. The intensity in his dark eyes stripped what little confidence Moses felt at the time. He'd left Nichols for Memphis to try out for a losing baseball team and wondered if he had the magic to help the Eagles win more games than they lost. The man extended his hand and Moses took it, his hand disappearing into a much larger one.

"Odell Nelson. But everyone calls me Coach."

Moses felt some of his apprehension fading and managed to smile. "It's nice meeting you, Coach."

Odell released Moses's hand, took out a handkerchief from the pocket of his pants, pushed back his battered baseball cap, and wiped his forehead. "This heat is too much. That's why I want you to take batting practice before it gets any hotter. I'm parked on the street behind the house, so let's get going."

Picking up his duffel, Moses followed the man around the house to where he'd parked a battered pickup truck. He got in and nearly gagged from the smell of hay and horse manure. Thankfully, the windows were open, and he turned his head to breathe in the stifling air that was preferable to the odors in what was obviously a farm truck.

"I know it stinks," Odell said, "but it's the best I could get because the bus is being repaired before we go on the road again, and if you're as good as Edgar says you are, then you'll be traveling with the team."

Moses noticed he'd said *Edgar* and not *Mr. Donnelly*. Judging from the way he spoke he didn't sound like a Southerner. It was obvious both men were raised up North. "I am good."

Odell gave him a sidelong glance. "How good, son?"

"I think I could be as good as Ty Cobb or even Babe Ruth."

"You think or you know?"

"I don't understand you, Coach."

"What's there to understand? Either you believe you're good or you'll never be. What surprises me is that you mentioned White ballplayers. What about the Colored boys who play for the Negro Leagues? Haven't you heard of Josh Gibson and Satchel Paige?"

"Yes, sir."

"Well, if you did, then why did you mention those two White boys? Cobb was not only violent, he was still fighting the Civil War, and despite Ruth's accomplishments on the field, he was a drunk, smoked and ate too much, and cheated on his wife. Not the best reputations for hero worship, son. If you are good enough to join the team, then you will have to act accordingly, and that means no drunkenness, fighting, and above all no betting on games. We don't want a repeat of the Black Sox Scandal, when eight members of the Chicago White Sox were accused of throwing the 1919 World Series against the Cincinnati Reds in exchange for money from an illegal gambling syndicate set up by Arnold Rothstein. The first time you break one of the rules you will be fined five dollars. The second time is ten. There will not be a third time because you'll be cut from the team. What you do on your own time when we don't have scheduled games is your business."

Moses felt as if his face was on fire, and it had nothing to do with the relentless late-spring temperatures that did not abate even after the sun had set. "I didn't know about Ruth and Cobb. I suppose I admire them because they made lots of money playing ball."

Odell downshifted as he maneuvered up a steep hill, the cab shaking and rattling until he reached the top. "Money don't mean shit, son, when you know you're as good as the next man. Even though we're not allowed to play on teams like the Boston Braves, New York Giants, Yankees, or the Pittsburgh Pirates, we know the players in the Negro Leagues are as good or even better than theirs. They didn't want us, so we had to organize our own teams. Are you aware of how many Negro Leagues teams there are?"

"No, sir."

"Almost one hundred. And they come from at least twenty-five states, and that's not counting the traveling teams. I suggest if you're planning to be a ballplayer, then you should read up on the various minor Negro Baseball Leagues, as well as the independent teams that were called proto leagues. If you want to read up on Negro baseball, then you should buy copies of the

Pittsburgh Courier and the *Chicago Defender*. Both have a team of reporters who write about Negro baseball."

Moses wanted to tell Odell that he didn't have much access to Black newspapers and even less exposure to reading about Black baseball players. Although an avid reader, Moses had to admit to himself that he didn't know as much as he should have about the history of Negro baseball. Rather than devouring stories about gangsters, he should have read the sports sections of Black-owned newspapers.

The pickup bumped over the unpaved rutted road lined on both sides with trees growing so close together that it was impossible to see what lay beyond them. The topography was nothing like the area surrounding Nichols, where coal mining had become a way of life for Blacks and Whites for several generations, despite the many hazards faced by miners each time they ventured down below ground to extract the coal for heating and industrial processes to fuel power plants for electricity. Coal production in Tennessee was small when compared to Kentucky, Pennsylvania, and West Virginia, but the coal was of higher quality than in some of the other states.

"We're not that far from the Mississippi River," Odell said, after a pause.

"I've never seen the river," Moses admitted.

If he were telling the truth it would be to say he hadn't seen much of anyplace beyond the environs of Nichols. He'd played games either at his school or at two others. All the players were Colored, but that didn't stop White people from coming to watch the games. If he were to join the Memphis Eagles, then he'd get to travel to other cities, not only in Tennessee but other states too. Becoming a Memphis Eagle would also allow him the option of playing winter ball in another country.

"You'll get to see it when we play in Arkansas and Missouri. Oh, I forgot to ask if you had breakfast."

"Yes sir, I did."

"That's good, because you need to change into a uniform and begin batting practice soon after we arrive and before it gets too hot."

"It's hot now," Moses said.

"Memphis is in southern Tennessee, so it's a lot hotter down here than where you come from."

He wanted to tell the man the heat would've been tolerable if not for the cloying stench of old manure. He couldn't wait to get out of the pickup and inhale a lungful of clean stifling air. Minutes later his fervent wish was answered when Odell drove along a road that led to a two-story white shingled house with a wraparound porch.

"This is where you'll room whenever we're in Memphis. You're one of two other boys who don't live around here."

"How often will I stay here?"

Odell drove around to the rear of the house and shut off the engine. "Probably no more than three or four times a month because most days we will be barnstorming in different cities."

Moses got out the pickup with his duffel, and that's when he saw the open field behind the house and men wearing baseball uniforms throwing and shagging balls. His heart rate quickened with anticipation. He'd come a long way from sitting in the stands with his grandfather to watch a baseball game in person for the first time. At that moment it didn't matter if baseball was segregated, because he would be with men who not only looked like him but played the game as well as or better than their White counterparts. The Memphis Eagles would have their own Christy Mathewson, Honus Wagner, Cy Young, and Babe Ruth.

He managed to tamp down his excitement when he followed Odell into the house with an expansive entryway and gleaming parquet floors and then into a parlor with a sitting area with sofas and chairs covered with floral fabrics in shades of blue, yellow, and green. Moses had never been inside a house as grand as the one where he'd live when the team wasn't traveling.

"I'll be outside when you're finished," Odell said, before he turned on his heel and left the house.

"You must be the new boy."

Moses turned to find a tall, slender woman wearing all white. Her gray-streaked straightened hair had a deep side part with sculpted waves that ended above her shoulders. He knew it was impolite to stare, but Moses couldn't help it. If he believed Winnie Chess attractive, she paled in comparison to the vision in white standing less than three feet away. It wasn't only her delicate features in her beautiful brown face, but the scent of her perfume wafting to his nostrils.

He nodded. "Yes, ma'am. I'm Moses Gilliam."

"Welcome to the Parker House. I'm Mrs. Lucille Parker, and my husband and I have opened our home to provide room and board for out-of-town Memphis Eagle players." She held up a manicured hand when he opened his mouth. "And before you ask. The owners of the team pay for your room and board, so I hope that puts your mind to rest that it will not come out of your salary."

Moses's lips parted when he smiled. It was apparent the woman had read his mind. "That's good to know, Mrs. Parker."

"We offer breakfast and dinner, and at no time is liquor permitted on the premises. I also have a fixed rule about gambling. I don't want cards or dice-playing, smoking, chewing tobacco, or dipping snuff. And then there's another rule. No women in your room. If you want to see a woman, then it must be outside."

Moses wanted to tell the woman that she had a lot of rules, but because it was her house, then she could make as many as she chose. "I don't drink or gamble, ma'am," he said truthfully.

He'd tried drinking whiskey the year he'd turned fifteen and didn't like the taste or how it made him feel. His mother had warned him about the pitfalls of gambling, that once he began, he might not be able to stop. And Mrs. Parker didn't have to concern herself about women. He didn't have a wife or girlfriend because at this time in his life they weren't a priority. He was only eighteen and Moses believed there would be time for him to become involved with women—even if only casually.

Lucille clasped her hands together. "Good. Now I'm going to have someone take you to your room where you can change into a uniform. There are some in the room, so try and find one that will fit you." Reaching for the bell on a side table, she rang it and within seconds a young boy appeared. "Jessup, please show Moses to his room," she said, smiling.

The boy, who couldn't have been more than a couple of years younger than Moses, nodded. "Yes, ma'am."

Moses followed him down a carpeted hallway, passing several doors and one with a sign that indicated it was a bathroom, and downstairs to a lower level. He paused to glance out the stained-glass window that overlooked the rear of the house.

"You are in here."

"Thank you, Jessup."

Moses opened the door and walked into a room with twin beds, a bedside table, a chest of drawers, and a cushioned armchair. Even though he had never been inside a hotel, Moses had seen photographs of luxurious lodgings for those with enough money to check in to. And as the son of a coal miner, he'd just checked in to his first hotel room. He spied a stack of faded gray uniforms on the chair and three pairs of worn cleats on the floor under the window.

He knew Odell was waiting for him to change out of his street clothes, so he left the bedroom and headed for the bathroom to relieve himself before he transformed into a tryout for the Memphis Eagles.

Moses did not encounter anyone when he walked out of the house and around to the open field where uniformed players were sitting on benches. He hoped they weren't waiting for him. The uniform was slightly too large, but at least the cap and shoes fit.

Odell's head popped up when he saw him. "It's about time you got here. Next time hustle your ass because this isn't about you, Gilliam. Your teammates, or should I say potential teammates, were sitting here baking in the fuckin' sun waiting for you to get all gussied up."

Moses felt as if he were being chastised when he hadn't lingered but had changed as quickly as he could, and wanted to tell the coach that, but decided it wasn't the time or the place to explain. "It won't happen again, Coach."

"Just see that it doesn't. Now grab a bat and stand at home plate, so we can see what you have to offer the Eagles."

Moses took a bat from several propped up against a barrel, and took several swings before reaching for another one. It took three bats before he found one that felt comfortable, and walked to home plate. At the same time a tall, skinny man, carrying a bucket of baseballs, made his way to the pitcher's mound. Another player, donning a catcher's mask, chest protector, and shin guards assumed a position behind him.

A hush fell over the assembly as the pitcher took a ball from the bucket and went into a full windup before releasing it. Moses recognized the fastball the second it left the pitcher's hand and his bat made contact, sending it soaring into the air far beyond centerfield. If there had been a wall or fence it would've cleared it.

The pitcher continued with a series of curveballs, fastballs, knuckleballs, changeups, and sliders. Moses was able to hit them all. He hit some directly to center field, while others were down the right- or left-field lines. Moses was oblivious to the cheering and shouting when he lowered the bat and stared at the pitcher as he approached him.

"Where did you learn to hit like that?"

He lifted his shoulders. "I did a lot of practicing."

The pitcher clapped a hand on his shoulder. "You must have been practicing day and night all of your life because most batters can't hit my curveballs."

The catcher wrapped both arms around the waist of Moses, lifting him off his feet. "The Memphis Eagles just got a winner." As soon as he set Moses on his feet, he was mobbed by members of the team, congratulating him on his hitting performance.

A feeling of accomplishment overwhelmed him when Coach extended his hand. "Let me be the first to welcome you to the Memphis Eagles."

Moses blinked slowly. "I'm on the team?"

"Damn straight, son. In all my years I've never seen anyone put on a hitting exhibition like you just did. You've just become the Memphis Eagles's best-kept secret. We have good pitching and fielding, and now probably the best newcomer batter in the Negro Leagues. Edgar told me you play outfield, so what position do you want?"

"It doesn't matter, Coach."

"I'll ask you again. Which one do you want?"

Moses pondered the question and wondered if he would be taking a position away from another player who would resent the rookie usurping him because of his batting prowess. However, he'd learned a team wasn't one person but several working together for a common cause. That cause was winning ballgames.

"Left field," he said after a long pause.

Odell nodded. "Then left field is yours. We have one more day in Memphis before we head out to St. Louis. We'll have practice tomorrow morning at ten o'clock with everyone on board for a game with team A against team B. You'll be on team B. So, suit up and be ready to play at exactly ten."

"Yes, Coach."

"I'm going to call Miss Chess, who will come by with your contract, and once you sign it, you'll be added to the list of team members and the payroll. In case no one has told you, you'll be paid on the fifteenth and the last day of the month. You have the rest of the day for yourself, so clean up and relax. Dinner is served at seven in the downstairs dining room and lights are out at ten. You should take advantage of your free time because once we go on the road life as you've known it will no longer be yours to control. The manager will be here tomorrow to watch the game, so it will be up to him to report back to the owner who to keep and who to cut from the team."

Moses nodded as a sense of dread swept over him; he didn't want to be responsible for anyone losing their position because he had supplanted them. Within seconds he realized baseball wasn't only a sport but also a business, and in business there were winners and losers and if a player wasn't delivering what he'd been paid to produce, then he would have to face the consequences.

He was unaware that in an instant he had mentally matured from a reticent boy into man with a clear-cut focus on what he needed to do as a ballplayer in the Negro Leagues. He was responsible for becoming the best, not only for himself but the team. He was now a Memphis Eagle, and that meant soaring to heights he had yet to experience.

Chapter 9

Moses read and reread every word on the typed contract before picking up a pen and scrawling his name on the line above the one where Winnie Chess would write her signature. She had typed up duplicate copies and backdated them to May 30th, the day he'd left Nichols and met Edgar Donnelly for the first time.

Winnie countersigned the contracts, then capped her fountain pen. "One contract is yours to keep, while I'll hold on to the other. And from what Coach said about your batting performance this morning, you'll be signing another contract before the end of the year with an increase in salary."

"Will it be for another six months?"

Winnie shook her head. "I doubt that, judging from what Coach told me about your batting exhibition."

"And what did he tell you?" Moses asked.

"He said that you were a phenom."

Moses knew that phenom was a shortened form of phenomenon, and that meant he was extremely talented. "If he believes I'm that talented and an asset to the team, then I would like a signing bonus in the next contract with terms that exceed six months or even a year."

Winnie sat straight as if she'd been pulled up with an invisible wire attached to the top of her head. Somehow, she had underestimated Moses Gilliam. Her first impression of the young man with the drawling speech pattern was that he would be all too happy to sign with the Memphis Eagles, as an alternative to attending college to study medicine or law.

"Tell me what you want, Moses."

"I want a two-year contract with a signing bonus."

"How much of a bonus do you want?"

"A month's salary. At the beginning of each year," he added.

Winnie lowered her gaze so she wouldn't have to look into Moses's eyes, which still sent chills right through her. "That's not a problem," she said. She was willing to agree to anything just to finish her business with Moses. However, she was grateful he hadn't asked for more money because there was no way she'd pay a rookie more than she paid her more veteran players.

She folded one of the contracts, slipped it into an envelope, and handed it to Moses, at the same time avoiding looking directly at him. "This is your copy."

"Thank you, Miss Chess."

Winnie stood and Moses also rose to his feet. "Once again, I welcome you to the Memphis Eagles."

He nodded. "Thank you."

Moses Gilliam had thanked her when she should have been the one to thank him. Even though she hadn't witnessed his batting practice, she had come to believe every word Edgar Donnelly and Odell Nelson had said about him. Moses Gilliam was the goose who would lay the golden egg to reverse the club's losing record.

She had invested too much money in the ball club

not to come out a winner. It was different with Edgar, because he owned the dress factory, while she had mortgaged the house she'd inherited, to purchase the team. Once the team became more profitable, she planned to buy out Edgar and become sole owner.

It wasn't that she didn't need Edgar—he was the White face fronting for her in the South—but if he was amenable to selling her his share of the team, then she would retain him as a scout. Knowing Edgar as well as she did, Winnie knew he'd agree because he was in love with her. But an interracial relationship, whether in the North or South, wasn't acceptable. She and Edgar were former classmates and friends, and that worked well for her. What she'd never told Edgar was that she preferred men of her own race, and at thirty-seven she had never crossed the color line to sleep with a man who was not Black.

She watched Moses's retreating back and seconds later Lucille Parker joined her in the parlor. Winnie smiled at her cousin. "What do you think of him?"

Lucille took the chair Moses had vacated. "He's quite a looker."

"I'm not talking about his looks, Lucy."

"If it's not his looks, then what are you talking about?"

Winnie ran a hand over the back of her neck. "You're a very good judge of character. Do you think he's going to become a problem?"

"Problem how?" Lucille had answered her question with another one.

"He's already making demands about how much he wants to be paid. He's also the first player who has requested a signing bonus."

Lucille pressed the palms of her manicured hands together in a prayerful gesture. "That's because he's different from the other men on the team. He's not only young, but he's also smart, Winnie."

"He gave up going to college to play baseball."

"And that bothers you?" Lucille asked.

"What bothers me is eventually he's going to become a problem whenever I offer him an extended contract. He knows his worth, and if I don't give in to his demands, then he'll leave the team for one that is willing to pay him what he wants."

A beat passed before Lucille said, "That doesn't have to happen if you sign him to a long-term contract."

"How long, Lucy?"

"An exclusive contract where he would have to play for the team for at least, say, five years. You can also include a proviso of increases in increments of whatever amount you think is comparable to the team's winning record."

Deep in thought, Winnie angled her head. She'd asked her cousin's advice because she had a head for business; she had learned from her husband, who owned and operated an insurance company and a funeral parlor business with his brothers. Unlike herself, who, as registered nurse, was focused on healing. However, it was her love of baseball—along with Edgar's urging—that had led to her decision to become a businessperson; a businessperson who was still navigating what it would take to become adept in making her investment profitable.

"But what if the team has a losing season?" she asked Lucille.

"Then that must be written into the contract. His increases in salary should be increments of, say, two hundred dollars each year. For example, if you were to pay him four thousand the first year, then he would get forty-two hundred the second year and forty-four the third, and so on. I know two hundred a year comes out to less than twenty dollars a month, but you're going to have to decide what he's worth to the team."

"You didn't answer my question, Lucy. What if the team loses more than it wins?"

"Then there won't be any raises. And that's for everyone on the team, Winnie. You shouldn't have to reward folks who don't do their jobs. The Eagles have lost how many games since the season began?"

"More than half."

"Which means you've been paying losers. Why should they strive to win if they're still being paid? I know Coach has been working hard to get the batters to improve, but he can't do it alone. It's up to the manager to make them a winning team, and if he can't do the job then fire him. Better yet, have Edgar fire him. Even though you are equal partners, it would look better coming from a White man than a Black woman. But make certain you have someone else in mind to manage the team."

Winnie knew her cousin was right. She nodded. "I'll tell him that he must meet with the manager and let him know that his job is on the line if the team continues their losing streak. And I plan to think about what you said about Moses's future contracts."

"Don't think too long, cousin, because you shouldn't underestimate Moses Gilliam. I'm willing to bet if he had gone to college, he would have become one fine lawyer."

Winnie smiled. "You're right about that."

Winnie knew she had to stay one step ahead of Moses or he would get more than she was willing to give. Once she'd divorced her husband, she had vowed she would never let another man use her. Not only was she young when she'd married, she had been completely in love, but unaware that her husband had used her to conceal his homosexuality. And for Winnifred Chess, once burned, twice shy. Her intent wasn't to use a man but deal with him on an equal footing.

"Are you leaving now or staying the night?" Lucille asked.

"I think I'm going to stay and then get up early to drive up to Chicago. I'll stay there for a few days before I head out to New York. Meanwhile, I want to use your phone to call Edgar to let him know about coming back down for a face-to-face with the manager. If you don't mind, I'd like to have dinner in my room tonight." Winnie had made it a practice never to eat in the dining room whenever the team was in town.

"I'll tell the cook to prepare a separate tray for you. Do you plan to drive without stopping along the way?" Lucille asked.

Resting her head against the back of the armchair, Winnie closed her eyes. As a Black woman, she loathed coming south. Whenever she saw the WHITES ONLY and COLORED ONLY signs it was a blatant reminder of why so many Negroes were leaving the South. Jim Crow and not the US Constitution had become law in the Southern states.

"I don't know. It all depends on how I feel. What I do know for certain is that I'm not going to stop until I'm out of the South."

"I don't think any redneck policeman will stop you, because you have Tennessee plates. It would be different if you were driving a new car with New York license plates."

Winnie nodded. When she had purchased the used car, she had made certain to register it using her cousin's address, because if she was going to do business in the South, then she wanted to blend in. Being related to the Parkers was an advantage because not only were they well-known in the Negro community, but they were also respected by prominent White elected officials to whose political campaigns they had generously donated.

"Are you okay, Winnie?"

She opened her eyes. "Yes. It's just the heat. I know it gets hot in New York City, but not like this. At least not this early. There are years when it's still cool at the end of May."

Lucille smiled. "There's nothing like Dixie in the summer because it can get so hot that you can fry an egg on the sidewalks." She paused, meeting her cousin's eyes. "I don't think it's the only thing that's bothering you."

Winnie froze. "What are you talking about?"

"I think that boy is bothering you, because I've never seen you so uneasy when dealing with one of the players."

Winnie wanted to lie but knew she wouldn't be able to fool Lucy. At least not for long. She didn't know if her cousin had second sight, and if she did, then Lucy would never admit it. "You're right. I've always felt in control when negotiating with the other men, but it's different with Moses Gilliam."

"It's because he's had more book learning than the others. More than half the players on the team can't read above the third-grade level, so when they sign their contracts, they are relying on you to explain what is written."

"Are you saying I'm cheating them?"

Lucille held up a hand. "There's no need to get huffy, Winnie. I'm not saying you cheat them."

"Then what are you saying?"

Winnie knew she sounded defensive, but when she'd purchased the team, she vowed never to cheat any of the players. They'd had enough of that with the former owner, who had gambled away almost all the team's profits, so he didn't have enough to cover the semi-monthly payroll.

"It's just that you look flustered, and I'm wondering what's wrong."

"There's nothing wrong except that I've never had to negotiate with a player who decided to make demands beyond what I am offering him. It's the first time I've been challenged since taking ownership."

Lucille nodded. "Do you think it would've been better if Edgar had discussed the terms of the contract with him?"

"No! That's one responsibility I refuse to relinquish to him, because despite his liberal views about Colored people, there's never a time when I can forget that he is a White man in America. When we decided to become co-owners, we agreed that he'd travel to scout for the best talent, while I managed everything else."

A sly smile flittered over Lucille's features. "So, the boy has looks and brains along with talent. That's a winning combination. Once the team starts barnstorming, I predict there will be a noticeable increase in women—young and old—buying tickets to get a glimpse of Moses Gilliam."

Winnie's light brown eyes shimmered like polished gold citrines. "I just thought of something."

"What is it?"

"I'm thinking of calling a few Black-owned newspapers to ask that they send their reporters to cover our games now that we have a player who has the potential of hitting as many home runs as Babe Ruth."

"Now you're thinking like a businessperson, Winnie. There's nothing better than free publicity."

"After I call Edgar, I'm going upstairs to my room and take off all my clothes and take a nap."

"Don't forget to lock your door. You don't want one of the men walking in on you."

Winnie gave her cousin an eye roll. "You know that's not going to happen. They are not allowed upstairs." When she'd told Lucille she would pay her for putting up players who didn't live in Memphis, her cousin agreed but had relegated them to rooms on the lower level, while the first and second floors were off-limits.

"I only mentioned it in case one of them decides to see why they're not allowed upstairs."

"They're lucky, Lucy, because if they didn't live here, they would have to pay folks for room and board. I told you when I decided to buy the team that I didn't want to take advantage of the men like the previous owner, who treated them as chattel. He fined and cheated them for every infraction, and they got back at him by losing games. They may have forced him to sell the team, before he blew his brains out, but they haven't changed their attitude when it comes to losing, because they're still being paid. That is something that must change."

"I believe you signing Moses Gilliam will spark a change, Winnie. He's going to be the catalyst that will make the Memphis Eagles soar."

Winnie nodded, smiling. "I think you're right, Lucy." If what Coach had told her about Moses was true, then there was no doubt the Memphis Eagles would become a winning team because now they had good pitching, fielding, and a newcomer home-run hitter. "If I don't see you later, then it will be tomorrow morning." The heat was sapping all her energy, and she planned to call Edgar to tell him about their next move before going upstairs. She pushed off her chair. "I'm going to call Edgar, and my friend in Chicago, then I'm going to rest for a few hours."

Lucille rose to her feet and pointed to the telephone on a table. "It's all yours," she said, walking out of the room to give Winnie some privacy.

Winnie dialed the number to the factory and waited a full two minutes before Edgar picked up the receiver. "How was he?"

She knew he was talking about Moses. "You're right, Edgar. Coach told me that he's a sure winner."

"I told you. When I saw him hit a home run for the first time, I thought he got lucky because the ball was right over the plate. But luck had nothing to do with it. He managed to hit everything thrown at him whether it was a fastball, curveball, and even a knuckleball. The kid is our secret weapon."

"I'm glad we were able to sign him before another team did. I know you just got back home, but I need you to talk to the manager. Coach told me that he's not doing his job. That he rarely shows up for practice, and he wasn't here today to see Moses take batting practice."

"Do you want me to fire him, Winnie?"

"Fire him before we have a replacement?"

"We already have a replacement."

"Who, Edgar?"

"Odell Nelson. All the players like Coach, and he knows them better than any of us."

"Do what you have to do, Edgar."

"Are you telling me to fire him?"

She closed her eyes, wondering why she wasn't getting through to her partner. It wasn't as if they hadn't discussed finding another manager to replace the one who had made it known he resented that the new owner of the team was a woman.

"Fire him, Edgar. And please do it before the fifteenth of June so I can give him his last paycheck." Winnie knew she didn't have to pay him beyond that date because, unlike the players on the team, he'd refused to sign a new contract once she and Edgar purchased the team.

"Consider it done, boss. I'm looking at the schedule now and see that the team will be in Missouri for a couple of days. I'm going to call to reserve a flight as soon as we hang up and meet them in St. Louis. I'll pay him in cash and give him enough money to travel back to Memphis." There came a pause before Edgar said, "I'm seriously thinking of traveling with the team to keep a close eye on things now that we've signed Gilliam."

Winnie was slightly taken aback with Edgar's suggestion. "What about your family? Your other business?"

"My mother-in-law is staying with us for the summer, so she can help out the wife with the kids, and now that my brother is assisting me at the factory, he knows enough to oversee the day-to-day operation."

"Why now, Edgar?" Winnie questioned.

"Once folks get a look at Gilliam and the sports reporters start following him, there will a lot more behinds in the seats in the ballparks. I want to make sure we're not cheated when it comes to getting our percentage of ticket sales."

She smiled. It was obvious that he wanted to closely monitor their latest acquisition. "That sounds good. How long do you intend to travel with the team?"

"Probably until the end of the summer."

Winnie wondered if Edgar's willingness to travel with the Eagles was because things were not going well at home between him and his wife. Well, that was no concern of hers, because if he was having marital problems, then that was something he had to work out for himself. "I'm glad you've decided to travel with the team." She didn't tell him his becoming more involved, beyond just scouting for players, would free her up so she wouldn't have to travel South so often. "Thank you."

"Anytime, my love."

"Love your wife and children," she said, frowning.

His chuckle came through the earpiece. "I love them, but I also love you, Winnifred Chess. You're the best friend a man could have without feeling guilty that he's cheating on his wife."

She wondered if Edgar had ever cheated on his wife, and if he had it was of no import to her. "It's the same with me, *friend*." She'd made certain to stress the word.

"When are you returning to New York?"

"Not until the weekend. I'm planning to spend some time in Chicago to see some friends, before I come back home." She'd refused to tell Edgar who the friends were she occasionally saw in Chicago, because for Winnie it was too personal to disclose to him, or even to her cousin. It wasn't friends but a special friend who she did not get to see often enough.

"I'll call your house until I get you, so safe travels."

"You too," she said, before ending the call. She then made another call, leaving a message with the person who had answered that she was coming to Chicago and would call again when she got into town.

Winnie was glad she had signed Moses Gilliam to the team and had resolved the problem of finding a new manager. Odell Nelson would be perfect for the position because of his no-nonsense attitude when interacting with the players, despite her telling Moses that he was all bark and no bite. Odell had been hired as a coach for his ability to motivate the players without humiliating them, something the current manager tended to do too often.

Running a business was challenging work, but Winnie had told herself she was up to the task; for her, failure wasn't an option. She walked out of the parlor and up the staircase to one of the guestrooms Lucy had set aside for visiting family. She kicked off her heels and made her way to the ensuite bathroom to remove her clothes and makeup. She wound the clock on the bedside table, setting the alarm for five o'clock, and then got into bed.

Winnie wasn't as physically exhausted as she was mentally. She hated traveling to the South, where she had to adhere to a distinctly different set of rules and laws from those she'd known all her life. Although racism did exist in New York, it wasn't as blatant or overt as it was below the Mason-Dixon Line. When she'd explained this to Edgar, he offered to make the trips South. And she appreciated that he rarely turned down her requests because he was grateful that they had gone into business together.

She closed her eyes and began breathing slowly until she was relaxed enough to fall asleep.

Chapter 10

Reaching for the pitcher of sweet tea, Moses refilled his glass. When he'd walked into the downstairs dining room, he could not believe the number of dishes lining a sideboard. He was one of three team members who didn't live in Memphis and were assigned rooms in what had been the servants' quarters for the former owners, who had been forced to sell the house and property when they lost everything during the 1929 Wall Street Crash.

Moses hadn't said much when he'd joined the others for dinner after showering and changing his clothes. He was more content to listen to the conversations floating around the table. He knew they were curious about him and decided the less he revealed about himself the better. He was hired to hit home runs, and that's all they needed to know.

"Why so quiet, Gilliam?"

Moses glanced up and stared across the table at the man everyone called Train because his first name was Lionel, like the popular model toy trains. Just like a runaway train the man didn't stop talking, even when his mouth was full of food.

"I'm trying to enjoy my dinner." He'd filled his plate with sliced ham, collard greens, potato salad, and buttery cornbread.

"You can't talk and eat at the same time?"

Moses shook his head. "No. It's impolite to talk and chew food at the same time."

Resting large fists on the table, Train glared at Moses. "Are you saying I ain't got no manners?"

"Let him be, Train," said the other man named Curtis Bullock, whom everyone called Bull, who was only few years older than Moses. "I don't know why you feel the need to mess with the rookies."

Moses knew he was physically no match for the taller, muscular ballplayer, and while he'd been warned against fighting, he did not intend to become a target of bullying and intimidation from anyone on the team. He'd had enough of that with his father. He was now his own man and had to stand up for himself.

"I'm not saying anything except that I don't talk when I have food in my mouth. Right now, I'm trying to finish my dinner, so I would appreciate it if you will excuse me while I eat."

A rush of color suffused Lionel Dean's light brown freckled complexion. "Well, well, well, pretty boy. Ain't you the fancy one."

Moses decided it was best if he ignored the man and continued eating. But something told him Train wasn't going to let up on him. It was obvious he was either embarrassed or felt insulted when Bull laughed loudly. Pushing back his chair, Lionel rose to stand, but before he could rise to his full height, Moses was on his feet, glaring at him. He didn't know what it was, but something about the man reminded him of his father. There were times when Solomon would goad him relentlessly until Moses was blind with rage. However, sanity had prevailed when he'd told himself to bide his time because each passing year brought him closer to leaving home.

Moses's fingers closed around the knife in his right hand. "One more word and I'll gut you like a fish." The words, though spoken quietly, were filled with a deadly threat that rendered Train and Bull motionless. He must have gotten through to Train because he sat down again.

Moses didn't want to tell the man that he wouldn't have cut him. He just wanted him to know that despite Bull's massive bulk, he didn't fear him, and refused to be intimidated.

"That's enough, Train," Curtis said quietly. "Don't start something you can't finish. Coach really likes this kid, and if you continue to mess with him, it will be you they cut from the team." It was obvious that Curtis Bullock had gotten through to Lionel Dean when he picked up his fork and began shoveling food into his mouth. "You did just fine, Gilliam. We usually put all the new guys through what we call an initiation to see if they have the guts to stand tall when we play other teams." He smiled. "We have our rivalries just like the White boys in their leagues. Right now, we are the laughingstock of the Negro Leagues because we just can't seem to bring in a run, even when there are no outs, and the bases are loaded."

"I hope to change that," Moses said, as he gave both men a level stare. They probably believed he was boasting, but there was one thing of which he was certain, and that was his ability to hit home runs.

Lionel shoveled a forkful of collards into his mouth. "From what I seen you do out there this morning, I don't doubt that we can begin winning a few games."

Moses averted his eyes because seeing his teammate

eat like he did served as a constant reminder of what he had experienced when seated at the table with his father. Now that he'd left home, everything he experienced up until that time seemed magnified. Moses knew he had to stop focusing on his past and look forward to his future as a baseball player in the celebrated Negro Leagues.

"Is everything all good, Gilliam?" Curtis asked.

Nodding and smiling, he said, "Yeah. Everything's all good."

Dinner continued without further conversations and Moses was relieved when someone came to collect the dishes on the buffet server. He finished eating, nodded to the two men at the table, walked out of the dining room and down the hallway to his bedroom. It wasn't until he closed the door that he realized the tension he'd been holding in had tightened the muscles in his neck and upper back, making movement painful. He chided himself for letting Lionel get to him when he'd had years of experience conjuring up ways to deflect his father's unprovoked taunting.

He hadn't understood why Solomon Gilliam was so filled with hate and resentment until he'd overheard his parents arguing about the man who had fathered him. It had come as a shock to Moses that Solomon Gilliam wasn't his birth father, yet it was Solomon and not his best friend who had claimed Daisy as his wife. He didn't want to think about Solomon now that Daisy had finally stood up to him. And he'd meant it when he'd warned his father about laying a hand on his mother. If Moses heard that he had, he'd return to Nichols and make his father regret the day he'd been born.

Moses loved his sisters and had wanted to protect them, but he hadn't been able to. When they confided in him that they were dropping out of school to marry local coal miners, he kept their secret. When Solomon returned home one day and discovered his daughters were missing, he sat outside the house all night drinking moonshine until he collapsed in a drunken stupor. It was the first time Moses had glimpsed a modicum of remorse in his father. However, Solomon refused to admit he was responsible for their leaving home to escape his wrath.

Moses stripped down to his underwear and picked up a notebook and pencil off the bedside table. He wanted to jot down events of the day while they were still fresh in his mind. He'd lost track of time as he filled pages with what he had experienced, when he heard a tapping on his bedroom door.

He sat up straight. "Who is it?"

"Train."

Moses blew out a breath. "What do you want?" He'd had enough of the loudmouth during dinner.

"I just want to talk to you," came the voice on the other side of the door.

Moses didn't know what his teammate wanted, but decided it was better to get everything out in the open. "Hold on." Reaching for a pair of shorts, he slipped them on over his underwear before walking on bare feet to open the door.

"What do you want?"

Lionel lowered his eyes. "I came to apologize for how I treated you."

Moses glared at him. "It wasn't how you treated me, but what you said. But as I said before, everything is all good."

"I'm sorry about that." He paused. "May I come in?"

"Sure." Taking a step back, Moses opened the door wider. He wanted to hear what his teammate had to say and hopefully call a truce.

Lionel walked in and sat down on one of the twin beds. He extended his legs, crossing his feet at the ankles, while Moses closed the door and retook the chair.

"You read all these books?" Lionel asked, pointing to the stack on the bedside table.

"Yes. Are you familiar with them?" Moses had packed several of his favorite novels that included *The Count of Monte Cristo*, *The Three Musketeers*, and *Les Misérables*. Moses didn't know why, but he had fallen in love with the works of French writers. He had also packed a worn Bible that had belonged to his late grandmother.

Lionel shook his head. "No, because I can't read. At least not well," he added when Moses gave him an incredulous stare.

"How much schooling have you had?" Moses asked.

"Not much?"

"How much is not much?"

"I stopped going to school when I was nine because I had to help my father harvest sugarcane."

"You were sharecroppers." The question was a statement.

Lionel scowled. "We were worse. We were slaves. Every year my daddy worked his ass off, but he couldn't earn more than a hundred dollars for all the work he'd done once the owner deducted what he said was expenses for us working and living on his land. Even when I quit school to help him in the fields it still didn't help much. In the end I gave up schooling just to help my family survive."

"Why are you telling me this, Train?"

"I want to be like you, Gilliam. I want to be able to read and write so once I stop playing ball I won't end up like my father."

"Have you thought about going back to school during the offseason?"

Lionel shook his head. "No, because I play winter league ball to make money to send back to my family." He paused. "I have a wife and two kids, with another one on the way."

Moses didn't know what to say to the man. It was obvious he had a lot of responsibility and couldn't afford to stop playing ball once the regular baseball season ended. "Why are you telling me this?" he repeated.

"I . . . I want you to help me to read." He lowered his head. "I can't pay you—"

"There's no need to pay me, Lionel," Moses said, interrupting him. "I'll help you any way I can." He'd known too many Black kids who'd had to drop out of school to help their parents keep a roof over their heads or put food on the table years before and during the ongoing Depression.

Lionel ran a large hand over his face. "I'm sorry I came at you like I did. We usually mess over the new guys, but I know I took it too far. I suppose I was jealous because I heard Coach say that you were smart."

Moses forced a smile. He wanted to tell his teammate that if he truly was smart, then he would have elected to attend college rather than become a baseball player. He could have benefitted his race much better as a doctor or lawyer, and not as someone providing amusement for those with money to spare to come to a ballpark and cheer for their team.

"I don't know about smart," he said to downplay his intelligence, "but I've learned a lot by reading. My mother taught me to read before I began school, so whenever I wasn't playing baseball, I would read. Books allow me to travel to different countries and learn about people who lived a long time ago."

"Do you also read the Bible?"

Moses smiled. "Yes. It is filled with stories about faith, sacrifices, war, adultery, prostitutes, slavery, and political intrigue."

"I never went to church. My father didn't believe in God, so he wouldn't let my mother or any of us go."

Moses thought this odd because practically every

Black family he knew attended Sunday services. "If you want to read, then we can start with the Bible." He believed it would be easier for Lionel reading Bible stories than introducing him to French history. "Can you answer one question for me?"

Lionel gave him a direct stare. "What?"

"Why do you want to read now that you're a grown man?"

"My kids are getting older, and whenever they ask me to help them with their homework, I tell them to ask their mother, with the excuse that after being on the road playing ball I'm too tired to look in a book."

"Your wife is able to help them?"

Lionel nodded. "Most times she can. She managed to finish the seventh grade before she had to quit because her mama died, and she had to help her stepdaddy take care of her younger brothers and sisters." Lionel paused, as he stared at the floor. "I married her because she told me he started pestering her to sleep with him."

"How old was she, Train?" Moses asked, his voice barely a whisper.

"She was twelve going on thirteen."

"You married a thirteen-year-old girl?"

"No. She managed to avoid him until she turned fifteen, and that's when she left school in the eighth grade and ran away from home. She was my sister's friend. When she told my sister what she was going through, my mother let her stay with us. When my father came home and found her, I lied and told him she was my girlfriend and that her daddy had gotten drunk and beat her. Even though my father claimed he didn't believe in God, he was against any man who would hit a woman because of what his father had put his mother through. I waited until she turned sixteen, then I married her right after I signed with the Eagles."

Moses smiled. "So, now you are a married man with kids?"

"Yeah. We just get by with my playing ball and Ella working in a hotel laundry." He smiled and stared at the floor. "She's a good woman. Whenever I'm home I go to church with her and the kids. She made me promise before she married me that I would go to church because she didn't want a husband and the father of her kids to be a heathen."

"She does sound like a good woman." There was hardly a Sunday when Moses, his mother, and sisters did not attend services, while Solomon rarely joined them. "Where do you live?" Moses asked.

"New Orleans. We're scheduled to play there sometime in August, and you are welcome to stay with my family before we leave for Texas."

Moses, who had never traveled outside of Tennessee, was looking forward to seeing some of the other states and countries he'd read about. "I'd like that, and thank you for the invite, but are you sure I won't be putting you and your missus out?"

"No! The house isn't big, but we have a spare room Ella uses to store things. We keep a cot there for when some of our folks come to visit."

Moses knew Lionel inviting him to stay with his family in New Orleans meant he was offering him an olive branch. Although Curtis Bullock had explained that new team members were subject to some hazing, it was apparent Train had gone too far. "I'm looking forward to meeting your family."

Lionel stood and pointed to Moses's pencil and open notebook on the bedside table. "I'm going to let you get back to your writing." He paused. "By the way, would you have cut me if I didn't stop mouthing off at you?"

A beat passed. "No, Train. I wouldn't have cut you. It was just that you reminded me of my father, who is mean as a coiled rattlesnake ready to strike. Solomon Gilliam is a man who is so mean and evil that even the devil wouldn't let him into Hell."

"That bad?"

Moses nodded. "Yeah. That bad. And I told myself if I ever get married and have kids, I will never put them through what my family had to put up with from him."

"How old are you, Gilliam?"

"Eighteen."

"Damn. You're still a kid."

"You can't be that much older than me," Moses countered.

"I'm twenty-five, and in another month I'll be twenty-six, and that's enough to make me your older brother."

"I've always wanted an older brother," Moses said truthfully.

"Well, now you have one. Gotta go and get ready to turn in before it's time for lights-out. See you in the morning."

"Good night."

Moses waited until the door closed behind Lionel before he went over and locked it. He hoped not to have any more interruptions because he wanted to finish writing in his notebook. His mother suggesting he write down what he'd experienced each day was like what he'd read about Catholics talking to a priest. They were able to clear their conscience, and after saying a few prayers their sins were forgiven.

He didn't believe he had sinned that much in his young life. The exception had been on occasion wishing his father dead, but that would come sooner rather than later. There was no doubt Solomon had come down with black lung and it was just a matter of time before he would succumb to the debilitating disease that had afflicted too many coal miners.

He finished writing, then left his bedroom to go into the bathroom to brush his teeth and shower. Coach told him lights went out at ten and he wanted to be in bed before that. He also wanted to get a restful night's sleep so he could be alert as the newest member of the Memphis Eagles.

CHAPTER 11

Moses had gathered with his teammates on the field and struggled not to lose the contents of his stomach. He had eaten light that morning because he'd awoken sometime during the night in a panic after having dreamt that he couldn't hit a ball. Each time he swung and missed, Solomon's laughter grew louder and louder. He'd managed to curtail his anxiety when he realized it was nothing more than a nightmare. He had to stop thinking about Solomon's hateful prediction, because he'd proven that he could hit a baseball.

Coach was busy dividing the players into team A and team B. It was another hot day and Moses was grateful the game would only go six innings rather than the regulation nine. He was on B and had been assigned to the clean-up batter position. If the bases were loaded, then it would be his responsibility to bring in at least one or more runs. Lionel was playing right field because of his strong throwing arm. The top of the first inning ended quickly when two of the three batters struck out and the third popped out to the short stop.

It was the bottom of the first for team B. The lead-off batter was hit by the pitcher and given first base. Batters two and three struck out and it was up to Moses to try to either move the runner on first base or bring him in. He let two pitches go by—a ball and strike—before contacting the third pitch and hitting it over the head of the center fielder into the area designated for home runs. He was greeted at home plate with players from A and B before Coach shouted for everyone to retake their positions.

Moses sat on the bench to catch his breath after rounding the bases, and accepted a cup of cold water from the man who was responsible for the team's equipment. The water felt good going down his throat and he exhaled an audible breath that released all the tension he'd experienced since waking up earlier that morning.

In that instant, Moses realized his decision to become a baseball player rather than a doctor or lawyer was the right one. Moses didn't know why, but he felt alive—as if he'd become a different person the instant he walked onto a baseball field. He knew his ability to hit home runs was integral to the team's success. He was also aware that he wasn't one of the fastest runners with the ability to steal bases, nor did he have the fielding range of a center fielder to cover enough ground to catch fly balls. He didn't have the quickness of infielders to execute a double play, and that was why he'd opted to play left field.

The game ended after two hours with team B winning by five runs—two that were hit by Moses. He was running a towel over his face when Coach approached him.

"That was some pretty fine hitting, Gilliam."

Moses smiled. "I'm just glad I was able to bring in a few runs."

Odell Nelson folded muscular arms over his chest. "I've coached a lot of hitters over the years, but you are exceptional. You have a good eye and don't swing at every pitch like some who only want to hit home runs. Do you have a trick up your sleeve you don't mind telling me?"

"It's not a trick, Coach. Even though the pitcher is hiding the ball in his glove before he throws it, I can identify the pitch from the point of release. Then there is the speed and movement, or if there's a break as it reaches home plate."

Odell closed his eyes for several seconds. "Are you saying you can track the movement of the pitch before it reaches home plate?"

Moses nodded. "I don't know what it is, but it's something I realized I could do when I first started playing back in school."

"So, you know when he's going to throw a four-seam or two-seam fastball?"

"Yes, sir."

"Do you think you could teach it to some of the other players?"

Now Moses was confused. He had signed a contract with the Memphis Eagles as a player, not a coach. "You want me to be a coach?" he asked, voicing his thoughts aloud.

"Oh no," Odell said quickly. "I just need you to show the others how to track the ball. I will make sure you get paid extra for helping me," he added when Moses hesitated.

Moses wanted to tell the man it wasn't about money, even though he could use every penny. It was more about time. Whenever he had a day off, he wanted to relax and possibly do and see things he never had before. But then, he was also a Memphis Eagle, and he wanted to become a member of a winning team.

"Okay, Coach. What I will do is draw diagrams for you of different pitches for the guys to study, so they won't waste their turn swinging at the ones they can't hit." Moses knew he did not have the skill to teach pitching, but he would do what he could to help batters identify different pitches.

Odell flashed a wide grin and rested a hand on his shoulder. "Let me know what you will need, and I'll get it for you."

"Okay."

"Gilliam?"

"Yes, Coach."

"Thank you."

Moses gave him a direct stare. "There's no need to thank me. I'm a Memphis Eagle and it's my job to help the team win."

"Now if all the boys had your attitude, we could be winners. Enough chitchat. Why don't you go and get washed up. Even though I wouldn't recommend it to you, I heard that some of the boys will be going into town later tonight to let off some steam before we board the bus tomorrow morning for St. Louis. Just make certain you're back here before ten or you will find yourself in the dark. Oh, I forgot. Don't take too much money with you because some of the boys have had their pockets picked. Unfortunately, where you're going isn't on the best side of town, but it's the only place where Colored folks are allowed. It has a lot of juke joints, flophouses, honky-tonks, and dive bars. Most of them are owned by a family of cousins who think nothing of taking advantage of folks."

"Are they White?"

Odell grunted under his breath. "It wouldn't bother me so much if they were, but the truth is they are Colored. I just don't understand how Negroes feel the need to mess over their own folks when we have enough with Jim Crow that controls our very lives here in the South."

"I suppose it takes all kinds," Moses remarked, not knowing what else to say. He wanted to tell Coach there were good and bad folks of all races, and that many Blacks fleeing slavery would not have found freedom if it hadn't been for White Northern abolitionists.

"Sure, you're right," Odell said, smiling.

Moses was aware that he, Lionel, and Curtis Bullock had a curfew while other team members could stay out longer because they lived in and around Memphis. "Yes, sir. And thanks for the advice."

He returned to the house and went into the bathroom to shower before Train and Bull. He was exhausted from playing ball in the intense heat and beginning to feel the effects of not having had a restful night's sleep. He planned to take a nap and then get up and join the others when they went into town.

Moses knew he was out of his element within seconds of walking into Tommy's Joint, a dimly lit, smoke-filled, noisy juke joint. It was his first time venturing into what his mother would've referred to as a *bucket of blood* because a fight could break out at any time and end up with someone being stabbed or shot.

The sound of a blues trio was nearly drowned out by the hooting and hollering of the patrons.

"Whatcha having, pretty boy?"

Moses turned and stared at the upturned face of the young woman clinging to his arm. She called him pretty when she was the most beautiful woman he had ever seen, even prettier than Winnie Chess. The girl's nut-brown complexion was flawless and was the perfect canvas for large, expressive, velvety dark eyes and a short nose. However, it was her full lips that drew his rapt attention. His gaze lingered on her black straightened hair, which was parted off center in a cascade of waves ending above her shoulders.

"Who's asking?" he questioned, not knowing what else to say.

The young woman licked her ruby-red lips, bringing his gaze to linger on them. "Buy me a drink and I'll tell you."

Moses thought she was young to be drinking, but who was he to judge? "What do you want?"

"Pop."

He gave her an incredulous stare. "Pop?"

She nodded and smiled. "Yes. If my uncle saw me drinking anything stronger, he'd tell my daddy, who would skin my hide."

"How old are you?"

"Sixteen. And I'm not going to tell you my name until I get my drink."

Pretty, young, and sassy. There was something about the girl that Moses liked. What he couldn't understand though was why she was spending time in a place where adults came to drink liquor, listen to live music, and behave like they'd never had any home training. Some couples were dancing together, their movements suggestive of people having sex.

He wanted to tell the girl flirting with him that he also didn't drink hard liquor because of the way it made him feel dizzy and not in control of his surroundings. "Stay here and I'll bring you your pop." Moses inched his way through the throng, managing to get the attention of one of the bartenders and ordered two Coca-Colas. The man had walked to the opposite end of the bar to get the pop when Moses felt movement behind him.

"She's off-limits, Gilliam."

Moses recognized the voice in his ear and turned to look directly at Lionel. "Who is she?" he whispered back.

"Her name is Sallie Ann and she's the niece of one of the owners."

"What is she doing here?"

Lionel grunted. "I'm not sure, but she's always here on the weekends to flirt and make sure the liquor keeps flowing."

Moses wanted to tell Lionel that he didn't mind a little flirting, but drinking alcohol wasn't going to happen. The bartender returned with two bottles and Moses placed two dimes on the bar. He could buy a soft drink for a nickel, but it was apparent the establishment had doubled the price. He picked up two ice-cold bottles. "She's out of luck because I don't drink."

A hint of a smile lifted one corner of Lionel's mouth. "Good for you. I drink, but I never have more than two. If I was to show up for practice or a game hungover, then Coach would not only bench me, but I'd lose money, and that is something I cannot afford. Not with another baby on the way."

"How about having one, then cut it off," Moses suggested. He didn't want to tell his teammate that if he wanted to save money, then buying one less drink meant more money in his pocket.

"You're right, Gilliam. Even though there are times when I need to blow off steam and relax with a couple of drinks after barnstorming for weeks, I need to save money so I can stop renting and buy a house for my family."

Lionel had plans for the money he earned playing baseball and so did Moses. He wanted to buy his mother an electric sewing machine. After that he wanted to put away enough for his own future. He'd given playing winter ball a lot of thought, and aside from adding to his meager savings, he wanted to travel. Not only in the States, but also out of the country.

"Let me know when you're ready to leave and we can go back together." He, Lionel, and Curtis had come to the Colored part of downtown Memphis in a taxi.

Moses wanted to get back to the house before the lights were turned off downstairs. He didn't know if Lucille Parker wanted to save on her electric bill or if she had an agreement with Winnie Chess that her players had to abide by a ten o'clock curfew. Moses didn't mind the curfew; he needed structure, being away from home for the first time in his life. He'd heard stories of young men and women who had gone down the wrong path and ended up either broken or dead.

Moses walked back to Sallie Ann and handed her the soda pop. "Drink up, Sallie Ann," he said, smiling. Her arching eyebrows lifted at the same time her jaw dropped. It was apparent that he had beaten her at her own game. "I would've bought you a drink even if you hadn't challenged me."

Sallie Ann lowered her eyes. "So, you saw through me."

"I didn't until someone told me your name and that your uncle owns this place." Moses wanted to tell Sallie Ann that the men in her family were pimping her to increase business, but if they weren't careful, it could backfire. She was young and vulnerable, and there were men who would resent being conned into buying more liquor than they normally would and might physically take it out on her.

Sallie Ann took a sip and stared at Moses. "Are you some kinda teetotaler? Why don't you drink?"

"It doesn't agree with me."

Looping her arm through his, she steered away from the crowd to an area where they could talk without having to shout to each other. "What's your name?"

Moses stared at her under lowered lids. "Moses Gilliam."

"Do you play baseball like the others? I don't remember ever seeing you here before."

He took a swallow from the bottle, then set it on a

shelf. There was something about it that didn't taste right. It was different from the one he'd ordered at the restaurant his first night in Memphis.

"You don't remember me because I just joined the team."

Sallie Ann pointed to his bottle. "Is there something wrong with your pop?"

Moses thought about lying and saying nothing but decided to tell the truth. "Yes. It tastes funny."

"Funny how?"

"I don't know, but I don't want to drink it." Picking up the bottle, he poured out the contents in a nearby bucket. "Aren't you going to drink yours?" he asked Sallie Ann.

A smile parted her vermilion-colored lips. "I will in a while. I usually wait for the bubbles to go away because they make me burp. It's going to be a while before it goes flat, so I'm just going to hold on to it."

Moses didn't want to think of himself as paranoid, but something wasn't adding up. The woman had asked him to buy her a nonalcoholic drink, then was reluctant to drink it. He wondered if the bartender had put something in the bottles to make him dizzy or sick so that he would become a victim of a robbery. Well, if someone was waiting to take advantage of him, they were in for a surprise. He hadn't brought more than three dollars with him, thanks to what Coach had said about pickpockets.

Moses stared over her head. "Why don't you try and work your magic on some other unsuspecting mark, because I'm going to go over and hang out with some of my teammates." He was surprised when Sallie Ann's eyes filled with tears. "What's the matter?"

Sallie Ann leaned in close to Moses. "I didn't want to do it."

"Do what?"

"Set you up to be robbed," she whispered.

Reaching for her arm, Moses steered her down a narrow hallway to a side door and opened it. The hot, cloying night heat was like a blast from a fiery furnace. "Talk to me, Sallie Ann."

He listened intently as Sallie Ann told him how she had been selected to set up unsuspecting men to buy drinks laced with drugs that made them less steady on their feet. They would become easy targets to have their pockets picked.

"Why do you do it?" Moses asked her. "You're young. Sixteen, so you should be either in school or hanging out with your friends instead of being forced to pimp for your uncle."

Her eyes grew wide. "Is that what you think? That he is pimping me?"

"What else can it be, Sallie Ann? There is the possibility that after he sets you up with men that he will force you to start sleeping with them."

Sallie Ann sniffled. "How do you know this?"

Moses shook his head. "I don't know. But if he is willing to use a sixteen-year-old girl who is blood, then there's nothing he wouldn't do to drug and rob his customers. And that includes turning his niece into a whore."

Clasping her fingers together in a prayerful gesture, Sallie Ann closed her eyes. "I like you, Moses Gilliam, and I hear what you are saying."

"You hear it but are you listening?" he countered.

She nodded. "Yes. When are you coming back?"

"Why?"

"Because I would like to talk to you—away from here. I will give you a phone number to reach me so we can set up a time and place to meet whenever you come back."

Moses didn't know what it was about Sallie Ann, but she was so different from the other girls he had met in and out of school. There was a weariness about her that made her appear much older than sixteen, but underneath there was a young, frightened girl on the cusp of womanhood whose life was going in the wrong direction. He was only two years older than her, yet he'd be willing to bet there were things she had experienced that would take him years to encounter—if ever.

"Okay, Sallie Ann. The team is scheduled to spend time in St. Louis before we travel to other states. What I do know is that we will be back in Memphis the first week in July. I will meet you here then."

Sallie Ann nodded. "Okay." Reaching into the pocket of her apron, she took out a pad and pencil and wrote down a series of numbers and tore off a page. "If I don't pick up, then leave a message with my mama."

Moses took the sheet of paper, wondering what he would say if her father answered the phone. He leaned closer and rested a hand on her shoulder. "Try and stay out of trouble until I see you again."

Sallie Ann smiled. "I'll try."

He returned her smile. "I'll see you when I get back."

Moses turned on his heel and returned inside, where he found some of his teammates sitting at a table listening to the band. The lyrics sung by the guitar player were filled with pain and suffering, but also love and happiness. It was as if there was a battle for supremacy and in the end the pain was victorious.

Although he hadn't spent more than an hour in the place, Moses was ready to leave when it appeared as if Lionel and Curtis were not only enjoying their drinks but also the music. However, there was nothing he could do but wait until they were ready to go back to the Parker House. They were his teammates and if they'd come together, then they would leave together.

CHAPTER 12

Winnifred Chess parked along a street with a row of stores and then walked into a luncheonette to use a pay phone. She was exhausted and wanted nothing more than a bath and a clean bed. When she told her cousin she planned not to stay overnight anywhere in the South she had been truthful. She'd stopped in Kentucky to refuel, then sat in the car along the side of the road and ate the box lunch Lucille had fixed for her. Then she stopped again near a secluded spot off a local road to relieve herself before getting back in the car. She refueled once more in Indianapolis, Indiana.

People sitting at a lunch counter barely gave her a passing glance as she opened and closed the door to the phone booth. Depositing several coins, she dialed the number that was imprinted on her brain like a tattoo, counting off the number of rings before she heard someone pick up on the other end.

"Erskine residence. Who may I ask is calling?"

Winnie folded her body down on the worn seat. "Winnifred Chess. Is it possible to speak to Mr. Erskine?"

Frederick Erskine's housekeeper had answered the phone.

"Please hold on, Miss Chess, and I'll see if he is available to speak to you."

Winnie bit her lip to keep from telling the pompous woman that whenever she called, and if Frederick—or F. Douglas Erskine, as he preferred to be addressed—was at home, he would drop everything and take her call.

The seconds ticked by before she heard, "Hello, Winnie. How are you?"

"I'm in Chicago and I want to know if I can come and spend a few days with you."

A deep chuckle caressed her ear. "Of course. I was thinking about you when you left the message that you were coming to Chicago."

A tired smile flitted over her features. "Well, you will get to see me in about fifteen minutes. I just drove practically nonstop from Memphis to get here."

"You must be hungry and exhausted. I'll have Miss James prepare your room and something for you to eat before you get here. I have a meeting with some of my business associates at two, so try and get some rest before I get back and then we'll talk."

"Thank you, Douglas." Winnie always thought calling him F. Douglas was a mouthful, so she'd decided to use his middle name.

"There's never a need to thank me, beautiful. I'll see you later."

Winnie nodded although he couldn't see her. "Later."

She returned to her car, started it up, and drove in the direction of a neighborhood populated by professional Black residents. Winnie had been introduced to Douglas when they both were married to other people. Her ex and Douglas had attended the same law school, and despite her divorce, she and Douglas had remained friends. When she'd disclosed to him why she was filing for divorce, he'd encouraged her not to reveal her husband's homosexuality because it would ruin his career, but proposed she ask for a generous settlement to guarantee her silence. Winnie thought of it as blackmail; however, after rethinking Douglas's suggestion she had followed through with his recommendation, receiving more money than she'd earn in a year as a nurse, and her ex was left with his reputation intact as a much-sought-after Black attorney.

Although her marriage hadn't survived two years, it was different with Douglas. He and his wife had tried unsuccessfully to have children and five years ago, after several miscarriages, she died from what had been diagnosed as puerperal or childbed fever. Winnie had to explain to the devastated widower that puerperal sepsis due to a streptococcal infection had been introduced into his wife's vagina following her last miscarriage.

Despite living in different states, she and Douglas had managed to maintain a close friendship. Not only was he her friend, but also her legal advisor. She drove slowly through an area of ramshackle houses with rickety second-story porches. The neighborhood was reminiscent of the one in Memphis where she'd purchased several shotgun houses, but with a distinct difference. Here the streets were paved, lined with streetlights, and had indoor plumbing and electricity. However, poverty was still visible; even with the election of a new president and his New Deal policies, the country was struggling to overcome the ongoing crippling grip of the Great Depression. Even before the Depression, Black neighborhoods had suffered when city government prioritized services for White residents who had moved to the suburbs.

There were millions across the country who had been affected by the economic devastation of losing their jobs and homes, yet there were a select few who had managed to maintain their normal lifestyle. It had been that way for Winnie because she'd had a choice of either working in a hospital or becoming a private-duty nurse for those willing to pay personal medical professionals to care for their loved ones. The latter had proven to be beneficial for her. She wasn't wealthy or even well-to-do, but she had enough capital to make conservative investments.

She owned the historic brownstone along a tree-lined street in Harlem. She'd taken over the first floor, sharing it with her parents, as her principal residence, and rented out several apartments on the second and third floors. She co-owned the Memphis Eagles and had recently purchased the dilapidated row houses that would eventually generate even more rental income for her.

Winnie slowed and maneuvered into the horseshoe driveway leading to Douglas's elegant two-story brick home at the end of the cul-de-sac. A smaller structure built slightly behind the main house doubled as his housekeeper's residence. She parked in front of a carriage house that had been converted into a three-car garage. Douglas had confided to Winnie that most of his income did not come from representing clients willing to pay his hourly rate, but from a company paying to lease oil deposits on the land that had been in his family following the Civil War.

Douglas had also revealed to her that his former slave ancestors had been duped into purchasing nearly fifty acres of land in Texas where the only thing that would grow was tumbleweed. They'd managed to scratch out a living raising hogs until natural oil deposits were discovered under the barren soil. The oil company had offered to purchase the land for three times what they had paid for the property, but they rejected the offer in lieu of leasing. Now, more than sixty years later, the Erskines were reaping the bounty of the flow of oil reserves.

The front door opened as Winnie alighted from her car. She picked up her handbag and luggage off the rear seat and nodded to Douglas's resident housekeeper. "Good afternoon, Miss James."

"Miss Chess," Felicia James said, with a barely perceptible smile that appeared more like a grimace. "Please come in. I've readied your room and prepared something for you to eat after you have settled in."

Winnie was unaware what she had done to the middle-aged spinster to garner her resentment other than she couldn't help thinking that maybe Miss James fancied herself becoming the next Mrs. Erskine; but whenever she observed Douglas with his housekeeper, there was nothing in his behavior that indicated he was remotely interested in his employee. There was no reason for Miss James to see her as competition for her boss, because Douglas was her friend, not her lover.

Tightening her grip on the handles of her luggage, Winnie followed the woman through the entryway and up a winding staircase to the second floor and into the bedroom suite with an adjoining bathroom. She set her bag down next to a closet. "I'll be down right after I take a bath." Even though the sight of the bed beckoned her, brushing her teeth and taking a bath had become a priority.

Winnie woke hours later, totally disoriented. She'd drawn the drapes in the bedroom, and she wasn't certain of the time of day. She left the bed and opened the drapes. There was waning daylight. Reaching for her wristwatch, she noted the time. It was after eight. She'd been asleep for more than five hours. She went into the bathroom and splashed water on her bare face before brushing her hair and pinning it into a twist at the nape of her neck. Dressing quickly, she exchanged her nightgown for a white sleeveless blouse, tan cotton pants, and white tennis shoes. Winnie preferred wearing pants to dresses, suits, and skirts. Then there was the makeup, which she had learned to apply with the skill of a movie makeup artist. But again, if she had a preference then it would be to go out barefaced.

Winnie headed downstairs and found Douglas in a room off the screened-in back porch, listening to the radio. His head popped up when he noticed her presence. Smiling, he stood and approached her.

"How do you feel?"

She smiled at the tall and handsome man who had become one of Chicago's most eligible bachelors. Everything about F. Douglas Erskine radiated confidence. Her gaze lingered on his strong masculine mouth with a neatly barbered mustache, smooth dark brown complexion, and close-cropped hair with a feathering of gray. It didn't matter whether he was casually or formally dressed, he always cut a fine figure.

"Wonderful, Douglas."

Leaning to his right, he turned off the radio. "Are you hungry?"

Winnie shook her head. "No. What Miss James prepared for me earlier was more than enough to sustain me until tomorrow."

He gestured to a chair facing the one he had just vacated. "If that's the case, then please sit with me."

Winnie thought there was something off with her friend. In the past whenever they met, he would hug her and kiss her cheek, but not this time, and she wondered if he had met someone with whom he was serious. The glow from several table lamps illuminated the space with warmth, throwing long and short shadows over

Douglas's face. She wondered what was going on behind his large dark eyes as he sat and crossed one leg covered with sharply creased trousers over the opposite knee.

The seconds stretched into a full minute before he asked, "How was Memphis?"

She told him everything, from meeting Moses Gilliam for the first time and signing him to the contract Douglas had drawn up for her. She also mentioned Edgar Donnelly traveling to St. Louis to fire the current manager, but not that Edgar had decided to travel with the team for the summer.

Stroking his mustache with his forefinger, Douglas gave the woman sitting a few feet away a direct stare. When he'd told Winnie that he had been thinking about her, he'd wanted to openly admit there were times when she had occupied his thoughts to utter distraction.

It hadn't been that way when he was married, or even after losing his beloved wife, but lately something had changed. She was his friend, and what he didn't understand is why he wanted more than an occasional meeting or telephone call. He wanted more, although nothing in her behavior communicated to him that she did.

"How would you like to become the sole owner of the Memphis Eagles?"

She gave him a wide-eyed look. "What are you talking about, Douglas?"

"If what you are saying about this new player is true, then the—"

"It is true," Winnie said, interrupting him.

Douglas tented his fingers, a gesture those who were familiar with him saw often whenever he was deep in thought. "I was about to say before you cut me off," he said, his voice lowering as he glared at Winnie, "that the

Eagles will probably generate a lot of talk with your newest player, and hopefully make the team as popular as the Kansas City Monarchs, the Washington Homestead Grays, or even the Pittsburgh Crawfords. That means you will make a lot of money that you'll be forced to share with your partner."

Winnie rested her hands on the arms of her chair. "That is what makes me and Edgar partners. We have decided to split the profits down the middle."

"The man owns a factory and has the means to own a team outright, so why does he need you to invest in his business scheme?"

Her eyelids fluttered. "It's not a scheme, but something we both agreed to."

"Can you afford to buy him out?"

A hint of a smile tilted the corners of Winnie's mouth. "I would if I hadn't purchased those rundown row homes in Memphis. And I add, it was at your recommendation." She hadn't told Douglas that she didn't want to become sole owner at that time, because she was already involved in enough business ventures to look after. And she needed Edgar to front for her in the South.

"I will always recommend buying real estate because it doesn't depreciate, but what I'm attempting to say is that I'm willing to give you the money to buy out Edgar Donnelly."

She blinked. "That would make us partners."

Douglas nodded. "Yes, it would."

"Why, Douglas? When I first told you about going in with Edgar, you didn't object."

"It was because you were so hellbent on becoming his partner. I know your friendship goes back to when you were in high school together, but you and times have changed, because you've proven to be a very astute businesswoman, and one I would like to go into business with."

"So, now you've changed your mind about me being in business with Edgar?"

Douglas stared at the toe of his shoe, hoping what he planned to say to Winnie wouldn't shatter their friendship. "I've changed my mind because my feelings for you have changed."

She went completely still. "Changed how?" Winnie asked.

"I'm forty and I have been widowed for more than five years, and that translates into wanting to make changes in my life. I'm not going to lie and say that I don't see women, but it's just that. Seeing is not the same as sharing things I like and what we would be like—together as a couple."

"But we are friends," she whispered. "And we've been friends for a very long time."

Douglas nodded. "That's true, but I want us to become more than friends."

Winnie sucked in her breath and held it until she was forced to exhale, the audible sound like a long sigh. "When did your feelings about me change?"

"I don't know, Winnie," Douglas admitted. "There was something I always liked about you even when you were married to Henry. Even before I discovered he'd preferred men, I was of the belief that you loved him more than he loved you."

"But I did love him, Douglas. In fact, I loved everything about him."

She hadn't lied. There was something about Henry Gaskin that had drawn her to him at first sight. She wasn't certain whether it was his intelligence and urbane demeanor, but he was everything she'd sought in a husband. He'd recently graduated from Howard

Law School, while she had graduated from nursing school. They began dating and were married a year later in a small private ceremony that included their families and close friends.

Meanwhile, she had secured a position at New York City's Harlem Hospital, an institution that made history when they hired Dr. Louis T. Wright as not only the first Black physician on the staff, but the first in any city hospital. Winnie, who had been born in Brooklyn, had come to love Harlem. The Black population swelled appreciably between 1910 and 1930, despite Black residents having been present in the Harlem community since the mid–seventeenth century.

As a couple in their twenties, she and Henry were caught up in the Harlem Renaissance that had become an intellectual and cultural revival of Black music, literature, dance, politics, fashion, art, and theater. It was the Roaring Twenties when Whites traveled uptown to Harlem to eat, drink, dance, and listen to jazz. It had also become a time of cultural awareness and political activism for Black Americans. Those who had come North during the Great Migration and settled in Harlem had discovered a newfound freedom away from the oppression and harsh economic conditions they had experienced in the South.

Winnie, when she was nineteen and in her second year of college, had promised her parents that she would do whatever she could to make them proud of her. Her father worked two jobs and her mother had become a domestic to save enough money to send her to nursing school. Just a year ago, she was finally able to convince her father to quit his job as a janitor at a midtown warehouse, and he and her mother moved into a first-floor apartment in her brownstone, where her father had assumed the responsibility of maintaining the property and collecting rents from her tenants. Her parents were able to live rent-free and enjoy the outdoor space at the rear of the property during the warmer weather.

"Are you saying that being married to a man who was living a double life has soured you on love and marriage?"

Douglas's query broke into Winnie's musings. "No," she admitted truthfully. "It's just that I like being single. I have a sense of freedom I wouldn't have if I were married. Do you think my husband would approve of me being in New York for a few months, and then pick up and go to Tennessee, or even here to Chicago?"

"I would, Winnie."

She stared at Douglas as if he had suddenly taken leave of his senses. Her heart was beating so fast she was able to feel it outside her body. "Frederick Douglas Erskine, are you asking me to marry you?"

He nodded, his gaze locked with hers.

Winnie slowly shook her head. "No, Douglas. Marrying you would spoil everything we have. Not only are you my friend, but I'm also your client." Winnie did not understand why men wanted more than friendship from women with whom they were involved. Why couldn't they be friends without sex becoming part of the equation?

"You only became my client when you insisted on paying me for legal advice."

"If I didn't pay you, then I would be forced to pay another lawyer. And he might be one I couldn't trust to look after my interests the way you do."

A beat passed before Douglas asked, "Do you have a lover?"

Winnie went completely still, wondering when and why Douglas sought to change their easygoing relationship from friends to something more. She did see someone with whom she was intimately involved, but that was something she wasn't willing to admit to him. Not even her parents were aware that she was sleeping with a man who shared her attitude toward marriage.

"I . . ."

Harper's fingers stilled when her cell phone rang. She glanced over to see her mother's number on the screen, as her mind went completely blank. Martell had called at the wrong moment, and although she wanted to ignore the call and have it go directly to voicemail, she decided it was best she talk to her mother. She tapped the speaker feature.

"Hello, Mom. How are you?"

"I'm fine. I should be the one asking how you are. I haven't heard from you in nearly a week."

Rolling her head from side to side to relieve some of the stiffness in her neck and shoulders, Harper closed her eyes for several seconds. "I'm doing well. Grandpa went away with a few of his army buddies for the holiday."

"So you're there by yourself?"

"Yes."

"If that's the case, then why don't you drive up and hang out with me and a few of your cousins who are coming in from Ohio?"

"I can't because I'm writing."

"How's that coming?"

Harper smiled for the first time since answering the call. "It's really coming together well." She wanted to tell her mother that she'd been typing nonstop, that the words were barely formed in her brain before they transmitted to her fingers on the keyboard.

"That's good to hear. I called for two reasons, the first to know how you're doing and the second is to tell you that Zion stopped by the other day. He told me that he couldn't reach you at the newspaper and you had blocked his number."

Harper smothered a groan. "He's right about me blocking his number because I don't want to see or hear from him again."

"Why, Harper? He seems like a wonderful young man."

"Yeah right. A wonderful young man for someone else. Mom, I know you want me to settle down and live happily ever after like you and Dad, but right now I'm not ready for that."

"When are you going to get ready, Harper? When you're fifty and the only men left are the ones who are widowed or have been married and divorced multiple times? Or maybe you'll hook up with a man who has five or six kids from two or three different baby mamas."

"Mom! Stop with the melodrama." She knew her mother was looking forward to seeing her only daughter married, but that wasn't going to happen until Harper found someone she could love and trust unconditionally. It wasn't only her love life she had to get back on track but also her career.

"I know I can sometimes get a little too dramatic, but I worry about you, baby. You go to work, come home, and then stay in on weekends. You don't have any girlfriends—"

"I don't have any girlfriends because I don't want or need them. Not when they seem to hit on every man who has shown an interest in me. Thanks but no thanks, Mom. I like me, and I don't mind spending time alone."

She wanted to tell her mother that she coveted her alone time when she could sleep in late, cook her favorite dishes, and spend hours watching classic movies. Yes, she liked Harper Lauren Fleming and enjoyed spending time with her.

"I've lost count of the number of women who openly flirted with your father even though they knew he was married."

"That's because Dad was and still is a celebrity. It goes with the territory."

"I suppose it does," Martell said in a quiet whisper. "Well,

I'm not going to keep you, but try and call me a little more often to let me know that you're still alive."

Harper laughed. "What if I send you a text?"

"That will do. Love you, baby."

"And I love you, Mom."

She ended the call and set the phone on the table beside her laptop. Harper had wanted to finish the scene between Winnie and Douglas but realized the telephone call had shattered her concentration. If the caller had been anyone other than her mother, she would have let it go to voicemail. But knowing Martell Fleming, she would have continued to leave voicemails until she picked up.

Saving what she had typed, Harper powered down her computer, turned off the desk lamp, and walked out of the sunroom and into the house. She had to decide whether to cook something or eat leftovers. Two days ago, she had made lentil soup with diced carrots and thinly sliced kielbasa, and it had come out better than she'd expected. Even her grandfather had raved about it. She would pair the soup with a salad of tomatoes and cucumbers. Warming the soup in the microwave would prevent heating up the kitchen.

An hour later, after eating and cleaning up the remains of her dinner, Harper returned to the sunroom, tapping a button on a remote device to lower built-in shades to watch television. The sun had set, taking with it most of the daytime heat as she sat on a recliner and channel surfed until she found one featuring classic black-and-white films. She didn't know why, but she preferred the films from the '30s, '40s, and '50s because of the plotlines and the talented actors who were able to make the characters come alive on the screen.

Although she had seen *Sunset Boulevard* before, she settled down to watch it again; William Holden was one of her favorite actors from Hollywood's golden age. A wave of fatigue washed over her as the movie credits filled the screen, and Harper knew if she didn't get up, then she'd fall asleep where she lay.

She managed to brush her teeth, wash her face, and apply a moisturizer before stripping off her clothes and getting into bed without putting on a nightgown. It wasn't often that she slept in the nude, but this night was going to be one of them, now that she had the house to herself.

CHAPTER 13

Harper felt exhilarated once she had set up her printer. As promised, it had been delivered along with a carton of paper and ink cartridges that would last for several months. She'd spent more than three hours reading, editing, and then printing out what she had written.

Her creative juices were flowing again as she took a break to prepare a chef's salad to sustain her. She planned to write nonstop until waning energy reminded her it was time to eat again.

She reread the scene with Winnie and Douglas and then picked up where she had left off.

"I . . . I . . ." Winnie stuttered, not wanting to believe that Douglas would ask her something so personal. In all the years they'd known each other, they had never talked about their sex lives. It was as if the subject was taboo. "I can't believe you would ask me that," she finally said.

Douglas uncrossed his legs, planting both feet on the carpeted floor. "I'm asking because I need to know if

I'm coming between you and another man by my asking you to marry me."

Winnie thought about lying about having a lover, then changed her mind. She and Douglas were friends, and if they were to remain that way, then she felt honesty was best.

"If you claim you're seeing someone, then so am I," she admitted truthfully. "What he and I have is beneficial to both of us. I don't want to get married, and it's the same with him."

Douglas stared at the floor. "Has he been married before?"

Winnie nodded. She did not intend to disclose to Douglas that the man she had been seeing *was* married and his wife had spent the past four years of her life in a mental hospital. She'd been diagnosed as a paranoid schizophrenic who'd purported hearing voices telling her to kill herself. After two failed suicide attempts, subsequent shock treatment therapy had left her in a vegetative state.

"Don't you want children, Winnie?"

A gentle smile parted her lips. "I did at one time, but now at thirty-seven I can't see myself as a mother. I'm involved in too many things. It wouldn't be fair to a child to have a mother who would tell him or her that their mama must go away on business and promise to bring something back for them. I don't intend to have a child or children resenting me for neglecting them because I value business over them."

Leaning back in his chair, Douglas stretched out long legs, crossing his feet at the ankles. "I see what you mean."

"Do you really, Douglas? Are you saying it to placate me, or to convince yourself that I'm not wife material?"

His inky-dark eyebrows lifted slightly. "Damn, woman, you don't bite your tongue, do you."

"You've known me long enough to know that I say whatever is on my mind." She paused. "You're the only male friend I have, and I would like it to stay that way."

"What about Edgar Donnelly?"

Winnie shook her head. "What I have with Edgar is different from what you and I share. You know more about me than he will ever know. He is aware that I was married before, but not why I decided to divorce my husband. He also knows that I own a brownstone in Harlem but not how I came into possession of it. I don't get involved with his wife and children because I don't need her to think that I'm after her husband. The only thing Edgar and I share is the Memphis Eagles. Don't forget I need him because of his color. He can go places in the South where I as a Black woman am not allowed to go. Besides, almost all the teams in the Negro Leagues are owned by White men, and with Edgar fronting for me, it's no different."

"Not all the teams are White owned. What about Gus Greenlee?"

Winnie rolled her eyes. "The man's a gangster and a bookmaker and it's rumored that he purchased the Pittsburgh Crawfords to launder money from his numbers games."

Douglas grunted under his breath. "Greenlee is no different from Cumberland Posey, who is one of the shrewdest Black businessmen in the Negro Leagues. The man has an innate gift for evaluating talent when signing players to the Homestead Grays. Don't forget that he saw financial opportunity in barnstorming."

"The difference between Greenlee and Posey is that Posey did it legitimately," Winnie countered, frowning. "What's frightening is what if Greenlee is arrested and charged with bookmaking? What happens to his team?"

"That's a risk he'll have to take, Winnie. The man

invested a hundred thousand in a new ballpark and called it Greenlee Field. Now, that's what I call risky, but it was what his team needed to boost their morale. Don't forget that he has the most marketable pitcher-catcher battery—Satchel Paige and Josh Gibson—in all Negro baseball."

Winnie wanted more Black people to own teams in the Negro Leagues, but legitimately, and not give White people the satisfaction of asserting that Black folks weren't astute businesspeople. If one of the teams in the Negro Leagues got involved with game-fixing, like the famous Black Sox Scandal in 1919 involving White teams, the Black owner and his entire team would be out of business.

"You're right, Douglas. That is a risk he must take," she agreed.

Every business venture a Black person went into was filled with risks. Even when Negroes established all-Black towns with thriving businesses, they were risky endeavors. The two-day-long White supremacist massacre in Tulsa, Oklahoma, in 1921, had destroyed the Greenwood District, which had come to be known as Black Wall Street.

A racially motivated massacre of Black people also occurred in Rosewood, Florida; and in Ocoee, Florida, it was estimated that mass racial violence had killed eighty Black people, and their businesses and residences were burned to the ground.

Winnie knew she had taken a risk when she'd agreed to go into partnership with Edgar Donnelly to assume co-ownership of the Memphis Eagles. However, she hadn't put all her apples in the same proverbial basket because she did own property. The Harlem brownstone had become a rental property, and she had paid her cousin Lucille to monitor the renovations and collect rent on the Memphis row houses. Lucille also had become her eyes and ears when it came to the finances for the Eagles. Lucille had soaked up all aspects of business like a sponge, from her husband and brothers-in-law, and Winnie trusted her implicitly and paid her well for looking after her Tennessee business interests.

"How long do you intend to grace me with your beauty, intelligence, and wit?"

Winne wanted to tell Douglas to save the sweet talk for some of his lady friends. "If you don't mind, I'd like to stay for a couple of days."

"Stay as long as you like, Winnie."

Smiling, she nodded. "Thank you."

She would stay, take in a few sights, and then drive back home.

Moses stared out the window in awe when seeing the Mississippi River for the first time. He thought it was the most breathtaking sight he had ever seen.

"What do you think of it?" Lionel asked.

Moses turned to look at Lionel, who had elected to sit next to him when they'd boarded the bus earlier that morning. He saw the team's manager for the first time, once everyone was onboard. Lionel had whispered to him that Teddy Reed rarely showed up for practice but was always present whenever the team traveled.

Teddy, a short, squat, dark-skinned man with a large head, had given the obligatory speech about how he expected them to behave regardless of whether on or off the field. He had planned for some of the team to stay in a Black boardinghouse, while others with family, friends, and relatives in St. Louis were exempt. He also recommended everyone purchase a copy of the *Green Book* that had come out that year and listed bars, gas stations, hotels, and restaurants where Black travelers would be welcomed. He claimed it had become the Black travelers guide to Jim Crow America.

Moses knew for certain he would purchase a copy; he was more than aware of "sundown towns," all-White towns and neighborhoods that excluded Blacks, who were warned to leave before sundown.

"It's a sight to behold," Moses whispered.

Lionel nudged him with his shoulder. "There are a lot more sights to behold now that we are going to be barnstorming for the next month."

Moses nodded. He'd been given the schedule, and the team wasn't due back in Memphis until the first week in July. They would barnstorm in Missouri, Ohio, Indiana, and Illinois before returning to Tennessee. Moses, who at eighteen had never been outside the state where he'd been born and raised, now would get to visit places he had read about but had never seen.

Although he was excited about seeing other states, it was the talk of playing winter ball in foreign countries that had enthralled him. Hearing people speaking a language other than English, and sampling dishes with ingredients he was unfamiliar with, were things he could not wait to experience.

Moses gathered with the team in the backyard of the boardinghouse, listening intently to a pep talk from Coach, who was now officially the Memphis Eagles's manager. Edgar Donnelly had been waiting for them to arrive and summarily fired Teddy Reed, much to the shock of many of the players. A few had even applauded when Edgar announced that Odell Nelson would take over as manager. Their enthusiasm for having Coach as their manager was overshadowed when Edgar announced he would be traveling with the team for the remainder of the summer. He had also promised new uniforms with numbers on the back of the shirts to identify the different players, while his intent to travel with them was to keep a close eye on ticket sales and become the point person for the team if or when they encountered problems with local law enforcement.

This disclosure made Moses feel more secure. Being away from home and all that was familiar had left him slightly fearful. He was aware of the boundaries, as a Negro, and what he could do and where he could go in Nichols, but he was still attempting to navigate the world outside his hometown with a more stringent set of rules he was forced to follow to ensure his day-to-day survival. Unfortunately, it was a burden he was forced to experience as a Black man in the American South.

Coach cleared his throat after Edgar had finished with his short speech, stood, and clasped both hands behind his back. "Half the season is over, and it's time we either shit or get off the pot. I know many of you have been playing the best you can, while others are just dragging their feet. For those who claim they love this game but aren't willing to play hard, then let me warn you that you'll be let go so fast that you won't know what hit you." He paused as his gaze lingered on each player as they sat on several benches. "I know we've had a hard time bringing in runners, but I believe we can offset that with more batting practice. I was given diagrams of different pitches, which I will share with you so you can recognize what the pitcher is throwing."

"How will that help us, Coach?" someone called out.

"If you pay close attention when the ball is released, then you will be able to track the movement, hand or wrist position and even the arm angle of the pitcher."

"But that sounds impossible," Lionel said.

"It's not impossible, Train," Odell countered. "Do you have a problem seeing and hitting the ball?"

Lionel shook his head. "No."

"Then you shouldn't have a problem learning to recognize a two or four-seam fastball along with a curveball, or a screwball when it's coming at you."

"Will the rookie have to take extra batting practice?" Curtis teased, pointing at Moses.

Odell glared at Curtis Bullock. "Every man on the team will take extra batting practice, and that includes Moses Gilliam. Now, I want everyone suited up and at the ballpark by eleven. We will have batting practice for an hour before the game begins at one, so let's see if we can stop this losing streak and show everyone that we are winners."

Moses was grateful that Coach hadn't announced he was the one who had drawn the diagrams depicting the different pitches, because as a rookie he'd wanted to stay in the background and not show up the veteran players. He didn't want to become the object of resentment. He had joined the Memphis Eagles because he loved playing baseball and not to become a hero like Babe Ruth or Satchel Paige. However, what he did not plan to do was downplay his ability to track and hit different pitches. It was a gift he had been blessed with and Moses intended to exploit it every chance he got.

He settled into the room he shared with Lionel. Even without saying anything they had become official roommates. The space, although small, was clean and functional with twin beds, a nightstand with a table lamp separating the two, and a four-drawer chest. There were two bathrooms on each floor of the three-story building, with posted signs that showers were not to exceed ten minutes.

He'd admitted to Lionel that it was his first time traveling outside his home state and the first time he'd become a roommate. There were only two bedrooms in the house in Nichols, where his parents slept in one and his sisters in the other, while he had been relegated to sleep on a fold-up cot in the storage room. The cramped space was either too cold or sweltering. He'd gone to bed fully dressed during the winter and slept completely nude in the summer.

Moses sat on the side of his bed, watching Lionel as he removed his uniform and cleats from a small satchel. "I can't believe we are going to play a game in Sportsman's Park." It was the home ballpark of the St. Louis Cardinals, who were formerly known as the Browns.

"That's because things are different when a White owner is traveling with the team. Most times we wind up in raggedy, broken-down ballparks that seat less than five thousand folks. And if ticket sales are low, then what we get from the box office doesn't amount to a hill of beans."

"I suppose if we can play in major league stadiums with a lot more seats, then the owners will make more. But does that trickle down to us being paid more?" Moses asked.

Lionel sat facing Moses. "No. We get paid what is written on our contracts."

Moses was focused on making money, not only for himself but for his family. A new sewing machine for his mother would allow her to sew not only for the wife of the owner of the mine, but for other women who had complimented her sewing skills. Daisy Gilliam was able to look at a picture of a dress in a catalogue or fashion magazine and duplicate it until it appeared to be an original. There had been a time when Daisy had confessed that she wanted to be like Coco Chanel and design her own clothes. She wanted to be a clothing designer and market her clothes to Black women. "Do you believe Donnelly when he says that he wants to buy a new bus and uniforms with numbers on our backs?" Lionel asked, breaking into Moses's musings.

"I don't know, Train. I suppose we will just have to wait and find out."

"What do you make of him, Moses?"

"Even though he's White, he's different from the other crackers down here. He is willing to shake hands with us, and we don't have to say yes sir, and no sir. And we can look him straight in the eye without the fear of being whipped or lynched. I suppose it's because he's from up North that makes him different." He didn't tell his roommate that Donnelly had referred to him as a nigger.

Lionel sandwiched his hands between his knees. "Don't let him being from up North fool you. There are as many White folks living in Ohio and Indiana who hate Colored people. What you must do is ignore them when they start calling you nigger, coon, and everything but a child of God. It doesn't matter where you live in this country, we can't escape folks who hate us for no reason other than the color of our skin."

Moses recalled his grandfather talking about the 1919 Red Summer in which White supremacists terrorized Black people in more than three dozen states in the country. It had started in Chicago with the death of a Black boy who had been rafting on Lake Michigan with friends and accidentally drifted over to the area reserved for Whites. He was hit in the head with a rock thrown by a White man standing on the shore, and drowned after being knocked unconscious. Black folks insisted the police arrest the man, but they refused, and the aftermath was rioting between mobs and gangs from both races.

"What about when the team travels to Mexico or the Caribbean?" he asked, wanting to know beforehand what he would have to encounter.

Lionel smiled. "That's a whole different world. We are treated with respect, and it's the only time that I can completely relax as a Black man. Then there is the music and food. Once we cross the border you will know exactly what I am talking about. And if I wasn't married, I would think about taking up with a señorita."

Moses's eyebrows lifted slightly with Lionel's pronouncement. "Are you talking about fooling around or marrying one?"

Lionel leaned forward. "Come on now, Moses. You know there are women you can fool around with and others that you marry." He paused. "Have you ever been with a woman?" Moses nodded. "Then you know what I am talking about. There are whores and then there are good girls."

Moses nodded again. He didn't need Lionel to school him on the differences. "Have you ever cheated on your wife?"

Lionel gave him a direct stare. "No. Never. Once I married her, I swore never to take up with another woman."

"Have you been tempted?"

"Hell, yeah. Many times, but I think about what I have and could lose if my wife found out about it. She warned me before we were married that if I cheated on her then she'd be gone faster than a cat could flick its tail. You are still young, Moses, so you have time before you think about settling down. But most guys on the team are married, because after being on the road for weeks they want something and someone to come home to. And that is a wife and kids."

Although he didn't have a girlfriend, Moses thought about Sallie Ann and how much he liked looking at and talking to her. He had promised to meet her again when the team returned to Memphis, and he hoped she wouldn't stand him up.

CHAPTER 14

I'm not going to be sick. I can't embarrass myself by throwing up. An attack of nerves had made it impossible for Moses to draw a normal breath, while his entire body was awash with sweat, and for the first time since becoming a Memphis Eagle he was scared. Scared beyond belief. It hadn't been that way when he'd played high school baseball or when he came up to bat during the practice game back in Memphis.

That was then and this was now. He had become a professional ballplayer, paid to play the game. He wasn't competing against his teammates; now they were scheduled to play another professional Negro League team that was one of the best in country.

Moses, sitting in the dugout, concentrated on the billboards advertising Royal Crown Cola, Quaker State Motor Oil, and Champion Spark Plugs. He smiled. Sportsman's Park was sure a fine baseball park. Although it had opened during the turn of the century, the stadium had been renovated and updated where wooden bleachers were replaced by concrete stands, including a covered pavilion from the right-field foul line to the center-field bleachers. He noted the distances of 426 feet to dead center, 310 to right, and 351 to left field. Although the length of his home runs hadn't been measured, Moses knew as a right-handed hitter he could easily clear the left-field fence. A seating capacity of 30,000 meant more ticket sales.

Moses took deep breaths to slow down his runaway pulse. He was assigned to hit fifth, and that meant if batters were able to get on base, then he was expected to bring them in. He hadn't realized he was tapping his left foot until he felt Lionel's hand on his knee.

"It's all right, man. You will do okay."

Moses shot him a sidelong glance. "I don't know why I'm so nervous."

"Everybody goes through it whenever they play in their first game."

"You?"

Lionel smiled and nodded, exhibiting several teeth ringed in gold. "Yeah. I almost shit my drawers when I was first called to bat. I was lucky because I got on base when the pitcher threw four straight balls. It must have been a bad day for him because he had trouble finding the plate. The next batter hit a double and I came in to score. After that it never happened again."

Moses forced a smile, hoping he was only experiencing heebie-jeebies because he wanted to do everything he could to help his team win. The Eagles were the visiting team, so they were first up. He couldn't forget that the home team was on a winning streak of seven consecutive games.

He didn't know how it happened, but as soon as he heard the call to play ball, Moses felt as if he had entered another zone, where he was able to shut out the sounds of fans in the stands to concentrate wholly on the game. The first and second batter were able to get on base, while the third popped out to the short-stop. With one out the fourth batter strolled up to the plate. He was able to bunt for a hit and the bases were loaded. Lionel lined out to the second baseman.

Moses strolled into the batter's box, appearing calmer than he felt. He had dreamt of this moment from the first time he'd picked up the broomstick that had doubled as a baseball bat. He made eye contact with the runner on third base, and then raised his bat and looked directly at the left-handed pitcher. A slight smile parted his lips. As a righty he loved hitting off left-handed pitchers. He heard the catcher pat his glove and Moses relaxed his shoulders. The umpire called the first pitch a ball when it sailed slightly off the plate. There came two more balls, and Moses knew the pitcher had expected him to swing at them. It was now three balls and no strikes, and one more would result in walking in a runner.

The pitcher was throwing screwballs and Moses knew he wasn't about to throw another one. It had to be a four-seam or two-seam fastball. Although he couldn't see the grip of the ball the pitcher hid in his glove, he was ready for whatever he threw. The pitcher went into a windup with a high leg kick and let the ball go, and Moses's bat contacted the two-seamer. The sound of it coming off the bat was like an explosion as it carried over the heads of the center fielder and into the stands. He remembered circling the bases, but not much after that when he was mobbed by his teammates once he entered the dugout.

His grand slam seemed to have energized the Eagles, and with good pitching and excellent fielding they were able to win the game with a score of 8 to 5, ending the Kansas City Capitals' winning streak.

The mood on the bus back to the boardinghouse was jubilant as everyone seemed to be talking at the same time, while Moses lost count of how many times he'd been slapped on the back for hitting a home run that had cleared the bases. He was quick to remind them that it was a team effort, to which they shouted him down saying modesty wasn't becoming to a professional athlete and that he had to learn to accept all the accolades because fame was fleeting.

The mention of fame had Moses thinking that hitting a home run in one game did not equate to fame. Hopefully it was the first of many more to come to make the Memphis Eagles a winning team. He returned to his room and made his way to the bathroom to shower. Although Negro teams were permitted to play in the major league ballparks, they couldn't use their shower facilities. Jim Crow had controlled every phase of Black life like an invasive disease. The exception was money. If Blacks spent their money in White establishments while being denied the same opportunities, then everything was okay. Not only were there separate water fountains, but also separate entrances to eating establishments; there were segregated schools, waiting rooms, and public transportation. He had to pay the same fare as a White person but was relegated to a separate section in a bus or train. Moses felt if he was forced to use inferior accommodations, then he shouldn't be forced to pay full price for the same service.

He thought about what Lionel had said regarding encountering racism and prejudice in northern cities, but at least Black folks could experience a modicum of freedom without the overt shackles of Jim Crow. After showering and changing his clothes, Moses retreated to his bedroom to write to his mother. He had promised to write to her at least once a week to let her know how he was faring. He'd just finished putting the letter in an envelope addressed to Daisy Gilliam, with a return address in care of him at the Parker House, when Lionel entered the room.

"I was wondering where you had disappeared to."

Moses smiled. "I needed to clean up and relax before dinner."

"I was about to do the same but the bathrooms on our floor are occupied. I'm fixing to try the ones on the other floors." Lionel pointed to the notebook on Moses's bed. "What you writin' in that book?"

"It's my journal. I'm writing down everything that's happened to me since I left home."

Lionel blinked slowly. "Everything?"

"Yes, everything."

"You writin' about me?"

Smiling and nodding, Moses said, "Everything and everybody."

An expression of confusion spread over Lionel's face. "Are you gonna write a book?"

"No, Lionel. I'm not writing a book. This is something I can look back on once I stop playing ball. It will become a book of memories."

"So, you're not going to show them to anybody?"

"No. At least not now. I want to save them for my future children, for them to read after I'm gone so they will be able to see what their daddy experienced as a player in the Negro Leagues."

A sly grin tugged at Lionel's lip. "So, you are looking to take a wife?"

Several seconds went by before Moses said, "I'm not ready, but just saying I would like to get married and start a family one of these days."

Moses thought about Sallie Ann. She was only sixteen and still in school. He didn't want her to commit to anything before she graduated. And just because she had smiled at him, it didn't mean she liked him.

Moses would be the first to admit he didn't have much experience with women. When he wasn't studying, he was playing baseball. He hadn't had a girlfriend in high school like many of his classmates, and some of them were forced to marry in a hurry because they'd gotten their girlfriends pregnant. He wasn't a virgin; he'd slept with a woman who had lost her husband during the Great War. Moses met her when he had delivered a sack of groceries she'd ordered from the general store. There was something about her he couldn't resist, and whenever she invited him into her bedroom, he'd encountered unbridled lust inside her warm, supple body. It wasn't that he didn't have sexual urges—there were times when they were more frequent than he wanted—yet he had to keep his wits about him when it came to sleeping with women.

"You need to get ready when you come home with me, because New Orleans has some of the most beautiful Colored women in the country," Lionel said to him.

Moses wanted to remind Lionel that there were beautiful Negro women all over the country, but he held his tongue. He wasn't certain whether there was any truth to it, but he had read about a time in New Orleans when there were infamous quadroon and octoroon balls hosted by Negro women who paraded their mixed-race daughters like slaves on auction blocks for wealthy White men to select as mistresses.

"I've read a lot about gumbo, crawfish, and jambalaya. Are they as delicious as folks rave about?" Moses asked.

Lionel rolled his eyes upward. "I ain't got nothing against fried chicken, collard greens, and cornbread, but once you have a bowl of gumbo, jambalaya, or red beans and rice you will crave it like a drug."

Throwing back his head, Moses laughed when Lionel

rubbed his belly and smacked his lips. "I like the sound of that."

Lionel also laughed. "I'm not joking when I say that my wife is a fabulous cook. Her fried shrimp and catfish will melt in your mouth. Every Sunday morning, we have fried fish, grits, and biscuits. I don't know if you will like our coffee because it's made with chicory, but it goes well with beignets. I'm gonna let you go back to writin' while I can see if I can't shower off some of this dirt."

To say Moses was looking forward to going home with Lionel was an understatement. He waited until Lionel left the room to write in his notebook. He underlined the date, because not only had he played his first game, but he'd also helped to win the game for the Memphis Eagles.

Slumping back in the chair, Harper massaged her eyes with her fingertips. She could not believe she'd written nonstop until she had been forced to turn on a lamp because dusk had given way to nightfall.

Moses Gilliam had come alive in her head and had become a living, breathing character who dictated what he wanted her to write. As she developed him, Harper realized he was idealistic almost to a fault. That he was not only optimistic but also a romantic, easily taken in by a pretty face. If Sallie Ann's uncle had set her up to get customers to buy more drinks, then why would she be above luring men into more devious plots?

Harper had read all her great-grandfather's notebooks, and had changed every name, while she knew how the life of Kelton Fleming aka Moses Gilliam would turn out. Her great-grandfather had left Nichols, Tennessee, in 1936, at the age of eighteen, as an innocent, idealistic young man; however, he would not be the same toward the end of his life.

She saved what she had typed, deciding to wait until the

following day to reread and edit what she'd written. Powering down her laptop and turning off the lamp, she made her way through the house and into her bedroom. Even though her head was still filled with ideas about what she planned to write, Harper knew she had to take time to relax before the novel consumed her every waking moment.

I'm going to take the weekend off. It was a holiday weekend, the official beginning of the summer season, a time when families went to amusement parks or the beach or got together for backyard barbecues. She walked into her bedroom and stripped naked before going into the bathroom. Now that she had the house to herself, she didn't have to concern herself with her grandfather walking in on her. It was what she liked about living alone—the freedom to be herself.

Her mother had called her selfish when she told Martell that she wasn't ready to share her life with a man, that the men she'd met had wanted her to change into someone she couldn't become. She'd only had two serious relationships, and both ended without regret. One wanted her to become a stay-at-home mother like all the women in his family, and the other talked about moving to a country in Africa where he'd planned to start a business. When she'd questioned him about starting a business in the States before branching out overseas, he claimed his lack of credit made it impossible for him to secure business loans. That was when he'd asked if her father was willing to invest in his start-up. That, for Harper, had been an easy decision. If she didn't ask her father for money for herself, then she wasn't going to do so for a boyfriend. When she told him she wouldn't, it was the last time she heard from him.

The year she turned thirty her mantra was she didn't want a man because she didn't need one for her day-to-day existence. Now, after quitting her job, it was time for Harper Lauren Fleming to figure out what she wanted to do with the rest of her life. She would celebrate her thirty-fourth birthday in another two months, and she would give herself until thirty-five to settle into a career that she hoped to enjoy and find gratifying.

She filled the bathtub with lukewarm water, added a capful of lavender-scented bath oil, and got in, sighing as she closed her eyes. It felt good to relax, where she didn't have to think about the next day. Now she knew why some people elected to check out of life—out of their day-to-day existence to become a nomad. After her bath, she lay in bed luxuriating in the cool air filling the bedroom as she willed her mind blank. However, images of Moses and his teammates flooded her head when she least expected. If she couldn't turn them off, she wasn't going to get a restful night's sleep. Even though she'd written copy for the newspaper, this was the first time she'd attempted to write a novel, especially about someone whose bloodline she carried.

Harper thought it ironic that both her father and great-grandfather had been baseball players, while it had skipped a generation with Bernard. Despite Bernard admitting that his father had talked about baseball ad nauseam, his son had taken up the sport. Whenever Daniel Fleming was interviewed by reporters, he admitted baseball was in his blood because his grandfather had played in the Negro Leagues before Jackie Robinson broke Major League Baseball's color barrier.

She smiled when she thought about how times had changed since that momentous day in April nearly eighty years before. Major League Baseball was no longer an all-White sport, but teams had added Blacks, Latinos, and Asians to their rosters. Many Black players had also dominated basketball and football, while baseball had honored Jackie Robinson by retiring number 42—a number that would never be assigned to another player in the history of the sport. It had taken decades for the Majors to right the wrongs, inducting thirty-seven players from the Negro Leagues into the National Baseball Hall of Fame, while on Jackie Robinson Day every player on every Major League team wears number 42 to honor him.

It was in December 2020 that Major League Baseball officially recognized the Major League status of seven professional Negro Leagues that operated from 1920 to 1948. Jackie broke the color barrier in 1947, but it wasn't until 1971, after a public plea from Ted Williams, that the Hall inducted Satchel Paige as its first Negro Leagues star.

Whenever she discussed baseball with her father, Daniel did not hesitate when he said Satchel Paige was the greatest pitcher who ever lived. Like his grandfather, Daniel would go on and on about the incredible skills of Buck Leonard, Josh Gibson, Monte Irvin, and Cool Papa Bell. Harper, unlike her grandfather, never tired of her father talking about the baseball greats who were denied the same privileges as their White counterparts because of the color of their skin.

Then she thought about her last boss, who had denied her becoming the sports reporter for the paper, not because of her race but her sex. The Fifteenth Amendment to the Constitution had given all men, regardless of their race, the right to vote, but not women. It had taken years and the Nineteenth Amendment to the Constitution for women to be allowed to vote, while it wasn't until the 1965 Voting Rights Act that it became a reality for Black women in the South.

Harper had become sick and tired of asking to cover sporting events. Eventually she reached her breaking point upon realizing she had been relegated to begging. She didn't mind asking, but it wasn't in her personality to beg—not for anything or to anyone. Not once since she'd walked out of the newspaper office with her personal belongings had she had regretted her decision. Perhaps if she hadn't then she wouldn't have been given the opportunity to read her great-grandfather's notebooks and draft his story.

Harper sighed, the sound echoing in the silence of the

room as she thought about Cheney Sanders. He had invited her to his home on Sunday for a cookout. Spending time away from the house would give her the opportunity to separate herself from writing, which had started to feel like an obsession. Spending time with Cheney would become a welcome distraction, which she was looking forward to.

Her last thoughts weren't of Moses Gilliam but Cheney before she finally fell asleep.

Chapter 15

Harper inserted a toothpick into the top of the golden-brown Bundt cake, smiling and sighing in relief when it came out clean. Thankfully she hadn't lost her touch when it came to baking her late grandmother's celebrated sour cream pound cake that had always garnered raves from everyone whenever Nadine donated her dessert for a church social. Despite countless requests for the recipe, her grandmother had remained as closemouthed about it as a covert undercover agent, and after a while most stopped asking. She'd found the Bundt pan with six wells for individual cakes.

Despite getting up early to bake the cake to take to Cheney's house later that morning, Harper had promised herself not to dwell on what she wanted to write next, but she'd failed. Miserably. She couldn't stop thinking about fictional Moses reuniting with Sallie Ann, and how she wanted to develop Sallie Ann's family dynamics. A teenage girl working in what Harper thought of as a dive bar wasn't a good look in the mid-1930s; it would have been frowned upon because women who were thought of as possessing low morals were not expected to find a so-called decent husband.

The more she wrote the more Harper thought of the parallels between her life and some of the women in the novel. Unconsciously she had become Winnie Chess, living her life by her own set of rules. Winnie was a woman almost one hundred years ahead of her time. She was educated, divorced, and solvent—things that were out of the reach of many Black women during the 1930s and at least another thirty or forty years that followed.

Harper had allowed Winnie to live in both the Black and White worlds, in order to achieve success. Winnie was more than aware of her effect on men and used her wiles, albeit subtly, to achieve what she wanted from them. She knew she could have convinced Edgar Donnelly to leave his wife and children for her, but she wasn't willing to start with a White man, whether Northern or Southern, when Black men and women were being lynched for so-called Jim Crow infractions. Lynching had become something of a spectator sport, where thousands of Whites gathered to picnic, watching her people being tortured while hanging from trees, solely for the crime of being born Black in America.

When she'd written the scene between Winnie and F. Douglas Erskine, Harper was reminded of the interaction she'd had with the man who had wanted her father to bankroll his business startup. Despite Douglas's success as an attorney, Harper felt that he had an ulterior motive for proposing marriage to Winnie, because he was privy to her net worth. And if they were to marry and combine their resources, then he would be able to achieve millionaire status—something he sought but had eluded him. He had wanted to become one of a few Black millionaires in the country. Harper had found herself laughing when she wrote Winnie's response to his marriage proposal. She knew if Winnie married Douglas, then she would, despite his denial, forfeit her independence. It was the same with Harper. If she had elected to marry, then she doubted whether her husband would've agreed to her leaving him for months so she could find herself. Harper had allowed mid–twentieth century Winifred Chess to become a twenty-first-century woman of independent means.

Kelton Fleming had written in explicit detail about people, places, and events spanning eleven years of his life. It was like turning on a faucet to let the water of his experiences flow unchecked, but once he stopped playing baseball, that water dried up. However, there were other entries that were related to the game once he was no longer able to compete. Harper wondered if life as Kelton had known it up to that time had become mundane after he no longer was able to experience the rush of excitement of stepping up to the plate to bat. When Harper had asked Bernard about his father, he would say that Kelton had resigned himself to being a husband, father, and a farmer; that when Kelton wasn't tending his land, he would talk endlessly about his time playing ball in the Negro Leagues. Bernard suspected he had belabored the subject because he'd refused to talk about his experiences as a soldier in World War II. It was then Harper recalled the occasion her grandfather had become emotional when he told her about seeing his father cry for the first time in his life when Bernard's draft number came up in during the Vietnam War. Bernard survived when so many American soldiers lost their lives in the jungle, fighting a war they had no chance of winning, and now he and his friends had gotten together to bond and reminisce about their past lives.

She waited for the cake to cool enough to turn out onto a rack before she retreated to her bedroom to find something to wear before Cheney came over to pick her up. A day following their initial meeting she had sent him a text with her grandfather's address and her brothers' email addresses. Cheney had returned the text with a thumbs-up emoji.

Harper vacillated between wearing a sleeveless cotton dress ending at her knees or a pair of cropped pants with a camp shirt, then at the last minute decided on the latter. Although there was a forecast of rain later that afternoon, she had found the outdoor morning temperatures unbearable. This is not to say Chicago didn't have death-defying summer heatwaves, but Harper found the heat in Nashville relentless.

She walked out of the bedroom and into the ensuite bath to shower before Cheney arrived. His text message said he was going to pick her up around noon, and she had less than an hour to shower, dress, and pack up dessert before he arrived.

When Cheney saw Harper standing on the front porch as he came to a complete stop, he realized he was looking forward to seeing her again. The image of a very grown-up Harper Fleming had popped into his head when he least expected it. Bumping into her in Nashville was shocking. Their sharing a meal had conjured up memories of when he'd been invited to sit and eat with the Flemings and got to witness firsthand why Miss Nadine had earned the reputation as one of the best cooks in Memphis.

But that was then, and this was now. Miss Nadine was gone, they were no longer in Memphis, and he wasn't a teenage boy and Harper a preteen girl. They were adults. Even when he'd accompanied his father and uncle to the Fleming farm there hadn't been a time when he'd thought of Harper as other than Danny and Craig's little sister. He knew she'd wanted to hang out with them, but her brothers thought of her as an annoyance because they didn't want her to overhear what they were talking about—and most times it was about sex and girls.

Back then Cheney had found Harper quiet and shy, which he attributed to her having two rambunctious older brothers. The present-day Harper Fleming was poised and exuded confidence. He hadn't met many women who were willing to leave a job before securing another. But then again, there weren't many who were the daughters of a former professional baseball player turned sports commentator. What he admired about her was her wanting to do things on her own terms. However, it wasn't the only thing he found himself admiring as he watched her when he stepped out of his vehicle. Harper Fleming had matured into a beautiful woman with an incredibly husky, sexy voice. That, along with her natural beauty, was a winning combination.

Granted, he had dated women following his divorce, some whom he saw platonically. A few others he slept with, but since moving to Nashville he'd become somewhat of a recluse when it came to dating. Cheney wasn't certain whether he had matured when it came to women, or he'd simply become more discriminating when choosing someone to spend time with.

Like most men, he liked being in love and enjoyed being married. But he hadn't realized until it was too late that he hadn't been the best husband for a woman who needed more from him than he was willing to give. That selfishness and blind ambition to make law partner had made it impossible for him to focus on anything or anyone but himself.

He'd left that life behind and everything that went with it to become an attorney taking on pro bono cases for women in crisis. The agency received city and state funding as well as donations from charities advocating for women's rights. For him, it wasn't about how much he'd earn from winning a case, or billable hours, it was all about giving back. He had the proceeds from the sale of the house in Falls Church to fall back on. Even after purchasing and renovating the house in Nashville, and with proceeds from investments, he still had enough money left on which to live comfortably.

How lovely and refreshingly feminine she is, Cheney thought as he approached Harper. He couldn't pull his gaze away from her bare face radiating good health. Her hair was brushed away from her face and styled in a ponytail. Even without a hint of makeup, he found her ravishing.

Cheney had grown so used to women with meticulously applied makeup and coiffed hair that seeing one without these accoutrements made him realize he much preferred natural beauty. Harper was a throwback to the grandmother she so closely resembled, who had turned the heads of men whenever they were in her presence. Nadine Fleming was one of the most strikingly beautiful women in their Memphis community with her dark brown complexion, large expressive dark eyes, and evenly balanced features. Cheney thought Harper the perfect likeness of her grandmother.

He lowered his head and pressed a kiss to her cheek, the lingering scent of her perfume wafting to his nose. "How are you?"

Tilting her chin, Harper smiled up at him. "Wonderful."

Cheney wanted to tell her that she looked and smelled wonderful, but he decided to keep that to himself. He pointed to the cake carrier. "What did you make?"

Harper smiled, bringing Cheney's eyes to linger on her full lips. "My grandmother's recipe for sour cream pound cake."

Cheney closed his eyes for several seconds as he moaned under his breath. "Hot damn." It was like turning back the clock to when Miss Nadine baked for their church's bake sales. Her cakes were always the first to sell out, while the kids had to stand around and watch adults devour slice after slice. It wasn't until he was able to sit at Miss Nadine's table and sample her cakes that he knew why they'd sold out so quickly. "What other recipes do you have that were hers?" he asked.

Harper lowered her eyes and glanced up to look at him through her lashes, unaware of how sensual Cheney found the gesture. "All of them."

"You know what that means," Cheney countered.

She gave him a direct stare. "No. What does that mean?"

"That I, with your permission of course, will invite myself over for dinner at least a couple of times a week."

"I can remember you inviting yourself to eat with us a couple of times a week when we were kids," Harper remarked.

Cheney took the cake carrier from Harper and cupped her elbow with his free hand. "Now that I look back, I realize how shameless I was, begging to eat with your family. My mother was a good cook, but compared to your grandmother she was fair-to-middling."

"Your mother couldn't have been that bad, Cheney."

He led Harper down the steps to his car. "I'm not saying she was bad. What I'm saying is your grandmother was phenomenal."

"That's because my grandmother was a perfectionist. Her claim was she didn't want to do anything that she'd call half-ass. She would make me crack eggs in a separate bowl before adding each one into the cake mix to make certain they were good."

"You're right about Miss Nadine being a perfectionist. She was a no-nonsense teacher who expected nothing but excellence from her students. Even when some kids couldn't grasp a subject or math problem, she would have them sit with her during our lunch period to give them extra help."

Cheney opened the passenger door to his Infiniti QX50 for Harper, waiting until she was settled and belted in before setting the cake carrier on the rear seat. Then he came around the SUV to sit behind the wheel. He started up the engine, wondering if inviting himself to Harper's grandfather's home to share a meal with her was presumptuous. He had assumed Mr. Bernard would not resent his intrusion when he showed up at his door after so many years, to sit at his table as he'd done more than twenty years before.

Many things had changed in twenty years and Cheney knew he couldn't turn back the clock and relive his childhood summers when he'd helped his father and uncle do contracted renovations. He'd learned as much as he could to please his father, but in his heart he knew he didn't want to take over James and Jack Sanders Construction once his father and uncle retired. It had taken a great deal of soul searching to tell his father that although he enjoyed working with his hands, he wanted to study law.

James Sanders had given him a long, penetrating stare before he nodded and wished him well, whereas Cheney had expected a long, drawn-out lecture about not wanting to continue with the family business. However, he did make his parents proud when he was accepted to attend Morehouse College and graduated with honors. Once he'd received his law degree, his parents boasted to everyone that their son had become the first lawyer in the family.

Two decades later, his life had changed and so had he. He told Harper that after his divorce he realized it was time for him to come home, and now that he'd settled down in his childhood home state he felt as if he'd come full circle. Somehow reuniting with Harper made it complete.

"I can't believe you live in the boonies."

Harper's dulcet voice shattered his musings, and he gave her a quick sidelong glance before redirecting his eyes back on the road. He had been driving for more than a quarter of an hour. "It's a little way from downtown Nashville."

"It's more than a little, Cheney."

He smiled. "I like living in the country because it's where I can get away from the noise, hustle and bustle of the city."

"You don't like city living?" she asked.

Cheney gave her another quick glance. "I don't mind working and hanging out in the city for the nightlife, but when it comes to where I want to lay my head at the end of the day then it's in the country. What about you, Harper?"

"What about me?"

"Do you live in the city?"

"Close enough. I've always worked in the city, so that's why I decided to rent an apartment about a fifteen-minute drive from downtown Chicago."

"Do you think you could get used to living in the country?" Cheney asked as he left Nashville's city limits.

"I probably could. When I was a kid, I couldn't wait until school was out to come down to my grandparents' farm. During my first summer I'd sit on the window seat at night marveling that the entire countryside was so quiet. The only sounds were the chirping of crickets, an occasional hoot of owls, and the croaking of frogs from the nearby ponds. Even though the house where I'd grown up was in a suburb, you still could hear passing cars or the wail of sirens from emergency vehicles."

Lines fanned out around Cheney's eyes when he smiled. "So, as a city girl you really liked spending your summers on a farm."

"Yes, but I must admit it took some getting used to being around the animals. The first time my grandmother sent me to the chicken coop to gather eggs, the hens attacked me something furious and I ran back to the house crying uncontrollably. Grandma managed to calm me down, then took me back to the coop and showed me how to get the eggs without disturbing the hens."

Cheney chuckled under his breath. "They didn't attack her?"

Harper shook her head. "No. I don't know what it was, but she had a special way with animals where they were always calm around her."

"Maybe they knew if they acted up, then they would end up on her table."

Harper landed a soft punch to Cheney's shoulder under the black T-shirt molded to his toned upper body like a second skin. "That's not nice."

"You have to know that some of Miss Nadine's yardbirds ended their lives as fried or roast chicken."

"If they did, then I never saw my grandmother kill a chicken or my grandfather butcher a pig."

"That's because they wanted to spare you from experiencing that. I grew up witnessing a lot of people wringing chickens' necks or cutting up hogs. My grandfather raised hogs and our freezer was always stocked with ham, bacon, pork chops, sausage, and ribs."

"What about chitlins?"

Cheney chuckled, the sound rumbling in his chest. "There

was never a Thanksgiving or Christmas when we didn't have chitlins. My mother would spend hours cleaning, cutting and then soaking the intestines in buckets that were left outside the back door. She would change the water over and over, and then she'd bring them into the kitchen and wash them many more times."

"Did you like them?" Harper asked him.

"They were good, but personally I don't think all the work to make them edible was worth the effort."

"My grandmother refused to have them in her house and my mother never ate them, so it wasn't until I was in college when my roommate invited me to spend a week at her house that I had them for the first time. It was also the first time that I sampled pigs' feet and tails."

Throwing back his head, Cheney laughed loudly. "How did you like the trotters?"

Harper also laughed. "They cooked the pigs' feet with barbecue sauce and served them with braised cabbage and potato salad, and I must admit I made a pig of myself. However, once we returned to campus, I gave up eating pork for the next month because I'd overdosed on divine swine."

"Folks cook and eat the pig from the rooter to the tooter."

She stared at Cheney's profile as he focused his gaze on the narrow road lined on both sides with towering trees. "Did it bother you when your grandfather butchered hogs?"

"No, Harper. It was an integral part of life that's repeated over and over on farms all over the country."

"I enjoyed every summer I spent on my grandparents' farm," she admitted, "but I don't think I would've been able to deal with them killing their animals, even if it was to put food on the table."

"If that's the case, then you'd never make it as a farmer's wife," Cheney countered as he decelerated around a curve in the road.

Harper wanted to tell Cheney that she didn't think she would make a good wife for any man. She was über-opinionated and the older she became, the more set in her ways she became. There had been a time when she'd been willing to compromise, but now she doubted she'd ever want to. She'd given so much to make her relationships work, but when they ended, she had no regrets.

Harper smothered a gasp as Cheney approached a sprawling two-story brick house with a red-tiled roof that had been constructed on a wooded lot atop a small hill. He had told her the house was more than four thousand square feet, and judging from the exterior it had been meticulously restored to its original magnificence. Hipped roofs and broad overhangs were constructed to keep the rain off the screened-porch windows.

Cheney came to a stop alongside the house. "Are you ready to see inside my humble abode?"

Harper curbed the urge to roll her eyes at him. Cheney's house was the epitome of elegance, hardly humble. "Yes."

That was the last word that came out of her mouth when she stared, awestruck as Cheney led her in and out of the carefully constructed balance between communal and private spaces. Windows were set low near the floor to offer views of the woods, while sturdy timbers, a cathedral ceiling, and an entire wall of stone displayed the enormous scale of the great room. She lingered over the second-floor balcony leading to the suites Cheney had designated for his guests. The balcony also provided an unobstructed view of the heart of the house, which he'd admitted to not wanting to be a cookie-cutter design.

Cheney had set up his home office on the basement level adjacent to a space for entertaining. It had been outfitted with the requisite large wall-mounted television, a mahogany bar with a half dozen stools, a pool table, and black leather reclining chairs with cupholders. A fully stocked bar and a wine cellar with bottles of red, white, and rosé took up one entire wall. There was another room that had been set up as a gym with weights, an elliptical bike, and a treadmill. There was even a wall-mounted TV he could view while working out. He told her that he was planning to install an inground pool before next summer.

Harper was enthralled when Cheney revealed that the original owners of the house had commissioned it to be built during the Gilded Age. The owners had made a fortune when competing with Jack Daniel's, distilling whiskey, but the passage of the Volstead Act had led to the enforcement of Prohibition, and they were forced to go out of business. Once Prohibition was repealed, they were unable to recover and had resorted to selling off parcels of the more than one-thousand acres they'd claimed until their last surviving descendent listed the four-thousand-square-foot house, which sat on six acres, with a realtor. The house had been updated to include central air and heating, while Cheney had commissioned all the fireplaces be converted from wood-burning to gas.

When Cheney had asked Harper if she'd be content living in the country before seeing his house, she hadn't given him an unequivocal yes. But now that she'd toured his house, she could imagine herself sitting on the screened porch watching the change of seasons as she read or wrote. It would become her favorite place where she would be content to begin or end her days, while occasionally enjoying afternoon tea.

Harper knew her imagination was running away with her because she had planned to stay in Tennessee for the summer, and then she'd be returning to Chicago. Times had changed and so had she. Despite these changes, she still harbored an attraction to Cheney. The attraction wasn't purely physical as it had been years ago, now she was more drawn to his character. He'd given up the cutthroat world of corporate litigation to take up the cause of protecting women and children from domestic violence, and she couldn't help but admire that about him.

"I love your home," she said reverently.

Cheney took a step, bringing them less than a foot apart. "Do you really?"

His hazel eyes bored into hers behind his lenses, his expression slightly disturbing to Harper. "Yes. Do you doubt me?"

He blinked slowly, and the gesture reminded her of what Winnie might have felt when Moses stared at her.

A chill washed over her body and in that instant Harper thought maybe her imagination was getting the best of her; fiction and reality had merged to where she wasn't certain where they began or ended.

Smiling, Cheney lowered his eyes, shielding his innermost feelings from her. "I don't doubt you as much as I need to know whether you're being truthful."

"Why is that so important to you?" she asked.

Cheney met her eyes. "If I were truly honest, then I'd have to say I don't know. There's something about you that makes me want to relive a time when the only responsibilities I had were to go to school, earn good grades, and come hang out with your brothers, swimming and shooting hoops."

"What I don't understand is whenever you came to the farm you barely gave me a passing glance. I remember all the times I said hello to you, and you never even acknowledged me," Harper said.

The seconds ticked before Cheney said, "That's because I liked you, Harper. Liked you the way a boy likes a girl. But I knew nothing would come of it because your brothers had warned me that you were off-limits, and I didn't want to do anything to mess up my friendship with them."

It was Harper's turn to stare before she was forced to blink. "How old were you when you realized you liked me?"

"I was fifteen and randy as a goat."

She smiled as a rush of heat suffused her face with his admission. "And I'd turned twelve that summer. Besides, isn't it a known fact that most teenage boys are randy as goats?"

Cheney angled his head. "I was, though I can't vouch for most boys. It's just that you appeared to have grown up that summer. From that point on I looked at you differently."

"That's because my body had changed," she countered.

"It wasn't just your body, Harper. It was everything about you. And I'm just realizing now that it's your confidence and poise that comes so naturally to you. As a kid, that frightened me more than your brothers' warning to stay away from you."

Harper's eyebrows lifted slightly. "I frightened you?"

"Yes. Because I wanted to spend time with you whenever I came to your grandparents' farm, but your brothers warned me away. Then there was Miss Nadine. She'd been my teacher, and I don't think she would have taken kindly to one of her former teenage students asking to date her twelve-year-old granddaughter."

"I had no idea I'd become a dilemma for you."

"You were more than a dilemma, Harper, because I kept asking myself why you and not some of the other girls I knew and went to school with."

Harper wanted to tell Cheney that he wasn't the only one conflicted, because she had found herself fantasizing about him. He was someone she could fall in love with, marry, and live happily ever after with, like the heroines in the romance novels her mother read secretly and hid from her.

"Are you still in a quandary?" she asked after a lapse of silence.

There came another long, pregnant pause before he said, "No. Because I still like you. Now I don't have to concern myself with your brothers' interference that won't permit us to become friends."

Harper was aware that he'd said *friends* and not something more. When she thought about it, friendship seemed more fitting for her than their becoming lovers. She hadn't come to Tennessee to get involved with a man when she'd established an expiration date for completing her book before returning to Chicago.

"And I like you, Cheney. You have the honor of being the first man I will be able claim as a friend."

"Wow! I suppose that makes me very special."

Harper took a step, wrapped her arms around his waist, and going on tiptoe, she kissed his cheek. "You have no idea how very special you are."

CHAPTER 16

It was late afternoon when Harper opened her eyes to find Cheney reclining on a matching chaise, staring at her. "I'm sorry that I'm not good company, but champagne always seems to do a number on me and I find it hard to keep my eyes open."

Cheney had demonstrated that he was an adept cook by topping creamy stone-ground hominy grits with grilled shrimp, andouille sausage, and smoked ham. After eating the shrimp and grits and drinking several glasses of champagne with freshly squeezed orange juice, Harper had excused herself, folded her body down to a cushioned chaise, and dozed off and on. She acknowledged having eaten and drunk too much, to the point of being so totally relaxed that she'd fallen asleep where she lay.

He winked at her. "There's no need to apologize. There are times when I eat too much that I need a nap afterwards."

Shifting on her side, she smiled. "Your shrimp and grits were some of the best I've ever eaten."

"I can't take credit for the recipe. When I left home to attend college, the extent of my cooking was making toast, peanut butter and jelly sandwiches, and instant coffee. At the time, my parents were struggling to keep their businesses afloat while paying tuition and room and board for me, so to help them out I decided to get a part-time job."

"Wasn't your mother a schoolteacher?"

Cheney nodded. "Yes, but she left teaching to open a day-care center. My dad had bought an abandoned building and renovated it for her. He installed a kitchen, bathrooms, a play area, and a couple of offices. She advertised and had hired staff a month before parents began registering their children. She didn't have to pay rent for the building, but there were ongoing expenses for salaries, food, cots and cribs, kitchen and laundry equipment and supplies, so her attempt to stay in the black depended on how many kids were registered. I can remember my parents talking about having to pay tuition for both my sisters to attend college at the same time."

"That couldn't have been easy for them."

"It wasn't, Harper, so to ease some of the financial burden on them I decided to get a job on the weekends. I found one at a diner that was very small, seating no more than thirty folks at any given time, and there was always a line outside for people waiting to get in. I was hired as a busser and dishwasher, but things changed when one of the cooks didn't come one Sunday. That's when the owner, Mister Louis, asked me to fill in for him. Of course, he had to tell me everything to do but I managed to fry eggs without breaking the yolk, and grill bacon until it was well-done crispy.

"I hadn't realized up until that time that I really enjoyed cooking. That's probably because I'd learned from one of the best short-order cooks in Atlanta. When I asked him why he didn't move into a larger space, he claimed the diner had been in his family for years and he wasn't certain whether he'd have his regular customers if he moved away."

"How long did you work for him?"

"All four years I was at Morehouse. He used to call me Malcolm because I wore glasses and he claimed my complexion and eyes reminded him of Malcolm X. I didn't have the heart to tell him that Brother Malcolm was lighter in complexion, and was two inches taller than me, that he had reddish-brown hair, and grayish eyes."

"Did anyone else ever say you resembled Malcolm X?" Harper asked.

Cheney smiled. "No. Mister Louis used to tell me about the time he was involved in the Civil Rights Movement and that Malcolm, Martin Luther King Jr., Ralph Abernathy, and Andrew Young were his heroes. I stayed in touch with him even when I was in law school. Whenever I got the chance, I'd drive back to Atlanta to look in on him. That's when I realized he wasn't doing that well. He had diabetes and it was affecting his vision, so he was forced to sell the business."

"He didn't have anyone in his family that could take it over?"

Cheney shook his head. "He had a married daughter who lived in Baltimore, so he went to stay with her."

Harper realized how differently her life was from Cheney's. She and her brothers hadn't been struggling college students, because their father was a professional athlete with a contract that paid him millions of dollars a year for hitting a baseball. The Fleming kids had gone to elite private and prep schools and didn't have to apply for student loans for college. It wasn't until after she entered the real working world that Harper came to the realization that her childhood had been not only insular but one of isolation from many Black kids whose parents were forced to make supreme sacrifices to raise and educate them.

When offered the choice of teaching in a private school or public school, she had chosen the latter in what had been designated a high-risk district. While she taught English and literature, she had sought permission from the head of the

English Department to expose her students to writers of color during Black History Month, because they had complained about only reading books written by White authors.

Harper knew some of the titles she had selected could've been viewed as subversive, but her students eagerly devoured the literature of James Baldwin, Richard Wright, Claude Brown, Elridge Cleaver, Zora Neale Hurston, and Angela Davis. Some of the books contained profanity, but most of the students were not offended because of their exposure to explicit rap lyrics. All bemoaned when the month ended and she had to go back to the regular curriculum to discuss the works of Shakespeare, F. Scott Fitzgerald, Dickens, and Hemingway.

Then she thought about her fictional Moses Gilliam reading Dumas and Hugo, French writers who wrote about the injustices heaped upon France's downtrodden. Moses lived in Nichols, his own insular world, whereas the son and grandson of coal miners and former slaves was confident of who he was and what he could and could not do. It wasn't until he left Nichols to play baseball that what had been a predictable life had become not only unpredictable but threatening.

"Why did you decide to become a lawyer?" she asked Cheney, following a comfortable pause.

"I didn't know that I wanted to study law until in high school I read about Thurgood Marshall, who had won twenty-nine of thirty-two cases he argued before the Supreme Court. Social change only came about when laws were changed."

"But you didn't become a civil rights lawyer," Harper countered.

There came a another pause before Cheney said, "No I didn't. I was in my last year at Georgetown Law when one of my professors approached me about clerking for him once I graduated. To say I was shocked is an understatement, because he was a partner at one of the most prestigious D.C. law firms. He told me to think it over and give him an answer the next day. His offer included paying off my student loans and a starting salary that left me speechless."

"You took it."

He nodded. "I did, but only after I'd talked it over with my parents. They said the firm probably needed a Black attorney, and that I'd be a fool to reject his offer. I gave the firm eleven years of my life, and once I decided to resign it was as if I could finally stop running on the hamster wheel."

"It was that bad, Cheney?"

"For me it was. There were times when I loathed getting out of bed, and that's when I started thinking about leaving. I came back to Memphis for the funeral of a high school classmate who had been murdered by her boyfriend. I was approached by another classmate who was a social worker here in Nashville, and she asked if I'd be willing to come work for her agency as its legal counsel. She quoted a salary that was one-tenth of what I'd been earning, because her funding came from federal, state, and local sources, and I told her I'd think about it."

"How long did it take for you to think about it?" Harper asked him, unaware she'd slipped into the role of a journalist working on a story.

"It took a couple of months because I wanted to finish the cases that I'd been working on. I called Sabrina to ask if the position was still open, and when she said it was, I accepted. I arranged for a realtor to find a house that was large enough for the furniture I'd put in storage after selling the house in Falls Church. I was renting in Alexandria, so I decided not to renew the lease. She found this place, and my first impulse was to tear it down and start over, but an engineer said the foundation was good, so any changes could be relegated to the interior. I packed up my apartment and put that furniture in storage with the other stuff and moved here mid-February. I rented an apartment at an Extended Stay America until the renovations were completed, then arranged for the furniture in Virginia to be shipped here."

"The furnishings are exquisite," Harper commented.

"I can't take credit for anything in this place because I hired a professional to decorate." Harper wanted to ask him about his ex-wife and why she didn't want the house or the furnishings once their marriage ended. However, she decided she'd asked Cheney enough questions and didn't want him to think that she was prying. If he wanted to reveal things about his past, then she would wait for him to be forthcoming. This is not to say she wasn't curious about the woman he'd fallen in love with and married. While revealing he'd been married, he hadn't said anything about a child or children.

"As I said before, your home is lovely, and I hope you will get to spend many, many happy years here."

Cheney took off his glasses and massaged his eyes with his fingers. "That's what I'm hoping."

Sitting up, Harper swung her legs over the chaise. "It's been wonderful hanging out with you and I promise to return the favor, but I need to get back and do a few things before I turn in for the night."

Cheney put on his glasses, stood up, and extended his hand to assist Harper to stand. "I'm going to hold you to that promise. And thank you again for the cake."

In turn, Harper wanted to thank him for being the man he had become. He had been candid about his feelings toward her as a teenager and because of his respect for her family those feelings had become his secret—until now. She didn't know if she would've been as open to him about admitting he was the first boy she'd had a crush on, because somehow it would complicate things between them. Cheney admitted he still liked her, but he only meant it as a friend. Harper didn't trust herself to want more if his reaction toward her changed. Her becoming involved with a man now would be tantamount to what Superman experienced whenever he came in contact with kryptonite. It spelled disaster. Cheney was her childhood friend who was now her adult friend. And for Harper that was a win-win.

Harper sat on the rocker in the sunroom, vacillating between whether to go inside the house or stay and write. Several weeks ago, she wouldn't have had to make that decision. She would soon turn thirty-four, but it would be the first time since she'd graduated from college that she was unemployed.

She had given herself a timetable for writing and completing her novel, and once she returned to Chicago, she'd have to decide where she wanted to take her career. Fortunately, she had options and one of them was returning to teach high school English. Many of the city's public schools were experiencing a teacher shortage, with educator retirees outpacing new hires. She had taught for three years at an inner-city school before resigning to return to college to pursue a degree in journalism.

Writing *Home and Away* was about tying up the loose ends of her family's legacy. The question that remained was whether she planned on submitting to a traditional publishing house or self-publishing. That was something she didn't want to dwell on because she had a lot more writing to do before Moses Gilliam's story came to its conclusion.

A wry smile parted her lips when she thought about the three men who had unconsciously become a part of her everyday thoughts: Bernard Fleming, Moses Gilliam, and Cheney Sanders. Two were real while one was imaginary. It was the imaginary one who had consumed her, awake or asleep. Moses had invaded her dreams, nagging her to continue to tell his story. He had become an addictive drug, one she wasn't able to shake or resist. He was a specter invading her very existence, and only after reading his notebooks had she felt compelled to let the world know what this talented baseball player had gone through in his quest to be acknowledged not as a Negro, but as a man with full rights afforded him in the Constitution. He'd had to fight for equality on and off the baseball diamond.

Although Harper had promised herself to take the entire day off, she knew that wasn't possible, not when she imagined Moses whispering in her ear to get up and write. Listening to the voice in her head, she pushed off the rocker and walked over to the table where her laptop was. She booted it up, inserted the thumb drive in the port and picked up where she'd left off.

One day blended into the next and after a while Moses learned to sleep on the bus as the team barnstormed from one dusty town to another. Some days they played one game, and others it was two or occasionally three. The word had gotten out that the Memphis Eagles were on a winning streak, and as their wins increased so did the crowds who came out to watch the games.

During downtime, of which there was little after playing other teams along with batting and fielding practice, Moses wrote in his notebooks and helped Lionel improve his reading. Lionel seemingly had surprised himself once he realized he could recognize many of the words in the Bible. Those he didn't he was able to sound out phonetically until getting them right.

Moses had purchased a copy of the Green Book and was astounded by the number of places where Negroes were welcomed, including hotels, restaurants, barber shops, taverns, roadhouses, night clubs, and beauty parlors. The detailed entries listed names, addresses, and places of interest for Negroes in more than forty states, including New York City and the District of Columbia. Moses was surprised to see states like Montana and Wyoming listed, and it was obvious that his people lived and/or were welcomed in what he'd thought of as the most unlikely places.

Lionel had warned him about racism in Ohio. Moses wanted to believe it wasn't as overt in the North, but he had become an eyewitness and a victim once they took the field in Cleveland to play another Negro Leagues team. Negroes and Whites had come to the ballpark to view the game.

He had just taken his position in left field when a White man leaned over the fence to heckle him. "Hey, nigger, nigger, nigger. You should be picking cotton instead of trying to play baseball."

Something in his head told him not to pay attention to the ignorant fool, but after a while Moses had had enough, and he shouted back, "Shut up, dumbass, and watch the game."

What ensued was the fan attempting to crawl over the fence while Moses threw down his glove and was prepared to hit him if he came any closer. The Eagles' center fielder came over to pull Moses back as several fans held the heckler before he could scale the fence. Play was held up until everyone settled down, and Moses hadn't realized how close he had come to being fined for fighting or possibly even arrested if he'd injured the loudmouth racist. At that point he hadn't cared because he'd had to swallow and accept the racist taunts in the Jim Crow South, and he didn't want to put up with them in the so-called free states.

Later that night Coach had taken him aside and lectured him sternly about losing his temper, reminding him to get used to being called a nigger, coon, boy, and worse. "You're too good a player and much too smart to let some ignorant-ass redneck get to you, Gilliam," Odell said quietly. "You're going to have to grow a thick skin when folks get in your face, or you will never survive.

Not only will you hear it from crackers, but also from Black folks who are jealous because they want to know who is this kid that everyone is talking about. And if you live long enough, you'll realize that our folks are like crabs in a barrel who aren't happy unless they are starting shit. It's sad that we have to prove to White folks that we're as good as they are, but we must also do the same with our folks."

Moses digested what Coach was saying and nodded. "I'm sorry I lost my temper."

"It's understandable, but if you had knocked the shit out of that man you would be in a jail cell instead of sitting here talking to me."

"I know that, but it wasn't as if I went into the stands to assault him."

"Don't matter, Gilliam. There are laws for Whites and those for Negroes and we know which one holds all the power. He could've gotten some of his buddies to say you were the one calling him names and he couldn't stand it and decided to teach an uppity nigger a lesson."

Moses apologized again for losing his temper, not because he meant it, but because it had cost them the game. He had been so rattled by the confrontation with the fan that it had taken him off his game. It was the first time since joining the Memphis Eagles that he didn't have a hit.

"You're right, Coach. It will never happen again."

Later that night when he lay in bed, resting his head on folded arms, he stared up at the ceiling. It had taken hours for him to regain control of his emotions after his talk with the team's manager.

"Was Coach hard on you?" Lionel asked as he flopped down on his own bed.

"No. He just warned me about losing my temper."

"Coach is right," Lionel said. "Because if you had hit that bigot all hell would have broken loose. I'm certain cops would have been on the field and the Eagles would've busted a few heads."

Moses turned to look at Lionel. "Are you saying the team would have backed me up?"

"Oh, hell yeah! The entire team probably would have got locked up, but with Edgar Donnelly traveling with us, he would've paid the fine so we could keep to the game schedule. There's no doubt he also would have docked our pay, but I say it would have been worth it to knock a few White heads and not have to worry about being lynched."

"Our folks aren't only lynched in the South, Train. It happens up here, but not so often or publicly."

Moses had begun the practice of buying Black-owned newspapers whenever he could, and he read every article from the front page to the last. Moses cut out and saved the articles he found profoundly interesting before discarding the rest of the paper.

"What you need to do, Mo, is concentrate on the game and not think about what you can't control."

A beat passed. "I'm trying, but I keep wondering if the White teams will ever allow us to play with them."

"I don't know, but if or when it happens, we will probably be too old by then."

Moses wanted to agree with Lionel, but something nagged at him. It wasn't that he was anxious to play on White teams, as much as he wanted them to acknowledge that Negro players deserved to play in the majors.

Growing up he hadn't had much interaction with White people because the mining town was segregated. The White kids went to the White schools and the Colored kids attended Colored schools. Even sports were segregated. The closest he had come to involvement with the other race was when the owner of the general store hired him to stock shelves, clean up, and occasionally deliver groceries to White and Colored people. He discovered that the owner charged Black folks a delivery fee, when there was no charge for his White customers. In other words, different rules for different folks.

Moses lowered his head and kept his mouth shut because he had a purpose. He needed money. Even if he had accepted the scholarships to attend college, he would still have needed money to buy books and pay for his room and board.

Moses didn't want to think about what he had given up to play baseball, because it was the past. What he hoped was if he did have children, that they'd take advantage of what he'd been denied and had to sacrifice to make life better for them.

"It will happen, Train, and I'm willing to bet in our lifetime. It's not as if Colored men didn't play in Major League Baseball in the past, before the owners got together to establish a color line. What they don't know is if they did allow us to play, they would make a lot more money than they do now."

Lionel snorted. "I'm willing to bet some of them would rather go bankrupt than allow us to play on their teams."

"I doubt that," Moses countered. "This country was founded on greed and is sustained by greedy men. Look at the number of men who either jumped to their death or committed suicide when the stock market crashed in 1929 because they lost their so-called fortunes. I'm willing to bet that the lifestyles of the Fords, Rockefellers, Carnegies, and Morgans did not change much. They still had roofs over their heads and food on their tables. Even gangsters became millionaires as bootleggers during Prohibition. It doesn't matter how greedy men make their money, whether it means kidnapping Africans and selling them as slaves or taking advantage of immigrants who come to this country for a better way of life, or like the men in my family who risk their lives every time they go down in a coal mine while the owners of the mining companies live in mansions as if they were royalty."

"That may be true, Mo, but I am still better off than my great-grandpappy who was born a slave."

Moses wanted to ask his teammate who he was kidding. Yes, there were Negroes who were educated and had become professionals, but that still didn't make them equal to their White counterparts. Black doctors and nurses worked in Colored hospitals, teachers taught in Colored schools, and the Whites Only and Colored Only signs were blatant reminders that many regions in the country were separate and unequal.

"What I don't understand, Mo, is why did you get so mad at that redneck calling you a nigger when folks down South call us that all the time?"

"I don't like it when anyone calls me a nigger, but I find it worse when some White person who lives above the Mason-Dixon line does it. If you hate Colored people that much then pack up and move down South with the rest of the White supremacists."

Lionel grunted. "As far as I'm concerned, all White people feel they are better than Colored folks."

Again, Moses wanted to disagree with Lionel, but he held his tongue. There had to be some good White people, otherwise there wouldn't have been a Civil War or the Thirteenth, Fourteenth, or Fifteenth Amendments to the Constitution.

"We have a couple of games in Indiana and Illinois before we go back to Memphis," he said, deftly changing the topic of conversation.

"Yeah," Lionel drawled. "We are scheduled to spend a few days there before heading down to New Orleans. I can't wait to see my wife and babies."

Moses wanted to tell him that he couldn't wait to return to Memphis. He had memorized Sallie Ann's phone number and hoped she would be as anxious to see him as he was to see her again.

Thinking about Sallie Ann helped him to forget about the chaos he'd experienced on the field earlier that day. He lowered his arms as he turned over and turned off the lamp on the nightstand next to his bed. Lionel turned off his lamp, plunging the room in darkness, and minutes later Moses surrendered to the comforting arms of Morpheus.

CHAPTER 17

Sallie Ann Thompson pushed out her lips as she glared at her father. She knew she was being insolent and overtly disrespectful, but she was beyond caring. He had broken both legs after falling off a ladder and a doctor had encased them in plaster for two months to aid healing. She'd filled in for him every weekend at Tommy's Joint during his recuperation.

The doctor had removed the casts two weeks ago and declared him healed enough to put weight on his legs. However, he had cautioned him to sit whenever he tired or if he was experiencing discomfort.

"But, Daddy, the doctor said you can go back to work."

Jimmie Thompson exhaled an audible sigh. "I told you I'm going to wait another couple of weeks before I go back. Now get up off your butt and git to work."

Sallie Ann met her mother's eyes but knew she wasn't going to get any support, so she turned on her heel and walked out of the parlor. Jimmie and his brothers had gone into business together to open the bar within months of the repeal of Prohibition. They served alcohol, barbecued chicken and pork, with the ubiquitous sides that included coleslaw, potato salad, baked beans, and collard greens. Lately they'd added biscuits and cornbread to the menu.

She thought it was wrong and a sin that the Thompson brothers occasionally spiked the drinks to render their customers unstable so that nimble-fingered waitresses could pick their pockets. Although it didn't happen often, Sallie Ann didn't like it one bit. They were making a profit, so she didn't know why her father and uncles felt the need to cheat and rob their customers, because the juke joint had earned the reputation of offering good booze, food, and music. Tommy's Joint also held the distinction of being the only Colored-owned bar with a jukebox.

Curbing the urge to suck her teeth, Sallie Ann went to her bedroom to change clothes and ready herself for a night filled with leering men, loud music, and choking cigar and cigarette smoke. Sallie Ann hated leaving the bar with nauseating odors clinging to her clothes and hair. The one time she attempted to tie her hair up with a bandana, her mother complained that she didn't want her daughter to look like someone who had been working in the cotton fields and forbade her from doing it again.

Sallie Ann was changing out of her skirt and blouse when Maddie Thompson entered her bedroom. She met her mother's eyes. "Mama, you know that Daddy is ready to go back to work, so why won't you tell him that?"

Maddie narrowed her eyes as she folded her arms under her breasts. "Sallie Ann Thompson, I will not have you questioning me about your father. After all, he's grown and you're not. He will go back when he feels he's ready. Unless you have forgotten, Tommy's Joint is a family business, and that means every Thompson must pitch in. Including you. Where do you think I get money to buy you those fancy shoes and dresses you wear to school?"

Sallie Ann knew her mother was going to launch into a tirade about how ungrateful she was. Her mother dressed her better than many of the girls at her school just so she could brag to her friends that her daughter was one of the smartest and best-dressed girls at the private school for Colored girls. It hadn't been Sallie Ann's choice to wear the same outfit no more than twice a month, but her mother's. Maddie had thought herself fortunate that she had caught the eye of Jimmie Thompson, who with his brothers operated an illegal still, selling moonshine while successfully evading the federal revenue agents who were unable to shut down their operation because it had been deftly concealed in a forested area populated by rattlesnakes and black bears.

"I told you before, I have too many shoes and dresses."

Maddie lowered her arms and fisted her hands. "You ungrateful heifer. How dare you stand there and tell me what you don't want. Now, let me tell you what you're going to do. You are going to fill in for you father on weekends, and now that school is out, you're going to get up early and help me cook. You will start with peeling potatoes for the salad, cutting up cabbage for slaw, and cleaning collard greens. You're sixteen and it's time you get involved in the family business instead of hanging around the house doing who knows what."

Sallie Ann felt like crying but decided not to give her mother the satisfaction of knowing she was upset. She thought she'd be free of the juke joint now that her father had healed enough to return to assist his brothers. But her mother had recruited her to help cook. Maddie got up every morning before dawn to begin cooking for the customers who came to Tommy's for dinner.

Fifty-pound sacks of potatoes, bushels of cabbage and collard greens were delivered to the shed behind the house a couple of times a week, once the Thompson brothers had decided to add food to the bar menu. They'd hired a cousin to smoke chickens, whole hogs, and sausage links, while Maddie had volunteered to make the sides. Tommy's Joint wasn't just a family business but an enterprise that included only those claiming Thompson blood, of which Sallie Ann was one.

She thought about the handsome baseball player who had promised to call her when he returned to Memphis, but with her spending all morning and afternoon cooking with her mother, she knew it wasn't possible for them to spend an appreciable time together.

Sallie Ann forced a smile. "Yes, Mama." She knew it was better to placate her mother than attempt to reason with her.

Maddie nodded. "Good. Now hurry and change because it's getting late. The bar will be getting crowded and I'm going to need you to help me serve dinners tonight."

She didn't know where her mother got her energy. Maddie got up before dawn to begin cooking, and then she'd load up the car with the pots of food to drive two blocks to the bar. She'd come home to take a nap before returning to work in the kitchen filling dinner orders. Once the food ran out, she went back home and went to bed to sleep soundly until the next morning.

Sallie Ann wanted to ask her mother why she had spent money to send her to a private school only to have her daughter work in a juke joint. It was a dive where regulars congregated to sit at the bar, drinking and eating peanuts while listening to music coming from the colorful jukebox. Once the morning and afternoon crowds left, it was time for food, live music, and dancing. And if a patron became too drunk or rowdy, he was unceremoniously escorted out with a warning not to come back until he sobered up.

The only employees who didn't claim Thompson blood were members of the band. Even the waitresses and kitchen help were Thompsons by blood or marriage, and all kept to the strict protocol of family first.

Sallie Ann slipped into a pair of tan wide-legged, high-waisted trousers with a white, short-sleeved blouse and a pair of white tennis shoes. She preferred the casual shoes to Mary Janes. Since Tommy's Joint didn't have a uniform dress code, she could wear whatever she chose.

Fifteen minutes after her mother left the house, Sallie Ann walked along the road to the rear entrance of Tommy's Joint. Maddie and another cousin were busy filling plates with sides while barbecued chicken and pulled pork from a whole hog were heaped on large serving platters. Reaching for a bibbed apron, she put it on and began ladling collard greens, potato salad, baked beans, and coleslaw on a row of plates on a low table.

Maddie read the order the servers handed her and added chicken and cornbread to one of the plates on the table. The assembly line filling dinner orders continued until Sallie Ann lost track of time as she alternated with one of the servers, setting down plates on the table in the bar's dining area. The cacophony—raised voices, shouting, and the band playing at a higher decibel than usual—assaulted her as she served the diners. Her father and uncles' decision to serve food along with live music was ingenious and had made Tommy's Joint a popular hangout along the strip with other Colored bars.

She took a break and slipped out the back to escape the heat and cloying smell of smoke and sweaty bodies.

Leaning against the side of the building, she noticed a man standing close by, smoking a cigarette. Night had fallen and a dimly lit bulb over the door wasn't sufficient to make out his features.

"Hey, baby, you looking for company?"

"No!" she snapped angrily when she wanted to tell him that she wasn't his baby. Sallie Ann didn't know how it had happened so quickly, but before she could blink, he was next to her, imprisoning her arm. "Let me go!"

"Is that really what you want?" he whispered in her ear as he pushed his groin against her hip.

Sallie Ann thought she was going to be sick from the stench of his unwashed body, but her fear escalated when he fumbled with the front of his pants with his free hand and took out his penis. She did not want to believe she was going to be raped outside the door to her family's business, and somehow she found the strength to extricate herself and punch him in the face at the same time she recovered her voice to scream. One second he was there, and in the next he wasn't. She didn't know if it had been her scream or hitting him in the face that had sent him running in the opposite direction and disappearing into the night.

Sallie Ann waited until her heart slowed to a normal rhythm to go back inside. It was apparent that when she screamed no one had heard it, or if they had, they'd chosen to ignore it because this part of town was filled with screams and hollering that escalated with the onset of sunset. Although her family lived in a Colored neighborhood in Memphis with a sprinkling of shacks and proliferation of juke joints, there were other sections in the city where professional Negroes had created fine homes and businesses.

Although she attended school with their children, Sallie Ann was more than aware that they would never permit her to date or marry their sons because of how the Thompsons earned their money, and no Thompson had graduated from college. If there was a mandate in the South for separate-but-equal between Coloreds and Whites, it was also in effect among Black folks. In other words, she had to stay in her social place.

"Where were you?" Maddie questioned accusingly.

Sallie Ann's hands curled into fists. "I was outside taking a break."

"You can take a break after we finish serving. Then you can go home."

She stared at the woman she knew resented her station in life. Madeline Thompson née Duncan wanted to live like the women whose daughters attended the private school Sallie Ann went to, but by accident of birth she hadn't been permitted to join their social circle. Maddie was tall, slender, and attractive, with large deep brown eyes, an enchanting pug nose and rosebud mouth that could have been a prototype for a doll. She had a sienna-brown flawless complexion and thick black hair that when straightened with a hot comb reached her shoulders. Maddie may have had the looks and bearing to join what she called the *mucky-mucks*, but not the pedigree, and that was something she'd wanted for her daughter once she enrolled her in the exclusive school for Colored girls. However, Sallie Ann knew she would never be accepted in their world without a college degree, and certainly not as the daughter of a juke joint owner. And now, with Maddie talking about her becoming involved in the family business, Sallie Ann would have to let go of her dream of attending college.

She had one more year before she graduated, and that was more than enough time to plan her future. And if she were to stay in Memphis, it wouldn't be to work in Tommy's Joint.

* * *

Moses returned to Memphis and within minutes of walking into the Parker House, Lucille Parker handed him a stack of letters that had been addressed to him from his mother.

He thanked her and retreated downstairs to his room to shower and change out of the grimy uniform before reading them. It felt good not to share a room with Lionel; despite their becoming close while traveling, there were times when he craved his privacy, to read at his leisure and write in his notebooks.

After shaving, showering, and changing into a pair of clean underwear, khakis, and a white shirt, Moses sank down on his bed to read the letters. Both his sisters were pregnant and would make Daisy a grandmother for the second time the following year. Solomon wasn't doing well. His coughing spells were more frequent and violent, yet he refused to see a doctor. Relations were still icy between Daisy and Solomon after she'd threatened to shoot him, but she preferred it that way because he was less argumentative. She was still sewing on the treadle machine and had taken on another customer who wanted her to make her blouses, skirts, day dresses, and evening gowns to take with her on a transatlantic cruise.

In that instant, Moses knew he had to purchase an electric sewing machine sooner rather than later. He'd researched a catalogue and saw they were priced from eighty-five and upward to one hundred fifteen dollars. Moses was willing to pay more if the machine contained functions that would assist his mother in completing her projects more quickly.

He opened his duffel and took out the piece of paper with an order blank he'd ripped from a catalogue advertising Singer sewing machines. Spending more than one hundred dollars would deplete some of his savings, but that wasn't important. He was playing ball and getting paid for it. He had the machine's model number, so all he had to do was purchase a money order and mail it to the company with instructions where he wanted the sewing machine delivered. The team was scheduled to remain in Memphis for almost two weeks and that gave Moses enough time to go to the post office and hopefully spend time with Sallie Ann.

Now that he had committed to purchasing a sewing machine for his mother, the next purchase on his wish list was an automobile. It didn't have to be brand-new, but one that was dependable enough to get him around locally without his having to rely on taxis.

Moses spent the next hour writing his mother before he picked up his notebook to jot down the results of the last game the Eagles played in Chicago. They'd won the game, but instead of staying in the city following it, Edgar Connelly had shocked everyone when he informed them they were going back to Memphis. After gassing up the bus, the driver drove southward, stopping only at Black-owned service stations to purchase gas. He'd stopped twice, once at a roadhouse and again at a hotel for food and bathroom breaks, where Edgar had covered the cost for the entire team. His generosity was appreciated, and he had unknowingly gained the respect of everyone connected with the Memphis Eagles.

CHAPTER 18

Sallie Ann had returned to the house after delivering the food to the bar and headed for her bedroom to relax before going back later that evening to work in the kitchen. Getting up before sunrise and standing on her feet for hours cooking and baking had left her physically and mentally exhausted. She couldn't understand why her mother hadn't hired a cook, or cooks, to prepare the dinners. Even family-owned businesses had employees to perform certain tasks to keep the operation viable and profitable. However, it was different with the Thompsons. They had a tight grip on every phase of the operation, and that included controlling members of their own family.

Sallie Ann sank down to the cushioned rocker and closed her eyes. She had chosen the rocker rather than the bed because she knew she would've fallen asleep within minutes of her head touching the pillow.

This can't continue. She didn't want to spend her summer vacation serving in a bar. It was no place for a teenage girl who had to use everything in her limited protective arsenal to thwart the advances of men who'd accidently brush up against her body or whisper ribald suggestions as to what they wanted to do to her. The sixteen-year-old girls she went to school with were either vacationing with their families or attending afternoon teas with their peers.

Sallie Ann knew her life would never mirror theirs, and she had resigned herself to it. She was the descendant of both slave and free Thompsons; however, what she did not understand was why her father and uncles were running their business like a plantation. They were like White plantation owners who, despite fathering mixed-race children, saw them not as human beings but chattel. When her mother enrolled Sallie Ann in Memphis's elite Colored all-girl school, she had believed it would elevate Maddie's social status among her peers. Madeline Duncan may have been able to lord it over the girls with whom she had grown up that she'd "made it." However, it hadn't mattered to those from whom she really sought acceptance, because she'd become the wife of a saloonkeeper. So much for her upward mobility.

Sallie Ann was aware that the country was still struggling to emerge from the Depression, and while President Roosevelt's New Deal government programs were instituted to assist in providing relief for millions of unemployed Americans, they weren't of interest or help for her. She lived in a state where Jim Crow laws predominated every phase of her life, and without a college education she would never be able to throw off the shackles to elevate herself to the social status that had been denied her mother, grandmother, and great-grandmother.

On the other hand, she didn't envy her classmates or want to mirror their lives. Sallie Ann wanted more options where she hoped to take her future into her own hands, rather than marry a boy her parents had selected for her from their coveted social circle. Her independence was less likely now that Maddie Thompson had decided she would probably spend the rest of her life working for Tommy's Joint.

She opened her eyes and stared at the tattered teddy bear on the top of the chest of drawers. The bear had become her best friend to whom she'd whispered her heartfelt secrets. Sallie Ann missed her little brother who had choked and died from ingesting a plug of chewing tobacco her father had left on a table. The teddy bear had been her brother's favorite toy and Sallie Ann had rescued it from the pile of clothes and toys her mother had packed up to give away. She was too young to know what had transpired between her mother and father prior to her brother's passing. However, she knew it was the last time her parents had shared a bedroom, and eventually attributed it to Maddie's blaming her husband for the death of their son; she had pleaded incessantly with him to give up what she said was the disgusting habit of chewing tobacco.

Sallie Ann was suddenly alert when she heard the telephone ringing. Pushing off the chair, she hurried to the living room to answer it. She stopped short when she saw her father leaning on a pair of crutches with the receiver pressed to his ear.

"Who did you say you wanted to speak to? Sallie Ann. Who are you and why are you calling her?"

Sallie Ann went still. She knew who was on the other end of the line asking for her. It had to be Moses Gilliam. He had promised her he would call once he returned to Memphis.

"Are you the ballplayer Moses Gilliam?" Jimmie Thompson continued with his questioning. "Hey now. I can't believe I'm talking to a hometown hero."

Registering the change in her father's attitude, Sallie Ann walked into the room. "Daddy, please give me the phone."

"Yes, son. My daughter's here."

Jimmie handed her the receiver, and she gave him a look that spoke volumes. She wanted to talk to Moses without her father overhearing what she would say to him.

Covering the receiver with her hand, she whispered, "May I please have a little privacy?"

Jimmie nodded. "But I'm going to need you to tell me where you met him and why he is calling you."

It was Sallie Ann's turn to nod and wait until her father left before removing her hand. "I can't believe you remembered to call."

Moses's chuckle caressed her ear through the earpiece. "I told you I would."

She smiled. "Yes, you did. How was barnstorming?"

"It was good. We won almost all our games."

"How long are you going to be in Memphis?" she asked.

"Ten days. Only two won't be game days. I was wondering if we can't get together and maybe take in a movie during my off days."

Sallie Ann sank down to an armchair, struggling not to lose her composure. It was the first time a boy had asked her out on a date, and she wanted to say yes, but there was still the problem of her getting time off from work.

"I would like that. But I must first talk to my parents."

"Okay. When can I call back?"

"Tomorrow," Sallie Ann said quickly. She knew from her father's response that she would be going out with what he'd called a hometown hero, but it was her mother she had to convince to give her time off from working at the bar.

"Can I call you around this time tomorrow?"

"Yes," she said quickly.

"Okay, Sallie Ann. I'll talk to you tomorrow."

She held on to the receiver for several seconds after Moses had hung up. Moving as if in slow motion, she set down the receiver on the cradle, her heart pumping a runaway rhythm, as she went to look for her father. She found him on the screened front porch sitting on a chair with his sock-covered feet resting on a footstool.

She took a chair opposite his. "He asked me out."

Jimmie Thompson gave her a long, steady stare. "What did you tell him?"

Sallie Ann smiled at the man who could have easily passed for the Negro version of Santa Claus. He was tall and plump with fleshy cheeks. He'd begun losing his hair in his twenties and had instructed his barber to cut what was left close to his scalp.

"I told him I had to talk to my parents."

Jimmie nodded, smiling. "I'm glad you told him that."

A slight frown appeared between Sallie Ann's eyes. "Why?"

"Because I don't want him to think that my daughter is easy because he's a baseball star."

"Easy how, Daddy?"

"That he could take advantage of you because folks see him as a celebrity."

It suddenly appeared to Sallie Ann what her father was talking about. That she would allow Moses to charm her and he would get her to have sex with him. Well, if that was his intent, then he had selected the wrong girl. She had no wish to end up like some of the girls in their neighborhood who either had to drop out of school because they were pregnant, or were forced into so-called shotgun marriages to avoid bringing disgrace on their families. Then there were those folks who whispered about who'd had abortions to rid themselves of unwanted babies.

"That's not going to happen, Daddy. There's no way I would allow a boy to take advantage of me in that way."

"Good for you." Jimmie paused as he stared at his legs under a pair of shorts. "Where did you meet him?"

Sallie Ann wanted to ask her father if he was kidding. Her only contact with men was at Tommy's Joint. "I met him at the bar. He had come in with some of his teammates from the Memphis Eagles. He'd ordered pop and it only took a swallow for him to know it had been spiked."

"Oh shit!" Jimmie whispered under his breath. "What happened?"

"If you're asking if he made a scene, then the answer is no. I don't know why you and my uncles are still spiking drinks, because one of these days it's going to backfire when someone gets sick, or worse, dies. You're already making a profit by charging more for drinks than the other bars, and now that you're selling food the business is doing well."

"You're right, Sallie Ann. I'm going to tell my brothers to stop messing with the drinks because if Moses Gilliam decides to put the word out that he was drugged, then we may as well close the doors. And you're right about us making more money than we had expected once we stopped selling moonshine."

"Do you think they will listen to you?" she questioned.

"I'm hoping they will after I tell them about Moses Gilliam being on to us. And if he were to tell his teammates, then there's no doubt we would be in hot water. The girls also must stop picking pockets."

"What I don't understand, Daddy, is why you did it in the first place. It's not as if you're not making money."

Jimmie lowered his head, appearing remorseful. "We

did it when we first opened up to compete with the other bars, but even after we were able to turn a profit we didn't want to stop."

"It's time to stop, Daddy, because it's illegal and dangerous."

Jimmie's head popped up. "You're right, honey. I'm going to call my brothers and tell them it stops today. I can't have my daughter date a man who has attracted the attention of Colored folks not only in Memphis but all around the Negro Leagues."

Sallie Ann sat straight. "Are you saying I can go out with him?"

"Of course."

"But, what about Mama?"

"Don't you worry yourself none about your mother. I'll take care of her."

"You'll take care of me how?"

Sallie Ann and her father were unaware of Maddie's presence before she spoke. "How, Jimmie?" Maddie repeated, as she walked in and sat next to her husband.

"I was just telling Sallie Ann that you wouldn't have a problem with her going out with Moses Gilliam."

Maddie looked at her daughter with wide eyes. "You know him?"

Sallie Ann flashed a Cheshire cat grin. "Yes. And he's only going to be in Memphis for ten days and during that time he wants to take me to see the moving pictures."

"What did you tell him?" Maddie had repeated the same question as her husband.

"I told him that I had to talk to my parents. Daddy has already said yes, so—"

"Of course you can go," Maddie said, interrupting her. "I can't wait to tell everyone that my daughter is dating a popular baseball player."

"Stop, Mama," Sallie Ann said, smiling. "It's only one date."

"One date that can turn into more and hopefully marriage."

She shook her head and closed her eyes. She did not want to believe her mother was not only looking for attention but also wanted to lord it over her friends. If her daughter couldn't marry a doctor or a lawyer, then why not a popular Negro athlete.

"Enough, Mama," she whispered. "I don't know if he's been married or if he even has a girlfriend, and you already have us walking down the aisle together. Please give me time to get to know the man and vice versa."

"She's right, Maddie. Don't go and count your chickens before they hatch."

Maddie rolled her eyes at her husband. "You are a fine one to talk. You have been running off at the mouth ever since the Eagles started winning again."

"They are winning, Maddie, because of Moses Gilliam. The sports reporter for the *Memphis Herald* wrote that opposing pitchers have intentionally walked him to keep him from hitting."

Sallie Ann realized she knew nothing about baseball and if she was going to date a ballplayer, then she needed to read about the sport. She'd told Moses to call her tomorrow, and she hoped the time would go quickly so they could establish a day and time to see each other again.

She stood up and walked off the porch, leaving her parents to discuss what Sallie Ann thought of as her uncertain future where it concerned Moses Gilliam. The promise of one date did not guarantee something more, and she was glad he had mentioned taking her to the movies. The year before, several businessmen had invested in a theater that was forced to close in 1930.

They renovated it, installing an air-cooling system, and showed some silent films along with some popular talkies. Seating was segregated, with the balcony designated as the Colored section. Whenever the heat became oppressive, people went to the movies in droves just to stay cool, making it a popular place to gather during the summer months.

Sallie Ann had become obsessed with motion pictures, and her fervent wish was to travel to a city with considerable Colored populations to view Oscar Micheaux's all-Black films in hundreds of theaters that were called the "ghetto circuit." She'd read that Micheaux's films offered an alternative to the ongoing stereotyping of Colored people in movies produced by Hollywood studios, in which Negro actors were depicted as subservient or frightened, bug-eyed stooges.

Although she'd planned to take a nap, the notion that she was going on a date with Moses wouldn't allow her to completely relax as she thought about what she wanted to wear and how to fix her hair. He'd promised to call her again the next day and she knew she would count down every hour until she heard his voice again.

Jimmie waited until he was certain Sallie Ann was out of earshot to reveal to his wife what their daughter told him about her encounter with Moses Gilliam. "I'm going to need you to drive me over to the bar so we can have a family meeting to talk over a few things."

Maddie narrowed her eyes. "I have told you so many times about messing with the customers that I have lost count. It's the same thing I told you about chewing tobacco and—"

"Woman! I don't want to hear about something that happened a long time ago."

Maddie froze. "Either you call me Maddie or Madeline, because *woman* isn't my name. Maybe that's what you call your whores, but in case you have forgotten, I happen to be your wife and not one of your women."

"You stopped being my wife the day you moved out of our bedroom."

"You're lucky it was only the bedroom I moved out of."

"What the hell are you talking about?" Jimmie countered angrily.

"I could have taken my daughter and moved out of this house, Jimmie Thompson, because I pleaded and begged you over and over to stop that nasty habit of chewing tobacco, leaving the pouches all over the house. But it took the death of my son for you to quit. It's the same with you and your hardheaded brothers messing with folks' drinks for you to decide it's time to stop. Why? I'll tell you why," she continued without giving him time to respond. "Because a young man who just happened to take a liking to your daughter decided to keep his mouth shut. A young man who everyone in Memphis is talking about and if he wanted could ruin everything you and your greedy-ass brothers have worked so hard to achieve. Yes, Mr. Jimmie Thompson, I will drive you over to Tommy's Joint so y'all can stop being criminals."

Jimmie clenched his teeth so tightly that the pain in his jaw surpassed that in his legs. He wanted to tell Maddie that he'd had to take his pleasure with other women because she had denied him what was expected of a wife. He thought he'd been discreet, but apparently he hadn't been able to fool her.

However, he had been forced to stop his tomcatting and think about the state of his marriage when he'd fallen off a ladder and broken both legs. Maddie had gone above and beyond what was expected when she fed, bathed, and dressed him until he was able to get around with the aid of crutches. She was a good woman and he realized he should've listened to her when she'd nagged him about his chewing tobacco. She had loathed the habit ever since her father had taken it up. The only difference between him and his father-in-law was that he'd used a spit cup, while Leon Duncan spat out tobacco juice wherever he chose.

"You're right, Maddie."

She gave him a startled stare. "I am?"

Jimmie forced a smile. "Yes, ma'am, you're right that it's time for us to stop being criminals. It's just that we have had to scrimp and scrap for every dollar to keep a roof over our heads. And if we hadn't made and sold moonshine, then we would have lost this house. It's called survival, Maddie. That's what it has been since Europeans kidnapped Africans and brought them to this country as enslaved people. If that ain't criminal, then I don't know what is."

"Of course it was criminal, but what's worse is Colored folks stealing from their own people, Jimmie. You and your brothers are no different from White people who cheat Colored sharecroppers who work their land, or factory owners who pay Black workers less than the White ones for the same job. Now, tell me if I'm wrong, but would you have thought about stopping if Moses Gilliam hadn't asked to date our daughter?"

"Probably not," Jimmie admitted. "But as I said before, you're right. It's time we quit while we can."

Maddie grunted. "You don't want to hear it, but breaking your legs and laying up on your back has allowed you time to think about a lot of things."

"What things?"

"That you had to depend on your wife and not your whores to take care of you."

Jimmie anchored a hand under his knees as he lifted one leg, and then the other off the footstool. "Enough talk about whores. Please help me up so I can get my crutches. I want to get to the bar before the dinner crowd comes in."

He'd wanted to thank Maddie for what she'd done to help him following his accident but didn't know how, because he'd never witnessed a tender moment between his mother and father. Leroy Thompson had been lord and master of his home; his wife had always been at his beck and call, acquiescing to his every demand.

In that instant he knew that, to be a better husband and father, he would have to be a better man. And he would start with giving up sleeping with other women.

CHAPTER 19

What Moses hadn't been able to see in the smoke-filled and dimly lit Tommy's Joint was revealed in the brilliant sunlight when Sallie Ann opened the door to his knock. Initially he'd thought her pretty; however, he was only half right. She was delicate and very pretty, like the bud of a flower whose petals were just beginning to open to exhibit nature's beauty. She appeared young, every inch a sixteen-year-old girl with her face scrubbed clean. The mascara and brilliant red lipstick were missing.

"Good afternoon. Will you please come in."

Moses hadn't been aware that he had been holding his breath until she spoke. He smiled and took off his panama hat; he had seen it in a men's shop in Chicago and couldn't resist purchasing it because he'd seen pictures of fashionable men wearing them. He had chosen one made with the authentic circular rose on the center of the crown in a soft beige shade. After purchasing the hat and a sewing machine for his mother, he had depleted most of his savings, and he was forced to remind himself to budget his earnings carefully so he could save enough to buy a car.

"Good afternoon. And thank you." He extended his left hand with a bouquet of flowers that he'd concealed behind his back. "I thought I'd bring a little something for your mother."

As someone born and raised in the South, he'd heard over and over that you were never to go to someone's home empty-handed. And because he didn't cook and wasn't familiar with a shop that sold baked goods, he decided flowers would be an appropriate substitute.

Sallie Ann inhaled the scent of the bouquet of roses, carnations, and daisies in varying shades of yellow, not meeting his eyes. "They are beautiful. I am certain my mother will love them. She's been trying to grow a flower garden for years, but there's something wrong with either the seeds or the soil."

Moses's gaze swept over the screened-in front porch. A round table with two pull-up chairs, a rocker, and another couple of armchairs were covered with the same off-white fabric stamped with colorful blue and yellow flowers. When he'd called Sallie Ann back as she had requested, and she informed him that her parents had agreed to let her go out with him, he had curbed the urge to shout at the top of his lungs. He wasn't certain what there was about Sallie Ann that had him thinking about her whenever he wasn't concentrating on a game. Hopefully he would find out what it was after they were able to spend several hours together away from the bar.

"Are you going to introduce me to your mother?"

Sallie Ann shook her head. "Not today. She had to take my father to the hospital because when he woke up this morning one of his legs was swollen. He fell off a ladder a couple of months ago while trying to remove a bird's nest off the roof of the house, and broke both legs. Although the casts were removed several weeks ago, he's still in pain and then there was the swelling today."

"I hope it's nothing too serious."

She smiled, the gesture not reaching her large expressive eyes. "I'm praying it's not." She paused. "We can leave right after I put the flowers in water."

Moses clasped his hands behind his back as he waited for Sallie Ann to return. Her reaction to him was wholly different from their first meeting. Then she had been seductive because men would be inclined to spend more money if they believed she liked them. But when he'd accused her of putting something in his pop it was as if the curtain had come down on her staged performance and she had admitted she didn't want to set him up so someone could rob him. He didn't know if she was still working weekends at the bar and hoped she had taken his warning to heart about her uncles using her as a lure to make money.

Sallie Ann was sixteen, the same age as one of his sisters; however, unlike them she hadn't married to escape a volatile home situation. His sisters had been thrust into adulthood as wives and mothers when they should have completed high school, dated boys they liked, and then married if that was what they had chosen.

A silent voice reminded Moses that he'd just met Sallie Ann, and her parents were responsible for her. Although he'd mentioned that her uncles were pimping her, he knew that was none of his business, and no doubt her family would resent his interference. He'd returned to Memphis, and as promised contacted her, offering to take her to the movies. It was to be a date, and hopefully, after spending a couple of hours together, he would be able to discover why he'd found himself so attracted to her.

As Sallie Ann walked in the direction of the kitchen to

find a jar large enough for the flowers, she couldn't stop smiling. *I'm going to marry him.* She wasn't certain where or when it was going to happen, but prayed it would become a reality.

When she'd opened the door and saw Moses standing on the front steps, tall, dark, and incredibly handsome, casually dressed in a crisp white short-sleeved shirt and pressed dark slacks, her heart had stopped beating for several seconds. She didn't know which smelled better—the bouquet or the aftershave on his lean, clean-shaven jaw.

If someone were to be touted as a hometown hero, then Moses Gilliam had the qualities to be judged one. He was the type that men could admire, and women of all ages would want to pursue. Sallie Ann could not believe he had asked her to go out with him.

After she met him, which now seemed so long ago, she'd thought about him calling her once he returned to Memphis, chiding herself because it wasn't ladylike for her to give him her telephone number even before they'd gotten to know each other. She knew if he hadn't become a local baseball celebrity her mother would have severely punished her for being *loose*, although Maddie didn't seem to have a problem with her daughter wearing makeup and enticing customers to buy drinks at the bar. And loose was a word Sallie Ann had come to resent. She wanted to remind her parents that loose women offered their bodies to men without the benefit of marriage, or if they were married, they had no qualms about sleeping with men who weren't their husbands. She was neither; she hadn't even kissed a boy yet.

Not wanting to keep Moses waiting too long, Sallie Ann set the jar with the flowers in the middle of the table, then turned on her heel to retrace her steps where she had left Moses on the porch. From a table she picked up a small, quilted bag that doubled as her purse, which contained cash, a handkerchief, and her house keys. His back was to her when she reentered, allowing her to admire his ramrod-straight posture. He was a perfect male specimen, with broad shoulders and a slim waist and hips. Sallie Ann cleared her throat and Moses turned to look at her. There was something in his gaze that made her slightly uncomfortable, but not enough to cancel their date. What, she mused, was he thinking as he stared at her? Had he regretted asking her out when he could have taken any girl he chose?

"I'm ready, Moses." As soon as the words came out of her mouth she wondered if she were truly ready. Ready for her first date with a man whose exploits on the baseball field had all the Colored population of Memphis talking about him. And, if she was ready for the attention.

Moses stared at the petite girl wearing a skirt, blouse, socks, and a pair of patent leather Mary Janes, and smiled. He had to admit to himself that he was more than ready for the Sallie Ann Thompson who looked more like the schoolgirl, with her hair braided in a single plait, than the provocative one he'd met at the bar.

He waited for her to lock the door, then took her hand and led her to where he had parked Odell Nelson's car. When he had mentioned to Coach that he was taking a local girl out on a date, the older man had volunteered his vehicle, saying if he wanted to impress the girl, then a set of wheels was better than two legs.

"You have a car?" Sallie Ann asked, her voice filled with what he interpreted as surprise.

Moses opened the passenger door. "No, it's my manager's. He let me borrow it for the day." The Ford Model A was ten years old, but Coach, as an amateur mechanic, had kept it in tip-top running shape. He waited until Sallie Ann was seated before rounding the car to take his seat behind the wheel. He started the engine, then slowly let out the clutch at the same time he applied pressure to the gas pedal.

He concentrated on the road rather than the young woman beside him. Moses was still attempting to figure out how Sallie Ann could shift from a seductress to a schoolgirl so easily. He couldn't help but wonder which was the real Sallie Ann and what image she preferred.

"What are you doing now that school is in recess?" he asked her.

"I'm helping my mother cook for the bar."

His eyebrows lifted. "You're still working at the bar?"

"Yes and no."

"Why yes and no, Sallie Ann?" He was hard-pressed to keep a hint of annoyance out of his tone. Moses didn't know why, it was none of his business where she worked; but he just couldn't let it go.

"I'm no longer serving drinks but helping in the kitchen serving dinners. Customers don't have to worry about something being put in their drinks because that ended yesterday."

Moses gave her a quick glance. "What happened for your uncles to stop?" He struggled not to laugh when Sallie Ann recounted the conversation she'd had with her father when she informed him that Memphis's latest sports hero was aware that his drink had been spiked, and he feared if Moses went public with his suspicions, it would be bad for business.

"So, it took my asking you on a date to make them mend their ways?" he asked, chuckling.

Sallie smiled, nodding. "I'm willing to bet that the news that Moses Gilliam is dating Sallie Ann Thompson will be all over town before the sun goes down. I don't know anything about baseball, but whenever men get together that's all they talk about. A few follow the White players, but it's the Negro players they follow religiously. When Daddy mentioned that pitchers were intentionally walking you to keep you from hitting, I had no idea what that meant."

Moses sobered. "Will it bother you if folks talk about us?"

"No. Why would you ask me that?"

"I asked because I need to know. I'd like you to become my girlfriend."

"You're kidding, aren't you?"

"Do I look like I'm kidding, Miss Sallie Ann Thompson?"

A beat passed. "No, Moses, I know you're not kidding. We haven't spent one hour together and here you are asking me if I will be your girlfriend. How many other girls have you asked the same question?"

"You're going to have to give me time to think about it."

"Stop the car! Stop the car this minute!" Sallie shouted.

"For what?"

"So I can get out."

"Why would you want to get out?"

"Because I don't have any intention of dating someone who has another girlfriend or should I say *girlfriends*. How would you like it if I dated more than one boy at the same time?"

"I wouldn't like it," Moses countered, "and I was just teasing you, Sallie Ann. I don't have any other girlfriends because I only want one. And that's you."

"Why me, Moses?"

"Why not you?" he asked, answering her question with one of his own. "Haven't boys asked you out before?"

Sallie Ann wanted to tell him that she'd had lots of dates, but that would be a lie, and if she was going to trust him, then he had to trust her. "No. You are the first boy who has asked me out. And please don't look at me like that."

"Like what, Sallie Ann?"

"Like . . . like . . . I am not worthy enough for . . ." Her words trailed off at the same time her eyes filled with tears. She didn't know what was wrong with her. Without warning he slowed the car, maneuvered over to the side of the road, and shut off the engine, then rested his right arm over her shoulders.

"Why are you crying, Sallie Ann?"

She untied the drawstring to her purse, searching for a handkerchief to blot her tears, but Moses was quicker when he removed his arm, pulled a handkerchief from his pants pocket, and blotted her face. The concern in his voice and gentle touch elicited another wave of tears, and Sallie Ann feared she had ruined any chance of Moses asking her out again.

After several minutes she was able to compose herself enough to tell Moses that the boys she knew thought her beneath them. She told him everything. Her mother enrolling her in Miss Cora's School for Girls because she believed it would allow her daughter to marry well. All the pain and humiliation she had encountered for the past sixteen years poured out when she revealed that the professional, college-educated, successful Negroes would never accept her because she was the daughter and niece of moonshiners, bootleggers, and saloonkeepers.

"How important is it that you marry the son of a doctor or lawyer, Sallie Ann?"

She managed what passed for a smile. "Not as important for me as it is for my mother. What she doesn't realize is that the lives of those who live in what we call 'the Heights' aren't perfect. I've overheard a few of my classmates talk about their fathers fooling around with their nurses and secretaries while some even have outside families they attempt to hide from their wives. The only thing that sets them apart from us is they are better educated and have more economic opportunities."

"Folks are folks, Sallie Ann, and it doesn't matter how much or how little money they have. And I'm glad those egotistical boys believe you are beneath them, because I never would've been given the chance to ask you out."

With wide eyes, she said, "Really?"

Moses nodded. "Yes, really, Miss Sallie Ann Thompson." He started up the car. "We better go so we don't miss the beginning of the movie."

Chapter 20

Not only had they missed the beginning of the film, but a sign on the marquee indicated the theater was closed for repairs. Moses overheard some people milling on the sidewalk say the air-cooling system was blowing hot air, making it impossible for anyone to remain inside.

He escorted Sallie Ann back to where he had parked the car. "We have a few hours to spend, and because I am new to Memphis, you are going to have to tell me where you would you like to go." He had planned to spend at least a couple of hours watching a movie, but now that was not going to happen. Moses wasn't ready to take her back home.

"Do you like ice cream?" she asked.

Moses smiled as he reached for her hand. "I love it. Why?"

"There's an ice cream shop that we passed on the way here that folks claim serves the best homemade ice cream in the city."

"Have you eaten there?"

Sallie Ann shook her head. "No."

"Well, pretty girl, this is going to be a first for both of us."

Even if she hadn't believed she was pretty, at that moment Sallie Ann felt more than pretty. She felt beautiful. Whenever she was among her classmates, she saw them as Cinderella's stepsisters who would subtly remind her that she wasn't their equal. That none of their brothers or cousins would ever consider her good enough to dance with, date, or even marry. That not even wearing the latest fashions was enough to change her social status.

"What made you decide to become a baseball player?" she asked Moses after they were once again seated in the car.

Sallie Ann listened intently, enraptured, as Moses revealed he had come from a generation of coal miners, and while he'd earned partial scholarships to attend two prestigious Black universities, he had given it up to pursue his true passion, which was baseball. She didn't know, if she'd been given the opportunity to attend college to become a teacher or a nurse, whether she would've turned it down to take up her secret passion: photography.

She had read everything she could find about the evolution of modern photography, beginning with Mathew Brady, whose photographs of Civil War battles depicted the horrors of war, slavery having ripped the country apart. Sallie Ann saw the photographic images as communicating silent messages to viewers, stirring their emotions. And it was moving pictures, with the release of D. W. Griffth's *The Birth of a Nation*, that had resurrected the Ku Klux Klan throughout the South, with the depiction of a White man in black face assaulting a White woman.

Maddie Thompson had already determined her daughter wouldn't attend college, because she wanted her to become involved in the operation of Tommy's Joint. And while she knew debating the issue with her mother was futile, Sallie Ann couldn't imagine what more could be done to the business to make it more profitable.

Sallie Ann closed her eyes as Moses drove slowly over the rutted road, signaling they had entered the Negro section of downtown Memphis. Her mother had been a fool to believe if she sent her daughter to a private all-girl Colored school that she'd be able to attract a boy who would elevate her social standing. Maddie failed to realize that as the wife of a saloonkeeper, the doors to those living in the Heights would forever remain closed to the Thompsons.

However, Sallie Ann had to thank her mother for allowing her to attend a school where she rubbed shoulders with Colored people who had become socially and economically successful, despite systemic racism, allowing her to experience both worlds. Worlds that were defined by education and money, but not morals. And if or when she married, whether to a college or non-college-educated man, she wanted it to be based on love and respect.

"Why so quiet, Sallie Ann?"

Moses's query shattered her musings. She opened her eyes. "I was just thinking about you turning down college scholarships to play baseball."

"You think I was wrong?"

Turning her head, she stared at his profile, committing it to memory. She still could not believe this tall, handsome, and talented young man had asked her out on a date, a man who had admitted he didn't have a girlfriend.

"It's not whether you were right or wrong, Moses. You did what was best for you."

"If I had come to you before I decided to become a baseball player and told you what I had been offered, what would you have said?"

"I probably would have asked if you could do both. Play baseball and attend college at the same time."

Moses shook his head. "That wasn't a possibility. I'd received partial scholarships, and that meant I would have had to work to make up the difference. I wouldn't make any money playing college baseball."

"Couldn't you have finished college, then joined the Negro Leagues?"

"That's not how it works, Sallie Ann. I finish college, then go on to medical or law school to become a doctor or lawyer. When would I get the time to play ball? Not when I'm on house calls or preparing to defend someone in court. White players in the Major Leagues play for six months, beginning mid-April and ending early October, while those of us who play in the Negro Leagues also play winter ball in Latin American countries where professional baseball isn't segregated."

"Do you plan to play winter ball?"

"Yes, because I need to make enough money to buy the things that I want."

Sallie Ann stared out the windshield. "What things are those?"

"Land, Sallie Ann. I want to own property that I can pass down to my children and grandchildren. I know nothing about farming, but I intend to learn everything necessary to care for cows, chickens, and how to grow my own food."

"That sounds daunting."

Moses smiled. "Daunting, but attainable. What have you planned for your future?"

"It won't be attending college, because my mother wants me to eventually take over from her, cooking for the bar."

Moses decelerated enough to give her an incredulous stare. "She paid to send you to a private school so when you graduate you won't go to college, but will work in a bar—even if it is family owned."

"Yes. She thought sending me there would end with me being introduced to the brothers or cousins of my classmates and eventually marrying one of them. Once she realized that wasn't going to happen, my fate was sealed. As a Thompson, it's always family first."

"Would that also apply if you were married?"

Moses's question gave Sallie Ann pause. "I don't know," she admitted. "It would depend on my husband."

"Depend how?"

"If he objected to his wife working in a bar."

"Do you like working in a bar, Sallie Ann?"

She pulled her lower lip between her teeth to stop spewing curses. "No. I hate everything about it. I don't think I will ever get used to men standing so close that I can smell their liquored breath on my face, or their feeble attempts to rub up against me, believing I like it."

"A bar, saloon, tavern, beer garden, or whatever it's called is no place for a schoolgirl," Moses stated.

Sallie Ann smiled. "I agree."

"I know I want to be a farmer once I stop playing ball, but what would you do if you didn't have to work for your family's business?"

Sallie Ann felt a spurt of excitement wash over her with his question. "I want to become a photographer, Moses. I want to travel to take pictures of people, places, and things I've never seen. I want to take a train to Chicago and visit the movie houses showing Oscar Micheaux's all-Black films so I can forget about the Hollywood films depicting Nego actors in buffoonish roles."

"What would you do with your photographs?"

"I would hope to sell some of them to the *National Geographic* magazine or compile a personal collection for myself. Now that I'm dating a baseball player, I would like to attend a game and see for myself why the sport is so popular."

"You've never been to a game?"

"No, Moses."

"The rules are easy to follow."

"Easy for you, but not for me," she admitted.

"Baseball is a game of numbers. There are nine players on the field: pitcher, catcher, first, second, and third baseman. Then there is a shortstop who plays between the second and third bases. The outfield consists of a left-, center-, and right-fielder. There are three bases, four including home plate. The game is divided into nine innings, with the home team batting at the end of each inning. Three strikes are an out, and four balls allows the batter to take a base."

"How many outs end an inning?"

"Three. And if the score is tied at the end of the ninth, then the game goes into extra innings."

"You're right, Moses. That is a lot of numbers."

He laughed softly. "A lot, but easy to follow. There are also umpires who are the officials and whose job is to make certain the rules are followed. The home plate umpire is responsible for calling balls and strikes thrown by the pitcher, and the other umpires are there to see if a player reaches a base safely. They also monitor the right- and left-field foul lines to determine whether a ball is in play or out. Balls that hit an outfield wall are usually doubles, or if the runner is fast, then maybe a triple. Balls hit over the wall are home runs, and if there are runners on bases, then all can reach home plate."

"I guess I'm going to have to attend a game to see what the excitement is all about."

"The Eagles are playing tomorrow, and if you want to

come to the game, then I can arrange to have tickets for you and your parents at the box office."

"Oh my gosh! My father would love that."

"What about your mother?"

Sallie Ann couldn't stop grinning. "I don't know about Mama, but I know me and Daddy will be there even if I have to get someone to carry him."

"That settles that. Now where is this ice cream shop you were telling me about?"

"Go past the next street and then turn right into an alleyway. There will be space in the back where you can park the car."

Moses wasn't disappointed they weren't able to see a movie, because it gave him more time to talk with Sallie Ann.

He had found her open, forthcoming about her life and what she wanted for her future. She was only sixteen, but there was something about her, notwithstanding her youthful appearance, which made her seem older. Her mother had paid to have her educated at a private school in the hope she would attract a young man of impressive means, and it had backfired. It could have become a reality if she hadn't forced her daughter to serve drinks in a dive bar. What, Moses mused, had the woman been thinking?

Even he, coming from a family of coal miners, would have been reluctant to marry a woman who'd earned money seducing men so they could buy booze at her family's bar. But that was before he'd met Sallie Ann. There was something about her that appealed to his protective instincts that he hadn't been able to act on when he lived with his parents; he hadn't been able to protect his sisters from their father whenever he'd gone into one of his rages and beat them. He should've interfered to stop the whippings, because if he had then he was certain his sisters wouldn't have dropped out of school to become wives of generational coal miners. Daisy Gilliam's letters were filled with the news that her daughters were enjoying their lives as wives and mothers.

His thoughts drifted from his mother and sisters to Sallie Ann, who he had discovered was an enigma. While most young girls talked about becoming secretaries, nurses, or teachers, she wanted to become a photographer, an occupation conventionally reserved for male photojournalists, and not a Colored woman. He'd read about James Van Der Zee in a Black magazine. He had made a name for himself during the Harlem Renaissance photographing Negro men and women in all phases of Black life.

Sallie Ann had also talked about wanting to travel, while in the past five weeks he had been to places he could never have imagined if he'd stayed in Nichols. Travel had changed him in so many ways. He'd traveled to other states and cities and had become an eyewitness to how his people were able to live without the obvious shackles of Jim Crow hindering their very existence. When he rode a bus in Chicago, he could sit anywhere he chose and not be relegated to the designated Colored section in the back.

Moses had followed through on his promise to give up reading about mobsters, gangsters, and outlaws to search out Black bookstores and newsstands where he could purchase books, magazines, and newspapers dedicated to the Negro reader. He had picked up a copy of *Opportunity: A Journal of Negro Life*, which highlighted the art and literature of the Harlem Renaissance, and read it several times cover to cover.

He was given the address of a bookstore in a Colored neighborhood and found old, backdated copies of *The Crisis* magazine, created in 1910 by W. E. B. Du Bois, and the official publication of the National Association for the Advancement of Colored People. Reading about his people and the advances they had made since gaining their freedom had filled him with a sense of pride that made him almost giddy.

When Lionel had mentioned about them playing in the Major Leagues, the only upside for Moses would be the possibility of earning more money. But after the confrontation with the White fan in Cleveland, Ohio, Moses preferred competing with and against players in the Negro Leagues. He didn't want to join a White team where he might face ongoing hostility from not only other teams but also his teammates. The owners of White teams had instituted a color line in baseball, and Moses was more than content not to cross it—not even for money.

He found the ice cream shop and noticed when he had opened the door to let Sallie Ann precede him, it was as if all movement and conversation stopped. At first Moses thought he had been recognized but saw that it was Sallie Ann who had garnered everyone's rapt attention.

Lowering his head, he pressed his mouth to her ear. "What's going on?" he whispered.

Chapter 21

Sallie Ann wanted to tell Moses that the tiny shop was crowded with kids from her school and their brother school. It was the first time any of them had seen her in the company of a boy.

She smiled up at him. "I'll explain it to you once we can find somewhere to sit."

He rested a hand at the small of her back. "You go and find two seats while I order for both of us." He stared at the flavors written on the blackboard. "Which flavor do you want?"

"Strawberry."

"Cone or cup?"

Sallie Ann paused. "I'll have a cup."

Whenever she came in, she ordered a cone and left. But not today. She was going to sit with Moses and enjoy the frozen dessert at her leisure. The shop had become a familiar hangout for most school kids. They usually gathered there after classes and on weekends when school was in session, and almost every day during summer recess.

She found a table with two chairs near the rear door, sat and waited for Moses. A girl in her math class came over to join her. She was grinning so wide that Sallie Ann swore she could see her tonsils.

"How are you doing, Sallie Ann?"

Sallie Ann flashed a saccharine smile. "I'm doing well, Diane." Diane Wells, the daughter of a Memphis dentist, barely spoke or acknowledged her in class or whenever they passed each other in the halls. Now, because she saw her come into the ice cream shop with a boy, Diane wanted to get into her business.

"Is *he* the reason you stopped coming to the school dances?"

Not today. Not ever. None of the stuck-up girls who wouldn't give her the time of day would get anything out of her about Moses. "I stopped going because they were always the same." She wanted to tell her it was the same snotty girls and snobbish boys who acted as if they were doing the girls a favor whenever they asked them to dance.

"The last two weren't the same," Diane said, as her eyes shifted from Moses and then back to Sallie Ann. "The Valentine's Day and Spring Frolic turned out better than the year before."

"It's okay, Diane. I had better things to do than waste my time standing around at a boring school dance."

Diane recoiled as if she'd been struck across the face. "Like working in your family's juke joint. Everyone in school knows that you work there on weekends. And that's why none of the boys at Calhoun want anything to do with you."

"That's where you are wrong, because she's too good for them."

Sallie Ann's head popped up when she heard the familiar male voice. She was so focused on Diane that she hadn't heard Moses's approach until he stood over the table. "Moses." His name was a whisper.

"Excuse me, miss, but I would like to sit down with my girlfriend."

Diane rose slowly to her feet, her eyes meeting Moses's before she walked back to where she sat with her friends.

Moses set a dish with strawberry ice cream on the table in front of Sallie Ann, then took the chair Diane had vacated. He set down his own dish of chocolate ice cream and handed Sallie Ann a spoon. "Are they always so cruel and nasty to you?"

Sallie Ann picked up her spoon, nodding. "I've heard whispers behind my back, but this is the first time anyone has said anything to my face."

Reaching for his spoon, Moses met her eyes. "The only thing I'm going to say is your classmates' parents are wasting their money sending their daughters to that fancy school. What happened to good manners?"

"Good manners and proper decorum only surface when necessary," Sallie Ann said in a hushed tone. "Otherwise, they are like pit vipers. Once they decide they don't like someone, they go in for the kill."

"Don't worry about them, Sallie Ann. They hide behind their parents' money, believing they are better than others. Money doesn't equal class."

She knew what Moses was talking about firsthand, because even with their fashionable clothes and fake smiles the girls were no better than those living in her part of town. So many of them had tongues like rapiers that would sever a person's confidence if they uncovered something unsavory about them. There had been rumors that a recent enrollee's family had moved from Mobile, Alabama, to Memphis because her father had been caught in a compromising situation with another man. The poor girl had been ostracized, and anonymous notes were left in her desk accusing her father of being a sodomite. Whether it was true or not, Sallie Ann believed it was none of their business and whatever his sexual predilection, it had nothing to do with his daughter. Then there were more rumors that the school board had accepted the girl's application for admission because her mother, a mulatto, had inherited a small fortune from her White father. Again, it was money that allowed board members to look the other way to keep the school viable.

"I have almost become immune to their nastiness, Moses. It's as if they get giddy when insulting or making fun of someone."

Moses swallowed a mouthful of ice cream. "It's probably because they feel the need to attack before someone attacks them or points out their faults."

"Now you sound like my grandmother, God bless the dead."

"Grandmothers and wisdom go together."

Sallie Ann gave Moses a lingering stare. "How old are you, Moses?"

He smiled. "Eighteen. Why?"

"There is something about you that makes me think you are so much older."

"How much older?" he asked.

"Like someone in their twenties."

"Well, I will be twenty in two years."

"That's not what I meant," she countered.

Placing an elbow on the table, Moses rested his chin on a fist. "What exactly do you mean?"

"I don't know how to explain it, but you talk as if you have experienced so much more than a boy who is eighteen."

"I think it's because I love books. Reading has allowed me to travel back in time and to countries I have heard of and will never travel to."

"How many books have you read?" Sallie Ann asked.

"Too many to count. It's not only books but newspapers, and now magazines."

"I suppose that's why you got good grades and were offered scholarships to attend college."

Moses shrugged his shoulders. "Could be."

"Now why are you being modest? You are smart and a talented baseball player. That's a winning combination."

His eyebrows lifted. "If you say so."

Reaching across the table, Sallie Ann rested her hand on his shoulder, encountering solid muscle under the cotton fabric. "I say so, Moses Gilliam."

A shadow fell over the table, and she glanced up to see a boy who attended her brother school. There had been a time when she'd had a crush on him, but that was in the past.

Richard James cleared his throat, his protruding Adam's apple bobbing up and down in his throat. "Excuse me, Mr. Gilliam, but is it possible for you to give me your autograph? My father is a fan of the Eagles."

Moses looked up at the tall, skinny, eyeglasses-wearing boy who kept glancing over his shoulder at a table filled with kids who were watching him. "I would, but that depends on something."

"What's that, Mr. Gilliam?"

"I want the girl who insulted my girlfriend to apologize to her."

The boy's eyelids fluttered wildly. "You mean Diane?"

Moses nodded. "If that's her name, then yes."

"I'll ask her if she will."

"Not ask," Moses retorted. "Tell her or I'm not signing anything."

"Was that necessary, Moses?" Sallie Ann whispered when the boy turned on his heel to return to his friends.

"Very necessary, Sallie Ann. Do you think I'm going to

sit here and watch you being insulted and ridiculed to your face? If you're going to be my girlfriend, then be prepared for me to protect you whenever I can. And I meant what I said about her apologizing. What she said to you was not only nasty but unnecessary."

Moses wanted to tell Sallie Ann because he hadn't been able to protect his sisters from their father's wrath, and he did not intend for that to happen to her. He liked Sallie Ann Thompson, and asking her to be his girlfriend wasn't something he took lightly.

He'd told Lionel that he had time to think about marrying and settling down with a family; that at eighteen he knew he wasn't financially able to take care of a wife but if he continued to play ball and save his money, then it could become a reality in a couple of years. He would turn twenty in two years, and Sallie Ann eighteen, and if they were still dating, then there was the possibility they could have a future together.

Pushing back his chair, he stood when Diane approached the table. Her eyes were filled with tears and her hands were fisted. It was obvious she was angry and embarrassed.

Moses angled his head, glaring at her. "Yes?"

She exhaled an audible sigh. "I'm sorry, Sallie Ann, for what I said to you."

Moses watched Sallie Ann's reaction to the apology. There was no expression on her face. "I hope it won't happen again."

"Oh, it won't," Diane said quickly.

"Okay. Now you can tell your friend I will sign something for his father."

Sallie Ann felt like Cinderella in the fairy tale when the prince came to her house to rescue her from her evil stepmother and sisters. Moses had reversed the attitudes of her classmates when he'd insisted Diane apologize to her. Not only had he signed autographs for Richard's father, but for everyone who approached him. She watched in awe at his patience as he chatted briefly with each one before scrawling *MoGil*, the nickname sports writers had given him, on scraps of paper. All the kids who had shunned her now were grinning in her face.

As far as she was concerned, their feeble attempts to befriend her were false; she would never be accepted into their privileged social circle because of her family origins. Saloonkeepers did not rub shoulders with medical doctors, lawyers, nurses, teachers, or legitimate businessowners.

She had known early on that she was accepted at Miss Cora's School for Girls because her mother was willing to pay the tuition, which was needed to keep the school open following a drastic drop in enrollment during the Depression.

"Do you think they will treat you differently now?" Moses asked as he pulled into the driveway leading to her house and parked behind her father's car.

"It wouldn't matter if they do. I still don't want anything to do with them. One incident isn't enough for me to forget how they've treated me these past few years. I was happier at my old school where the teachers were stricter and demanded respect."

Moses shut off the car's engine. "You only have two more years before you graduate."

"I don't have two years, Moses. When the school year resumes next month, I will be a senior. I will graduate a month after celebrating my seventeenth birthday."

Her disclosure that she would finish school earlier than he'd believed meant Moses had to rethink his plans. He'd just begun playing ball, and he had depleted nearly half his savings purchasing the sewing machine for his mother. That meant it wasn't possible for him to save enough in one year to support not only himself, but a wife.

"Are you willing to wait two years?"

"For what?" she asked.

"For me."

Her lips parted as she smiled. "A lot can happen in two years."

He shifted on his seat to give her a direct stare. "You're right. It may be too soon to ask you, but are you willing to wait a couple of years to see if we can make a go of it as man and wife?"

Sallie Ann's heart was beating a double-time rhythm, making it difficult for her to breathe and think straight. "Do you realize what you're saying, Moses?"

He blinked slowly at the same time he nodded. "I know exactly what I am asking, Sallie Ann Thompson."

"But . . . but," she stuttered, "what if you meet someone in a couple of years and forget all about me?"

"That's not going to happen."

He had said it with so much conviction that Sallie Ann believed him. "I want to say yes, but that's something you should talk about with my father."

"Of course." Moses got out of the car and came around to assist her.

When he reached for her hand, she was certain he felt her trembling. Sallie Ann wanted to believe she was dreaming, and when she woke, she would be alone. That Moses Gilliam had been just a figment of her imagination. He was a hometown hero and a recognizable celebrity. His asking her to wait for him was a proposal of marriage, and she found it more frightening than exciting.

Her parents were relaxing on the porch, a cane resting against her father's favorite chair. Jimmie reached for the cane and hoisted himself to stand, as a smile swept over his fleshy features.

"Welcome, son. When my Sallie Ann told me you wanted to take her out, I couldn't believe I was talking to *the* Moses Gilliam."

Sallie Ann shared a smile with her mother when Moses shook her father's hand. Walking over to Maddie, she took her mother's arm and led her off the porch and into the parlor. "Moses wants to talk to Daddy about something," she whispered.

Maddie looked as if she was going to faint when she clutched her chest. "He wants to marry you?"

"No, Mama," she said, laughing. "He wants to ask Daddy if he would object to my marrying him after I complete high school and he's saved enough money playing ball to take care of a family."

Maddie sank down to a chair and closed her eyes. "Thank goodness for that." She paused. "What did you tell him?"

"I told him he had to speak to my father," Sallie Ann said, as she folded her body down to the sofa. "I like him, Mama. But so many things can happen in two years; however, there is one thing I know for certain and that is I'm never going to date or marry any of the boys who go to the Calhoun School." She told Maddie about the incident at the ice cream shop and felt sorry that she had revealed it when her mother looked as if she was going to cry.

"I never realized it was that bad," Maddie said.

"I stopped complaining because you thought I just wanted to go back to my old school. Those girls are horrible, and the boys aren't much better."

Maddie took her hands, holding them gently. "Do you want to go back to the public school?"

Sallie Ann shook her head. "No, because I don't want

those heifers to think they got the better of me. I'm going to stay and graduate and then if Moses still wants to marry me, I will become his wife."

A sad smile flitted over Maddie's mouth. "I'm glad he stood up for you."

"What he did was protect me, Mama. And that's what men are supposed to do if they care about a woman. Protect her from any and everything."

"He sounds like a nice boy and I'm glad you like him."

Sallie Ann wanted to tell her mother that she was glad Moses liked her, and she was more than willing to wait for him even though she wasn't so naïve to believe he wouldn't attract women everywhere he went. He was a celebrity and was expected to pose for photographs with his fans. It was something she not only had to accept but also get used to if she hoped to become Mrs. Moses Gilliam.

Jimmie Thompson, leaning on his cane, limped into the parlor, Moses following. He sat down heavily on an armchair, and motioned for Moses to sit on the sofa next to Sallie Ann.

"I just had a chat with your young man," he said, smiling at his daughter, "and he's asked my permission not only to date you, but if I would object to his marrying you in the future."

Sallie Ann held her breath. "What did you say, Daddy?"

"I said yes to both." Jimmie sighed. "He also asked that you no longer work at the bar."

"What did you say?" she repeated.

"I told him okay."

Sallie Ann blew out an inaudible breath as she reached for Moses's hand, lacing their fingers together. "Thank you, Daddy."

She didn't know how Moses did it or what he had said

to her father to make him change his mind about her working at Tommy's Joint. She would continue to help her mother cook but would no longer work as a server.

"Moses has offered to give us tickets for tomorrow's game, and the timing is perfect because we don't open for business on Sundays."

Maddie smiled. "I have never been to a baseball game, so this is going to be a treat for me."

It was not only going to be a treat for her mother but also for Sallie Ann. She was going to the ballpark to see her boyfriend play and to witness why folks were calling him a hometown hero.

She walked Moses to the door when he announced that he had to leave. He kissed her cheek when it was her mouth she'd wanted him to kiss, and she watched as he backed out of the driveway and drove away.

Her parents were still in the parlor when she walked past and headed for her bedroom, closing the door. The events of the day whirled around in her head like a spinning top. When she'd gotten up earlier that morning to help her mother cook, she never could have imagined her date with Moses would end with an anticipated marriage proposal two years from now. If she was dreaming, then she never wanted to wake up.

Even though she wasn't in love with Moses yet, everything about him made it so easy for her to like him. She was also glad that she had two years in which to make up her mind if she would be ready to marry a celebrity.

"I've got two years," she whispered.

Opening a drawer in the dresser, she removed the diary she had concealed under a stack of lingerie. She unlocked it with a key and flipped to a blank page. Sitting with her legs crossed on the bed, she uncapped a fountain pen and wrote down what she had experienced with her first and hopefully her last boyfriend.

Sallie Ann drew hearts around his name when she finished writing. She read and reread what she had written, then closed and locked the book, before secreting it in the drawer.

Only days before, the United States had celebrated its one hundred sixtieth birthday while for Sallie Ann Thompson, she was beginning her first with the man she hoped to spend the rest of her life with.

CHAPTER 22

Harper reread what she'd typed, editing and tweaking as she went along before printing the pages and adding them to the stack on the table next to her laptop. It had taken three days to come up with what she'd wanted to create for the Thompsons. First there was Sallie Ann, followed by her mother and father. She was more than familiar with mothers like Maddie Thompson because of the girls who'd attended the same private school where her mother had enrolled her.

Martell had risen above her family's working-class, blue-collar existence when she'd become the first to attend and graduate from college. However, it hadn't been her intent to marry a professional ballplayer, while Maddie had dreamed of her daughter marrying up. That meant she wanted Sallie Ann to marry a boy who came from a prominent Colored family. As she was creating the characters, Harper hadn't realized until she reread what she'd written that there were parallels between the fictional Madeline Thompson and the real Martell Fleming.

Although her mother had never openly voiced it, Harper knew Martell enrolling her in the private all-girl school had set her on a course where, if she did meet someone from a prominent family, she would easily be able to navigate within their world.

There was also an acute difference between the economic status of the two women. As an educated professional, Martell could earn enough to sustain whatever lifestyle she chose, while Maddie was forced to rely on her husband and brothers-in-law for financial security. Martell had married Daniel Fleming for love. Maddie had married Jimmie for financial survival.

When Harper read the notations in her great-grandfather's notebooks, she realized Kelton Fleming had been awestruck, mesmerized even, by the teenage girl he'd encountered for the first time. After sharing only one date, he knew he wanted to marry her. It hadn't taken Daniel Fleming two years but only three months after being introduced to Martell Shepherd to make her his wife.

"Harper, don't you think it's time that you get ready to greet your dinner guest? It's three, and Cheney should be here any minute."

She glanced over her shoulder to find her grandfather standing in the doorway to the sunroom. He'd returned from his weeklong outing with his former military buddies more animated than she had seen him since she'd come to stay for the summer. Harper had listened patiently while he talked about touring Civil War battlefields, the Great Smoky Mountains, and the Natchez Trace Parkway.

Harper caught him up on what she'd been doing while he was away. She told him about running into Cheney Sanders, who was now working and living in Nashville. She explained that Cheney had invited her to his home for Sunday brunch and she had promised to return the favor. Her grandfather said he was anxious to reunite with the young man who had come to his farm to hang out with his grandsons, which now seemed so long ago. She had sent Cheney a text, inviting him to dinner, and he accepted with a smiley face emoji.

It had taken hours to decide what she wanted to prepare. Still cognizant of her grandfather's elevated blood pressure and cholesterol levels, Harper had decided to roast a turkey with all the trimmings. She ordered a fresh ten-pounder from a local butcher, recalling that her grandmother had brined all her chickens and turkeys before cooking them. Collard greens, potato salad, turkey sausage cornbread stuffing, and giblet gravy completed her dinner menu.

She had been in a quandary when it came to dessert, vacillating between pie or cobbler, but in the end, she'd decided on strawberry shortcake after pushing the shopping cart down the aisle in the supermarket's produce section. The berries were large, ruby-red, and not overly ripe.

"Yes, Grandpa. I'm coming." The words were barely off her tongue when the chiming of the doorbell echoed throughout the house.

Bernard winked at her. "I'll get the door."

Cheney felt as if he had stepped back in time when greeting Bernard Fleming for the first time in almost two decades. With the exception of the silvering of his hair and a fine network of lines around his eyes, not much had changed about the tall man with the ramrod posture.

He extended his right hand. "It's good seeing you again, Mr. Bernard, after so many years."

Nodding, Bernard shook the proffered hand. "Same here. Look at you. All grown up."

Cheney laughed softly. "Time has a way of doing that to a person." He became serious. "I'm sorry that Miss Nadine can't be here to make this reunion complete."

"You're right about that," Bernard said as he opened the door wider. "Come on in and rest yourself."

Cheney handed him a colorful shopping bag. "I can't remember what you drink, but there's some libation in that bag."

"You can't remember because Nadine would never let me drink around you kids. She used to say it was in bad taste."

"Miss Nadine had something there," Cheney said as he followed Bernard through the entryway of the ranch-style house constructed with an open floor plan. A family room flowed into a dining area and beyond that a kitchen. He sniffed the air. "Something smells good."

"I never thought I'd say this, but my grandbaby girl can cook as well as my Nadine."

He wanted to tell the older man that he'd sampled Harper's baking skills and in two days he had devoured the four remaining servings of sour cream Bundt cake she'd baked for their Sunday brunch.

Cheney hadn't taken more than a half dozen steps when Harper walked into the family room. He knew it was impolite, but again he'd found himself staring at her, unable to look away as if he'd been pulled into a forcefield from which there was no escape. She appeared utterly feminine in an ice-blue linen sundress ending at her knees. He managed to pull his gaze away from her bare legs and feet to her hair styled in a twist behind one ear. She smiled, shattering the spell she had unknowingly woven whenever they shared the same space.

"Hello again."

Cheney returned her smile. "Same here."

Bernard handed Harper the shopping bag. "Cheney brought this."

Her eyebrows lifted slightly when she peered into the bag. "Nice. Grandpa, I know you're going to enjoy the bourbon. Thank you, Cheney."

He nodded. It had taken him a while to go through his wine collection to select bottles of red and rosé and an aged bourbon. He had become a connoisseur of wines and liquors after attending a wine-tasting event hosted by the law firm's managing partner. Cheney began collecting bottles of domestic and foreign red, white, and blush wines to add to his collection of aged scotch, whiskey, and bourbon. Once he'd sold the house in Falls Church, he'd packed the bottles in crates and stored them in a spare room at his Alexandria rental, rather than in the storage unit with the household furnishings.

Bernard clasped his hands. "Cheney, I will show you where to wash up before we sit down to eat."

Nothing had changed over the years. Whenever he was invited to eat at the farm, Mr. Bernard or Miss Nadine had ordered everyone to the bathroom to wash up before sitting at the table.

Harper had set out a platter with the turkey, serving bowls with collard greens, potato salad, cornbread-sausage stuffing, and a gravy boat with giblet gravy on the table by the time her grandfather and Cheney entered the dining area. Wine and water goblets, and chilled bottles of white wine and rosé, and two bottles of Perrier were the offered beverages.

"Wow," Cheney said under his breath. "This looks like a feast."

"It's just Sunday dinner," Harper countered. "You do remember sharing Sunday dinner with us at the farm?"

Cheney tapped his forehead with his index finger. "It's tattooed on my brain."

Bernard chuckled. "I must confess that I'm spoiled, because I wake up every morning wondering what Harper is going to cook. I really don't know what I'm going to do once she goes back to Chicago."

Harper glared at her grandfather. "What I don't want is for you to take up with that woman again who used to cook for you."

Bernard lowered his eyes. "I must admit I feel a lot better since you've been feeding me."

She wanted to remind her grandfather that she had taken great pains to prepare health-conscious meals for him, while limiting the amount of fat and sodium in his favorite recipes. "Grandpa, will you please carve the turkey?"

Bernard pulled out a chair and seated her, indicated where

Cheney should sit, then picked up the carving knife and fork and began carving the golden-brown bird with the skill of a surgeon.

Serving dishes were passed around the table and, as if it had been decades ago, Harper, Bernard, and Cheney held hands while Bernard said grace. He blessed the food, the hands that had prepared it, and the farmers who had grown it.

Harper knew his reference to farmers was to honor his father, Kelton Fleming, who had fulfilled his dream to become a farmer. Her great-grandfather had written in his notebooks that owning land meant having power. Wars were fought to gain more land, and he felt the more land Negroes owned the more they could seize and control economic power. Bernard had inherited his father's farm and had continued to work it in-between his shifts at the prison.

I'm truly home. Cheney had moved back to Tennessee after twenty years, but sitting at a table with Bernard and Harper made it real. He hadn't moved back to Memphis, but Nashville, and the odds of him reconnecting with Harper's grandfather were slim to none. It was as if everything was in suspended animation where he was a teenage boy and Bernard and Nadine were his adoptive grandparents who'd treated him no differently than they did their grandsons and granddaughter. Mr. Bernard was more tolerant, while Miss Nadine was like a drill sergeant barking orders and expecting them to be followed without question. She was the opposite of his mother, whose mantra was *if not today, then tomorrow*.

"Mr. Bernard, Harper told me you reconnected with some of your old army buddies."

Bernard stared at Cheney over the rim of his water goblet. "We had a blast."

"How long had it been since you all had gotten together?"

"Let's see now," he said, seemingly deep in thought, "it has to be at least fifteen years."

"Fifteen years is a long time, Grandpa," Harper remarked.

"You're right. We were talking about getting together again every other month. They said they want to come and stay with me when they come to Nashville next month, because with all of us on fixed incomes, it's somewhat prohibitive to stay in hotels while having to pay for food."

"What did you tell them, Grandpa?"

"I told them that can't happen at this time because you're staying with me, and that means one less bedroom."

"You all can stay with me," Cheney said, as soon as the thought entered his head. "My house is big enough for you and your buddies to have their own bedrooms and bathrooms." He noticed Harper and Bernard staring at him as if he'd suddenly grown an extra eye. "What's the matter?"

"Do you know what you are saying, son?"

Cheney smiled. "I know exactly what I said, Mr. Bernard. My house is too big for one person. No, let me correct that. Six bedrooms, and seven bathrooms are too big for two or even three people. I've always thought of myself as your adopted grandson, so Grandpa Flem, will you accept my offer to open up my home to you and your army buddies?"

Bernard shook his head, smiling. "Now I know why you decided to become a lawyer, because you can be pretty persuasive."

"Is that a yes, Mr. Bernard?"

"Which one am I, Cheney? Mr. Bernard or Grandpa Flem?"

Cheney adjusted his glasses as he stared at Harper. "I like Grandpa Flem." It was what she and her brothers called Bernard because they'd had two living grandfathers.

Bernard flashed a sheepish grin. "Nadine used to say, 'That boy is going to weasel his way into our family one way or another.'"

Cheney wanted to tell Bernard that his late wife was right. He hadn't known it at the time, but he had preferred Craig and Danny's friendship to the boys he'd grown up with. Perhaps it was because their father was a professional baseball player in a big city with two professional baseball teams. He'd become enthralled with Harper's brothers' stories about criminals who had become the models for gangster movies, and the rumors of corruption that was pervasive in Chicago's politics, while he had grown up in a state with a history of Jim Crow, having had the odious distinction of being the birthplace of the Ku Klux Klan and also bearing the shame of being where Martin Luther King Jr. had been assassinated. Although they would occasionally try to top one another with stories about their home states, it would be overshadowed whenever they issued challenges as to who was the fastest swimmer or who could stay underwater longer. They were teenage boys with out-of-control hormones that could only be assuaged with physical activity.

Ironically, instead of Bernard Fleming inviting him to share a meal with his family, it was Cheney who had offered to open up his home to the elderly man and his friends who were bonding over their experiences in a war that had taken more than fifty thousand American lives.

"Miss Nadine is right, because now that I'm a part of your family you can't get rid of me."

Bernard nodded. "And I don't want to."

"And before your friends come and spend the week, I'd like to invite you and Harper over for a weekend. I seem to remember that someone is having a birthday soon, and it would be a good time to celebrate."

"I can't believe you remembered my birthday," Harper said to Cheney.

He smiled. "Are you kidding? Miss Nadine always made a big deal about your birthday when she would bake a cake and cook all your favorite dishes."

"She sure did," Bernard confirmed.

"What's it going to be?" Cheney asked. "Are y'all coming for that weekend?"

Harper lowered her eyes. "Okay. Count me in."

Bernard chuckled under his breath. "That's a yes for me, too."

Cheney gripped the handles of a bag filled with containers of leftovers as Bernard walked him out to his car. Harper had outdone herself with dinner and he hadn't been embarrassed when he had second helpings of everything. Dessert was homemade strawberry shortcake topped with freshly whipped cream that literally melted on his tongue. Bernard had opened the bottle of bourbon, and poured a small amount of the golden liquor into warmed snifters that had enhanced its smoky essence.

"I didn't want to belabor the point in front of Harper," Bernard said in a quiet voice, "but are you serious about my friends hanging out at your place for a week?"

"I don't know how more serious I can be, Mr. Bernard."

"I thought I was Grandpa Flem."

Cheney narrowed his eyes behind the lenses of his glasses. "Why are you trying to be obstinate, Grandpa? I told you before that my home is open for you and your friends to stay, and I don't intend to debate my decision with you. You'll have the complete run of the house inside and out. There's a gym, media room, and game room in the basement if you decide to work out, watch television, or shoot pool. There's also an outside kitchen where you can grill and a loggia if you decide you want to relax and do absolutely nothing more than inhale and exhale."

"Are you doing this for me or for Harper?" Bernard asked.

"What are you talking about?" Cheney hadn't bothered to disguise his annoyance as he questioned Harper's grandfather.

"I may be old, Cheney, but I'm not blind nor stupid. You've got a thing for my granddaughter, and it didn't start when you ran into her a couple of weeks ago. It started a long time ago when you used to come to the farm to play with my grandsons. I'd see you staring at her, and I knew then that you liked her the way a boy likes a girl. And because she was too young for you, I told my grandsons to warn you to stay away from her."

"Is that what you're saying now? That I should stay away from her?"

"No, Cheney. I will not interfere in my granddaughter's life, because she's a grown woman capable of making her own decisions."

"Even if you were to interfere it wouldn't make a difference to me because I've already told Harper how I feel about her." Cheney nearly laughed when he saw Bernard's shocked expression. "She knows I like her, not like a boy likes a girl, but as a man likes a woman."

"What did she say to this?"

"You'll have to ask her that for yourself."

Bernard shook his head. "You know I'm not going to do that."

"Then, let everything take its course. I'm aware that Harper is only going to be in Nashville through the summer, and hopefully that will give me enough time to convince her to stay."

"Stay for what?" Bernard questioned.

"To see if she's willing to let me share what I have with her."

A beat passed. "Are you saying that you are in love with my granddaughter?"

There came another pregnant pause before Cheney said, "Right now I don't know. Whenever I think of Harper, I can't put my emotions into perspective when I reflect on how I reacted to her when we were teenagers. Now there is the adult Harper, who's so independent and confident that it frightens me. Everything about her says she doesn't need a man, while I want her to not only want but also need me."

"There are different degrees of wanting and needing, son.

We want women to need us because we are raised to protect women, and we want them to love us as much or more than we love them."

"Why more?"

A faraway expression flitted over Bernard's features. "There are times when we mess up and we count on their love because we want forgiveness."

"I know you're not talking about cheating on your wife."

Bernard lowered his gaze. "Yes. I messed around with a woman, and when Nadine found out she was ready to leave me, but I begged, groveled, and pleaded with her to stay and promised it would never happen again."

"Did it?"

"No. Once was enough for me to come to the realization whatever was in those streets wasn't worth losing what I had at home."

Cheney was shocked by Bernard's revelation that he had cheated on his wife; he had thought they were the perfect couple. "I'm glad you came to your senses before you lost a good woman."

"And that she was. She was the best wife, and I knew I'd been blessed when she decided to stay with me."

Cheney thought about his own marriage. Although he hadn't cheated on his wife, he wasn't what he'd thought of as a good husband. He neglected Michelle for far too long and his inability to give her not what she wanted but what she needed drove her into the arms of another man.

"I never make promises, because I'm not certain whether I will be able to keep them, but I will promise you that I won't cheat on Harper. I never cheated on my ex-wife or on any woman I ever dated."

Bernard angled his head. "I love my granddaughter, and only want the best for her, so I wish you luck in convincing her that you two can be happy together."

"Thank you, Grandpa."

Pressing a button on the fob, Cheney unlocked the door to his vehicle, and placed the bag on the floor behind the driver's seat. He drove home replaying his conversation with Bernard in his head. The man had known of his attraction to his granddaughter and had instructed his grandsons to keep them apart. That was then and this was now because Cheney's attraction for Harper was stronger than ever. They weren't kids faced with interfering adults, and while he didn't know if Harper wanted more than friendship, he was willing to wait until she decided if she wanted to stay in Nashville or go back to Chicago.

CHAPTER 23

Harper paced the length of the sunroom as she attempted to compose her thoughts enough to continue writing. Pacing was something she did whenever she was deep in thought, but lately it had become more frequent. She had gone over the history of Black baseball, highlighting dates in her notes. Although her novel was a work of fiction, Harper wanted some of it to be factual. Before 1946, Blacks played in separate leagues because of the color of their skin, so in the Negro Leagues "only the color of the ball was white."

She stopped pacing and closed her eyes. Who was she fooling? It wasn't writer's block that was preventing her from writing but her inability to stop thinking about Cheney Sanders. Why, she thought, did he have to possess most of the qualities she was looking for in a man with whom she could have an open and ongoing relationship?

A relationship wasn't what she wanted or needed now. There were other things she had to sort out before agreeing to see someone exclusively. When she'd met Zion Robinson, Harper liked that he wanted them to see each other casually. While she'd gone along with his suggestion of casual, she hadn't anticipated that seeing each other several times a month would turn into lapses of two and occasionally three months. He would turn up unexpectedly and ask to see her, and she did. Until one day she realized she'd become a booty call. Even if she'd had her doubts about his using her for sex, it was confirmed when he called her by another woman's name in the throes of climaxing. What really took the rag off the brush—an expression she'd learned from her grandmother—was his denial that he knew a Jameeka. She wasn't Jameeka and didn't want to be either. The mystery woman did not have to share Zion with her, because Harper banished him from her bed and her life.

Harper had to admit she was shocked when Cheney had offered to open his home for Bernard and his former military friends to get together. She recognized a change in her grandfather after he'd returned from his weeklong reunion when he talked incessantly about the number of Civil War battles that were fought in Tennessee. He claimed to have felt an immense sadness when he visited Shiloh National Military Park. He experienced the same when he paid a visit to the Vietnam War Memorial in D.C. and recognized the names of some of his fallen comrades. She didn't like war stories because two of her brothers were active-duty military, and both had completed several tours in the Middle East.

Harper realized that pacing while thinking about Cheney and her grandfather was preventing her from writing. She had to get out of the house, if only for a few hours, to clear her head. Sallie Ann, her parents, Moses, and his teammates had become living, breathing people who had begun communicating with her, telling her how they felt and what they wanted to say. They now lived in her head, but there were nights when they wouldn't permit a restful night's sleep.

"If you keep pacing like that, you'll wear a hole in the carpet."

Harper stopped her pacing to find her grandfather standing at the entrance to the sunroom. She'd been so deep in thought she wasn't aware that he had been watching her. "I was just thinking about something."

Bernard walked in. "Something or someone?"

Harper smiled. "Both," she said, as he reached for her hand and led her over to a love seat, waiting until she sat before folding his body down beside her.

"You've got to lighten up yourself, grandbaby girl. You get up before the sun comes up to make breakfast, then you come in here to start writing. You get so into it that I must remind you to eat. I know you're excited about writing a book about my father, but don't let it become an obsession where you don't leave room for anything else in your life."

"Other than you, right now there isn't anything else I want or need in my life."

"That's not true, Harper," Bernard countered. "You're a beautiful, talented young woman who should be dating, going on girl trips, and having the time of her life before she . . ."

"She what, Grandpa?" Harper asked when his words trailed off. She met his eyes. "Before I settle down to become some man's wife and the mother of his children?"

"I don't understand you, Harper."

"What is there to understand, Grandpa?"

"Why you make excuses as to why you can't or won't do something because you're so single-focused on becoming a sports reporter. What if it never happens?"

Harper bit her lip to stop the acerbic words on her tongue from spewing out. "I won't know that unless I try," she said between clenched teeth.

Bernard gently squeezed her fingers. "But you did try. When you applied for a position at that biweekly it should have been to cover sports and not the social and political beat. That's where you made your first mistake."

"I told the editor during my first interview that I wanted to cover sporting events. He told me to wait because the sports reporter had hinted that he was going to retire and relocate in a couple of years once his kids graduated from college, then I would take over from him."

"I shouldn't have to tell you that talk is cheap. People say things, then change their minds. What you did, Harper, was stay at the party even after the lights were turned off."

"Did you expect me to call my boss a liar to his face once I discovered I was never going to replace the sports reporter because the man had no intention of retiring or relocating?"

"Yes. You should've confronted him. But you stayed, hoping and praying what you wished for would become a reality. It was only when you'd had enough that you left. When Daniel called and told me that you'd quit, I told him it was about time. He also told me that he could've gotten you a position at one of the television networks, but you turned him down."

"That's because I didn't want folks to say I got it because of my father's influence."

"Do you think it bothered Ken Griffy Jr. that his father was also a professional baseball player when he decided he also wanted to play baseball? And that they made baseball history by becoming the first son and father to play on the same team at the same time? It happens all the time in sports, so it shouldn't be any different in sports broadcasting."

"Grandpa, I'm aware of fathers, sons, and even grandsons who have played generational sports, but it's different for women. If I must interview any of them, then it would have to be conducted along sidelines, while male reporters are allowed to conduct their interviews in locker rooms."

"Come on now, Harper. No man wants to be interviewed by a woman while he's standing in front of her butt naked."

Harper made a sucking sound with her tongue and teeth. "The ones I've met are hardly modest."

She had lost count of the number of athletes she'd been introduced to who had hit on her when she accompanied her father to sporting events, Some would take the hint and leave her alone, while others were more persistent until she was forced to say that she just wasn't into him.

"There will always be inequities between the sexes, Harper, so you must choose your battles. Have you given any thought to going back to teaching?"

"Believe it or not, I have, when I was talking with Cheney about assigning books written by people of color to my students during Black History Month. I gave the class a list of titles and authors to read, and the last week of the month each student was given five minutes to critique what they'd read."

"How did it go?"

"It was wonderful. Those interested in poetry and hadn't read Langston Hughes, Nikki Giovanni, or Maya Angelou were writing their names down so they could check their books out of the library."

"Do you realize that you became an inspiration for another generation of readers?"

"That was what I was hoping."

"Think about it, Harper. You seemed happiest and content when you were teaching, so that could be your calling."

"Even though I enjoyed teaching I recognized it wasn't my passion. I wanted to become a journalist."

"You are a journalist, but, like teaching, you've walked away from that."

It suddenly hit Harper since graduating from college she'd left teaching to intern for a magazine, then worked for two newspapers, and now she was attempting to write a novel. Her career mirrored her love life, with her inability to form positive relationships. She had this rule that she had to date someone for at least three months before taking their relationship to the next level. The men who had admitted they were attracted to her complained that she tended to control their relationship with a set of conditions, and it was thanks, but no thanks. Had her life become the adage of a rolling stone gathering no moss?

"I'm still a journalist, Grandpa," she retorted defensively. "It's just that I haven't found my niche."

"Find your niche, or find yourself? It's time you stand still long enough to take stock of who Harper Lauren Fleming is and what she needs to make her life fulfilling. You're blessed, grandbaby girl, because nowadays many thirty-something working women don't have the option of walking away from one job before having another one to go to. I'm talking about those who are married, divorced, or even single mothers. You grew up with a platinum spoon in your mouth because your father was a professional athlete making millions for working an average of six months a year. You grew up in a large house in an affluent suburb and attended private schools all your life. When you graduated it wasn't with a boatload of student loans that would take years for you to pay off. You're living the dream many young women wish they could have, yet you sit here and bitch and moan because the one thing you want most has eluded you. Have you thought that perhaps it's not for you? That maybe you should go back to teaching, even though teachers don't get the pay or appreciation they deserve?"

Harper sat, stunned and unable to speak because her grandfather had just chastised her—something he had never done in the past. No, she thought. It wasn't chastising, but more like a dressing down. His words had cut like a knife, and she wondered if her complaining to him about not becoming a sportswriter was the straw that had broken the proverbial camel's back.

"I know I'm blessed, Grandpa."

"Then dammit, act like it, Harper. Stop beating yourself up about what you don't have and concentrate on what you do. Stop with the rules you've set up when dealing with men. Nadine told me that you treat your relationships like baseball, with balls and strikes, and if you, as the umpire, decide you don't like that he has challenged a third strike, then you throw him out of the game."

Harper felt tears prick the backs of her eyelids and bit her lip to regain her composure. "That's not fair," she whispered.

"You think I'm not being fair because you don't want to hear the truth? Nadine loved all her grandchildren, but even though she wouldn't admit it, she loved you more than your brothers. She wanted the best for you. She wanted you to be financially independent and not have to rely on your parents to take care of you. That's why you were the beneficiary of her life insurance. I didn't want to tell you, but after I buried Nadine, I revised my will to make you the beneficiary of everything I own, and that includes this house and the monies I received from the sale of the farm."

Waves of shock washed over Harper as her breath caught in her lungs. "Why, Grandpa?" she asked, recovering her voice.

"You shouldn't have to ask me why, Harper. You're going to be thirty-four and you still don't have a chick, child, or a man in your life. And with you job hopping, you're going to need some financial stability. I purchased this house without a mortgage with a portion of the money I got from selling the farm, so it will go to you when the good Lord calls me home. You don't have to be a senior citizen to live in this community, so you can either elect to keep the house or sell it."

"What about my brothers? Will you leave them anything?"

Bernard shook his head. "No. Me and your father agreed some time ago that Nadine and I would take care of you, while he had set aside trusts for his children and grandchildren. Once he retired from playing ball, he set up an annuity for Martell. The Flemings have come a long way from being slaves and scratching out an existence as coal miners. My father had to fight two wars—one as a baseball player in a segregated league, and another on foreign soil to stop fascism from taking over the world. Two decades later, I was drafted to fight in a war we had no chance of winning. It's like baseball and the military is in our DNA. Your father was selected as a third-round pick to play for the White Sox, and his sons, my grandsons, decided they wanted a career in the military.

Harper, you are the only one who isn't a professional athlete or in the military, so you're going to have to figure out how to distinguish yourself as a Fleming."

"How can I do that, Grandpa?"

Bernard pointed to the table with her laptop and printer. "Finish your book. You are a journalist, and no one else will be able to write our family's story. You claim it's going to be fictional, so write whatever you want."

"Even if it's scandalous?" Harper asked, aware that some of Kelton's entries about his interaction with women were inexcusable.

"No one is perfect. We all have our faults and some of us have a lot of crosses to bear. Kelton Fleming was my father, and even though I loved him, I knew he was an imperfect man just like I am."

With wide eyes, Harper stared at her grandfather, wondering if he had cheated on Nadine. She shook her head as if to banish the thought. She had always believed what went on between a man and his wife was of no concern to others unless they chose to share it.

"We all are imperfect, Grandpa."

Bernard smiled. "You too?"

Throwing back her head, Harper laughed. "Yes. Me too."

Bernard also laughed. "Not according to Nadine." He released her hand and pushed to his feet. "I've taken up enough of your time, so I'm going out for a drive."

Harper watched his retreat. "Be careful out there, Grandpa. And make certain there's no lead in your right foot."

"I've stopped speeding," Bernard said, glancing over his shoulder.

"Only after the judge threatened to suspend your license after umpteen citations."

Bernard stopped and turned to look at her. "If that's the case then you'll be forced to move here and drive me around."

"That's blackmail!"

"Wasn't it Malcolm who said by any means necessary?"

"Oh no, you didn't go to Malcolm."

"Speaking of Malcolm, the older Cheney gets, the more he looks like Malcolm X."

Harper didn't know why, but she didn't see the marked resemblance between Cheney Sanders and the late firebrand civil activist. They both wore glasses and had similar eye color, but Malcolm was taller, and his complexion was lighter than Cheney's. Perhaps it was because she continued to see Cheney as the boy she'd had a crush on and not as the man who, if she wasn't careful, would become someone she liked too much when she had an expiration date to return to Chicago.

"Will you be back in time for lunch?"

"Nah. I'm going to the recreation center to swim a few laps, and then I'll grab something at that little café that opened a couple of weeks ago advertising healthy salads and smoothies. Do you want me to bring you something back?"

"No, thanks, Grandpa. I'm good."

Harper had told her grandfather that she was good when she really wasn't. She'd just had a therapy session with someone who hadn't held back when confronting her with issues that needed to be resolved. He addressed things she didn't want to acknowledge as the truth, because she did have a plethora of rules and conditions when it came to forming relationships. It was as if she couldn't allow herself to become emotionally involved with a man because it would interfere with her focusing on her career—a career that, if she was honest, was going nowhere.

She had held three positions in ten years, and none, except for teaching, had given her a sense of purpose and fulfillment. Bernard had reminded her that baseball and military service were intrinsic to generations of Flemings, like automobiles were to the Fords. Kelton had played baseball and served in World War II; Bernard had served in Vietnam; Daniel Sr. played baseball and was inducted into the Baseball Hall of Fame, while his sons Craig and Daniel Jr. were committed to life in the military. What Bernard had failed to mention was that Harper had followed Nadine, who'd become an educator, and Martell, who was a school psychologist.

Most people are considered adults at the age of eighteen, but for Harper it was taking much longer. Now that she was quickly approaching thirty-four, she had to decide how she wanted to live the rest of her life. Did she want to continue bouncing from different companies and positions or select one where she would spend the next thirty years before retiring?

Harper asked herself if she wanted to fall in love and experience her happily-ever-after like the heroines in her mother's romance novels. And the resounding answer was yes. Yes, she was still attracted to Cheney Sanders, but there were obstacles that would prevent them from becoming more than friends—that is, if he wanted more than friendship. She lived in Chicago and he in Nashville, and there could be problems with a long-distance relationship.

It was clear she'd had enough soul searching for one morning. If she didn't go back to working on the manuscript, then she would lose her momentum. Harper had to write about eleven years of Moses's life in baseball, and she had another three months to complete it. She opened the laptop and minutes later her fingers were flying over the keys, the words quickly filling up the screen.

CHAPTER 24

Moses felt as if he had come to another country when he stepped off the bus in New Orleans. Everything about the Crescent City looked and smelled different from the states and cities he had visited. The weather was hotter and more humid than Memphis, and he loathed having to practice and compete against other teams where his uniform, soaked in sweat, would be plastered to his underwear.

The driver had stopped in a Colored section of the city where the members of the team had reserved rooms in hotels, boarding houses and rooming houses. Moses was luckier than the others because Lionel had invited him to stay with his family for the weeklong stay.

Lionel had talked incessantly during the bus ride from Memphis to New Orleans, and while Moses had wanted to tell him to shut the hell up so he could get some sleep, he knew the man was excited to reunite with his wife and children even if it was only going to be for a week, before the team left Louisiana. They were scheduled to play in Texas and maybe Oklahoma during the months of August and September.

Moses didn't begrudge Lionel's overexuberance because it had been months since he'd seen his family, and it was only now that he understood it when Lionel said most of the Eagles were married because whenever they played in or near their hometowns, they were able to reunite with their wives and children. He didn't have a wife or children; just a promise from a girl that he could be her boyfriend.

He had asked Sallie Ann if he could see her, partly because he wanted to be like the other guys, have a woman greet him whenever he returned home. Nichols, a small mining town in northeast Tennessee bordering Kentucky, was no longer home. Memphis was, for the duration of his stint with the Memphis Eagles, and if he were to marry Sallie Ann, then they would live in her hometown.

Moses didn't believe he was using Sallie Ann; he really did like her. She was smart, pretty, and ambitious. She was also a dreamer, and unlike some young women who attended college or went into the workforce once they graduated from school, Sallie Ann wanted to become a photographer and travel to different states and countries to take pictures she could sell to newspapers and magazines. She said she wanted to make a name for herself as the female James Van Der Zee. Moses did not want to squash her dreams, but as a woman and more importantly a Colored one, she would be denied access to people, places, and things. He'd only seen Sallie Ann twice during his stay in Memphis; Coach had cancelled their second day off because the team's defense had begun to suffer. They'd lost two games to a low-scoring team because they failed to turn two routine double plays, and their catchers had let wild pitches go to the backstop without exhibiting aggressiveness in retrieving the ball.

He met with her and her parents after the game where he had arranged for tickets to be left for them at the box office and asked that she write him at the Parker House. In exchange, he promised to write her whenever he wasn't playing or practicing.

Moses wasn't certain what he had been thinking when he'd asked her to wait two years before they could be together. His request was akin to a marriage proposal. He had asked Sallie Ann to wait two years so he could save enough money for them to be married and settle down as husband and wife.

He'd asked himself over and over, was he being fair to her, asking Sallie Ann to put her life on hold for a stranger she had met in a bar? Moses wondered how Daisy Gilliam would react when she asked him how he'd met her future daughter-in-law. He would answer truthfully. Moses knew instinctually that if Sallie Ann's father hadn't been in awe of his status as a hometown baseball hero, he never would've agreed to Moses's request that she not work as a server at the family bar.

Moses wanted to be like his teammates who played ball and went home to their families at the end of the season. Even though his family lived in Nichols, he knew there was no way he could go back to living under the same roof as Solomon Gilliam.

He would return to Memphis and rent a room where he could come and go without the restrictions he had to follow at the Parker House; where he wouldn't have to adhere to the ten o'clock lights-out curfew, and where he and Sallie Ann could be together to talk and plan their future.

Two years.

That's how long he had given himself to save enough money before he would be able to marry Sallie Ann Thompson.

Moses stood up and smiled at Lionel's obviously pregnant wife when she entered the parlor. There was something about her smile that put him immediately at ease. "Please sit down. This is the first time Lionel has invited any of his teammates to stay with us." She took a chair opposite him.

"And I'm honored to be the first, Mrs. Dean."

She shook her head. "Please call me Ella. Mrs. Dean is Lionel's mother."

Moses smiled at the pretty, petite woman with a round face and rounded body. "Then Ella it is." He angled his head when he saw a small boy come into the room and hide behind his mother's chair. "And who is this little one?"

Ella eased her son forward. "This is Caleb. He's two going on five. My other son is Gabriel, and he's six and just finished the first grade." She rested a hand on her belly over a flower-sprigged sundress. "I don't know if I'm carrying another boy or a girl, but I already have names picked out for them. It's going to be Hannah if it's a girl or Jonathan if it's another boy."

"You've selected names from the Bible."

Ella smiled. "As did your mother when she named you Moses."

"My wife gives all our children biblical names because she's a holy roller," Lionel said as he walked into the room and scooped up Caleb. He sat next to Ella.

Ella rolled her eyes at Lionel. "Better a holy roller than a heathen. I want my children knowing the difference between right and wrong, good and evil. There's enough evil in this country and the world for the good Lord to say *enough* and end it like he did with Noah when He sent the flood."

"Ella, he's not going to send another flood," Lionel told his wife.

"How would you know? Whenever you go to church with me and the children you always end up sleeping during the pastor's sermon."

"I know because I have been reading Moses's Bible."

Ella gave Moses a direct stare. "Is that true?"

"Yes. Your husband has been reading my Bible. "

Ella clasped her hands in a prayerful gesture. "Praise be to the Lord. And thank you, Moses, for helping my husband to see the light."

Moses wanted to tell her he had nothing to do with Lionel finding faith, rather that he thought his reading the Bible would help to improve his literacy. Lionel had also taken an interest in reading the Black newspapers Moses bought. Most Americans got their news from radio, newspapers, magazines, and newsreels, while Negroes had to rely on Black-owned newspapers to report on what was happening in their communities.

"You're welcome," he said, hoping Ella wouldn't continue talking about her husband and his faith.

"I know y'all are exhausted from that long bus ride, so it's time to eat. I made all of Lionel's favorites and, Moses, I hope you brought your appetite."

Moses wanted to ask Lionel's wife if she was kidding. When he'd walked into the small, neat house, he had been bombarded with a plethora of mouthwatering aromas that had him practically salivating.

"Yes, ma'am."

Hours later, Moses lay on the cot in the space that had become his bedroom during his stay in New Orleans. Ella had outdone herself when she had prepared red beans and rice, fried catfish, and gumbo with chicken, shrimp, and sausage. He'd gorged himself on the gumbo and red beans and rice and was forced to push himself away from the table. Rather than sit with Lionel and listen to the radio, he had excused himself and retreated to his makeshift bedroom. To say Ella Dean was a good cook did not do her justice. She was an excellent cook, wife, and mother, and Lionel was blessed to have found and married her.

Ella had mentioned being eight months along in her pregnancy and she had been able to hide her condition from the owner of the laundry until she began showing. She admitted, laughingly, that because she always carried her weight in her middle, she was able to work until she'd earned enough money, and with Lionel's savings they now had enough to purchase a house in a better neighborhood. Lionel had returned to New Orleans in time to assist moving his family from the house with two bedrooms to one with three bedrooms and a backyard where their children could romp and play. Moses volunteered to lend a hand helping with the move.

He hadn't told the Deans, but he planned to visit the open markets to buy food for his hosts. After all, not only were they providing him with room and board, but also delicious meals. With a new baby on the way, coupled with purchasing a house, they had spent most of their resources. Lionel had announced that he also planned to play winter ball, which meant he needed the money to support his growing family.

Living with Lionel and his family during their stay in New Orleans would allow Moses to witness the responsibilities he would need to take care of a wife and children. Something he hadn't been privy to when growing up with his parents. He knew his father brought home his pay and Daisy paid the bills. She would give

Solomon what she thought he needed as his personal spending money. It was something his father had accepted because he knew that Daisy was better able to budget their household expenses. Her husband's salary and the money she earned from sewing and doing laundry had kept, as she was apt to say, "the wolf from the door." She claimed there were too many men who drank up their paychecks even before arriving home, leaving their families "without a pot to piss in and a window to throw it out." Moses did not know why, but he always seemed to recall Southern sayings like "Bless your heart," or "Pitching a hissy fit with a tail on it."

Moses had thought it would be different for Colored people when the team played in Ohio, Indiana, and Illinois, but after what he'd experienced in Cleveland with the White fan, he had concluded that he preferred living in the South. At least he knew Southern Whites didn't like his people. He wasn't so sure when it came to Northern Whites, and he preferred certainty to uncertainty.

Grunting softly, he shifted into a more comfortable position on the narrow cot. Despite being full and exhausted from the long bus ride, he was too wound up to fall asleep. He kept thinking about Sallie Ann and wondered how his life would be with or without her. He preferred not to think about the latter. She was nice, and when he compared her to the other girls who'd flirted with him while asking for his autograph—some were bold enough to ask to see him when he wasn't playing—that was when Moses knew he had made the right decision to ask that she wait for him.

The Memphis Eagles played an afternoon game in the sweltering heat and oppressive humidity and Moses, along with every member on both teams, thought it should have been postponed because some had complained of feeling sick. It was obvious that they were experiencing dehydration and possible heatstroke.

The night before he had helped Lionel move from his rental home into one with his name on the deed. It was an upgrade, with three large bedrooms, a kitchen, bathroom, and spacious fenced-in backyard. It had been constructed on stilts, which protected it from flooding during hurricanes or storms that usually formed in the Gulf of Mexico.

It had taken them most of the night along with three trips to load a pickup with boxes and furniture to transport them across town to the new house and it was only at eight in the morning when he and Lionel were able to catch a few hours of sleep before they were scheduled to be at the ballpark to begin practice before the scheduled one o'clock game.

Without warning, dark clouds and flashes of lightning followed with a roll of thunder sent spectators scrambling for safety. The umpires ordered all players off the field minutes before the skies opened and rain poured down on everything. There was grumbling from both teams that the game never should've been played; there had been a forecast of violent storms covering the region from Baton Rouge to New Orleans. The game was called after the third inning and rescheduled for another time, as the rain continued unabated.

It rained for three continuous days, with flooding conditions in some low-lying regions, and Moses knew the Deans had been blessed to have purchased a house built off the ground.

He took advantage of the downtime to write to his mother and in his notebooks. Although he was running low on stationery, he decided to write to Sallie Ann.

August 14, 1936

Dear Sallie Ann,

I'm in New Orleans and it has been raining for three days, making it almost impossible to be outdoors for any length of time. We are supposed to be here a week, and so far, all the games have been post-poned. They say we will have to make them up, but I don't know when that is possible, because we have a full schedule between now and September. Maybe we can fit in a few make-up games before the season ends in early October.

Now that the schedule has changed, I am not certain when we will be back in Memphis. Originally it was said that we would return for three days in September, but even that may change.

I'm staying with a teammate and his family. Lionel Dean and I are roommates on the road, and I have come to think of him as a brother. His wife is expecting a baby in another month, which will be their third. Right now, they have two boys, and they are hoping the next one will be a girl. Ella is a good wife, mother, and an excellent cook. The first time I ate her gumbo, red beans, and rice I had to stop myself from moaning aloud with each forkful. I've grown to love New Orleans cooking and could eat it every day. I wasn't much of a coffee drinker before now, but I really like the coffee here that is a little bitter but perfect when eating beignets. Beignets are fried dough covered with powdered sugar. I know if I hadn't been playing ball, I would gain at least ten, if not twenty pounds.

Enough about me. I hope you and your family are well, and please let them know I asked about them. If you write, then you must tell all that has been going on with you. I know I won't get to read your letters until I am back in Memphis at the Parker House, but hopefully whenever I get the chance I will write.

Sincerely,
Moses

He reread what he had written and decided not to include anything that could be construed as a love letter. After all, it was his first letter to Sallie Ann, and Moses wasn't certain of her feelings toward him. Now that he looked back, he realized he had put some pressure on her to agree to become his girlfriend and wait two years for something he hoped would come to fruition. Whenever he observed Dean with Ella, it strengthened his resolve that asking Sallie Ann to wait for him had been right. He didn't know her well, but something told him she would be good to share his life with and build a future together.

Chapter 25

"Sallie Ann, you have mail."

She scrambled off her bed and opened her bedroom door. It had to be important for her mother to come to her room with mail. "Who is it from?" Maddie handed her an envelope with a New Orleans postmark. When she saw the return address, she knew it was from Moses. "Thanks, Mama."

Maddie pointed to the envelope. "Aren't you going to open it?"

Sallie Ann forced a smile. "I'll open it later. Right now, I'm trying to finish reading a book."

"Since when is reading a book more important than a letter from your fiancé?"

"Moses Gilliam is my boyfriend and not my fiancé. Once we're engaged, then he will become my fiancé, so I'm not going to call him that now."

"Everyone in Memphis believes he's your fiancé."

"That's because you've been telling everyone that your daughter is engaged to be married to him." Sallie Ann wanted to scream at her mother that she was at it again. She was attempting to set her daughter up with a boy who would elevate her social status. If Maddie had been that focused on what she called "marrying up," then she never should have taken up with a family of saloonkeepers.

Maddie lowered her eyes. "I just happened to mention that you are dating Moses Gilliam and people jumped to their own conclusions."

"Conclusions you didn't bother to correct. Mama, please stop talking about me and Moses, because if we never get together then I'm going to have to live with the embarrassment and having folks ask me why we're not together."

"Okay, baby, I will stop. I don't know what it is, but something tells me that you are going to marry him."

Sallie Ann did not know who or what told her mother that she was going to become Mrs. Moses Gilliam, but in her heart of hearts she wanted it to be true. "After I read the letter, I will let you know what it says," she said, hoping to placate her mother enough to give her some privacy.

Maddie smiled, nodding. "Okay. I'll see you later."

She waited until her mother closed the door and then pressed her back against it. When she had jokingly told Moses that the news of them being seen together would probably spread around Memphis before sundown, Sallie Ann would not have suspected her mother would be the one to not only incite but keep the rumor mill going.

She went back to bed and carefully opened the flap of the envelope to find a single sheet of paper with Moses's neat handwriting. Sallie Ann read the letter, then realized he hadn't written a word indicating his feelings toward her. She wanted to brush it off that they hadn't spent enough time together for him to even hint that he really liked her. What he did was ask her to wait for him.

Sallie Ann wondered if she had been so in awe of him that she hadn't hesitated and said she would. He wanted her to write back, and she would. In fact, she would write him every day, and once he returned to Memphis there would be a stack of letters waiting for him.

Don't be a fool, Sallie Ann.

Don't chase him.

If he wants you, then he will let you know.

Sallie Ann wanted to ignore the voice in her head but found it so difficult to separate her feelings for a man who had made her feel special from the possibility that he may have strung her along because he needed a girl in every town or city where the team played. And that she would be his Memphis girlfriend.

She wouldn't write him every day. Instead, she would write him back and then wait for his next letter. Opening the drawer of the bedside table, she removed a fountain pen and box of stationery. She had purchased the stationery because the pages and the flaps of the envelopes were decorated with colorful flowers. They were perfect for love letters.

Sallie Ann uncapped the pen and wrote the date:

August 19, 1936
Dear Moses,

I received your letter today, and I was glad to hear from you. I am sorry about the weather in New Orleans and that your games had to be postponed, but we must remember that Mother Nature is the boss, and we must go along with whatever she wants.

Memphis is hot, and while you are having rain, it has been dry as a bone here.

The temperature doesn't go down much even after the sun sets. Farmers are complaining about their crops dying because of the lack of rain, while others are talking about a dust bowl like the one that is still ravaging the Midwest and Great Plains. Folks are praying for rain, while others say God is punishing us because of our wickedness. You should remember that just last year 20 of the worst black blizzards swept across the entire Great Plains from Canada and south to Texas.

We had an itinerant preacher come to Memphis and set up a tent for a revival meeting that was packed with both White and Colored folks. He performed all sorts of miracles, professing to have healed a woman who had been crippled from birth, but he turned out to be a charlatan when someone recognized the woman as someone he had met in a brothel in Louisiana and called her out. Folks attempted to attack the preacher, but his bodyguards managed to get him out of the tent and into a car before they could get to him. My mother said it was a sight to behold. After everyone left, somebody set fire to the tent and the fire department had to put it out before it spread out of control. I don't understand why someone would start a fire when everything is dry as kindling.

The farmers aren't the only ones affected by this heat, and business is down at the bar. Most folks don't want to venture out if they don't have to. School is about to start up again in a few days and there's talk that classes won't be held all day. They will begin at nine and end at one. The afternoon heat has been brutal.

I'm good. Now that I'm not working at Tommy's Joint, I have a lot of time to myself to catch up on my reading. I've read almost every book on my required reading list, so hopefully I will be ahead of the other girls when it comes time to discuss the books. I still haven't changed my mind about wanting to be a photographer and I have been researching the type of camera I would like to use. I found one I think would be perfect for me. It is called a Baby Rolleiflex and I can hold it against my chest to see an image in the viewfinder before taking the picture. The advantage is that I can photograph someone without them knowing it. They sell for about $250. My mother thinks the price is ridiculous when we could buy a new 1936 Buick for $700. I told her if I'm going to become a photographer, then I must buy a reliable camera.

I believe she is sorry that she told me that I wasn't going to college because I had to work for the family business. And even if she were to change her mind about me attending college it is too late because I haven't applied to any, and don't plan to.

I am going to end this rather lengthy letter before I run out of things to tell you.

I hope you are well and in good spirits when you do get a chance to read this.
Fondly,
Sallie Ann

She had ended the letter with *fondly* because it was the closest she could get to saying to Moses that he was someone very special and she could imagine spending the rest of her life with him.

Sallie Ann addressed the envelope and waited for the ink to dry completely before carefully folding the letter and slipping it inside. The Parker House was in the Heights where most of the prosperous Colored families lived. She had been surprised when Moses told her he stayed there whenever the Memphis Eagles were in town. Moses had a ten o'clock curfew there, and he wasn't allowed to entertain women in the house. That meant if she wanted to see Moses, then it wouldn't be at the Parker House.

Even if he had been permitted to have women visit him at the Parker House, Sallie Ann knew she would not be one of them. There was no way she was going to jeopardize her reputation by being discovered spending time in a man's bedroom. She had heard enough stories about girls who allowed themselves to be lured into situations where they had brought shame on themselves and their families. Shame was shame and someone's financial status didn't matter. Less fortunate girls were either forced to marry early or if not were left to raise their babies without the benefit of a husband, while the ones with money were either sent away to have their babies and put them up for adoption or undergo an illegal backroom abortion if the boys refused to marry them. Sallie Ann did not want to find herself in either situation. It was safer that she not open her legs to a man until they were married.

* * *

Moses returned to Memphis the last week in September and found a stack of letters in his room at the Parker House. He'd written Sallie Ann a half dozen times, catching her up on where he was and what he'd seen. Most were filled with what he called chitchat; chitchat because he still wasn't certain of her feelings for him, while he didn't want to tell her that she'd occupied his thoughts whenever he wasn't competing, and that he missed her.

However, the missing wasn't physical; he had assuaged his pent-up sexual frustration with a woman he'd met at a boxing match in San Antonio, Texas. They were in Texas to play the San Antonio Black Bronchos. Inez Cruz told him she lived in San Antonio and was an art student. They talked for several hours before Inez invited him back to the house she shared with three other students, and he spent the night with her.

Moses knew he wasn't the first man she had slept with, but that hadn't mattered because he had craved the company of a woman for far too long. She'd given him the address and telephone number of her relatives in Monterrey, Mexico, because she'd planned to leave the States at the end of the year for a fieldwork assignment that included studying pre-Columbian artifacts, and hoped he could look her up if he was ever in the country. He didn't give her his address, but promised he would. However, when he asked her if he would be confronted by a jealous boyfriend or lover, she smiled and reassured him that wasn't possible. Her heroine was a Mexican painter named Frida Kahlo who, although married to Diego Rivera, had slept with other men. There were rumors she also had affairs with women, and that's how Inez planned to live her life. Moses didn't tell her that he planned to play winter ball in Mexico, because that was his secret. Sleeping with Inez would become his secret from the other men on the team, and more notably from Sallie Ann. Once they were married, he planned to be a loyal husband.

He showered and changed into a pair of clean underwear and then lay on the bed to read Sallie Ann's letters, beginning with the earliest postmark. The first few were filled with what he thought of as mundane happenings in and around Memphis. Then her tone changed when she wrote about missing him and was counting down the days to see him again. Situations at her school hadn't changed—none of the girls were speaking to her—but that no longer mattered because she had what they didn't, and that was Moses Gilliam.

Her closings also changed from fondly, to affectionately, and then lovingly yours. It was as close as she could get to expressing more than affection for him. Moses knew if she were standing there, he'd tell her how much she had come to mean to him; and how this stranger he met, who worked in a bar, had gotten to him as no other girl or woman had before or since. When he slept with Inez it was something they both wanted and needed and nothing more. She didn't expect a declaration of love and he wasn't prepared to offer it.

After reading Sallie Ann's letters, Moses wanted to call her to let her know he was back in Memphis, but only for a few days before leaving to play winter ball in the Caribbean. When he had lived in Nichols, time seemed to go by at a snail's pace, but after playing nearly five months of baseball it was like the blink of an eye. One day merged into the next, then weeks and months. The Memphis Eagles had done well in their division, going from last to second, and it was enough for them to celebrate their meteoric rise and become contenders for next year's season.

Everyone was surprised when they were given year-end bonuses, and Moses was shocked when he received not only a bonus equal to his monthly salary, but an amended contract with an appreciable raise in salary. Winnie Chess had enclosed a note to him that he was not to reveal to any of the team members that he'd received a higher bonus because he had been instrumental in the team's success. He'd hit thirty home runs, twelve doubles, and two triples since joining the Memphis Eagles, and had earned enough to follow through with his plan to purchase a used car and give Lionel and Ella Dean a generous gift to celebrate the birth of their daughter. He wanted to mail off a check to the Deans before leaving for the Caribbean, while purchasing an automobile would wait until he returned for spring training.

His mother had also written him in his absence. Solomon's health was worsening, and despite his chronic coughing and loss of breath, he refused to see a doctor. Daisy said that she had stopped nagging him about taking care of his health and focused all her energies on her dressmaking business, with the aid of her new sewing machine. She had admitted to crying nonstop for hours once she answered the knock on the door to find a man with a box from the Singer Sewing Machine Company. Moses laughed when his mother wrote that she had stared at the machine for two days before attempting to use it, claiming she now knew the joy the Wright brothers felt when the Kitty Hawk lifted off and flew for twelve seconds.

Moses felt a lump in his throat as he tried to control his emotions. He realized the joy he was able to give his mother in return for her love and support to make his dream of becoming a baseball player a reality.

He put the letters in a drawer with his socks and underwear. Then he lay across the bed again to try and get some sleep before dinner was served. It felt good to be back in Memphis, and particularly the Parker House. Moses didn't mind the ten o'clock lights-out curfew because staying out any later might have made him an easy target for White police officers who were ordered to patrol Colored neighborhoods after dark. It was apparent the sundown rule, which declared it unlawful for Blacks to venture into White neighborhoods, didn't apply to Whites who occasionally ventured into neighborhoods populated by Blacks.

Moses still couldn't understand, if White men hated Black men, why were they unable to stay away from Black women when they had their own, whom they supposedly worshipped. Within minutes of turning off the bedside lamp and getting into bed, he heard a knock on the door and Lionel telling him to open it.

Getting off the bed, he walked to the door and opened it. "What's the matter?" he asked, not bothering to disguise his annoyance. He'd told Lionel that he planned to get some sleep before seeing him again at dinner.

Lionel pushed past him and stood in the middle of the room. "I'm not going with you guys to play winter ball."

"Say what?" Moses did not want to believe what he was hearing. Lionel had talked about playing winter ball when he first met him, and he wondered why the about-face.

"I can't go. Ella said the baby is sick."

Moses blinked slowly. "Is it serious?"

"I don't know. When I called her, she sounded hysterical and—"

"There's no need to explain, man," Moses said, cutting him off. "Go and be with your family." He paused. "I was going to send Ella something for the baby, but since you're leaving, I'm going to give it to you now." He returned to the chest of drawers, took out an envelope, and handed it to Lionel. I don't want you to open it until you get home."

Lionel gave him an incredulous stare. "You're kidding, aren't you?"

"No, Train," he said, using his nickname, "I'm not kidding." He gave his teammate a slight shove. "Now go and get your bus or train ticket. I'll see you when you get back in the spring."

Lionel chewed his lower lip. "You're the best, Gilliam."

Moses shook his head. "No. You're the best. You don't know, but watching you with your wife and kids showed me how I could be a good husband and father."

Lionel hugged him. "That's what big brothers are supposed to do. Show the little brother the right way to do things."

His teammate was there, then he was gone, and Moses felt the loss almost immediately. He was relying on Lionel to shepherd him though the ups and downs of playing winter ball in different countries. Even though he would be traveling with other members of the team, it wouldn't be the same. Not without Lionel "Train" Dean.

CHAPTER 26

Sallie Ann was certain anyone could see her heart pounding through her blouse as she waited for Moses to make his way up the porch steps. He'd called the house and left a message with her mother that he was coming by after school was dismissed for the day.

He had pulled the brim of his hat low on his forehead so she wasn't able to see all of his face, but when he glanced up it was as if her breath wouldn't leave her lungs. The summer sun had darkened his complexion from rich mahogany to a sable, and there was something about his face that reminded her of the photographs she'd seen of African masks. Moses wasn't just handsome. He was gorgeous.

The mercury had loosened its grip on the region and after much-needed rain a slight breeze had lifted the hem of his untucked shirt as he stood before her, tall and breathtakingly masculine. It was as if Moses had left Memphis a boy and had returned a man.

Her lips parted in an unconscious smile. "Welcome home."

Taking off his hat, Moses dipped his head and kissed her cheek. "It's good to be home."

She closed her eyes as the scent of his aftershave washed over her, along with the natural scent of his body that she found intoxicating. "How long are you staying?"

He blinked slowly. "Three days, then I'm on a train to Florida, where a boat will take us first to Cuba, then to Puerto Rico, and the Dominican Republic and Mexico, before we come back to the States."

Sallie Ann willed the tears filling her eyes not to fall. Why was it that the time they were able to be together was measured in days, and not weeks or months? How was she going to get to know him if he was in and out of her life like a bee flitting from flower to flower? He was present, then he was gone.

"Do you want to come in?"

"Are your parents home?"

Sallie Ann shook her head. "No. Why?"

"I think it's best if we sit out here on the porch."

Now she was confused. Moses had called to say he was coming to see her, and he didn't want to go into the house with her. He preferred sitting out on the porch where everyone passing by could see them.

"Why, Moses?"

"Because I don't want your mother or father to come home and believe I've compromised you."

Now, she was more confused. "Compromise me, how?"

Moses counted slowly to three, then said, "I don't want them to think that I've touched you inappropriately."

Her eyes grew wide. "That ain't going to happen, because I won't allow that."

"What you would allow and what they may perceive are two different things. Either we sit out here, or I'll leave."

Moses threatened to leave when it was the last thing he wanted to do. Seeing her face-to-face was a reminder of just how lovely she was. Being this close to her and catching the scent of flowers wafting from her warm body had sent his libido into overdrive. He had to sit before she noticed his erection. Sleeping with Inez had shattered his self-induced celibacy where he woke up with an erection and was forced to lie on his belly until it went down.

"Please sit down, Sallie Ann."

She complied and seconds later he took the rocker next to hers. He wasn't certain whether she could hear him when he exhaled a sigh of relief that he was able to conceal the bulge in the front of his pants by sitting and adjusting the hem of his shirt.

The seconds ticked by without them saying anything and when Moses felt more in control, he reached into the pocket of his pants and handed her a small velvet pouch. "I bought you a little something from my travels." He noticed her hands were shaking slightly when she untied the drawstring.

"Oh, it's beautiful," she whispered, holding up the length of delicate gold bracelet with a tiny heart charm. Sallie Ann held out her left hand. "Please put it on for me."

Moses fastened the bracelet around her tiny wrist. "The next piece of jewelry I will give you once you graduate will be an engagement ring."

Sallie Ann's eyes shimmered with unshed tears. "I love it, and I love you." Her eyelids fluttered wildly. "I would like to ask one thing of you, and I won't be upset if you say no."

Moses doubted if he could refuse anything she'd ask of him. Just hearing her admit that she loved him was enough. "What is it?"

"Can we go inside for no more than half a minute so I can kiss you?"

"Are you talking about thirty seconds?" She nodded. "That's a long time," Moses teased, smiling. "If you are willing to make it five seconds, then okay." It was apparent that she had never been kissed and thirty seconds was a long time—long enough for him get another erection.

Her smile was dazzling. "Okay. Five seconds."

They rose at the same time and Moses reached over her head to open the door to let her precede him. When the door closed behind them, he pulled her off to the side so anyone passing by wouldn't see them. He lowered his head at the same time, cradled her face, and touched his mouth to hers. Her lips parted slightly as he deepened the kiss and in that instant everything around him ceased to exist except the silkiness of her face against his palms. The warmth of her breath mingling with his, the crush of her breasts against his chest, and the sweetness of her mouth that he longed to devour in a kiss that went on forever. Moses didn't want to stop but knew if he didn't, then he'd break his promise to protect her, not only from other people but also himself. That meant not making love to her until they were married.

Breathing heavily, he ended the kiss. Sallie Ann hadn't opened her eyes as the sound of her breathing reverberated throughout the space. He looked down and saw the outline of her nipples through her white slip and blouse. It was obvious she had been aroused by the kiss, which told him that the girl he planned to marry would be a very passionate woman.

"I think it's best I leave now, Sallie Ann."

She nodded. "When are you coming back?"

Moses gave her a long, penetrating stare. He knew if he spent any more time around Sallie Ann before he left, it would spell disaster. Kissing her had been a mistake. "Not until spring. I'll see you again in April."

This time when her eyes filled with tears, they overflowed down her velvety cheeks, and rather than comfort her as he'd done with his sisters after their father's whippings, he turned on his heel and walked out of the house.

Sallie Ann had recovered from her crying jag by the time her mother returned home. She had splashed cold water on her face and then cold teabags to offset some of the puffiness.

"You just missed Moses," she told Maddie when she joined her in the parlor. She held out her left hand. "He gave me this. He said the next piece of jewelry will be an engagement ring."

Maddie pressed a hand to her breasts. "It's lovely. Why didn't he stay? When he called to say he was coming over, I told him I wanted to see him."

"He had to pack for his trip," Sallie Ann lied smoothly. She didn't know why he had left so abruptly, and it was the only excuse she could come up with.

"When is he coming back?"

"Not until April."

"April!"

"Yes, Mama. He's going to the Caribbean to play winter ball."

"When will he have time to court you properly?"

"That can happen once I finish school. You must remember that even after we are married, he will be away from home a lot whenever the team must travel. It's better I get used to it now, so I don't complain about it years from now. It will be the same with our children. They will have to become accustomed to not seeing their daddy come home every night like other fathers."

"And you're all right with that, Sallie Ann?"

"Yes, I'm all right, Mama, because I know who and what I'm going to marry. If you are thinking about him fooling around with other women when he's on the road, it's something I can't control. His loving and protecting me and our children is all I can ask." She wanted to remind her mother that she and her husband had had separate bedrooms for years, and it was only recently that Maddie and Jimmie had begun to sleep together again.

Maddie sighed heavily. "Men will do whatever they want, while most women must put up with it. And it doesn't matter whether she is White or Colored, because men are all the same under the skin."

"That's probably the reason some women prefer to remain single. They can come and go by their leave without having to answer to a man."

"I don't know any of those," Maddie said under her breath.

"A lot of bohemian women and suffragettes who were advocates for the right of women to vote opted not to marry."

"You're talking about White women, Sallie Ann."

"It doesn't matter, Mama. They are still women." Although she wanted to marry and have children, Sallie Ann admired what she called the "modern woman" who was able to determine her destiny without the benefit of a husband.

Sallie Ann wondered if she was becoming a modern woman when she had admitted to Moses that she loved him while he hadn't responded in kind. She had taken the initiative to ask him to kiss her. Some might call her brazen, but that didn't matter because Sallie Ann Thompson was in love.

If Moses believed he was in another country when visiting New Orleans for the first time, when the steamer docked in the harbor in Cuba it was as if he'd reached another world. He was in a foreign country where Spanish was spoken.

Four players on the Memphis Eagles team had opted to play in the winter leagues, and this buoyed Moses's confidence that he would be interacting with some of his teammates. George Edwards, who had assumed the responsibility as manager for their winter league team, spoke English and Spanish, which helped bridge the language barrier. When they boarded the train in Tennessee they were consigned to segregated cars until reaching Miami, Florida, where they boarded a Portuguese tanker sailing for the Havana harbor. Once onboard he endured twin smokestacks belching smoke, and the tropical sun. Despite the hat he wore, the unrelenting heat of the sun beat down on his head with a vengeance.

When the team was barnstorming, he'd gone to a Texas library and sat in the research section to go through encyclopedias to read about the countries he would visit when playing winter ball. Some of the Latin American countries were under the rule of dictators, and while there were distinct racial and social classifications, sporting events did not have a color line.

There were buses and taxis parked near the Malécon, the seawall built in 1901 when the United States government assumed control of Cuba. U.S. forces had occupied the island until 1902, when they allowed a new Cuban government to control their state's affairs. Waves crashed over the wall, soaking cars and strollers alike.

After dock officials had checked the steamer captain's manifest and cargo, they were able to clear customs. Moses boarded a bus with other baseball players and stared out the window at the Spanish Colonial buildings. The ocean, palm trees, colorful flowers growing in abandon and exotic birds had Moses believing he had come to paradise. He heard Spanish and English spoken by passengers crowding into the small, cramped bus.

The driver stopped to let off passengers, then continued in an easterly direction away from the center of the capital city. The skyline of Havana disappeared, giving way to small homes dotting the landscape off in the distance. The driver slowed and turned off on a rutted road leading to a quartet of small two-story salmon-colored structures several hundred feet from a plaza filled with an elaborate marble fountain, flowering shrubs, and palm trees. A small crowd had gathered around a group of musicians, the Latin music featuring rhythms that were unmistakably African. A lithe, dark-skinned woman dressed in an ankle-length white dress swayed and twirled sensuously in tempo with the hypnotic drumming. Moses was transfixed; her ruffled hem snapped and fluttered wildly as she danced as if caught up in a powerful spell.

Moses retrieved his luggage from an overhead rack and filed out of the bus to the building where the team would live during their stay. La Tropical, touted to be the best baseball park in Cuba, was built in 1929, with a seating capacity of 28,000. The stadium was newer and much larger than many in which Moses had played.

The team checked in and Moses discovered he didn't have to share a room with anyone in the converted convent. However, he did have to share the second-floor bathroom with those occupying the same floor; despite the heat, the interiors of the stucco building had remained cool.

They were instructed before disembarking from the steamer that they would be fed immediately after checking into their lodgings and everyone should be ready to board the bus by ten the following morning for the ride to the ballpark where they would practice before competing against a Cuban team later that afternoon. The manager had cautioned everyone to sleep well after the three days it had taken the team to arrive in Cuba, because they would need every bit of stamina to compete against the ballplayers in the Cuban League. Many Latin players were also prohibited from playing in Major League Baseball because of their color and were forced to establish teams in their native countries.

Moses decided to eat before unpacking. He went downstairs to the dining room after using the communal bathroom. Some of his teammates were already seated. White-clad women balanced trays on their shoulders carrying plates of white rice, black beans, grilled beef, and sliced avocado. He slid onto the bench seat beside one of the Eagles' pitchers.

"I'm hungry enough to devour a cow," he whispered. The box lunches they'd purchased during train stops contained enough to sustain a child, not a fully grown man.

"Tell me about it," the other man said *sotto voce*. "The one thing you can count on when playing winter ball is that you will eat well. It doesn't matter if you eat black beans in Cuba, pink beans in Puerto Rico, or red beans in the Dominican Republic, they are all delicious. There are two reasons why I sign up to play winter ball—the food and the money."

"I can think of worse reasons," Moses said. The words were barely off his tongue when a server set a plate in front of him. He nodded, thanking her, then picked up a knife and fork, cut into a piece of thinly sliced steak, and took a bite. The piquant spices with the distinctive taste of garlic melted in his mouth. He followed with a forkful of rice and beans, unable to suppress a moan of contentment. A slice of ripe avocado followed—a fruit he'd eaten for the first time when the team had traveled to

Texas, and it had become an acquired taste, like olives and mushrooms.

He had eaten sparingly to save room for dessert—custard known as flan, almond cake, and coffee. Rather than return to his room following dinner, Moses walked outside and sat on a stone bench. He nodded to an elderly woman who kept looking at him until she came closer, leaving less than a foot between them.

"*¿Habla español?*"

"I don't understand," he replied in English.

"*¿Inglés?*"

"Yes, English." That he understood. Without warning, she grabbed his right hand and dug her nails into the flesh. He immediately attempted to extricate himself. "Let me go!"

"No! Let me see *la mano*."

Moses stared at the woman who had a complexion that reminded him of aged tobacco. It was difficult to pinpoint her age. He predicted she had to be at least sixty. He knew he wasn't going to get away from her until he let her see his palm.

He nodded. "Okay."

There was only silence until she said haltingly in English, as if searching for the Spanish equivalent in each word, "You are very lucky. Good will follow you if you do good things." She paused. "I see two women in your life. Both will love you, but you must pick the one who is best for you." She paused for a second, staring intently at his palm. "See *bebés*—babies . . ." Her words trailed off as she released his hand. "*¡Basta!* No more. I can't see no more."

Moses wanted to tell the woman she was crazy, pretending to tell his future then demand that he pay her. Well, he wasn't about to fall into that trap and particularly not in a country where he didn't speak the language. He sat motionlessly, stunned when she got up and walked away. And because she hadn't insisted he pay her, it left Moses more unnerved than confused. He shook his head. *Forget about her. She's just trying to spook you.*

Moses waited for the woman to disappear from his line of vision, then got up and returned to his room, chiding himself for not going there once he'd finished eating. If he hadn't disobeyed the manager, he never would have had contact with the weird old woman. So much for his first day in Cuba.

Chapter 27

The next day, Moses stared at the passing landscape dotted with fields of tobacco and sugar cane, crops formerly cultivated with slave labor that had made European landowners wealthy. In Latin America cash crops were tobacco, sugar cane, and coffee, while during colonial times in the United States they were cotton, tobacco, sugar cane, rice, and indigo.

Cuban rum and cigars had earned reputations as some of the best in the world. He had made a mental note to purchase some to take to the States as gifts.

Moses was looking forward to batting practice in La Tropical before taking the field against one of the more popular Cuban teams. Lionel had told him the Caribbean island had produced some of the most talented baseball players in the world. If they were to compete against the players in the majors, they would annihilate them. This disclosure did little to boost Moses's confidence.

Well, he didn't have long to wait as the bus driver

pulled up to the entrance to the ballpark where they were going to play against the Cuban team. The park was large, expansive, and colorful. The seating was all benches, except for a few rows of individual seats in the infield. It was a marked difference from many of the small, dusty stadiums in which Negro teams were forced to play.

Moses had committed to spending two months in Cuba, one in Puerto Rico, another two in the Dominican Republic, and one in Mexico. After six months he would return home to begin another six months in the Negro Leagues. His introduction to Latin baseball was with the sound of fans playing bongos. It was a startling difference from cheering and clapping fans. He had become used to an occasional intoxicated fan screaming profanities, but not drumming. Under another set of circumstances, he would've enjoyed the music, but it reverberated in his head and shattered his concentration. The opposing pitcher was Cuba's answer to the Negro Leagues' Satchel Paige. Moses found it impossible to hit his pitches and for the first time since joining the Memphis Eagles he went 0 for 4.

Later that night when the team returned to their lodgings the catcher announced loudly, "They mopped the floor with us."

"Wrong," countered their manager. "What they did was kick our asses. What I saw out there today was disgraceful. I've seen eight-year-olds play better. And, Gilliam. What happened? You couldn't see the ball?"

Moses felt all eyes on him. "No, I couldn't see it because the pitcher tended to mix up his pitches with fastballs and curveballs. Those are his only two pitches, so when we face him again, I'll know what to expect."

He didn't tell the manager that the man had thrown a pitch he'd never seen. It started out as curveball, but then ended up on the outside of the plate for left-handers. As a right-handed hitter, he would have to reach across the plate to hit it.

"Gilliam, have you thought about becoming a switch-hitter?" the manager asked him.

"No, sir."

"Do you think it is something you'll be able to master?"

Moses shrugged his shoulders. "I don't know. It's worth trying." He was right-hand dominant, and learning to bat left-handed was something he had never considered. Maybe it was a good time to experiment while playing winter ball.

"I'll have the batting coach work with you on that. Not only was hitting bad but defense was even worse," George Edwards continued, glaring at the players who sat with downcast eyes. "Who the hell makes five errors in one game? I didn't bring you gentlemen down here to perform like buffoons. In case you didn't know it, everyone was laughing at you. Some of you don't know me, but I allow only one strike in my game. And you just had that strike today. I don't want to see the same shit tomorrow that I saw this afternoon. Now, get out of my sight before I really lose it."

Moses headed for the staircase that would take him to his room. The manager had given them a tongue-lashing that was well deserved. It was apparent the team had come to Cuba with the impression they could easily beat the Latin team. Well, they were wrong because they lost big-time with a lopsided score of 11 to 1. And the one run had come on a wild pitch.

Moses gathered a clean set of clothes and walked down the hall to one of two bathrooms to shower. He didn't want to dwell on what had happened that afternoon, because it was only one day and one game.

* * *

The days turned into weeks and the weeks into months, and then Moses found himself in Mexico. He had more than enjoyed playing winter ball in the Caribbean because Latin players had challenged and gone toe-to-toe with Negro Leagues players. He had worked religiously with the batting coach to perfect becoming a switch-hitter and the first time he at-=tempted it, he hit a double over the head of the center fielder. Now it felt natural to bat from either side of home plate.

He'd met Latin players who were as fair in complexion as White players, with blond hair and blue eyes, except they were named Garcia, Martinez, or Diaz. Like Negroes, they'd formed their own leagues with an endless coterie of talented athletes. Moses found himself playing baseball in a Mexican ballpark that was only four years old. The *Estadio Revolucíon*, located in the city of Torreón in the state of Coahuila, had less than eight thousand seats and was played on a grass surface.

He thought about Inez, who had predicted she would be in Monterrey on a fieldwork assignment. He took a chance and called the number she had given him and was pleasantly surprised when she picked up the phone. After exchanging inane pleasantries, he told her he was going to be in Torreón from late February to mid-March, then he was scheduled to return to the States for spring training and the new baseball season. Inez said she had cousins who lived in Ciudad Juárez, about 520 miles from Torreón. Whenever she had a break in her studies, she would visit him before he returned to the States.

After spending four months in Spanish-speaking countries Moses had picked up enough of the language to become conversational. He was able to order food, ask for directions, and negotiate prices with merchants whenever he wanted to purchase an item. He had made it a practice to buy something for Sallie Ann and his mother in each of the countries he visited.

He'd found the return trip from Mexico to the United States harrowing. Once they arrived in Miami, the team boarded a train for a weeklong trip across five Southern states. After arriving in South Texas, they boarded a bus to take them across the border and into Mexico. It was the first time in a week that he'd been able to exhale and lower his guard because he wasn't confronted with the overt racism he had encountered in Georgia, Alabama, Mississippi, Louisiana, and Texas.

George had asked if anyone objected to forfeiting three games in lieu of spending a week in Mexico City, and not one hand went up. Everyone was exhausted and frustrated from getting on and off trains, while spending long hours in Colored waiting rooms for a connecting one. The entire team had reached their breaking point when a train that was more than three hours behind schedule pulled into a tiny town in Mississippi that barely made the map, for a connecting one going south to Louisiana. The entire station had closed for the night, forcing the team, with their equipment, to bed down on the floor in the Colored waiting room.

George had taken the no-show of hands as approval and announced he'd arrange for the team to stay in Mexico City for a minimum of five days to allow everyone to recover from their exhausting travel schedule.

Moses discovered Mexico's topography and its people were a study in contrasts. There were mountains, valleys, deserts, and active volcanos. The racial makeup of the people in the country was varied, some people with

European ancestry and native groups who were Mayan, Zapotec, and Nahuatl. Inez Cruz had revealed that she was a descendant of Zapotecs, a pre-Columbian civilization that flourished in the state of Oaxaca.

He had taken advantage of the team's layover in Mexico City to attend a bullfight, visit a Catholic church for the first time, and sample enchiladas, tamales, chiles rellenos, guacamole, and mole. Some of the spices used in Mexican cuisine had overwhelmed his palate and whenever he ordered a dish, he asked the server to ask the cook not to add so many chili peppers.

Moses was in awe when he witnessed *charrería*, an equestrian sport where men wore elegant costumes: sombreros with silver and gold embroidery and jackets and pants with silver buttons. Unwittingly, he had fallen in love with Mexico—its food, music, sports, ethnically mixed population, language, and the number of ornately decorated churches. He didn't know why, but he felt more at home in Mexico than he had on the three Caribbean islands. He even wondered if he'd had an ancestor who came from Africa to Mexico.

The team was in good spirits after leaving Mexico City for Torreón, and once they had faced their first Mexican team, they knew after the first inning they were facing their fiercest competitors. The Mexican baseball players exhibited a tenacity similar to the country's boxers. They refused to quit. Their offense was based on running. They stole bases when the pitcher was slow throwing a pitch, or when a wild pitch hit the backstop. Moses and his teammates were wholly frustrated when they'd lost several games as a result of the opposing team stealing home.

After the second loss, George had let loose with a string of profanities in English and Spanish that blistered everyone's ears. "Who the fuck loses a game because they allowed the runner on third base to steal home? Get your heads out of your asses, boys, and start playing baseball. You're being paid, so you are professional ballplayers. Now it's time for you to act like it." The balding middle-aged man with a fringe of white hair resembling cotton balls, sighed heavily. "I hate talking to grown men as if they were boys, but you're making me look bad and are a disgrace to the Negro Leagues. I'm certain those racist White boys in the Major Leagues would have a good laugh if they knew that Colored boys couldn't beat teams of Spanish ballplayers who can't even speak English." He paused and sighed. "I accepted the position to manage this team because I was told you men are the best in the Negro Leagues and when I saw the names, I thought I'd struck the mother lode. Please don't do this to me. Don't make me regret spending six months of my life with you when I could be back home in Little Rock with my wife and grandchildren."

"We feel bad enough about losing, Mr. Edwards, so chewing us out isn't going to help the situation," Moses said.

The manager glared at him. "If you think you can do a better job managing this team, then be my guest."

Moses chided himself for speaking his thoughts aloud. However, he felt compelled to say what was on his mind. "There's no way I could even begin to manage a baseball team, but it's not going to help if we are constantly ridiculed when we lose a game. No team, not even the ones in the Major Leagues, wins all their games every season. The Yankees may have had the most wins in 1932, but it didn't happen again for them until this year. It was the Detroit Tigers in 1934, and the Chicago

Cubs in 1935. I say this because there are always winners and losers, Mr. Edwards. Right now, we're on a losing streak but I'm confident that we will turn it around like we did in Cuba and the Dominican Republic."

"Gilliam's right," the second baseman chimed in. "You're talking to us as if we are a bunch of losers, and that's wrong. We know when we must do better and that means being better even if takes more batting and defensive practice."

"And I second that!" shouted one of the pitchers.

George's eyes appeared to bug out of his head. "What the hell is this? A mutiny?"

"No, Mr. Edwards," said the second baseman. "We're just trying to get you to see that badmouthing us is not going to prove anything. It's just going to make us more resentful of how we're not appreciated for what we do. I know I speak for everyone here that when we walk out onto that baseball diamond it's to win, not lose. But it's impossible to win every game, so if we lose, we tell ourselves it will be better the next time."

A smattering of applause followed when he stopped speaking, then increased as everyone began clapping when they saw their manager's expression change like a snake shedding its skin. It went from anger to an immediate softening of his features until one corner of his mouth was pulled into a slight smile.

"Well, damn. It's nice to see that you men are really a team and stick up for one another."

That's why we are a team. Moses exchanged grins and nods with his teammates. He had risked a tongue-lashing from his manager by speaking out, but fortunately he had been backed up by the second baseman, who had become the unofficial spokesperson for the team.

"You have a couple of days off before we play again, so perhaps we need to go into town and blow off a little bit of this shit that has kept us from winning. Just remember I want you sober and upright for Friday morning's practice."

Moses couldn't stop smiling. George giving them time off was perfect because Inez had called to say she was coming to Torreón to spend a couple of days with him.

Chapter 28

Moses reclined in bed, his shoulders supported by a pile of pillows. He stared at Inez as she peered through the lacy curtains in a bedroom of a farmhouse that had been converted into a hotel. He'd reserved the room for two days, and then he had to return to the ballpark for batting practice.

His gaze lingered on the abundance of straight black hair falling down her back. The blunt strands covered her butt, leaving only a pair of slim legs and thighs for him to admire.

Inez turned and came back to bed. She slipped in beside him, as he pulled her against his body. "Are you okay?" he whispered in her hair.

"I'm more than okay," she said, smiling. "When we first met, you couldn't speak a word of Spanish, and now you're practically fluent."

"It's taken a lot of hard work, but I was determined to learn. Spending months in Puerto Rico, Cuba, and the Dominican Republic has been the best teacher."

Shifting slightly to meet his eyes, Inez ran a forefinger

over the stubble on his jaw. "Most people become fluent after living in a country for a year, but it didn't take you that long."

"I'm not fully fluent, Inez."

"You could be if you decided to stay in Mexico."

He stared at the slender face, her large eyes the color of warm sherry. Moses thought Inez was more attractive than pretty, and it was her perfectly shaped feminine figure that had attracted him to her. Up close he'd found her features in a sun-browned face a little too strong for a woman, but once she struck up a conversation with him, he had fallen under her spell. They had talked for hours before he followed her like an obedient puppy to her house and into her bed.

"I stay in Mexico and do what?" he asked.

"Make love to me and play baseball."

Moses shook his head. Latin ballplayers made a lot less than Colored players in the Negro Leagues. "I don't plan to play baseball for the rest of my life."

"What do you plan to do?"

"Become a farmer."

Rising on an elbow, Inez gave him a direct stare. "You want to be a farmer?"

Moses heard a trace of disbelief in her voice. "Yes."

"Why, Moses? Why would you want to be a farmer when you can be so much more?"

"And you believe the *more* is playing baseball?" He answered her question with one of his own. "I've always wanted to own land, grow crops, and raise livestock that will support my family. And if there's a surplus, then I will either sell it or give it to needy families."

"But farming is so beneath you, Moses. You're still young enough to go to college to become a doctor or a lawyer."

Moses was annoyed. "Why do you believe farming is beneath being a lawyer or doctor? It's farmers who keep countries thriving by growing what we need to nourish our bodies. When the Europeans kidnapped my ancestors and brought them to the so-called New World in chains, it was to make them slaves to work in the fields cultivating cotton, rice, sugarcane, and tobacco. And don't forget coffee here in Mexico and Brazil. Even the Irish had to leave Ireland during the potato famine because they were starving to death. When you sit down at the table to eat your enchiladas or tamales, do you ever think about the people who worked long hours in the sun to work the fields and then harvest what they planted and tended? I do, Inez, because my ancestors were slaves in a country that still doesn't recognize their descendants as citizens with full rights granted them by the Constitution. Do you realize that my people are denied the right to vote in certain states because of Jim Crow laws? You live in Texas, so you know damn well what I'm talking about."

"Moses, darling, I didn't mean to upset you," Inez crooned.

He pressed a kiss on her hair. "I'm sorry I barked at you."

"It's all right. I like that you're passionate about something."

He wanted to tell her he was passionate about a few things, and at the present time, she happened to be one of them. He enjoyed their time together, especially making love to her.

"When do you have to be back in Monterrey?"

"Not until Monday. I'm going to leave in a couple of hours because I want to get back to Ciudad Juárez before nightfall. I'll spend some time with my cousins before leaving for Monterrey."

"How many more years do you have before you earn your degree?"

"I have one more year of fieldwork and then another

of classes. Then I'm finished. And once that happens, I would like us to get together because I plan to get all my friends together for a blowout celebration."

"Where do you plan to hold your celebration?"

"It will be in San Antonio at my parents' house. Promise me you'll come," she said, tickling his ribs.

"Okay," Moses said, laughing as he caught her hand. "You're going to have to give me your parents' number because I'm not certain where I will be living in two years."

"Do you still plan to get married in two years?"

"Yes." Moses had been upfront with Inez when he told her he was planning to marry in a couple of years. However, he had hesitated to tell her about Sallie Ann. "What are your plans once you graduate?"

"I have a position in an Austin museum waiting for me."

"Good for you."

Inez knew exactly where her career was going, while he had hoped to continue playing for the Memphis Eagles and eventually settle down with Sallie Ann. Once he returned to Memphis, he wanted to begin looking for parcels of land that were available for sale. Once he purchased the land, then he would wait a year to save enough money to put up a house and barn. The purchase of farm equipment and livestock would come later. Hopefully by that time he wouldn't be forced to play winter ball to make money and could stay at home to get his farm up and running.

"I've told myself that I don't want to marry or have children, but there is something about you that could make me change my mind."

"Why, Inez?"

"Would you believe I've fallen in love with you?"

"No, Inez, I don't believe it. What we've had is incredible sex and that doesn't necessarily translate into love."

Her fingernails made circular motions on his chest. "For me it does."

Moses exhaled an audible breath. He didn't want to talk about love when he wasn't certain whether what he felt for Sallie Ann was love or deep affection.

Sallie Ann didn't care who saw her when she threw her arms around Moses's neck and kissed him on the mouth. She moaned softly when he returned the kiss and at the same time tightened his hold on her waist, lifting her off her feet.

"I've missed you," he groaned against her parted lips.

"I've missed you more," she said, attempting to smother a giggle. "Come inside, because Mama is waiting to serve dinner." Reaching for Moses's hand, she practically dragged him inside the house to the dining room.

Maddie's head popped up and she smiled. "Welcome back."

Moses nodded. "Thank you, ma'am. It's good to be back."

"How did you like traveling?" Maddie asked as she set a pitcher of sweet tea on the lacy tablecloth.

"It was tiring. But once we got to our destination it was all good."

"Sallie Ann will show you where you can wash up before we sit down to eat."

When Moses had called Sallie Ann earlier that morning to let her know he was back in Memphis he hadn't expected her to invite him to dinner. He wanted to crawl into bed and sleep for hours.

Lucille Parker told him Lionel was expected back in Memphis in a few days and that Curtis Bullock had left the Eagles to sign with another team. Her disclosure about Bullock hadn't come as a surprise. The man had been hinting about joining a Texas team because he missed being with his family.

It felt good to be back in Memphis. It had become home. His mother had written him to say she was planning to come up later in the year to visit with him and hopefully meet the girl he planned to marry. He had let Daisy know he'd met someone with whom he planned to eventually settle down and marry.

Sallie Ann showed him where he could wash his hands and when he returned to the dining room, he was surprised to find her father waiting for him. He approached the older man and extended his hand.

"It's good seeing you, sir."

Jimmie grasped Moses's hand, shaking it vigorously. "Same here, son. You look as if you've gotten quite a bit of sun."

Moses was aware that his face was several shades darker than it had been before leaving the States. "The tropical sun was brutal."

Jimmie grunted. "You were basking in the hot sun while we were freezing our butts off here. We had more snow this winter than we've had in years. But I ain't complaining because we had a bitch of a summer."

"Daddy!"

"Jimmie!"

Sallie Ann and Maddie had spoken at the same time.

"Stop it," Jimmie chastised. "It's not the first time Moses has heard the word and I'm willing to bet it won't be last. Enough running off at the mouth. Let's sit down and eat."

Moses wanted to tell his future father-in-law he was right. He'd heard enough curses from George Edwards and his teammates to last him a lifetime. Jimmie blessed the table, then plates of honey ham, collard greens, sweet potatoes, and buttery cornbread were passed around the table.

He peered over his glass of sweet tea at Sallie Ann, sitting opposite him, wondering what she was thinking. She had this mysterious smile on her face as if she were hiding a secret. It didn't take Moses long to discover why the Thompsons had insisted he join them for dinner when Jimmie cleared his throat and said he wanted to make an announcement.

"Moses, my daughter told me that you plan to give her a ring once she graduates."

Moses sat up straight. "That's right."

"An engagement and not a wedding ring?"

He nodded. "Yes, sir."

"You claim you want to wait two years before marrying my daughter because you want to save enough money to buy land and a house."

"That's what I've planned."

Jimmie shifted on his chair. "Well, I'm going to make it easier for you. Me and Maddie decided to buy the land and house as a wedding gift. I found a parcel for sale about ten miles from here with a three-bedroom house set on eight acres that's large enough for you put up a barn and to grow whatever you want."

Moses shook his head, unable to believe what he'd just heard. "I can't."

"You can't what, Moses?"

"I can't accept it."

"Why not?"

"Because it's too much."

Jimmie frowned. "Are you saying my daughter isn't worth me giving her and her future husband a wedding gift?"

"I . . . I didn't mean it like that, sir."

The older man pounded the table with his fist. "Stop calling me sir. Now, I want to hear it—Is my daughter worth me giving her a wedding gift of my choosing?"

Moses felt as if he was being put on the spot and blackmailed. He wanted to marry Sallie Ann, and as her husband give her things she deserved, but her father had usurped him.

"She's more than worth it."

Jimmie sat back, grinning like a Cheshire cat. "That settles it. When you come by tomorrow, I will take you to see the property. Meanwhile, I will leave it up to Maddie and Sallie Ann to plan for a June wedding."

Moses's eyes shifted to Sallie Ann. When he saw the expression on her face, he realized she was as shocked as he. It was apparent her father had set up everything without her knowledge.

"Why, Daddy?" she whispered.

"Why what, baby girl?"

"Why did you do this without talking to me?"

"I didn't tell you because I wanted it to be a surprise."

"A surprise!" she said her voice rising. "It's a shock. It isn't fair that you didn't give me or Moses a chance to discuss this with you."

"You talk about fair, Miss Sallie Ann Thompson! What's not fair is Moses Gilliam asking you to wait two years while he is gone more than he's here and can't get to court you properly. I understand him traveling when he's playing ball, but then you don't get to see him for another six months because again he's traveling to play winter ball to get the money he needs to take care of a wife. Do you think it's fair when you sit home waiting for him when other girls your age are going to the movies or parties with their friends? And what if he meets someone else in two years, when you have put your life on hold for him?" Jimmie slowly shook his head. "I'm not willing to risk your happiness on a promise of two years." He shifted his angry glare from Sallie Ann to Moses. "What's it going to be? Either you tell me now that you're going to marry my daughter in June, or you can walk the hell out of my house and never come back."

Moses felt like a butterfly specimen pinned to a wall as he stared at Jimmie Thompson. He hated that the man had put him on the spot, but he wasn't wrong about some of the things he'd said. He had asked Sallie Ann to wait for him without an actual guarantee to marry her, because he'd wanted to wait until she graduated to give her an engagement ring.

Then he asked her to wait another year before they'd become husband and wife, and so many things could happen during that span of time. Not only he, but she, could meet someone with whom to fall in love and marry.

He'd asked himself over and over if he was being fair to Sallie Ann, and each time, he hadn't been able to answer definitively. Meanwhile, he was presented with a generous wedding gift from his future in-laws and he was vacillating whether he should be gracious enough to accept it.

"I will marry Sallie Ann in June, but only if she is willing to become my wife."

Tears were streaming down Sallie Ann's face and she held a hand over her mouth to muffle the sobs threatening to come out. "Yes," she said after an interminable length of time that had left Moses feeling as if he was in suspended animation.

Moses, who'd suddenly tired of Jimmie Thompson issuing mandates, said, "We will go and look at the property tomorrow, but only after I take Sallie Ann to the jewelry store, so we can select rings."

"Whatever you want," Jimmie said.

"It is what I want," Moses countered.

He wanted to remind Jimmie that he had only agreed because marrying Sallie Ann sooner rather than later was advantageous to both of them. He was still required to travel for away games, but when he returned to Memphis it would be to his wife and home instead of a room on the lower level of a house where he had to adhere to a set of rules, including a curfew. When he was off, he could begin working to put in a garden.

He was fond of Sallie Ann and with time would come to love her. She deserved to be loved.

CHAPTER 29

Sallie Ann sat on the sofa in the den of the house she would share with her husband in another two weeks, hand stitching the hem of a pair of curtains she wanted to hang in the smallest of the three bedrooms. Moses had been on the road traveling with the team on away games to Kansas and Missouri; he would return to Tennessee two days before their scheduled wedding. They had selected a date where there were no games, and that meant the entire team had been invited to attend.

It appeared as if she had entered an imaginary state fair, where one day she was riding in a runaway rollercoaster, then the next sitting in a Ferris wheel gondola that stopped with her suspended at the top, and there was a merry-go-round that refused to slow down so she could get off. The nonstop activity had begun to spin out of control the day Moses sat at the table with her family and had officially asked her to marry him. One day blended into the next when he selected a diamond engagement ring for her and matching bands they would exchange during the wedding ceremony.

The house her parents had selected as a wedding gift was a white clapboard farmhouse with a wraparound porch and a royal blue front door with matching window shutters. An expansive entryway, living and dining rooms, eat-in kitchen, den, and three second-floor bedrooms was perfect for several generations of Gilliams. Moses planned to turn the space at the rear of the house into a mud, utility, and laundry room.

When she returned to school with the ring on her finger, she'd experienced a personal victory because none of the other girls in her graduating class were engaged. She was the first and she'd overheard girls whispering about the size of the sparkly round diamond.

Sallie Ann had enlisted the help of her mother, who had also offered to pay for the wedding and the furnishings, when selecting furniture, and with the ongoing deliveries of lamps, chairs, sofa, beds, tables, rugs, dinnerware, linens, curtains, and pots and pans. Sallie Ann wanted the house to be fully furnished and decorated before the wedding. She and Moses would exchange vows at the local AME church, while Sallie Ann decided to host the reception under a tent on the lawn of her new home. Moses had selected Lionel Dean as his best man while one of her cousins had agreed to be her maid of honor. Her uncles had advertised that Tommy's Joint would be closed that day for a family celebration. She had mailed an invitation to his sisters. They declined because both had given birth earlier in the year, and they promised to send wedding gifts.

Moses had invited his parents, but his mother reported she would come alone because her husband's rapidly failing health wouldn't permit him to travel. Daisy Gilliam had written Moses to tell him that his father had stopped working because there were days when he hadn't been able to get out of bed.

Sallie Ann had wanted her future mother-in-law to stay for a week to become better acquainted, but Daisy claimed she had to return to Nichols to look after her husband.

The whirlwind of activity did slow down long enough for her to try on her mother's gown, and she had breathed a sigh of relief because it was a perfect fit. Maddie had wrapped the gown and veil in an airtight, moisture-proof bag and it looked as new as the day it had been made for her.

She heard a sound and went completely still, then let out a shriek when Moses walked into the room. "What are you doing here?" she asked, her heart beating double-time. "I thought you were in Kansas."

Moses sank on the sofa beside her and kissed her cheek. "We were headed there when we got the news that a tornado had touched down and nearly wiped out everything in the town."

"Oh, my goodness. That's horrible."

"It's a good thing it happened during the day and not at night when folks were sleeping."

Sallie Ann put aside her sewing. "So how long will the team be here before you leave again?"

Moses draped an arm over her shoulders. "At least three days before we head out to Missouri." He leaned closer and pressed a kiss on her hair. "That will give us three whole days to get used to each other before our big day."

She smiled. "We're already getting used to each other, because I get to see you more, now that you've moved into our new house."

Moses scooped her up and settled her on his lap. "And how many more weeks will it be before you move in?"

"Two, my love."

His eyebrows shot up. "My love?"

Sallie Ann scrunched up her nose. "You know I love you, otherwise I never would've agreed to marry you."

Moses closed his eyes as he inhaled the lingering scent of flowers on Sallie Ann's neck. He wasn't certain whether they were roses or lavender. It didn't matter because she always smelled delicious. "And I love you, Sallie Ann Thompson soon-to-be Gilliam."

She laughed softly. "That's truly a mouthful. What would you think if I hyphenated my last name like Thompson dash Gilliam."

Moses eased back, staring at the mouth he never tired of kissing. "Is that what you really want?"

"It's just a thought, Moses. I'd probably use it once I sell my first photograph."

She'd purchased her Rolleiflex camera and had begun taking pictures. Once they had been developed, Moses had to admit that they were incredible candid shots. She had even photographed him sitting in a chair breaking in a new glove. The lighting and angles were spectacular.

"Do you know what I want to do once we're married?"

"What?"

"I want to take a train ride up to Chicago and photograph the two Major League baseball parks."

"You mean Wrigley Field and Comiskey Park?"

She nodded. "Yes."

"Why Chicago, babe?"

"Because I can take a train to Chicago and shoot two stadiums during my stay. I would like to photograph every major and minor league ballpark in the country."

"That sounds very ambitious."

"True, but it's something I want to do when my husband is traveling around the country."

"Have you thought about your husband worrying about you traveling out and about when he's on the road and not able to contact you?"

"I'll leave you my itinerary, Moses."

"That's not enough. I don't want to become the type of husband who demands that you must do this or not do that, but I need you to understand what I would be going through not knowing if you are safe. You'd be a lone woman going places where you've never been. I love you, Sallie Ann, and because you've become everything to me, I don't want to lose you."

Moses didn't know when, how, or why, but he had fallen in love with the woman with whom he wanted to share his name and his life. She'd become so easy to love.

There was something about her that reminded him of his mother. Underneath her delicate exterior was an inner strength that communicated she would be all right if anything were to happen to him or the children he hoped they would have. As an amateur photographer she had an innate gift for taking spectacular pictures. Except for when she had demanded he stop the car to let her out, she'd never raised her voice to him again.

Yes, he had chosen well and he would be forever grateful to Sallie Ann for choosing him. "What if we compromise," he said after a pregnant pause.

"Compromise how?"

"When the team is scheduled to play in Chicago, you can take the train and meet us there. I'll reserve a room in a hotel where you'll stay with me. Then I'll act as your guide when you go to the North and South sides to take your photos of Wrigley Field and Comiskey Park."

Sallie Ann flashed a hundred-watt grin. "I like that."

"And I like you."

Moses was relieved that she had gone along with his

suggestion. A young woman traveling alone in a strange city could become a target for an unpleasant incident he refused to think about.

It was her wedding night, and although her mother had told her what to expect, it hadn't prepared Sallie Ann for the twin emotions of anticipation and passion eddying through her like a lighted fuse as she prayed not to dissolve into a maelstrom of fear that she wouldn't be able to please her husband.

Her wedding ceremony was nothing short of spectacular, with her wearing her mother's wedding finery and Moses tall and handsome in a dark suit that showed off his broad shoulders. After an exchange of vows and rings, they exited the church and were greeted by family and friends who had showered them with white and red flower petals.

A photographer had taken a series of pictures of the wedding party and the parents of the bride and the mother of the groom, while their guests were given directions to the house where caterers waited for them under a large white tent protecting them from the intense summer sun. Banquet tables were crowded with trays of food, with something for everyone, while her uncles had assumed roles as bartenders to serve potent drinks to those with enough courage to sample their reserves of homemade moonshine.

Sallie Ann walked on bare feet from the bathroom, where she'd changed into a floor-length silk and lace nightgown, and into the bedroom where Moses sat in bed with a mound of pillows supporting his shoulders.

Smiling, he swept back the lightweight blanket on the far side of the bed and patted the mattress. "Come get into bed."

She walked around the bed and got in beside him,

her foot encountering his bare leg. Sallie Ann swallowed to relieve the tightness in her throat. He was naked under the blanket.

"We don't have to do anything tonight," he whispered in her ear.

"What are you talking about?"

"I don't mind waiting to consummate our marriage until you're ready."

"I am ready, Moses. Let's do this before the effects of the moonshine I just drank wears off."

Moses gave her an incredulous look. "Is that what you were doing so long in the bathroom?"

Sallie Ann nodded. "Yes, because I needed something to fortify me."

"Are you afraid of me?"

"No, Moses, I'm not afraid of you. What I'm afraid of is that I won't be able to please you."

"You please me just by being you."

"I'm talking about sex, Moses."

"And I'm not," he countered. "Do you think I could have sex with someone I don't care about? No," he said, answering his own question.

Sliding lower, she closed her eyes. "I need you to make love to me."

Moses didn't know if Sallie Ann wanted him to consummate their marriage, or if it was the effects of the liquor. She had no idea how difficult it had been for him to keep his hands off her. He'd begun taking cold showers, and when that didn't work, he would pleasure himself to assuage the buildup of sexual frustration.

"Open your eyes, Sallie Ann. Please." He smiled when she looked at him. "I'm going to make love to you, and I'll try not to hurt you. And if there is anything you don't want me to do, then tell me and I'll stop."

"Okay." The single word was a whisper.

Moses took his time relieving Sallie Ann of her nightgown, then covered her mouth with his until her lips parted. He inhaled the lingering scent of the corn liquor on her breath.

He kissed her mouth, throat, shoulders and moved lower to her breasts. It was when she opened her legs to him Moses knew he had found everything he had ever wanted and needed with the woman who he had claimed as his wife.

CHAPTER 30

"When are you going to come up for air, Harper?"

Harper stared at the words filling the computer screen. "What are you talking about, Grandpa?"

"You know exactly what I'm talking about, Harper Lauren Fleming."

She spun around on her chair. "It must be serious if you had to address me by my government name."

"What are you trying to do, kill yourself? You've been working on that book nonstop for the past week. You only stop to shower and change your clothes, grab a bite, then go back to rat-a-tat-tat on those damn keys."

"I'm trying to finish the book before my birthday."

"If you keep going like you've been, you won't be around to celebrate your birthday. I don't know if you've looked in a mirror, but you've lost weight you can't afford to lose. And no man wants a bone."

Harper stood up. "What's going on with you, Grandpa?"

"I'm going to Chicago for a week to spend time with my boy. He says the Sox have a ten-day home game schedule, so after the games we're going to hang out together."

"Good for you. But what does that have to do with you biting my head off?"

"I don't want to come back here and find a scarecrow."

Harper narrowed her eyes. "Very funny, Grandpa."

Bernard pointed to the stack of printed pages. "What the heck are you writing? Another *War and Peace*?"

"No," she said, laughing. Harper wanted to admit to her grandfather that it had taken her longer than she had anticipated to introduce Moses Gilliam and develop his relationship with Sallie Ann and his teammates. "I've reached a point in the manuscript where it will go a lot faster now that I've set up the characters and situations I need to move the plot forward."

She had married Moses and Sallie Ann and now she could fast-forward their lives several years. It was now 1937, and in another four years the United States would be drawn into the Second World War. Two years after the end of the war the face of baseball would change forever when Jackie Robinson broke the color line by signing with the Brooklyn Dodgers. Not only would it be a history-making event, it would affect every Colored player in the Negro Leagues.

"When do you think you'll be finished?"

Harper bit her lip. "If I keep to the same pace, then I should be finished in a couple of days."

"Good, because I'm leaving in a couple of days. Meanwhile, I'm going to ask Cheney to check in on you."

Harper's jaw dropped. "I don't need anyone checking in on me."

"There you go again, Harper. Believing you don't need anyone but yourself. I'm not going to ask him to babysit you but invite you out to dinner so you can get out of this house for a few hours."

"Okay, Grandpa," she drawled.

"Okay what, Harper?"

"You can talk to him about taking me out. Now, if you will excuse me, I'd like to get back to writing."

"I'm going to bring you a dish of fruit. You're going to need the natural sugar to keep your energy up."

"Thank you. Grandpa?"

"Yes, Harper."

"You know that I love you."

Bernard shook his head. "That's something we never have to debate."

Harper knew he was right. There had never been a time when her love for her grandparents was debatable. Now that she was spending time with her with grandfather, the bond between them had grown even stronger. Leaning back in the chair, she thought about Bernard reconnecting with his former military buddies, and now his son. It almost seemed as if he was getting his house in order before . . . Her thoughts trailed off because she didn't want to think about losing her grandfather.

He shouldn't be living alone. It hadn't mattered that he lived in a semi-retirement community where the residents tended to look out for one another. He didn't need strangers, but family looking after him. It suddenly hit Harper that there was nothing and no one waiting for her in Chicago. She had quit her job, she rented an apartment and her lease was coming up for renewal at the end of the year, so her relocating to Nashville could be accomplished without a hitch.

Bernard had mentioned she didn't have to be a senior citizen to take up residence in his community, and that meant she could move in, with her grandfather's approval, and apply for a teaching position at one of the local high schools. It was time for her to stop running, settle down, and act like a responsible adult.

Bernard returned with a fork and a bowl of sliced melons.

"Thank you."

He bowed as if she were royalty. "You're quite welcome."

Harper took her time eating the fruit, as she thought about how she was going to tell her grandfather that she was planning to live with him—full time. What she didn't want to contemplate was his rejecting her offer because he thought she believed he was so old that he couldn't look after himself. She decided to wait until he returned from Chicago.

She picked up another notebook: *Property of Kelton S. Fleming—1940*, and thumbed through the pages. Although she'd read all of Kelton Fleming's notebooks cover to cover, she wanted to refresh her memory when it came to milestones in his life.

Moses sat on the side of the hospital bed and cradled Sallie Ann against his chest. "Everything is going to be all right. You're young and there will be more babies."

Sallie Ann closed her eyes as she shook her head. "No, there won't, Moses. This is the third baby I've lost in three years. I can't do this again."

He buried his face in her hair. "We'll wait a couple of years before we try again."

"I don't want to try again, Moses. The doctor said . . ."

He frowned. "The doctor said what, Sallie Ann?"

"He said that I should undergo a hysterectomy because the next time I miscarry I may not make it. Each time I lose a baby I lose more and more blood."

Moses swallowed painfully. There was a lump in his throat the size of a grapefruit. The day he and Sallie Ann celebrated their six-month anniversary, one day before New Year's Eve, was one he would remember forever when she told him she was carrying their baby.

He hadn't signed up to play winter ball, and once the regular baseball season ended, he had a lot of time to devote to his wife and starting the farm. A construction crew had put up a barn, with stalls for horses and an area for a bull and two heifers. Sallie Ann wanted chickens, so the next project was to erect an enclosed chicken coop with a half dozen laying chickens and a rooster. The rooster had become the bane of his existence when it began crowing with the first hint of daylight.

His life was as close to perfect as it could get, but with each miscarriage Sallie Ann appeared to lose her lust for life. "Is that what you want, Sallie Ann?"

"It's not what I want but what needs to be done. I want you to sign the paper so I can have the operation."

"And if I don't?"

"Then I will die, Moses. Because if I get pregnant and miscarry again, I will bleed to death."

Moses did not want to think of losing her; not when they had so much to live for. He'd wanted to mention adoption, but it wasn't the time to broach that subject. "Okay, sweetheart. I will sign the paper."

Sallie Ann underwent the hysterectomy, with a week-long hospital stay. Maddie had come to stay at the farm during her daughter's recuperation. There were days when Sallie Ann appeared to be in good spirits and then there were down days when she'd cry and refuse to get out of bed.

Moses was concerned about his wife, and about the political unrest in Europe. Germany had invaded Poland the year before, and France and Great Britain countered by declaring war on Germany. There were rumors that Germany had plans to invade the Soviet Union. So far, the United States had remained neutral. Moses had found himself fixated on war news coming out of Europe when listening to the radio or reading newspapers. Last month the United States had instituted the Selective Training and Service Act of 1940, and it required all men between the ages of 21 to 45 to register for the draft. Moses had recently celebrated his twenty-second birthday and he'd had to go to the local draft board to register.

He did not want to think of going to war or leaving his wife.

Not now.

Not when Sallie Ann needed him now more than at any time during their marriage. But if he had to go, then he would plan for her to stay with her parents.

The telephone rang and Moses got up to answer it. "Hello."

"Hello yourself."

He folded his body down to an armchair in the den. "And to what do I owe the pleasure of your call?"

"I just called to see how you're doing. From one old friend to another."

Moses hadn't spoken to Inez Cruz in years. The last time was when he'd called to decline her invitation to her graduation celebration because Sallie Ann had lost their second child.

"I should be the one asking how you are doing."

"I'm well, Moses. I just got promoted to assistant curator with a nice increase in salary. The reason I really called was to ask if you've registered for the draft."

"Yeah. At the ripe old age of twenty-two I had to register or get locked up."

"All my brothers and several cousins also had to register. My father, who just turned forty-six, managed to elude it, but that didn't stop him cursing up a blue streak in English and Spanish. I called to find out how you're doing and to let you know I'm putting together an exhibit of pre-Columbian art and antiquities for museums in Chicago and then New York next spring. And if you plan to be in either of those cities, I'd like you to come and check it out."

"I'll try, Inez, but I can't promise you anything because I haven't seen next year's game schedule. How long is the exhibition?"

"It's scheduled to run for two months in Chicago, and four in New York."

"If I'm not able to see it, then I'll ask Sallie Ann whether she would like to attend." He didn't want to tell Inez that Sallie Ann getting away from the farm for a couple of days would lift her spirits.

"Your wife is an artist?"

"No. She's an amateur photographer and I may sound biased, but she's very good."

"Maybe you could send me some of her photos to look over. The museum is thinking of creating space just for photography."

"I'll ask her."

"Please do. I forgot to ask, but how is your wife?"

Moses told Inez about Sallie Ann undergoing an operation that would prevent her from becoming pregnant again after miscarrying her third baby in three years. "Her mother's here with us, so she appears to be feeling better."

"I'm so sorry, Moses. Have you and Sallie Ann thought about maybe adopting a child?"

"Not yet. I'm going to wait before I bring that up. What I do know is that she wants to be a mother."

"What about you being a father, Moses?"

"I'm not going to lie and say I don't want that, but it's not as important to me as it is for my wife."

"I wish I could help you out, because I know of a few young girls from so-called good families who got themselves in trouble and their families sent them away, and once they delivered were forced to give up their babies."

"It happens here, too, Inez." Sallie Ann had told him that two girls she'd gone to school with had found themselves in the family way, and when the boys refused to marry them, their families sent them to relatives out of the state to have their babies.

"It's been happening since the beginning of time, Moses. The Bible is filled with stories about fallen women having sexual relations without benefit of marriage."

Lines fanned out around Moses's eyes when he smiled. "You're right about that."

"I can't promise you with any degree of certainty—"

"Only death and taxes are certainties in this life, Inez," Moses said, interrupting her.

"You're right. But what I was going to say is if I know of a young girl who is willing to give up her baby for adoption, you will be at the top of the list. I want you to mail me all the information that would go on a birth certificate, and that includes your wife's maiden name and age."

"Why are you willing to do this for me?"

"Don't you remember me telling you that you're the only man I've ever fallen in love with? I loved you then and I love you now. And people who know me are aware that I would do anything within my power to help those I love. That includes family and friends. I'll also make certain the girl I choose will be an American citizen and brown like his new mother and father."

Throwing back his head, Moses laughed so hard that his sides hurt. "You're unbelievable."

"I know. I'm going to end this call because the minutes are adding up and I'm spending more money on telephone calls than I do on food."

"Goodbye and thanks for calling, Inez."

"Love you, Moses."

"And I love you, too," he said, then hung up.

"Who were you talking to?"

Moses turned to see Maddie standing only a few feet away and wondered just how much of his conversation she had overheard. "A friend."

Maddie puffed up her chest, reminding him of a bantam rooster preparing to attack. "Is that friend a woman, Moses?"

"Yes," he said truthfully. "She's someone I met a long time ago and we relate to each other like sister and brother."

"So, there's nothing going on between you two?"

Not any longer. "No, Maddie. A man and woman can be friends without something going on between them." Maddie lowered her eyes and Moses knew she was thinking about what she had experienced with her husband. "How's Sallie Ann?" he asked, deftly changing the topic.

"She's changing her clothes. I've convinced her to go into town with me to do some shopping."

A smile spread over his features. Inviting his mother-in-law to come and stay with Sallie Ann had helped her recover more quickly than she had in the past. "I like the sound of that. Do you need some money?"

Maddie rolled her eyes. "No, Moses, I don't need any money."

"Okay, Mama."

He had begun calling his mother-in-law *mama* once he married Sallie Ann, while his own mother rarely left her husband's bedside as he lay dying from what had been diagnosed as black lung disease. Facing what had become inevitable death had changed Solomon from an angry, violent man into one who was weak and remorseful.

Moses had traveled to Nichols for the first time in years, and like a priest listening to a confession, Moses had listened to Solomon bare his soul, pleading for forgiveness. Moses did forgive him because there was no room in his own life for resentment and bitterness. He was reunited with his sisters, who had made him an uncle many times over and appeared happy with their lives as mothers and wives of coal miners.

He waited until he was alone in the house to pen a letter to Inez with the information she'd requested. He did not want to say anything to Sallie Ann about possibly adopting a child until she was fully recovered from losing the baby and healed from the surgical procedure.

CHAPTER 31

Harper printed what she'd saved and then did a happy dance. She was close to completing the manuscript but decided to take a break to prepare for her date with Cheney. Her grandfather had left for Chicago, and not having him looking over her shoulder to monitor the time she spent on the computer had allowed her to write uninterrupted for days.

However, she did take time out to respond to her mother's text messages, and Cheney's when he'd asked if she would accompany him on a night out on the town. He'd selected a restaurant featuring intimate dining and live music. Harper had less than three hours to wash her hair and blow it out before he arrived. She turned off the desk lamp and walked out of the sunroom to her bedroom.

Cheney couldn't believe his eyes when Harper opened the door. He stared at her like a deer caught in the blinding glare of headlights. Her little black dress didn't leave much to his imagination. The off-the-shoulder garment hugged her body like a second skin, and he forced himself to look at her face and not her chest. Four-inch stilettos put the top of her head level with his ear.

"You look incredible."

Harper lowered her eyes, the demure gesture more sensual than innocent.

"Thank you."

She turned to lock the door, and that allowed Cheney to view her body—all of it, from her exposed silken shoulders to her shapely bare legs and feet, without appearing to be a voyeur. He thought of her as elegant simplicity with her barely-there makeup and her straightened hair styled in a twist on the nape of her neck. Harper Fleming had enthralled him as an adolescent, and time hadn't changed his feelings toward her. Then it had been a boyhood crush, but now he was a man on a mission to let Harper know that his feelings for her hadn't lessened, but increased to where he wanted to convince her that she was what he had spent years searching for.

Every woman he'd had a brief encounter with following his divorce bored him to tears. Cheney wanted a woman to challenge him and not acquiesce to whatever he said or proposed. He wanted one who could make him laugh when he didn't feel like laughing, and sharing Sunday dinner with Harper and her grandfather was like reliving some of the best times in his young life. He held out his hand to take the keys from Harper, then cupped her elbow as he escorted her down the porch steps to his vehicle. When she hesitated getting in on the passenger side of the SUV, Cheney realized the fit of her dress wouldn't allow her to step up gracefully. Circling her waist with both hands, he lifted her effortlessly, and settled her on the seat.

Harper couldn't stop the wave of heat in her face and chest as she clutched the small evening purse in a death grip. She'd packed two dressy outfits, and much to her chagrin she'd chosen the wrong one to wear tonight. She had forgotten that Cheney's SUV was higher than hers, and the body-hugging garment ending at her knees would have made it impossible to get in without assistance unless she hiked the hem above her thighs, which would have exposed even more skin.

Cheney slipped in beside her. "Don't worry, Harper, I'll help you in and out."

She looked at him as he started the engine. Dressed in a custom-made white shirt with his initials embroidered on the cuff, a dark gray silk tie, and tailored suit pants, he appeared every inch the successful lawyer. "I suppose I wore the wrong dress for our date."

Cheney concentrated on backing out of the driveway. "No, you didn't. The dress is perfect. You are perfect."

She smiled. "Are you laying it on a little thick?"

"Is that what you think, Harper? That I'm trying to give you a swelled head because I have an ulterior motive?"

Harper sobered. "I don't know what you're thinking, because I don't have the gift of being able to read minds."

"Well, if you did then you'd know exactly what I'm thinking."

"And what is that?" she asked.

"That I lied when I said I liked you. That was when I was fifteen, but now at thirty-seven I realize that I fell in love with you back then and I still love you."

"Cheney," she whispered, as her breath appeared to congeal in her throat.

"That is my name."

Harper recovered with his quip. "I know it's your name, but I had no idea that you felt—no—feel this way about me."

"Does it bother you?"

"No, my feelings are similar to yours." Harper knew it was time she stopped fooling herself and told Cheney the truth. "You were the first boy and the last one that I had a crush on. I had a notebook where I wrote stories about a girl falling in love and marrying her prince. In every story, you were that prince, Cheney. And even when I began dating, I was always looking for someone who reminded me of you. It's probably the reason why I put up so many roadblocks that wouldn't allow me to have lasting relationships. It wasn't until I ran into you again that I realized that the boy who I had been crushing on had become a drug I didn't want to give up."

"Shit, Harper!"

"Why are you *shitting*, Cheney?"

"Because we've been wasting time dancing around each other for years, when if I hadn't been warned to stay away from you, I would've told you how I felt about you back then. And I wouldn't have attempted to seduce you because if your father didn't shoot me, then your grandfather would. I would've asked you to wait for me."

Just like Moses had asked Sallie Ann to wait for him.

Harper couldn't believe she was reliving what she gleaned from her great-grandfather's notebooks. Kelton had asked a woman he hardly knew to wait for him, and she had. She'd married him and they had a long and happy life together, and Harper wondered if it could happen for her and Cheney.

"Why don't you ask me now," she whispered.

Cheney's foot hit the brake, causing the car to stop short. They were lucky there wasn't another vehicle behind them. "Do you know what you're saying?"

"Yes, I know exactly what I'm saying."

"I'm willing to give you time to decide what you want to do before you go back to Chicago."

"Cheney, folks are honking behind us. I already know what I'm going to do before I go back to Chicago," she said when he started driving again. "I've already decided to give up my apartment and come live with my grandfather. I'll also apply for a teaching position at a local high school and do what I know I can do best, and that is teach. Now that I'm close to finishing my book, I'm thinking about writing another one, but only if I can come up with another plot."

"What about marriage and children?" Cheney questioned, giving her a quick glance.

"Those are definite possibilities. What I would do is get to know my childhood prince better before I decide to marry him and we live happily ever after."

Cheney's laughter echoed in the SUV. "I never figured I would fall for a romance writer."

Harper also laughed. "In case you aren't aware, Counselor, romance writers have incredible imaginations when it comes to writing love scenes. Most times the hero is left breathless and will do everything he can not to lose his heroine, and that includes making the staunchest anti-marriage man willing to turn in his bachelor card."

"Are you saying we're going to have fun acting out the love scene in your books?"

"That all depends on if you're willing to put down your law books long enough to begin reading romance novels."

Reaching for her left hand, Cheney cradled it in his right. "I'm willing to do whatever it takes to convince you that I want to spend the rest of my life with you."

Harper wanted to tell him it wouldn't take that much convincing, that whenever he proposed marriage she would accept. Making impulsive decisions was not in her character, but she didn't question this one.

"How long do you think it's going to take us to bring this unrequited love to its final conclusion?"

"I don't know, Cheney. But what I do know is that it will not take two years."

Moses had promised Sallie Ann two years, but something he had never anticipated stepped in to make it one. Harper knew she had to return to Chicago to tie up the loose ends of her life there before returning to Nashville to look after her grandfather, resume her career as a teacher, and plan a future with Cheney. She had a lot to look forward to for all her tomorrows.

Moses Gilliam knew exactly where he was and what he had been doing on April 15, 1947, when the foundations of Major League Baseball shook: The Brooklyn

Dodgers announced they had signed Jackie Robinson as their first Colored player.

He was sitting on his porch watching Sallie Ann bottle-feeding their son, who had recently celebrated his first birthday. Inez had kept her promise to find a child born out of wedlock and put up for adoption. What Moses hadn't known until a letter was delivered to him the day he'd driven to San Antonio to pick up the infant, was that Inez was the boy's mother and she reneged on her promise not to marry or have children. She hadn't married but had resigned her position once she'd discovered she was pregnant. She stayed with relatives in Austin, delivered the baby, then applied for a position with a museum in Mexico City.

The day she called Moses to tell him she was in possession of a baby boy named Bernard Gilliam and that he should come to Texas to pick up his son, he couldn't contain his joy. Inez had left Texas, leaving her son behind with relatives and a letter explaining the baby's existence. It had taken Moses a while to accept that a former lover had given him her child because, she professed, he was the only man she'd ever loved.

Once Sallie Ann was emotionally stable enough to discuss adoption, he was relieved that she was open to adopting a child. That was several months before he was scheduled to be shipped overseas to fight the Japanese in the Pacific. If he didn't make it back from the war, he hadn't wanted Sallie Ann to be alone. What he hadn't divulged was Inez's promise to find a baby by an unwed mother who was willing to give it up for adoption.

He had fought valiantly for his country and when he returned, Moses discovered nothing had changed. Negroes were still treated as second-class citizens. However, Branch Rickey had changed history when he signed Robinson to the Dodgers, and Moses knew it was to be the death knell for the Negro Leagues when other teams would eventually add the most talented Black baseball players to their rosters.

He'd been medically discharged from the army when a bullet had shattered the bones in his left shoulder, and the injury had ended his baseball career. He could no longer play for the Memphis Eagles, but he continued to work with them as a hitting coach. Traveling with the team was a part of his past, one he would ruminate on when working his farm..

Moses felt as if he had done a lot of living in twenty-nine years, and whenever he'd reminiscence about his past he recalled the old woman in Cuba who had predicted that two women would love him, and her mention of babies. She probably saw the children he and Sallie Ann would never have together. He smiled. It had taken the love of one woman to make him a better man and husband and the love of the other to make him a father.

"What do you think Bernard is going to be when he grows up, Moses?"

He smiled at his wife. "What else but a farmer, sweetheart."

She nodded. "It is a noble profession."

Yes, it is. And for Moses it was more than that because he owned land where his ancestors had worked for nothing. He had his wife, son, land, and the rest of his life to enjoy all of it.

CHAPTER 32

Two years later . . .

The entire Fleming and Sanders clans filled the loggia and had spilled out to the outdoor kitchen at Cheney and Harper's Nashville home. They came from all over the country to celebrate the release of her first novel *Home and Away*. It had become a double celebration because there was another first. She and Cheney were expecting their first child.

After she moved from Chicago to Nashville, she and Cheney decided not to waste any more time and they had a Christmas Eve wedding. It hadn't taken much convincing for Bernard to sell his house and move into the guest suite in their home.

However, it had taken longer for Harper to decide whether to send her manuscript to a traditional publisher or self-publish. In the end she looked up names of literary agents and submitted to one who had expressed an interest in the subject. She still didn't remember all that had been said to her when the agent called, but she did remember that a publisher had made an offer for it. Harper had Cheney read over the contract and with minor changes agreed upon by the publisher, she signed it.

There were some revisions, and her editor had given her a thumbs-up on grammar and syntax. When Harper told her she was an English teacher, the woman claimed she was a joy to work with.

Her life was full with teaching and looking after Bernard, who was beginning to show and feel his age. Harper knew she had too much on her plate to even think about writing another novel. She had just finished her first trimester and once the baby was born, she planned to take an extended maternity leave. By that time perhaps she'd be ready to write another book.

She detected the familiar fragrance of Cheney's cologne before his approach. He looped an arm around her rapidly expanding waistline. "Do you think everyone will enjoy the book?" she asked him.

"Of course. The other day I saw Bernard wipe away a few tears when he was reading it. Even though you changed names and dates, he was probably recalling some of the events his father had talked about."

Harper rested her head on her husband's shoulder. "There was so much I didn't include." What she couldn't tell Cheney was that her great-grandfather had an ongoing affair with the woman Harper had called Inez after he'd married Sallie Ann and that she'd had his baby. Moses Gilliam aka Kelton Fleming had a secret that had been buried with him. Sallie Ann never knew that her husband had been Bernard's biological father.

"Every family has secrets. It's just that some can keep them buried."

Harper looked up at Cheney, her eyes making love to his face. "What secrets are you keeping from me?"

"None. At least not yet."

"Oh, it's like that."

"Yup. Now, let's go and feed our guests or they'll think we're terrible hosts."

Trays filled with hot and cold foods lined two banquet tables in the expansive outdoor kitchen. Harper walked over to her mother and kissed her cheek.

"I need you to help me get everyone together so we can sit down and eat."

Martell smiled. "Of course. I hope you're not doing too much."

"Trust me, Mom, I know when to slow down. No one wants this baby more than I do."

"I think Cheney would debate that. That's all he talks about. I'm so glad you found someone like him who makes you happy."

"He didn't find me, Mom. It just took some time for us to rediscover each other."

If the characters in her book had discovered what they wanted for their tomorrows, so had Harper Fleming-Sanders. She had the love of her husband and their families. There was nothing else she wanted or needed as she awaited the birth of her son or daughter.

Book Club Questions

1. In *Home and Away*, Moses Gilliam is living in two worlds: one for Whites and another for Negroes. How was he able to navigate between both worlds to fulfill his destiny to become a baseball player?

2. Why do you think baseball wasn't segregated in countries outside the United States before Jackie Robinson broke Major League Baseball's color barrier in 1947?

3. Women characters play a pivotal role in this novel. Harper, Sallie Ann, Winnie, Martell, Inez, Maddie, and Daisy. Which one did you find most intriguing? And why?

4. Social mores were different for mid-twentieth century women than those of today. However, not all the women in the novel were willing to adhere to the rules of their day. Which ones challenged them, and who were the ones who were content to conform?

5. Do you believe Moses initially held any affection for Sallie Ann when he asked her to become his girlfriend? Or did he have an ulterior motive? And what was his motivation for accepting her father's wedding gift when he had professed to wanting to determine his own destiny?

6. How did Moses's relationship with his mother prepare him to become a husband to Sallie Ann?

7. What are the parallels and/or differences between married couples Daisy and Solomon Gilliam and Maddie and Jimmie Thompson?

8. Nine decades separate mother and daughter Martell and Harper Fleming, and Maddie and Sallie Ann Thompson. Are the mothers' aspirations for their daughters similar? Or do they differ? And why?

9. Although the main characters are fictional, there are many references throughout the novel to real and historical baseball figures, such as Cumberland Posey, Gus Greenlee, Effa Manley, Buck Leonard, Josh Gibson, Monte Irvin, and Cool Papa Bell. Were you unfamiliar with any of the real people who were mentioned in the novel? If so, which ones, and what did you learn about them?

10. Moses said it had taken the love of one woman to make him a better man and husband, and the love of another to make him a father. Did you suspect Inez was Bernard's mother before Harper revealed this to readers at the end of the novel?

11. Do you believe Harper's decision not to disclose the circumstances of Bernard's parentage in the novel was to keep readers guessing or to protect her family's name?